McCULLEN'S SECRET SON

BY
RITA HERRON

Harlequin (UK) Limited's policy is to use papers that are natural, renewable and recyclable products and made from wood grown in sustainable forests. The logging and manufacturing processes conform to the legal environmental regulations of the country of origin.

Printed and bound in Spain
by CPI, Barcelona

MILLS & BOON

Published in Great Britain 2015
by Mills & Boon, an imprint of Harlequin (UK) Limited,
Eton House, 18-24 Paradise Road, Richmond, Surrey, TW9 1SR

© 2015 Rita B. Herron

ISBN: 978-0-263-25317-7

46-0915

Rita Herron, a *USA TODAY* bestselling author, wrote her first book when she was twelve, but didn't think real people grew up to be writers. Now she writes so she doesn't have to get a real job. A former kindergarten teacher and workshop leader, she traded storytelling to kids for writing romance, and now she writes romantic comedies and romantic suspense. Rita lives in Georgia with her family. She loves to hear from readers, so please write her at PO Box 921225, Norcross, GA 30092-1225, USA, or visit her website, www.ritaherron.com.

To Aunt Nelda,
for her love of cowboys!
Love, Rita

Chapter One

The last place Brett McCullen wanted to be was back in Pistol Whip, especially on the McCullen ranch.

He pulled down the long drive to his family's ranch, Horseshoe Creek, his leg throbbing from his most recent fall. Damn, he loved rodeo and riding.

But maybe at thirty, he was getting too old to bust his butt on the circuit. And last week when he'd woken up in bed with one of the groupies, some hot, busty blonde named Brandy or Fifi—hell, after a while, they all sounded and looked the same—he'd realized that not a soul in the damn world really cared about him.

Or knew the Brett underneath.

Maybe because he was good at the show. Play the part of the bad boy. The fearless rider. The charmer who smiled at the camera and got laid every night.

Easier than getting *real* and chancing getting hurt.

He cut the lights and stared at the farmhouse for a minute, memories suffusing him. He could see him and his brothers, playing horseshoes, practicing roping on the fence posts, riding horses in the pasture, tagging along with their daddy on a cattle drive.

His oldest brother, Maddox, was always the responsible one—and his father's favorite. Ray, two years younger than

Brett, was the hellion, the one who landed in trouble, the one who butted heads with their father.

Brett could never live up to his old man's expectations, so he figured why try? Life should be fun. Women, horseback riding, rodeos—it was the stuff dreams were made of.

So he'd left home ten years ago to pursue those dreams and hadn't questioned his decision since.

But Maddox's phone call had thrown him for a loop. How could he deny his father's last request?

Hell, it wasn't like he hadn't loved his old man. He was probably more like him than Maddox or Ray. He'd always thought his father had a wild streak in him, that maybe he'd regretted settling down.

Brett hadn't wanted to make the same mistake.

He walked up the porch steps and reached for the doorknob, then stepped inside, back into a well of family memories that reminded him of all the holidays he'd missed.

Last year, he'd seen daddies shopping with their kids for Christmas trees, and mothers and kids at the park, and couples strolling in the moonlight, and he'd felt alone.

Mama Mary, his dad's housekeeper and cook and the woman who'd taken care of him and his brothers after their mother passed, waddled in and wrapped him into a hug.

"You're a sight for sore eyes," Mama Mary said with a hearty laugh.

Brett buried his head in her big arms, emotions churning through him. He'd forgotten how much he loved Mama Mary, how she could make anything feel all right with a hug and her homemade cooking.

She leaned back to examine him, and patted his flat belly.

"Boy, you've gotten skinny. My biscuits and gravy will fix that."

He laughed. Mama Mary thought she could fix any

problem with a big meal. "I've missed you," he said, his voice gruff.

She blinked away tears and ushered him into the kitchen. The room hadn't changed at all—still the checkered curtains and pine table, the plate of sausage and bacon left from breakfast. And as far back as he could remember, she'd always had a cake or pie waiting.

"Sit down now and eat. Then you can see your daddy." She waved him to a chair, and he sank into it. Dread over the upcoming reunion with his father tightened his stomach. Grateful to have a few minutes before he had to confront him, he accepted the peach cobbler and coffee with a smile.

Without warning, the back door opened and his little brother, Ray, stood in the threshold of the door. Ray, with that sullen scowl and cutting eyes. Ray, who always seemed to be mad about something.

Ray gave a clipped nod to acknowledge him, then Mama Mary swept him into a hug, as well. "Oh, my goodness, I can't tell you how much it warms my heart to have you boys back in my kitchen."

Brett gritted his teeth. It wouldn't be for long, though. As soon as he heard what his father had to say, he was back on the road.

A tense silence stretched between them as Mama Mary pushed Ray into a chair and handed him some pie and coffee. Just like they did when they were little, Brett and Ray both obeyed and ate.

"Maddox is on his way home now," Mama Mary said as she refilled their coffee.

Brett and Ray exchanged a furtive look. While the two of them hadn't always seen eye to eye, Ray and Maddox had clashed *big*-time.

Brett had always felt the sting of his big brother's

disapproval. According to Maddox, Brett didn't just leave but *ran* at the least hint of trouble.

Footsteps echoed from the front, and Brett braced himself as Maddox stepped into the kitchen, his big shoulders squared, that take-charge attitude wafting off him.

"Now, boys," Mama Mary said before any of them could start tangling. "Your daddy had a rough night. He's anxious to see you, so you'd best get upstairs."

An awkwardness filled the air, but Brett and Ray both stood. His brothers were here for one reason, and none of them liked it.

"I'll go first." Brett mustered up a smile. Pathetic that he'd rather face his father on his deathbed than his brothers.

Ray and Maddox followed, but they waited in the hall as he entered his father's bedroom.

The moment he spotted his father lying in the bed, pale, the veins in his forehead bulging, an oxygen tube in his nose, he nearly fell to his knees with sorrow and regret. He should have at least checked in every now and then.

Although he had come back once five years ago. And he'd hooked up with Willow James. But that night with her had confused the hell out of him, and then he'd fought with Maddox the next day and left again.

"Brett, God, boy, it's good to see you."

Emotions welled in Brett's chest, but he forced himself to walk over to his father's bed.

"Sit down a spell," his father said. "We need to talk."

Brett claimed the wooden chair by the bed, and braced himself for a good dressing-down.

"I want you to know that I'm proud of you, son."

Proud was the last thing he'd expected his father to say.

"But I should have come back more," he blurted.

His father shook his head, what was left of his hair sticking up in white patches. "No, I should have come to some of your rodeos. I kept up with you, though. You're just as talented as I always thought you'd be."

Brett looked in his father's eyes. Joe McCullen looked weak, like he might fade into death any second. But there was no judgment or anger there.

"I'm glad you followed your dreams," his father said in a hoarse voice. "If you'd stayed here and worked the ranch, you'd have felt smothered and hated me for holding you back."

Brett's lungs squeezed for air. His father actually understood him. That was a surprising revelation.

"But there is something you need to take care of while you're here. You remember Willow?"

Brett went very still. How could he have forgotten her? She was his first love, the only woman he'd *ever* loved. But his father had discouraged him from getting too involved with her when he was younger.

So he'd left Pistol Whip, chasing a more exciting lifestyle.

Willow had wasted no time in moving on…and getting married.

She even had a child.

Her last name was what, now? Howard?

"Brett?"

"Yes, I remember her," he said through clenched teeth. "I heard she's married and has a family." That was the real reason he hadn't returned to Pistol Whip more often.

It hurt too damn much to see her with another man.

"That girl's got troubles."

Brett stiffened. "Why are you telling me this?"

"Because I was wrong to encourage you to break up with her," his father murmured. "I've made my mistakes, son. I don't want you to do the same."

His father reached out a shaky hand, and Brett took it, chilled by his cold skin.

"Promise me you'll check on her and her boy," his father murmured.

"That's the reason you wanted to see me?"

"Yes." His father coughed. "Now send Ray in here. I need to talk to him."

Brett squeezed his father's hand, then headed to the door. If his father wanted him to check on Willow, something bad must have happened to her.

His heart hammered at the thought of seeing her again. But he couldn't refuse his father's wishes.

He'd pay her a visit and make sure she was okay. Then he'd get the hell out of Pistol Whip again.

When his father was gone, there was no reason for him to stick around.

Three days later

BRETT MCCULLEN WAS back in town.

Willow James, Willow Howard technically, although she was no longer using her married name, rubbed her chest as if the gesture could actually soothe the ache in her heart. Brett was the only man she'd ever loved. Ever would love.

But he'd walked away from her years ago and never looked back.

She sat in her car at the edge of the graveyard like a voyeur to the family as they said their final goodbyes to their father, Joe. Part of her wanted to go to Brett and comfort him for his loss.

But a seed of bitterness still niggled at her for the way he'd deserted her. And for the life he'd led since.

He'd always been footloose and fancy-free, a bad-boy

charmer who could sweet-talk any girl into doing whatever he wanted.

He'd taken her virginity and her heart with him when he'd left Pistol Whip to chase his dreams of becoming a famous rodeo star.

He'd also chased plenty of other women.

Her heart squeezed with pain again. She'd seen the news footage, the magazine articles and pictures of his awards and conquests.

She'd told herself it didn't matter. She had the best part of him anyway—his son.

Sam.

A little boy Brett knew nothing about.

If Brett saw Sam in town, would he realize the truth? After all, Sam had Brett's deep brown eyes. That cleft in his chin.

The same streak of stubbornness and the love of riding.

A shadow fell across the graveyard, storm clouds gathering, and the crowd began to disperse. She spotted Brett shaking hands with several locals, his brothers doing the same. Then he lifted his head and looked across the graveyard, and for a moment, she thought he was looking straight at her. That he saw her car.

But a second later, Mama Mary loped over and put her arm around him, and Brett turned back to the people gathered at the service.

Chastising herself for being foolish enough to still care for him after the way he'd hurt her, she started the engine and drove toward her house. She didn't have to worry about Brett. He'd bounce back in the saddle in a day or two and be just fine.

But she had problems of her own.

Not just financial worries, but a no-good husband who she was scared to death of.

Dread filled her as she drove through town and ventured down the side street to the tiny house she'd rented. Her biggest mistake in life was marrying Leo Howard, but she'd been pregnant and on the rebound and had wanted a father for her son.

Leo was no father, though.

Well, at first he'd claimed he was. He'd promised her security and love and a home for her and her little boy.

But as time wore on, she realized Leo had secrets and an agenda of his own.

They hadn't lived together in over three years, but last night he'd come back to town.

Hopefully he had the divorce papers with him, so she could get him out of her life once and for all.

Mentally ticking off her to-do list, she delivered three quilts she'd custom made from orders taken at the antiques store, Vintage Treasures, where she displayed some of her work. When she'd had Sam, she'd known she had to do something to make a living, and sewing was the only skill she had. She'd learned to make clothes, window treatments and quilts from her grandmother, and now she'd turned it into a business.

She did some grocery shopping, then dropped off the rent check. Earlier, she'd left Sam at her neighbor's house, hoping to meet with Leo alone.

She pulled in the drive, noting that Leo had parked his beat-up pickup halfway on the lawn, and that he'd run over Sam's bicycle. Poor Sam. He deserved so much better.

Furious at his carelessness, she threw her Jeep into Park, climbed out and let herself in the house, calling Leo's name as she walked through the kitchen/living room combination, then down the hall to the bedrooms.

When Leo didn't answer, dread filled. He was probably passed out drunk.

Fortified by her resolve to tell him to leave the signed divorce papers so she'd be rid of him for good, she strode to the bedroom. The room was dark, the air reeking of the scent of booze.

Just as she'd feared, Leo was in bed, the covers rumpled, a bottle of bourbon on the bedside table.

Anger churned through her, and she crossed the room, disgusted that he'd passed out in her house. She leaned over to shake him and wake him up, but she felt something sticky and wet on her hand.

She jerked the covers off his face, a scream lodging in her throat. Leo's eyes stared up at her, wide and vacant.

And there was blood.

It was everywhere, soaking his shirt and the sheets…

Leo was dead.

Chapter Two

Willow backed away from the bed in horror. The acrid odor of death swirled around her. There was so much blood… all over Leo's chest. His fingers. Streaking his face where he must have wiped his hand across his cheek.

Nausea rose to her throat, but she swallowed it back, her mind racing.

Leo was…really dead. God…he'd said he was in trouble, but he hadn't mentioned that someone was after him…

She had to get help. Call the police.

Sheriff McCullen.

Her head swam as she fumbled for the phone, but her hand was sticky with blood where she'd touched the bedding.

She trembled, ran into the bathroom and turned on the water, desperate to cleanse herself of the ugly smell. She scrubbed her hand with soap, reality returning through the fog of shock.

Where was the killer? Was he still in the house?

She froze, straining as she listened for signs of an intruder, but the house seemed eerily silent.

Sam… Lord help me. Her neighbor would probably drop Sam off any minute. She couldn't let him come home to this.

Panicked, she dried her hands, then ran for the phone

again. But a shadow moved across the room, and she suddenly realized she wasn't alone.

Terrified, she dived for the phone, but the figure lunged at her and grabbed her from behind. Willow screamed and tried to run, but he wrapped big beefy hands around her and immobilized her.

His rough beard scraped her jaw as he leaned close to her ear. "You aren't going to call the cops."

Fear shot through her. "No, no police."

He tightened his grip around her, choking the air from her lungs. "If you do, you'll end up like your husband."

Willow shook her head. "Let me go and I promise I'll do whatever you say."

A nasty chuckle rumbled in her ear. "Oh, you'll do what we want, Willow. That is, if you want to see your little boy again."

"What?" Willow gasped.

He twisted her head back painfully, as if he was going to snap her neck. She tried to breathe, but the air was trapped in her lungs. "Please…don't hurt him."

"That's up to you." He shoved her head forward, and she felt the barrel of his gun at the back of her head. "We'll be in touch with instructions."

Then he slammed the butt of the gun against her head. Pain shot through her skull, and the world spun, the room growing dark as she collapsed.

BRETT HAD MUDDLED his way through the funeral and tacked on his polite semicelebrity smile as the neighbors offered condolences and shared the casseroles that had been dropped off.

He didn't know why people ate when they were grieving, but Mama Mary kept forcing food and tea in his hands, and he didn't have the energy to argue. He'd grown accustomed to cameras, to putting on a happy face when his body was screaming in pain from an injury he'd sustained from a bull ride.

He could certainly do it today.

"Thank you for coming," he said as he shook another hand.

Betty Bane's daughter Mandy slipped up beside him and gave him a flirtatious smile. She looked as if she'd just graduated high school. *Jailbait.* "Hey, Brett, I'm so sorry about your daddy."

"Thanks." He started to step away, but she raised her cell phone. "I know it may not be a good time, but can I get a selfie with you? My friends won't believe I actually touched *the* Brett McCullen!"

She giggled and plastered her face so close to his that her cheek brushed his. "Smile, Brett!"

Unbelievable. She wanted him to pose. To pretend he hadn't just buried his old man.

He bit the inside of his cheek to keep from telling her she was shallow and insensitive, then extricated himself as soon as she got the shot. He shoved his plate on the counter, wove through the crowd and stepped outside, then strode toward the stable.

He wanted to be alone. Needed a horse beneath him, the fresh air blowing in his face and the wild rugged land of Horseshoe Creek to make him forget about the man he and his brothers had just put six feet under.

Or…he could take a trip down to The Silver Bullet, the honky-tonk in town, and drown his sorrow in booze and a woman.

But the thought of any female other than the one he'd left behind in Pistol Whip didn't appeal to him. Besides, if the press got wind he was there, they'd plaster his picture all over the place. And he didn't need that right now.

Didn't want them following him to the ranch or intruding on his brothers.

A heaviness weighed in his chest, and he saddled up a black gelding, climbed atop and sent the horse into a sprint. Storm clouds had rolled in earlier, casting a grayness to the sky and adding to the bleakness of the day.

He missed the stars, but a sliver of moonlight wove between the clouds and streaked the land with golden rays, just enough to remind him how beautiful and peaceful the rugged land was.

To the west lay the mountains, and he pictured the wild mustangs running free. He could practically hear the sound of their hoofs beating the ground as the horses galloped over the terrain.

Cattle grazed in the pastures, and the creek gurgled nearby, bringing back memories of working a cattle drive when he was young, of campfires with his father and brothers, of fishing in Horseshoe Creek.

He'd also taken Willow for rides across this land. They'd had a picnic by the creek and skinny-dipped one night and then…made love.

It was the sweetest moment he'd ever had with a woman. Willow had been young and shy and innocent, but so damn beautiful that, even as the voice in his head cautioned him not to take her, he'd stripped her clothes anyway.

They'd made love like wild animals, needy and hungry, as if they might never be touched like that again.

But he and his brothers had been fighting for months. His father had started drinking and carousing the bars, restless, too. He'd met him at the door one night when he'd been in the barn with Willow, and warned Brett that if he ever wanted to follow his dreams, he needed to leave Willow alone.

His father's heart-to-heart, a rarity for the two of them,

had lit a fire inside him and he'd had to scratch that wandering itch. Like his father said, if he didn't pursue rodeo, he'd always wonder if he'd missed out.

That was ten years ago—the first time he'd left. He'd only been back once since, five years ago. Then he'd seen Willow again...

He climbed off the horse, tied him to a tree by the creek, then walked down to the bank, sat down, picked up a stone and skipped it across the water. The sound of the creek gurgling mingled sweetly with the sound of Willow's voice calling his name in the moonlight when they'd made love right here under the stars.

He'd made it in the rodeo circuit now. He had fame and belt buckles and more women than any man had a right to have had.

But as he mourned his father, he realized that in leaving, he'd missed something, too.

Willow. A life with her. A real home. A family.

Someone who'd love him no matter what. Whether he lost an event, or got injured and was too sore to ride, or... too old.

He buried his head in his hands, sorrow for his father mingling with the fact that coming back here only made him want to see Willow again.

But she was married and had a kid.

And even if she had troubles like his father said, she could take care of them herself. She and that husband of hers...

He didn't belong in her life anymore.

WILLOW ROUSED FROM unconsciousness, the world tilting as she lifted her head from the floor. For a moment, confusion clouded her brain, and she wondered what had happened.

But the stench of death swirled through the air, and reality surfaced, sending a shot of pure panic through her.

Leo was dead. And a man had been in the house, had attacked her.

Had said Sam was gone...

She choked on a scream, and was so dizzy for a second, she had to hold her head with her hands to keep from passing out. Nausea bubbled in her throat, but she swallowed it back, determined not to get sick.

She had to find her son.

A sliver of moonlight seeped through the curtains, the only light in the room. But it was enough for her to see Leo's body still planted in her bed, his blood soaking his clothes and the sheets like a red river.

Who was the man in the house? Was he still here? And why would he kidnap Sam?

Shaking all over, she clutched the edge of the dresser and pulled herself up to stand. Her breathing rattled in the quiet, but she angled her head to search the room. It appeared to be empty. She staggered to the kitchen and living room.

Both were empty.

Nerves nearly immobilized her, but she held on to the wall and made herself go to Sam's room. Tears blurred her eyes, but she swiped at them, visually scanning the room and praying that the man had lied. That her little four-year-old boy was inside, safe and sound. That this was all some kind of sick, twisted dream.

Except the blood on the bed and Leo's body was very real.

At first glance, her son's room seemed untouched. His soccer ball lay on the floor by the bed, his toy cars and trucks in a pile near the block set. His bed was still made from this morning, his superhero pillow on top, next to the cowboy hat he'd begged for on his birthday.

But this morning his horse figurines had been arranged by the toy barn and stable where he'd set them up last night when he was playing rodeo. She was afraid he had his father's blood in him.

The horses were knocked over now, the toy barn broken. Sam was supposed to be at Gina's…

Her mind racing, she hurried to retrieve her cell phone from her purse and called her neighbor. *Please let Sam still be there.*

The phone rang three times, then Gina finally answered. "Hello."

"Gina, it's Willow. Is Sam there?"

"No, his father picked him up. I hope that was all right."

Willow pressed her hand to her mouth to stifle a sob. So Sam had come home with Leo.

Which meant he'd probably witnessed Leo's murder.

Fear squeezed the air from her lungs. The man who'd attacked her, warned her not to call the police, that she'd hear from him…

But when?

And what was happening to Sam now?

BRETT FELT WRENCHED from the inside out. He'd been living on adrenaline, the high of being a star, of having women throwing themselves at him, and everyone wanting a piece of him for so long, that he didn't know what to do with himself tonight.

He knew one thing, though—he did not want a picture of himself at his father's graveside all over the papers. He'd told his publicist that, and banned her from making any public announcement about his father's death.

Grieving for his father and returning to his hometown were private, and he wanted to keep it that way.

Night had fallen, the cows mooing and horses roaming

the pastures soothing as he rose from the creek embankment, climbed on his horse and headed back to the farmhouse. The ranch hands would have been fed by now, the days' work done, until sunrise when the backbreaking work started all over again.

If he had to stay here a couple of days to wait on the reading of the will, maybe he'd get up with the hands and pitch in. Nothing like working up a sweat hauling hay, rounding cattle or mending fences to take his mind off the fact that he'd never see his daddy again.

It made him think about his mother and how he'd felt at eight when she'd died. He'd run home from the school bus that day, anxious for a hug and to tell her about the school rodeo he'd signed up for, but the minute he'd walked in and seen his daddy crying, he'd known something was terribly wrong.

And that his life would never be the same.

Damn drunk driver had turned his world upside down.

Shaking off the desolate feeling the memory triggered, he reminded himself that he had made a success out of himself. He had friends…well, not friends, really. But he was surrounded by people all the time.

He'd thought that the crowd loving him would somehow fill the empty hole inside him. That having folks cheer for him and yell his name meant they loved him.

But they loved the rodeo star. If he didn't have that, no one would give him a second look.

The breeze invigorated him as he galloped across the pasture. When he reached the ranch, he spotted Maddox outside with a woman. Moonlight played off the front yard, and he yanked on the reins to slow his horse as he realized he was intruding on a private moment. He steered the animal behind a cluster of trees, waiting in the shadows.

Maddox was on his knees, and so was the woman he

was with. They were kissing like they couldn't get enough of each other.

The two of them finally pulled back for a breath, and Brett froze as he saw Maddox slide a ring on the woman's finger.

His brother had just proposed.

He should be glad for Maddox. His older brother had taken his mother's death hard, and he and their daddy had been close.

Maddox had obviously found love. Good for him.

He tightened his fingers around the reins, turned the gelding around and rode back to the stables.

Something about seeing Maddox with that woman made him feel even more alone than he had before.

WILLOW COULDN'T STAND to look at Leo's dead body.

She needed to call the police. But what if the killer was watching her and the sheriff came, and he saw her and hurt her son?

She paced to the living room, frantic. She needed help. She couldn't do this alone.

But calling Sheriff McCullen was out of the question.

Brett's face flashed behind her eyes. She hadn't talked to him since he'd left five years ago. When they'd made love that night, she'd thought that Brett might be rethinking his career, that he might have missed her. That he might have contemplated returning to her.

But the next day he'd left town without a word.

Still, he was Sam's father. Even if he didn't know it.

Heaven help her…he'd be furious with her for not telling him. Although years ago, he'd made it plain and clear that he didn't intend to settle down or stay in Pistol Whip. A wife and a child would have cramped his style and kept him from chasing his dreams.

And Willow refused to trap him. He would only have resented her and Sam.

Would he help her now?

She picked up Sam's photo and studied her precious little boy's face, and she decided it didn't matter. It might be a bad time for Brett, but her son was in danger, and she'd do anything to save him.

Her hand trembled as she phoned the McCullen house. Mama Mary answered, and she asked to speak to Brett.

"He's out riding, can I take a message or tell him who called?"

"It's Willow James. And it's important," she said. "Can you give me his cell phone number?"

"Why sure thing, Ms. Willow." Mama Mary repeated it and Willow ended the call abruptly, then called Brett's mobile. Nerves gripped her as she waited on him to answer. What if he didn't pick up? He might not want to talk to her at all.

The phone clicked, then his deep voice echoed back. "Hello."

"Brett, it's Willow."

Dead silence, then his sharp intake of breath. "Yeah?"

"I'm sorry about your father," she said quickly. "But I… need to see you tonight."

"What?" His voice sounded gruff, a note of surprise roughening it.

"Please," Willow cried. "I…can't explain, but it's a matter of life and death."

Chapter Three

Brett clenched his phone in a white-knuckled grip as he paced the barn. He hadn't seen or talked to Willow in years, and she hadn't attended his father's funeral today. Even as he'd told himself he didn't care if she came, he'd looked for her.

But now she wanted to see him?

It's a matter of life and death.

What the hell was going on?

He cleared his throat. Once upon a time, he'd have jumped and run at a moment's notice if Willow had called. But she was a married woman now. "What's wrong, Willow?"

"I can't explain on the phone," she said, her voice strained. "Please, Brett... I don't know what else to do. Who to call."

His gut tightened at the desperation in her voice. "Willow—"

"Please, I'm begging you. I need your help."

"All right, I'll be right there." He didn't bother to ask for her address. He knew where she lived. Mama Mary had managed to drop it in the conversation once when he'd had a weak moment and had called home.

He'd already unsaddled his horse, so he jogged back to the house and climbed in his pickup truck.

Thankfully, Maddox and his lady friend had gone inside, and he had no idea where Ray was, so he didn't have to explain to anyone. Not that he had to tell them where he was going.

He hadn't answered to anyone in a long time.

Well, except for his publicist and fans and the damn press.

He drove from the ranch, winding down the drive to the road leading into town, the quiet of the wilderness a reprieve from the cities he'd traveled to. A few miles, and he drove through the small town, noting that not much had changed.

At this late hour, the park was empty, the general store closed, yet country music blared from The Silver Bullet, and several vehicles were parked in the lot. He wasn't surprised to see Ray's. He was probably drowning his sorrows.

Inside, the booze and music was always flowing, the women footloose and fancy-free. Just his type.

Another night maybe…

He turned down the street toward Willow's, anxiety needling him. He'd never stopped loving her. Wanting her.

But she was taken. And he had a different life now. A life he'd chosen. Another rodeo coming up, another town…

Children's bikes and toys dotted the yards, suggesting the neighborhood catered to young families. The house at the end of her block, a small rustic log cabin, was Willow's and was set way back from the road, offering privacy. A beat-up pickup truck that had obviously run over the child's bike sat crooked, half in the drive, half in the yard.

His father had said Willow had troubles… Did it have to do with the man she'd married? Judging from the sloppy way the truck was parked, and the fact that he'd run over the bike, maybe he'd been drinking…

Not your problem, Brett.

Except that Willow said she needed him.

He scanned the outside to see if her old man was lurking around. Did he know that Brett and his wife had had a romantic relationship years ago?

He braced himself for trouble as he parked and walked up to the front door. Barring a low-burning light in the bedroom, the house looked dark.

The hair on the back of his neck prickled as he rang the doorbell. Something didn't feel right…

He waited several seconds, then knocked and called through the door, "Willow, it's me. Brett."

The sound of footsteps on the other side echoed, then the lock turned, and the door squeaked open. His breath stalled in his chest as Willow appeared, the door cracking just enough to see her face.

"Brett?" Her face looked ashen, and a streak of blood darkened her hair.

"Yeah, it's me."

Panicked at the sight of her disheveled state, he pushed open the door and stepped inside. "What the hell's wrong?"

She slammed the door shut, then locked it and turned to face him, her eyes wide with fear. "Help me," she whispered as she threw herself into his arms.

Brett's stomach churned as he pulled her trembling body against him and wrapped his arms around her.

WILLOW SANK INTO Brett's arms, the terror she'd felt since she'd arrived home pouring out of her as he held her. She tried to battle the tears, but they overflowed, soaking his shirt.

"Shh, it's all right," Brett murmured into her hair. "Whatever's wrong, we can fix it."

She shook her head against him. "That's just it, I don't know if I can."

Brett stroked her hair, and rubbed slow circles along her back. For the first time in years, she felt safe. Cared for.

But he was only being nice. He had his own life, and when she confessed the truth about Sam, there was no telling how he'd react. He might hate her.

Or he might leave town and not get involved in her troubles. A murder case could ruin his reputation.

But really—none of that mattered. Not when Sam was in danger.

"Willow," Brett said softly. "Honey, you've got to tell me what's wrong. What happened?"

Brett slipped a handkerchief into her hands and she wiped her face. Then she looked up into his eyes.

He had the darkest, most gorgeous eyes she'd ever seen. Eyes she'd gotten lost in years ago.

She wanted to soak in his features, but looking at that handsome, strong face only reminded her of her little boy who looked so much like him that it hurt.

He rubbed her arms. "Willow, talk to me."

"I…don't know where to begin." *With the body of her dead husband*? Or Sam?

"You said it was a matter of life and death. I know you're married, that you have a little boy." She squeezed her eyes shut, unable to look at him for a moment.

"I noticed the pickup truck outside and the crunched bike. Is that what this is about?"

"I wish it was that simple," she said on a shaky breath.

Brett led her over to the sofa and she sank onto it, her legs giving way. He joined her, but this time he didn't touch her.

"Your husband? Is he here? Did he hurt you?"

Emotions threatened to overcome her again, and she glanced at the phone, willing it to ring. Willing the caller to tell her how to get her little boy back and end this horror.

"Did he?" Brett asked, his voice harsh with anger.

She shook her head. "Not exactly."

Brett shot up from the seat, his jaw twitching. "Come on, Willow, tell me what the hell is going on."

"He's dead," Willow blurted. "Leo is...dead."

Brett went stone still and stared at her. "What do you mean, *dead*?"

"In there," Willow said. "When I got home tonight, I found him."

He glanced around the bedroom, then exhaled noisily. "How did he die?"

"Someone shot him." Her voice cracked. "There's blood...everywhere."

Brett released a curse and strode to the bedroom. Willow jumped up and raced after him, trembling as he flipped on the overhead light. The stark light lit the room, accentuating the grisly scene in her bed. Leo staring at the ceiling with dead eyes. Blood on his clothes and the sheets.

Brett choked back an obscenity. "Who shot him?"

"I don't know," Willow whispered. "I...found him and was going to call the police, but then a man jumped me."

Brett pivoted, his eyes searching her face, mouth pinched with anger as he lifted his hand and touched her forehead. She didn't realize she'd been bleeding, but he drew his hand back and she saw blood streaking his finger. "He hurt you?"

"I'm all right. He grabbed me from behind, and he said... He told me not to call the police, that he...had Sam."

"Sam?"

Willow's lungs strained for air. "My little boy. He has him, Brett. And he said if I called the police, I'd never see him again."

BRETT GRITTED HIS TEETH. "You mean he kidnapped your child?"

"Yes," Willow cried. "I have to get him back."

Brett stared at the man lying dead in Willow's bed.

Her husband.

He'd never met the man but had heard he was a businessman, that he'd done well for himself.

So why had someone wanted him dead? And why kidnap Willow's son?

"I don't know what to do," Willow said "I…can't leave Leo there. But if I call the sheriff, he'll send police and crime workers, and I might never see Sam again."

Cold fury seized Brett's insides. What kind of person threatened a small child?

"How old is Sam?" he asked.

"Four," Willow said. "He's just a little guy, Brett. He has to be terrified." Her voice cracked again, her terror wrenching Brett's heart. "And if he saw Leo murdered, then he may be traumatized."

He also might be able to identify the killer.

But Brett bit back that observation because it would only frighten Willow more.

If her son could identify her husband's shooter, the killer might not let Sam live anyway, no matter what Willow did.

Brett tried to strip the worry from his voice. "What does this man want from you, Willow?"

"I have no idea." She looked up at him with swollen, tear-stained eyes. "He said to wait for a call."

Brett turned away from the sight of the bloody, dead man. "I know you're scared, but think about it—why would this man take Sam? Did your husband have a lot of money?"

Willow shook her head back and forth, sending her hair swaying. It was tangled from where she'd run her hands through it, the long strands even more vibrant with streaks of gold and red than he remembered.

He tried to dismiss memories of running his hands through it, of the way it felt tickling his belly when she'd loved him, but an image teased his mind anyway.

"Are you sure? Maybe he had some investments? Stocks?"

"If he had any money, I didn't know about it," Willow said. "He didn't even have a savings or checking account in town. It's one of the things we argued about."

Brett arched a brow. He didn't have a bank account in town—which meant he was probably hiding one somewhere else? "One of the things?"

Her face paled. "Yes." She closed her eyes, a pained sound escaping her. "You might as well know. We weren't getting along. We hadn't for a while. Leo moved out three years ago."

Brett tried to assimilate that information. "What has he been doing?"

"I don't know," she said in a choked whisper.

"Was he giving you any money to live on? Helping out with the boy?"

Willow worried her bottom lip with her teeth. "No. He… didn't want to be a father to Sam."

An odd note crept into her voice.

"What kind of father doesn't want to be there for his kid?"

Willow didn't respond, making Brett even more curious about her husband and how he'd treated her.

"Willow, talk to me. What happened between you two? Was he abusing you and Sam?"

Willow cut her eyes away. "When we met, he was kind, charming. But the last year he'd been drinking too much, and his temper erupted."

"And he took it out on you and Sam?"

Willow shrugged. "At first it was just verbal. But...he hit me once. Then he started in on Sam, and I told him to leave." A fierce protectiveness strengthened her voice. "I would never let him hurt my son. I asked him for a divorce."

"How did he take that?"

"He was angry, but he left. Frankly...I think he wanted out."

"You don't know what he's been doing since?"

"No, I have no idea."

He was obviously in trouble.

Dammit. Even though he and his brother were hardly talking, Brett's first instinct was to call Maddox.

But that would endanger Willow's son.

Besides, Maddox had always been by the book. He'd want to call in the authorities, issue an Amber Alert, all the things they should be doing.

But if they did those things, Willow's little boy could end up dead like his father.

He couldn't allow that to happen.

So he made a snap decision. He'd bury Leo's body and protect Willow until they found Sam.

Chapter Four

Willow couldn't drag her eyes away from Leo's dead body. She couldn't believe this was happening.

She'd hated that her marriage had fallen apart, but it hadn't been right from the beginning. She'd never loved Leo and he knew it.

And truthfully, she didn't think he'd ever loved her.

But she'd been hurt with Brett, and lonely and a single pregnant woman with nowhere to turn. Leo had offered her security and comfort.

For a little while. Then everything had changed and the charming man who'd swept in like a hero had disappeared and become…someone she was afraid of.

Someone Sam was afraid of.

That was when she'd known she had to get out.

The blood on her hands mocked her. She hadn't loved Leo but she'd never wished him dead.

And where was her precious little boy? Was he safe? Hurt? Scared?

A tremor rippled through her. Of course he was scared. He'd been taken from his home.

"We'll bury him on the ranch somewhere," Brett said. "It's too dangerous to do it in your neighborhood."

Willow rubbed her hands up and down her arms as if to

warm herself. "But what about Maddox? He's the sheriff and...your brother."

Brett's look darkened. "I know that," Brett said. "I'll talk to him and explain once we get your little boy back."

Willow's heart constricted. "I'm sorry for putting you in this position, Brett. You could get in trouble with the law. But...I didn't know who else to call."

Brett clasped her arms and forced her to look at him. "Don't worry about me, Willow. I can handle whatever happens. But we can't go to Maddox yet. We have to play by this bastard's rules, until we find Sam."

How could she argue with that? She'd give her life for her son's.

And if Brett knew that Sam was his, he'd do the same.

He probably would anyway, just because he was a Mc-Cullen. Joe McCullen had taught his boys old-fashioned values, that men were supposed to protect women and children.

Brett moved over by the bed. "I need to get him in the back of my pickup."

"Why? Aren't we going to bury him in the backyard?"

"No," Brett said. "You live in a neighborhood. And if anyone comes asking about Leo and is suspicious, this is the first place they'd look." He glanced down at the floor and indicated the braided rug. "Let's wrap him in the sheet and I can use the rug to slide him outside."

"But what if a neighbor sees us?"

Brett's jaw tightened. "Your house is set far enough back from the road, so unless someone is in the drive, we should be all right. But I'll move my truck up to the garage and we can go through there just to be safe."

Willow agreed, although she knew what they were doing was wrong. *Illegal*. That they could both be charged.

But nothing mattered now except saving Sam.

BRETT HATED THE FEAR in Willow's eyes. If he had hold of the bastard who had hurt her and taken her little boy, he'd pound his head in.

He started to roll Leo in the sheet, but doubts hit him. He'd seen enough crime shows to know that as soon as he touched the man or the bedding, he was contaminating evidence. Evidence that could lead to the killer and the person who had abducted Sam.

Besides, he'd gotten in a sticky situation once. Had been accosted by the jealous lover of a rodeo groupie he'd dated, a man who'd tried to make it look as if he was the guilty party. He'd seen how the police handled the situation. If it hadn't been for a savvy detective who paid attention to detail, Brett might have gone to jail.

Maybe he *should* call Maddox.

But the kidnapper's warning taunted him. Willow's little boy was in danger.

He couldn't take the chance on that child getting hurt. Pain tugged at his chest. He'd once thought he and Willow would have a family together.

But he'd left and she'd met Leo, and their lives had gone down another path.

Still, her little boy shouldn't suffer.

He removed his phone and snapped some pictures of the man, the wounds to his chest, the blood on the sheets, and the room.

"What are you doing?" Willow asked.

"We'll be destroying evidence here," Brett said. "I should document how we found Leo to show Maddox when we tell him."

Willow's face paled. "I can't believe this is happening, Brett. I…don't know why anyone would want to kill Leo."

Brett clenched his jaw. "We'll talk about that once we take care of him." He studied the scene again, then snapped a picture of the bullet hole in Leo's chest. "Do you have plastic gloves?"

She nodded and hurried to the kitchen. Seconds later, she returned with two pairs of latex gloves and they both pulled them on. "Let's roll him in the sheet onto the floor. Then I'll wrap him in the rug and drag him outside."

Tears glittered in Willow's eyes, but she jumped into motion to help him. The man's shirt was soaked in blood, his eyes wide with shock, his mouth slack, one hand curled into a fist as if he might have been holding something.

If he had, the killer had taken it.

"Did Leo own a gun?"

"What man in Wyoming doesn't?" Willow asked.

"What kind?"

"A pistol and a shotgun," Willow said. "But he took them when he moved out."

"Look around for bullet casings. Maddox will want them to help with the case." Willow walked around, searching the floor and the bathroom, but shook her head. "I don't see any."

"How about you? Do you have a gun?"

Willow shook her head. "No, I didn't want weapons in the house with Sam."

Good point.

"When did you learn about crime scenes?" Willow asked.

Brett shrugged. He didn't intend to share the story about that debacle with the rodeo groupie. "Television."

She frowned as if that surprised her, but he wrapped the sheet around Leo, gritting his teeth as Willow's husband stared up at him in death.

Blood had dried onto the sheet and soaked through to the mattress. Rigor had set in and Leo was a deadweight. Willow gasped as he eased the man to the rug.

"Strip the rest of the bedding," Brett said. "And bag it. We'll keep it to give to Maddox later."

Willow looked ill, but she rushed back to the kitchen and returned a moment later with a big garbage bag.

While he wrapped the top sheet tighter around Leo, she stripped the fitted sheet and comforter and jammed it in the plastic bag. Her ragged breathing rasped between them as she added the pillowcases, then she stood and stared at the bed for a moment as if she'd never be able to sleep in it again.

Brett wanted to comfort her, but he needed to get rid of Leo's corpse before anyone discovered what they'd done.

THE SCENT OF the blood on her sheets and the image of Leo lying dead in her bed made Willow feel ill.

She didn't know how she'd ever sleep in this room again.

"What should I do with these?"

"We'll bury them with Leo."

The thought of digging a hole for her husband sent bile to her throat. But as Brett dragged Leo's body on that rug into the hall, she glanced in Sam's room again, and determination rifled through her.

That empty room nearly brought her to her knees.

Determined to bring her son home no matter what, she followed Brett with the garbage bag. He pulled Leo through the hallway to the kitchen. She opened the garage door, and he left Leo in the garage, then backed his pickup around to the exterior garage door, which faced the side of the drive.

Anger at Leo mushroomed inside her.

Leo had a temper, was manipulative and secretive and… he had gotten rough with her more than once. But the day he'd put his hand on Sam, she'd ordered him to leave and told him she wanted a divorce.

Nobody would hurt her baby.

Except Sam might be hurt now… All because of the man she'd exchanged vows with. She leaned over Leo and stared at him, a mother's temper boiling over. "What did you do to get my son kidnapped?"

Of course he didn't answer. He simply laid there with his mouth slack and his eyes bulging. If possible, his face looked even paler beneath the kitchen lights.

Brett appeared a second later, wiping sweat from his brow with the back of his sleeve. He planted his hands on his hips and looked down at Leo, then up at her.

"Are you okay, Willow?"

A sob caught in her throat, and she shook her head. "How can I be all right when Sam is missing? When he might be crying for me right now?"

Silence stretched full of tension for a minute. "Then let's get this done."

Brett sounded resigned, and Willow questioned again whether she should have called him. But what else could she do?

Brett knelt and grabbed the end of the rug, and Willow decided she couldn't allow him to do this alone. She set the garbage bag down, flipped off the garage light so they couldn't be seen through the front window, then grabbed the opposite side of the rug and helped Brett drag Leo through the garage.

She was heaving for breath by the time they reached the threshold of the exterior door. Leo's body was so heavy that she didn't know how Brett would lift him.

The garage door was situated on the side of the house and wasn't visible from the street, but in silent agreement they paused to check and make sure there weren't any cars passing or anyone walking by.

"It's clear." Brett stooped down, scooped Leo up—still wrapped in the rug—and threw him over his shoulder. She bit down on her lip to stifle a gasp as Leo's arm swung over Brett's back. The dried blood on his hand and face looked macabre in the moonlight.

Brett struggled for a minute with the weight, then maneuvered Leo's body into the truck bed. He climbed in and threw an old blanket over the body, and she tossed the bag of linens in the back with him.

"I'd tell you to stay here," Brett said, "but it's not safe, Willow. Come with me and I'll bring you back later."

The last thing Willow wanted to do tonight was bury Leo, but she had started this and she had to see it through. At least until she got Sam back.

"Let me get my phone in case the kidnapper calls tonight."

BRETT SAID A SILENT prayer that the kidnapper would call, but as Willow went to retrieve her phone and purse, he had a bad feeling. What did the kidnapper want?

Money? Or something else?

All questions to pursue once they got rid of Leo's body.

Damn, he couldn't believe he was doing this. Actively covering up a crime. If his agent and his fans found out, his career would be over.

Hell, if Maddox didn't help him out when he finally explained things, his life as a free man would be over.

But he couldn't let Willow down.

His phone buzzed, and he checked the caller ID. Kitty. Another pesky immature groupie.

Dammit, he'd slept with her twice, then broken it off, but she'd become obsessed with him. He'd warned her that he'd take out a restraining order if she didn't leave him alone.

He'd hoped coming home for a while might give her the time and distance she needed to move on.

Willow locked the house and closed the garage door and

he let the call roll to voice mail, then covered Leo's body in the bed of the truck. If he got stopped…no, that was not going to happen.

He removed the latex gloves and Willow did the same. He stuffed both pairs in his pocket, then opened the passenger side for Willow, and she climbed onto the seat, her hand shaking as she gripped the seat edge. The wind kicked up, stirring leaves and rattling the windows as he hurried to the driver's side, jumped in and started the engine.

The moon disappeared behind storm clouds as he eased onto the street. Senses on alert, Brett searched right and left, then in the rearview mirror, looking for someone who might be watching.

For all he knew, the killer/kidnapper might have hung around to see if Willow called the law.

Willow leaned against the doorframe, looking lost and shaken, and so terrified that Brett's heart broke. In spite of the fact that he was digging a hole for himself with the law and his own brother, he pulled her hand in his.

"We'll get Sam back, Willow. I promise."

"But what if—"

"Shh." He brought her hand to his mouth and kissed her fingers. "Everything will be all right. I swear."

Tears trickled down her cheeks, and she broke into another sob. Brett pulled her over beside him and wrapped his arm around her as he drove. She collapsed against him, her head against his chest, her arm slipped around his waist.

The two of them had ridden just this way in high school, hugging and kissing as they'd driven up to Make-Out Point. But tonight, they wouldn't be making out or…making love.

Tonight they were hiding her husband's body, and she was almost despondent over her missing son.

Still checking over his shoulder as he turned onto the

highway, a siren wailed from the right, and he tensed. A fire engine, ambulance, police?

Suddenly blue lights swirled against the night sky as a police car careened around the corner and flew toward them.

Brett's chest constricted. He was about to get caught with a dead body in his truck.

SAM CURLED INTO a little ball, hugged his knees to his chest and leaned against the wall. He was shaking so badly, he thought he might pee his pants. He hadn't done that since he was two.

Where was he? And why had that man with the bandana over his face grabbed him and thrown him in the trunk of his car?

Sam hated that trunk. He hated the dark.

Swiping at tears, he clutched the ratty teddy bear the man had tossed into the room with him. He didn't want the old dusty thing. He wanted his dinosaur and his mommy and his room with all his toys.

But he clutched the bear anyway because it made him feel like he wasn't all alone.

Outside the dark room, footsteps pounded and two men's voices sounded. Loud. Mad. They were barking at each other like dogs.

They had been mad at Daddy. Then one of them had pulled that gun and shot him.

Sam closed his eyes, trying to forget the red blood that had flown across the bed like a paintball exploding. Except it wasn't paint.

He couldn't forget it.

Or that choked gurgling sound Daddy had made.

He started shaking and had to hug his legs with his arms

to keep his knees from knocking. He had to be quiet. Make them think he was asleep or they'd come back and get him.

Daddy was dead.

And if he didn't do what they told him, he'd be dead, too.

Chapter Five

Willow clenched her clammy hands together as the sirens wailed closer. Dear Lord, had someone seen them leave with Leo's body?

Brett laid a hand over hers. "It'll be all right."

But they both knew it wouldn't be all right. They'd lose precious time explaining themselves to the police, and even then, they would go to jail and the kidnapper might hurt Sam.

Brett slowed and pulled off the road, but they were both shocked when the police car raced on by.

His relieved breath punctuated the air. "Whew, I thought they had us."

"Me, too." She wiped at the perspiration trickling down the side of her face, but she was trembling so badly a pained sound rumbled from her throat.

Brett pulled her to him for a moment and soothed her. "Hang in there, Willow. I'm here."

She nodded, those words giving her more comfort than he could imagine. She didn't think she could hold it together tonight if she was alone.

They sat there for several seconds, but finally Brett pulled away and inched back onto the road. By the time they reached the ranch, her breathing had finally steadied.

She had always loved Horseshoe Creek, but tonight she

found no peace in the barren stretch of land where Brett parked.

Brett kept looking in the rearview mirror and across the property as if he thought they might have been followed. The land seemed eerily quiet, the wind whistling off the ridges, whipping twigs and tumbleweed across the dirt as if a windstorm was brewing.

This rocky area was miles away from the big farmhouse where Brett had grown up, the pasture where the McCullen cattle grazed, from the stables housing their working horses and the bungalows where the ranch hands lived.

The truck rumbled to a stop, and Brett cut the engine. He turned to her for a moment, the tension thick between them. "His body should be safe out here until we get your son back."

Willow bit down on her lip as the full implications of what they were doing hit her. Not only was she compromising evidence and disposing of a body, but when the truth was revealed, she would look like a bitter ex-wife—one who might have killed Leo and then called an old boyfriend to help her dispose of his body.

She could go to jail and so could Brett.

It would also drive a bigger wedge between him and his brother Maddox.

But what other choice did she have?

She touched the knot on the back of her head where the intruder had hit her, then looked down at her cell phone, willing it to ring.

Poor little Sam must be terrified. Wondering where she was. Wanting to be home in his own bed.

Resigned, she reached for the door handle. "Let's get this done and pray the kidnapper calls tonight, then we can explain everything to Maddox."

Brett's eyes flashed with turmoil at the mention of his

brother, compounding her guilt. The men had just buried their beloved father and now she was asking *this* of him.

She hated herself for that.

But Sam's face flashed in her mind, and she couldn't turn back.

"WAIT IN THE TRUCK," Brett told Willow.

Brett jumped out of the pickup, walked to the truck bed and retrieved a shovel. Yanking on work gloves, he strode to a flat stretch between two boulders, a piece of land hidden from view and safe from animals scavenging for food.

A coyote howled in the distance and more night sounds broke the quiet. His breath puffed out as he jammed the shovel in the hard dirt and began to dig. Pebbles and dry dirt crunched, and he looked up to see Willow approaching with a second shovel.

"I told you to stay in the truck."

"This is my mess," Willow said. "I…have to help."

Brett wanted to spare her whatever pain he could. "Let me do it for you, Willow, *please*."

Her gaze met his in the dim light of the moon, and she shook her head, then joined him and together they dug the grave.

It took them over an hour to make a hole deep enough to cover Leo so the animals wouldn't scavenge for him. Willow leaned back against a boulder, her breath ragged. She looked exhausted, dirty and sweaty from exertion, and shell-shocked from the events of the night.

He returned to the truck, dragged Leo's body inside the rug from the bed, then hauled him over his shoulder and carried him to the grave. Before he dumped him inside, he retrieved a large piece of plastic from his trunk and placed it in the hole to protect the body even more.

Willow watched in silence as he tossed Leo into the

grave, then he shoveled the loose dirt back on top of him, covering him with the mound until he was hidden from sight.

But he had a bad feeling that even though Leo was covered, Willow would still continue seeing his face in her mind.

He smoothed down the dirt, then stroked her arm. "It's done. Now we wait on the ransom call."

She nodded, obviously too numb and wrung out to talk, and he led her back to the truck. He tossed the shovels in the truck bed, grabbed a rag and handed it to Willow to wipe her hands.

She looked so shaken that he decided not to take her back to that house. There were a couple of small cabins on the north side of the ranch that weren't in use because they'd reserved that quadrant to build more stables. Even though he was a bull rider, he also did trick riding, so his father had wanted Brett to handle the horse side of the business. But when Brett left town, Maddox and his father had put the idea on hold. "I'm going to take you to one of the cabins to get some rest."

Willow didn't argue. Her hand trembled as she fastened her seat belt, then she leaned her head back and closed her eyes. He drove across the property to the north, where he hoped to find an empty cabin.

Five minutes later, he found the one he was looking for just a few feet from the creek. He parked and walked around to help Willow out. The door to the place was unlocked—so like the McCullens. Trustworthy to a fault.

The electricity was on, thank goodness, and the place was furnished, although it was nothing fancy, but the den held a comfortable-looking sofa and chair and a double bed sat in the bedroom, complete with linens. He and Willow had sneaked out to this cabin years ago to make love in the afternoon.

Her eyes flickered with recognition for a moment before despair returned.

"Thank you for coming tonight," Willow said in a raw whisper.

He gestured toward the bedroom. "Get some rest. I'll hang around for a while."

She looked down at her hands, still muddy from the dirt and blood. "I have to wash up first."

He ducked into the bathroom and found towels and soap. The place was also fairly clean as if someone had used it recently. His father was always taking someone in to help them out so he wasn't surprised.He still felt like he'd walk into the main house and find him sitting in his chair. But he was gone.

Willow flipped on the shower, then reached for the button on her shirt to undress.

It was too tempting to be this close to her and not touch her, so he stepped into the hall and shut the door to give her some privacy. Self-doubts over his actions tonight assailed him, and he went to his truck, grabbed a bottle of whiskey and brought it inside.

As much as he wanted to comfort Willow and hold her tonight, he couldn't touch her. She'd only called him to help her find her son.

And he would do that.

But tonight the stench of her husband's dead body permeated his skin, and the lies he would have to tell his brother haunted him.

IMAGES OF DIGGING her husband's grave tormented Willow as she showered. No matter how hard she scrubbed, she couldn't erase them.

Leo was dead. Shot. Murdered.

And Sam was missing.

Her little boy's face materialized, and her chest tightened. Sam liked soccer and climbing trees and chocolate chip cookies. And he had just learned to pedal on his bike with training wheels. Only Leo had run over his bike.

Where was Sam now? Was he cold or hungry?

She rinsed, dried off and looked at the clock. It was after four. Was Sam asleep somewhere, or was he too terrified to sleep? His favorite stuffed dinosaur was still in his room...

She found a robe in the closet and tugged it on, then checked her phone in case she'd missed the kidnapper. But no one had called.

Tears burned the backs of her eyelids. Why hadn't they phoned?

Nerves on edge, she walked into the kitchen and spotted a bottle of whiskey on the counter. Brett had always liked brown whiskey. In fact, in high school, he'd sneaked some of his father's to this very cabin and they'd imbibed before they'd made love.

She couldn't allow herself to think about falling in bed with Brett again.

This was an expensive brand of whiskey, though, much more so than the brand Joe McCullen drank. Of course, Brett had done well on the rodeo circuit.

Both financially and with the women.

An empty glass sat beside the bottle, and she poured herself a finger full, then found Brett sitting in the porch swing with a tumbler of his own.

He looked up at her when she stepped onto the porch, his handsome face strained with the night's events.

"I should go home," Willow said from the doorway.

Brett shook his head. "Not tonight. We'll pick up some

of your things tomorrow, but you aren't staying in that house until this is over and Leo's killer is dead or in jail."

"But—"

"No buts, Willow." He sipped his whiskey. "It's not safe. Besides, we shouldn't disturb anything in the house, so when we do call Maddox in, he can process the place for evidence."

He was right. "I realize this is putting you in a difficult position with Maddox."

Brett shrugged. "That's nothing new."

Willow sank onto the swing beside him. She'd never had siblings although she'd always wanted a sister or a brother, especially when she was growing up. Her mother had died when she was five, and she'd been left with her father who'd turned to drinking to drown his problems. That alcohol had finally killed him two weeks before she'd graduated from high school.

Another reason she'd gravitated toward Brett and it had hurt so much when he'd left town. She had literally been alone.

"I know you've had issues, Brett, but your father just died, and you and your brothers should be patching things up." She took a swallow of her own liquor, grateful for the warmth of the alcohol as it eased her nerves. "Family means everything, Brett. When you don't have one anymore, you realize how important it is."

Brett's gaze latched with hers, but the flirtatious gleam she'd seen years ago and in the tabloids was gone. Instead, a dark intensity made his eyes look almost black.

"I'm sorry you lost yours. I know that last year with your dad was rough."

It was Willow's turn to shrug, although it was Brett leaving a second time that had sent her into Leo's arms. Made her vulnerable to his false charm.

"My family is Sam now. I can't go on if something happens to him."

Brett reached out and covered her hand with his. "We will find him, I promise. And I'll make sure whoever abducted him pays."

She desperately wanted to believe him.

"There's something I have to ask you, Willow."

A knot seized her stomach at his tone. "What?"

"Where were you earlier today?"

Willow tensed. "Why? You don't think *I* shot Leo, do you?"

He hesitated, long enough to make her think that he had considered the possibility. That hurt.

"No," he finally said. "But I have to ask, because the police will."

Willow sucked in a sharp breath. "I did errands, had to drop off some of my orders. Sam was staying with my neighbor Gina, but apparently Leo picked him up." That sick feeling hit her again.

"This other woman can corroborate your story?"

Willow pinched her lips together, angry. "Yes, Brett."

Would she need a more solid alibi to prove that she hadn't killed her husband?

THE PAIN IN Willow's eyes made Brett strengthen his resolve to help her. "Do you have any idea who abducted Sam?"

She shook her head, her hair falling like a curtain around her face. "I didn't recognize the man's voice. And he wore a ski mask."

"You said that Leo didn't have a bank account? Where did he keep his money?"

Willow traced her finger along the rim of her glass. "He kept cash in a safe when he lived with me. But he cleaned that out when he left."

"It seems odd that a businessman wouldn't have had bank accounts, maybe even a financial advisor."

"I thought so, too, but he just got defensive every time I mentioned it."

Brett rocked the swing back and forth with his feet. "Where did he go when he moved out?"

"I don't know."

"He didn't send child support?"

"No. And I was okay with that. When he left, I was so glad to have him out of my life, out of Sam's life, that I didn't want anything from him."

Brett willed his temper in check. The McCullen men had been raised to protect women, and to honor them. No man ever laid a hand on a woman or child.

"How bad was it?" he asked gruffly.

Willow sighed wearily. "At first it was just arguments. He wanted to control everything, from the money I spent, to how I took care of the house. I stood my ground, and he didn't like it."

"Good for you."

A small smile tilted her mouth. "He was nice in the beginning, Brett, but he changed once we married. Nothing I did was right. And he was always traveling and refused to tell me where he was going."

"You think he was having an affair?"

Willow shrugged. "It wouldn't have surprised me."

Brett contemplated that idea. What if Leo had been seeing another woman and she had killed him?

Still, why would that woman abduct Sam?

Unless she thought Willow had Leo's money.

"Tell me about his business," Brett said. "What did Leo do for a living?"

"When we first met, he said he'd made it big with some investment, something about mining uranium."

Made sense. Wyoming was rich in rare earth elements and mining.

"Did he say how much money he made? Thousands? A million?"

Willow bit down on her lip. "No. He just said he'd—we'd—be taken care of for life."

Brett considered the small house where Willow lived. "If he had so much money, why were you living in that little place?"

Willow frowned. "I moved there after Leo left. I wanted a fresh start."

"Where was your other house?"

"Cheyenne," Willow said. "But it was a rental, too. He said he was holding out to buy a big spread and build his dream house. But he never started anything."

"Did he have a business card? Or was there a business associate he mentioned?"

"No." Willow's voice cracked. "I'm sorry. I'm not being much help."

She obviously hadn't known much about her husband, which seemed odd to him. Willow had always been honest, trusting, and she valued family but she was also cautious because her father had had problems.

So why had she been charmed by Leo? Had his money appealed to her?

That also didn't fit with the Willow he'd known.

"Did Leo have any family? A sister? Brother? Parents?"

"No," Willow said. "He lost both his parents." Willow leaned against the back of the porch swing, her face ashen. "Looking back, Brett, I feel like I didn't know Leo at all."

Brett tossed back the rest of his whiskey. "You're exhausted now, but maybe tomorrow you'll remember more."

If he was lucky, he'd find something in the house to add insight into Willow's dead husband.

Knowing more about him might clue them in to the reason for his death.

He patted Willow's hand. "Go inside and try to get some sleep."

"How can I sleep when I don't know where Sam is? He must be scared…and what if he's hurt? What if that man did something to him?"

Brett cupped her face with his hands. "Listen to me, Willow. If this man wanted something from Leo, and he didn't get it, he's going to use Sam as leverage. So if we figure out what kind of trouble Leo was in, we can figure out how to save your son."

He coaxed her to stand. "Try to rest until he calls with his demands."

Willow glanced down at his hand. "Are you staying here?"

He wanted to. But that would be too tempting.

"No. I'll run back to the farmhouse to shower. I'll bring you some breakfast in a little while, then we can stop by your house for some of your things."

He opened the door and ushered her inside. "Now lock up. You'll be safe here. And when the kidnapper calls, phone me and I'll come right over."

Her golden eyes flickered with fear, but she nodded and slipped inside. He waited until he heard the door lock, then hurried to his truck before he went inside and crawled in bed with her.

Tension thrummed through him as he drove back to the farmhouse and parked.

Just as he let himself inside the house, Maddox was jogging down the steps. His gaze roved over Brett's dirt-stained clothes, a disapproving scowl stretching his mouth into a thin line.

"We just buried our father, and you went out partying,

huh?" Maddox muttered. "Some things never change, do they?"

Brett bit his tongue to keep from a retort.

Unable to tell him the truth, he let his brother believe the lesser of the evils, pasted on a cocky grin like he would after an all-night drunk and climbed the steps to his old room.

If his brother knew that he'd buried a murdered man on McCullen land, he'd lock him up and never talk to him again.

Chapter Six

Too on edge to sleep, Brett showered, anxious to wash the stench of Leo's dead body off him.

But all the soap in the world couldn't erase the memory of what he'd done.

He envisioned the headlines—Rodeo Star Brett McCullen Arrested for Covering Up a Murder, for Tampering with Evidence in a Homicide…

The list could go on and on.

If—no, *when*—it was revealed that he and Willow shared a past, people might think that the two of them had plotted to kill her husband so they could be together.

Perspiration beaded on his neck as he buttoned his shirt.

The only way to make sure the two of them weren't charged was to find out who had killed Leo. Then they could recover Willow's little boy and turn the situation over to Maddox.

He dressed in jeans, fastened his belt and yanked on his cowboy boots. Then he packed a duffel bag of clothes in case he needed to stay with Willow and stowed them in his Range Rover.

His eyes felt bleary from lack of sleep, but he couldn't rest right now. He had to find some answers.

Willow and her little boy were depending on him.

The first place he would start was Leo's truck. It had

been left in Willow's drive. Maybe there was something inside it that would give him a lead.

The scent of strong coffee and bacon wafted through the air as he entered the dining room. Mama Mary was humming a gospel song in the kitchen, but she had set out coffee and juice along with hot biscuits, bacon and eggs on the sideboard.

He poured himself a mug of coffee, then made a breakfast sandwich and wolfed it down. She ambled in just as he was finishing, her eyes probing his.

"How you doing this morning, Mr. Brett?"

He and his brothers always said Mama Mary had eyes in the back of her head, and a sixth sense that told her when one of them had been bad. She was giving him that look this morning.

He shrugged. "Okay."

"Hmm-hmm."

If guilt wasn't pressing against his chest so badly he would have chuckled. "It's hard being back here without Dad," he said, hoping she'd think his grief was all that was eating at him.

"I know. We're all gonna miss your daddy." She patted his shoulder and poured him another cup of coffee. "Best remember that and take care to make up with the ones still on this side of the ground."

He understood her not-so-subtle message.

Unfortunately his actions the night before would only create a bigger chasm and garner more disapproval from his older brother. He never could measure up to Maddox.

She cleared his plate. "Maddox wanted to check the fence on the west side before he went to the sheriff's office."

How Maddox handled being in the office and the ranch was beyond Brett. But then again, Maddox was the one who *could* do it all and make it look easy at the same time.

Hadn't his father told him that a million times?

"You know Maddox got engaged to this pretty lady named Rose?" Mama Mary said with a sparkle in her eye.

Brett nodded. "Is that her name?"

"Yeah, she's a sweetheart. Owns the antique store in town where Willow sells her quilts. Poor Rose had some trouble a while back, but Maddox handled it for her."

"I'm sure he did." He didn't mean to sound surly, but his tone bordered on sarcastic.

Mama Mary gave him a chiding look, and he grabbed one of the to-go mugs on the sideboard, filled it with coffee, wrapped an extra biscuit and bacon in a napkin for Willow and gave Mama Mary a peck on the cheek.

"Thanks for breakfast. I haven't had biscuits like that since I left here."

She grinned with pride, and he hurried away before she asked him where he was going. He could lie to Maddox, but it was harder to lie to Mama Mary because she could see right through him.

Wind stirred dust around his boots, and the temperature had dropped twenty degrees overnight. As he drove across the ranch, the beauty of the land struck him along with memories of riding with his brothers as a kid. The campouts and cattle drives. The horseshoe contests and trick riding.

When he'd left Pistol Whip, he'd been young and eager for travels, to see new places, to escape the routine of ranch life, and he'd enjoyed the different towns and women.

This morning, though, the land looked peaceful. The women's faces a blur.

There was only one woman he'd ever really cared about, and that was Willow.

By the time he reached her place, worry for her son dominated his mind.

Knowing Willow must be frantic, he scanned the outside of her rental house and the property when he arrived. Everything appeared as he'd left it the night before.

Leo's truck was still parked on the lawn, the little boy's bike mangled.

He yanked on a pair of work gloves to keep from leaving fingerprints, then climbed out and walked over to the truck. For a man who supposedly had landed a windfall, the truck was old and shabby looking. Barring a few tools, the truck bed was empty.

The door to the cab was unlocked, as if the man had gotten out in a hurry. Brett slipped inside and checked the seat. Nothing.

No papers, computer or cell phone. No gun.

He opened the glove compartment and found a wallet with a driver's license and a hundred dollars in cash.

He didn't find an insurance card, but found a tiny slip of paper with a name and phone number.

It was a woman's name. Doris Benedict.

Brett's instincts kicked in. If Leo had another woman on the side, maybe she'd killed him.

He jammed the paper in his pocket. It was a place to start.

WILLOW DOZED TO SLEEP but dreamed of her little boy and Brett, and woke up in a sweat.

In the dream, Sam looked so much like his father sitting on that horse that it nearly took her breath away and resurrected memories of watching Brett at the rodeo when he was eighteen.

She'd fallen in love with him that day. He'd looked so handsome with his thick hair glinting in the sunlight. When he'd turned his flirtatious smile on her, she hadn't been able to resist.

She had been alone so long. Dubbed poor white trash

because her father had been a mean drunk and she was motherless. The very reason she'd been determined to be a good mother to Sam.

But now he was missing because she'd been fooled by Leo's promises and wound up marrying a mean drunk herself.

But that day Brett had made her feel so special...not like poor trash. All the other girls at the rodeo wanted Brett Mc-Cullen, the up-and-coming rodeo star.

But after he'd received his buckle for winning, he'd walked over to her and kissed her right in front of the crowd.

How could she *not* have fallen in love with him?

It didn't matter.

Brett hadn't wanted her the past few years. He had plenty of women. And he certainly didn't intend to stay in Pistol Whip and settle down.

She had done the right thing. If she'd told Brett she was pregnant five years ago, he might have stuck around, but he would have resented her. And that would have destroyed their love.

She found some coffee in the kitchen and brewed a pot, then carried a mug and her phone to the front porch and sat down, praying it would ring with news about how to get Sam back.

BRETT DROVE BACK to the cabin, anxious to check on Willow. Hopefully the kidnapper would phone today with his demands.

But if Willow didn't have the money, what did they want?

Willow was sitting on the porch, sipping coffee and looking so damn lost and pained that his lungs squeezed for air. He'd do anything to make her happy again.

But the only way to do that was to put her son back in her arms.

He parked, then carried the biscuit in one hand as he walked up to the porch.

He handed her the food. "Any word?"

She unwrapped the biscuit, although she rewrapped it as if she couldn't eat. That, and the desolate look in her eyes, told him all he needed to know.

"I searched Leo's truck and found a woman's name scribbled on a slip of paper. Doris Benedict. Do you know her?"

"No. Who is she?" Willow ran a hand through her hair, the wavy strands tangling as the wind picked them up and whipped them around her face. Winter was blowing in to Pistol Whip with its cold and gusty windstorms.

"I don't know," Brett said. "But maybe she knows something about Leo that can help us."

Willow rose from the porch swing, her face even more pale in the early morning light. "I'll go with you."

"Are you sure? We don't know what we'll find—what her relationship with Leo was."

"I don't care if they were lovers," Willow said staunchly. "I was done with Leo a long time ago. But if she can help us find Sam, I have to talk to her."

Brett gave a clipped nod. She'd been done with Leo a long time ago—had she *loved* him, though?

At one time he'd thought she loved *him*. But when he'd left town, she'd completely cut him out of her life.

She disappeared inside the cabin and returned a moment later with her purse over her shoulder. But she kept her phone clutched in one hand. Her fingers were wrapped so tightly around it that they looked white.

She didn't look at him as she started down the steps. "Let's go."

Brett followed her, climbed in the truck and started the engine, the tension between them thick with unanswered questions as he drove toward the woman's address.

Doris Benedict lived in Laramie, in a stone duplex on the outskirts of town. Dry scrub brush and weeds choked the tiny yard. No children's toys outside, so she must not have kids. Although the duplex didn't look fancy or expensive, a fairly new dark green sedan sat in the drive.

Brett and Willow walked together to the front door. Willow folded her arms while he buzzed the doorbell. A car engine rumbled from next door while voices from another neighbor herding her kids out to the bus stop echoed in the wind.

He punched the doorbell again, and a woman's voice shouted from inside that she was coming. A second later, the door opened, and a young woman with a bad dye job and sparkling earrings that dangled to her shoulders stood on the other side.

He guessed her age to be about thirty-four, although she had the ruddy skin of a heavy smoker, so she could have been younger.

Her flirtatious smile flitted over him. "You're that rodeo star?"

He nodded. "Yes, ma'am. Brett McCullen."

When her gaze roved from him to Willow, her ruby-red lips formed a frown. "What do you want?"

Brett narrowed his eyes at the contempt in her voice.

"My name is Willow James, um Willow Howard—"

"I know who you are." Doris reached for the door as if to slam it in their faces, but Brett caught it with one hand.

Willow looked stunned. "How do you know me?"

Doris removed a cigarette from the pack in the pocket of her too-tight jeans. "Leo married you."

Brett frowned. "How do you know Leo, Ms. Benedict?"

The woman angled her face toward him, her eyes menacing. "He and I dated a while back."

"How far back?" Brett asked.

She lit her cigarette, tilted her head back and inhaled a drag, then glared at Willow. "About five years. I thought we were going to get hitched, but then he married you."

"You dated Leo?" Willow asked.

The woman pushed her face toward Willow. "What's that supposed to mean? You don't think he'd go out with a woman like me?"

"It's not that," Willow said quickly. "It's just that Leo never mentioned his prior relationships."

Doris chuckled. "Honey, there's a lot of things Leo didn't tell you."

Willow's breath rasped out. "Like what?"

Doris blew smoke into the air. "Why don't you ask him?"

Willow glanced at him and he gave a short shake of his head, silently willing her not to divulge that Leo was dead. Not yet.

"When was the last time you saw him?" Brett asked.

Doris shrugged. "About a month ago."

"You were seeing him while he was married to Willow?" Brett asked.

Doris poked him in the chest. "Don't judge me, Brett McCullen. Leo loved me."

"Then why did he marry me?" Willow asked.

Doris laughed again. "Because you were respectable. And Leo needed a respectable wife so nobody in town would ask too many questions."

"Why didn't he want them asking questions?" Brett asked.

Doris tapped ashes on the porch floor at Willow's feet. "Again—why don't you ask him?"

"Because I'm asking you," Willow said, her voice stronger. "You obviously don't like me and wanted Leo for yourself. So when I filed for divorce, did he come to you?"

Doris's eyes widened in shock. "You were divorcing Leo?"

Brett scrutinized her body language. She sounded sincerely surprised. But if she'd discovered he and Willow weren't together, and he still didn't want her, she might have killed him out of anger.

Although she didn't appear to be the motherly type. So if she had killed Leo, why kidnap Sam?

SAM HUGGED THE RAGGEDY stuffed animal under his arm and rubbed his eyes. He wanted his mommy.

But he remembered what had happened the night before and tears filled his eyes. Those bad men…two of them. One with the scarf over his mouth and the other with that black ski mask.

All he could see was their eyes. Mean eyes.

And the tattoo. Both of them had tattoos on their necks. One had a long rattlesnake that wound around his throat. The other had crossbones like he'd seen on some of the T-shirts at Halloween.

Those crossbones meant poison or the devil or something else evil.

Just like the bad men.

Red flashed behind his eyes, and he heard the gunshots blasting like fireworks. He covered his ears to snuff them out just like he'd done at his house.

But he'd peeked from the closet and seen his daddy and all that blood ran down his shirt. Then Daddy's eyes had gone wide, like they did on TV when someone was dead.

He didn't much care if he was dead, and he felt real bad about that. Kids were supposed to love their fathers. But he couldn't help it—his daddy had been mean to his mommy.

He didn't want to be dead, too, though.

He sat up on the cot and pushed the curtain to the side and looked through the dirty window. A spider was crawling across the windowsill, and a tree branch was beating against the glass.

He tried to see where he was, but all he saw was woods.

Big trees stuck together, so close that he couldn't see past them or even between them for a path.

He pushed at the window to open it and climb out. He was scared of the woods and the dark, but he'd rather run in there than be stuck here with these bad men with the tattoos and guns.

But the window wouldn't move. He pushed and shoved. Then he saw nails. They were hammered in the edge to keep it closed.

His chin quivered. They had locked him in here, and he was never going to get out.

Footsteps pounded outside the door, and he dropped back onto the bed, rolled to his side, grabbed the blanket and pulled it over him, then pretended to be asleep.

The door screeched open, then the snake-man's voice said, "What are we gonna do with the kid?"

"Dump him when we get what we want."

Sam pressed his hand over his mouth to keep from crying out loud.

Their boots pounded harder. They were coming toward him.

He squeezed his eyes shut, swallowing hard not to let the tears fall. Then one of them jerked the blanket off his head.

"Say *hi* to your mother, kid," Snake man said.

Sam couldn't help it. A tear slid down his cheek. Then the big man snapped a picture of him with his phone.

A second later, he tossed the blanket back to him, then

stalked across the room. The big man's words echoed in his head.

They were calling his mommy. Maybe she'd come and get him.

But they said something else. They were going to dump him when they got what they wanted. Would he ever see his mommy again?

Chapter Seven

Willow couldn't take her eyes off Doris.

Leo had been involved with *this* woman?

Doris was the complete opposite of her. Everything from her low-cut top to those red high-heel boots screamed that she liked the wilder side of life.

She'd considered the fact that during their marriage Leo had cheated on her. He was a womanizer and liked to flirt. And he'd lost interest in her early on, almost as soon as they'd exchanged vows.

But now she realized he and Doris had rolled in the hay while Willow had wondered what was wrong with her, if she didn't possess enough sex appeal to please him.

She certainly hadn't had enough to keep Brett in town. He'd wanted other women, too.

But Doris said Willow had been a tool to make Leo look good. For what reason?

Who had he wanted to impress?

And if Doris had killed Leo, why had she admitted that she knew *her*?

"Can we come inside for a minute?" Willow asked. "I need to use your restroom." What she really needed was to know if Sam was inside the house.

Doris glared at her, but waved them inside the foyer. "First door on the left."

Willow hurried down the hall, but she did a quick visual as she passed the small living room. Basic furniture, hair and makeup magazines on the oak coffee table, but no toys or children's books.

She ducked in the bathroom and closed the door, then checked the closet and cabinet. Sam wasn't hidden inside, and there were no kids' toothpaste or toys. She flushed the toilet, so as not to draw suspicion, then ran some water in the sink. When she finished, she slipped out and peered into the kitchen. Doris was handing Brett a cup of coffee.

She tiptoed down the hall to the bedrooms. One on the left that looked ostentatious with a hot-pink satin comforter, a silk robe tossed across a chaise and a door that probably led to a master bath. She veered into the second bedroom, which was filled with junk. Boxes of items Doris had obviously ordered online. She didn't see any signs of Sam or a child anywhere, though. She checked the closet and found more boxes stacked, many of them unopened. Many from expensive department stores.

How does the woman support her shopping habit?

Brett's voice echoed as she made her way back to him.

"Where were you yesterday, Doris?" Brett asked.

Doris tapped cigarette ashes into a coffee cup she held in her hand. "I was out. Why you want to know?"

"Out where?" Brett asked.

"Honey, you sound like a cop, not a cowboy"

Doris batted her lashes at Brett and traced a finger along his collar. Willow bit her lip. Surely Brett wouldn't be attracted to Doris like Leo had…

Brett winked at her, irking Willow even more. "Just indulge me, Doris," Brett said smoothly. "Were you with Leo?"

Anger flickered in the woman's eyes for a brief second. "No. I had to pull a double shift at Hoochies."

Willow inhaled to stem a reaction. Hoochies was a well-known bar where the waitresses offered dessert on the side.

"I suppose someone at Hoochies can verify that," Brett said.

Doris jerked her hand back. "You said that like I need a damn alibi."

Willow couldn't resist. She didn't like the fact that Leo cheated on her with this woman or that she'd touched Brett, and that Brett didn't seem to mind. "Maybe you do."

Panic tinged Doris's voice. "Did something happen to Leo?"

Willow shrugged. "Do you know anyone who'd want to hurt him?"

Doris took a step toward Willow. "Where is he? What happened? Is he hurt?"

For a millisecond, Willow almost felt sorry for the woman. Doris actually loved that lying bastard. "It's possible."

Doris grabbed Willow's arm. "What's that supposed to mean?"

Willow extracted herself from the woman's claws. "Just answer the question. Do you know anyone who'd want to hurt him?"

Doris glanced at Brett as if she wanted assurance that Leo was okay, but Brett maintained a straight face.

"Did he owe someone money?" Brett asked.

"Maybe." Doris's voice cracked. "I know he got in some trouble a while back."

"What kind of trouble?" Brett asked.

"Something with the law," Doris said in a low voice. "He never told me exactly what."

Willow grimaced. He'd certainly never shared that information with her either.

"And then there was his old man. The two of them didn't get along."

"His father?" Willow asked, her breath catching.

"Yeah," Doris said as she snatched another cigarette and lit up. "I don't know what happened between them, but there was some bad blood."

Willow forced herself not to react. Leo had claimed both his parents were dead.

Was everything he'd told her a lie?

BRETT SCHOOLED HIS FACE into a neutral expression, although it was all he could do not to punch his fist through a wall.

How had a man like Leo won Willow's sweet heart?

And why would a man cheat on Willow with Doris, when Willow was the most beautiful, tenderhearted, desirable woman in the whole damn world?

"What was his father's name?" he asked.

Doris shrugged. "Hell, I don't know. Every time I tried to ask him, he got mad. Told me it was none of my business."

Brett shifted. He wished she'd give him something concrete. Although this could be a lead. If Leo had been in trouble before, especially with the law, he probably had an arrest record.

Another thought occurred to him. One of his buddies had won thousands in the rodeo circuit, but he'd lost it all in Vegas.

"Was Leo into gambling?"

Doris inhaled and blew smoke into the air, her gaze fixed on him. "You're really scaring me now."

"Listen," Willow said. "Leo disappeared with my savings and I need it for medical expenses for my son."

Brett admired the way Willow told the lie without giving herself away. He watched Doris for a reaction, anything that might tip them off that she knew where Sam was being held.

"I have no idea where Leo is," Doris said instead. "But if I talk to him, I'll tell him about the kid." Her voice grew low, almost sincere. "I hope it's not too serious."

Willow gave a little shake of her head, but real tears glittered on her eyelashes.

"Was he into gambling?" Brett asked. "It could explain the reason he stole from Willow."

"He gambled some, but I don't think he was in big debt for it, if that's what you mean."

"Did he leave any money with you?"

Doris muttered a sarcastic sound. "If he left me money, do you think I'd be living in this dump or working doubles at Hoochies?"

Good point.

Brett crossed his arms. "Did Leo have any friends he might have been staying with?"

"You mean female friends?" She gave Willow a condescending look. "If he had other women, I didn't know about it. Then again, I never thought he'd marry *you*."

Brett cleared his throat. "How about male friends?"

"You mean friends who'd let him hide out with them?" Doris asked with a sarcastic grunt.

Brett nodded.

She stared at the burning tip of her cigarette for a long minute as if in thought. "He mentioned this guy named Gus a while back. But I don't know where he is. I think he might have been in jail."

Brett's instincts kicked in. If Leo and this guy were friends, they might have been in cahoots over something illegal.

He wasn't a cop, but his brother was. He wanted to ask

Maddox for his help more than he'd ever wanted to ask him anything in his life.

But the tears Willow had just wiped away haunted him. He couldn't turn to his brother now, not as the sheriff.

Although, if he could use Maddox's computer, he could research Leo's past. His father, his arrest record, this man, Gus...

That information might lead him to whatever Leo was involved in that had gotten him killed.

And then to Willow's son.

"Thank you, Doris." Brett handed her a card with his number on it. "If you think of anything else that might help us find Leo, let me know."

Doris caught his arm before he could leave, but she looked at Willow as she spoke. "If you hear from him, tell him I'm still here."

He expected Willow to show a spark of jealousy, but she gave Doris a pitying look and walked back to the car.

Brett followed, his mind ticking away. First they'd stop by Willow's house for her to pack a bag, then they'd go back to Horseshoe Creek.

Maybe he could sneak onto Maddox's home computer and access his police databases while Maddox was out.

WILLOW CHECKED HER PHONE as Brett drove away from Doris's. "Why haven't they called?"

Brett made the turn onto the highway leading back toward her rental house. "They're probably putting together a list of their demands."

She prayed they were. Although she had no idea what they would want from her. She had a couple of thousand in the bank, but that was all.

"Do you think Doris was telling the truth?" Brett asked.

Willow sighed. "She didn't seem to know Leo was dead.

If she had, why wouldn't she have hidden the fact that she knew me?"

"She was pretty up-front about that," Brett agreed. "Did you see anything in the house to indicate Sam was there or had been there?"

Willow shook her head no. "If Doris didn't murder Leo, who did?"

"That's what we're going to find out. I think the key is somewhere in Leo's past."

Willow heaved a breath. "I feel like such a fool, Brett. I thought I knew Leo when I first met him, but I didn't know him at all."

"He showed you what he wanted you to see," Brett said.

Humiliation washed over Willow. She'd made such a mess out of her life, while Brett had risen to success. "It's my fault Sam is missing," she said, her chest aching with guilt. "If anything happens to him…"

Brett squeezed her hand. "Nothing is going to happen to him. If he's anything like his mom, he's a tough little guy."

He was nothing like her and everything like Brett. But she bit back that comment for now. When they found Sam, she'd have to tell Brett the truth.

For now…she needed him focused and helping her. Because if he knew Sam was his, he'd blame her, too. And she couldn't bear any more guilt.

They lapsed into silence until they reached her house, and Brett parked. Leo's truck was still sitting in the drive, Sam's mangled bike beneath it. She gritted her teeth as they walked up to the front door. "Just pack a bag with some clothes. You can stay at the cabin until this is over."

The scent of blood and death permeated the air as Willow entered the house, then her bedroom. The bloodstain that had seeped through the sheets to the mattress looked even more stark in the daylight.

She rushed to the closet, grabbed an overnight bag, then threw a couple of pairs of jeans, a loose skirt, some blouses and underwear inside. In the bathroom she gathered her toiletries and makeup, then carried the bag back to the hall. Brett was kneeling in front of Sam's room with a dark look on his face.

"What is it?" Willow asked.

He gestured toward the floor. "A bloodstain. It looks like Leo might have initially been shot here, then moved to the bed."

"Why move him to the bed?"

"Perhaps to frame you."

Perspiration beaded on Willow's hand. "And when the police learn that Leo had another woman, they'll assume I killed him out of jealousy."

"It's possible. All the more reason we uncover the truth first."

Willow glanced up from the stain and into Sam's room. Horror washed over her as she realized that Sam could have easily seen Leo being gunned down from his room.

Poor Sam. What would witnessing a cold-blooded murder do to a four-year-old?

And if the killer knew that Sam could identify him, he might not let her have him back even if she did pay the ransom…

Chapter Eight

"Willow?" Brett gently touched her arm. "Are you all right?"

She blinked back tears. "How can I be all right when my little boy is in the hands of a murderer? What if they've hurt him, Brett?"

Brett made a low sound in his throat. "Don't think like that, Willow. We'll find him, I promise."

She nodded, although the fear was almost paralyzing. Finally, though, she stood and went into Sam's room. For a moment, she was frozen in place at the sight of his stuffed dinosaur and the soccer ball and the blocks on the floor. The top to his toy chest stood open, a few of his trucks and cars still inside although several of the toys had been pulled out and lay across the floor.

She ran her finger over the quilt she'd made for Sam. He'd picked out the dark green fabric because it was the color of grass, and he'd asked for horses on the squares. She'd appliquéd them on the squares, then sewed them together for him just a few months ago.

Would he ever get to sleep under that quilt again?

"We should go," Brett said in a deep voice. "I want to use Maddox's computer while he's at his office and see what I can learn about Leo and that man, Gus."

Willow grabbed Sam's dinosaur and the throw he liked, a

plush brown one with more horses on it, and clutched them to her. Brett carried her overnight bag, and she followed him outside to his truck.

Sam's sweet little-boy scent enveloped her as she pressed the dinosaur to her cheek, and emotions welled inside her. Last week they'd talked about Christmas and finding a tree to cut down on their own this year. They'd planned to decorate using a Western-themed tree with horse and farm-animal ornaments, since Sam was infatuated by the ranches nearby.

If only he knew his father lived on a spread like Horse-shoe Creek, and that he was a rodeo star…

One day, maybe. Although, Sam might hate her for lying to him about his father.

BRETT PARKED AT the ranch house, grateful Maddox's SUV was gone and Mama Mary's Jeep wasn't in the drive. She usually liked to grocery shop or visit friends from the church in the morning or early afternoon, but came home in plenty of time to make supper.

Maddox had another cook who prepared food for the ranch hands, and a separate dining hall for them to eat, as well.

He had no idea where Ray was. He'd made himself scarce since the funeral, probably biding his time until the reading of the will, after which he could head out of town.

"I'm sorry for taking you away from your family," Willow said. "I know this is a difficult time for you and your brothers, and you need to be spending time with them."

He hated to admit it, but he hadn't thought much about them since Willow's panicked phone call. "Don't worry about us. Our problems have nothing to do with you." Except of course, Maddox would disagree when he discovered Brett was covering up a murder, and he'd buried Willow's husband on McCullen land. Land as sacred to Maddox as it had been to Joe McCullen.

His conversation with his father about Willow having trouble echoed in his head, and he wondered if his dad had known more about Leo than he'd revealed.

The sound of cattle and horses in the distance took some of the edge off Brett's emotions as he and Willow walked up to the house. "You didn't eat your breakfast," Brett said. "I'm sure Mama Mary left something for lunch."

Willow paused to watch a quarter horse galloping in the pasture. "I'm not really hungry, Brett."

"I know, but you have to keep up your strength. I'll get us something if you want to relax in the office."

She mumbled okay, then he ushered her to the corner table in the gigantic office their father shared with Maddox, while Brett hurried to the kitchen and found meat loaf sandwiches already prepared, as if Mama Mary remembered their high school days when the boys had worked the ranch and come in starved.

He poured two glasses of tea and carried them and the sandwiches to the office. Willow nibbled on hers, while he consumed his in three bites. Their father's computer was ancient, but Maddox had installed a new one for the ranch business, one he also used for work when he was out of the office.

He attempted to access police databases, but doing so required a password. He tried Maddox's birthday, then the name of Maddox's first pony and their first dog. None fit.

He stewed over it for a minute, then plugged in their father's birthday. Bingo.

Determined to find answers for Willow, he punched Leo's name into the system. DMV records showed he had a current driver's license, then Brett ran a background check.

"Willow, listen to this. Leo Howard was born to Janie

and Hicks Howard thirty-two years ago, although Janie died when Leo was five. His father, Hicks, worked in a factory that made farm equipment, but he suffered debilitating injuries from a freak tractor accident on his own farm six years ago."

Willow nearly choked on the sandwich, and sipped her tea. "I still don't understand why he wouldn't tell me his father was alive."

"It's worth paying his father a visit to find out."

She wiped her mouth on a napkin and peered at the screen over his shoulder.

He ran a search for police records and watched as a photo of a man named Leo Stromberg, then Leo Hammerstein, popped up, both bearing Leo Howard's photo— both aliases.

Willow gasped. "Oh, my goodness. Leo had a police record."

"For stealing from his boss, a rancher named Boyle Gates, but apparently Gates dropped the charges." He scrolled farther. "But it says here he was implicated in a cattle-rustling operation. One of the men, Dale Franklin, was killed during the arrest. The other, Gus Garcia, is in prison serving time for the crime."

"How did Leo escape prison time?"

"Apparently Garcia copped to the crime. Although the police suspected a large cattle rustling operation, Garcia insisted that no one else except Franklin was involved. Franklin died in the arrest. Garcia is still in prison."

"You think he has something to do with Leo and Sam's disappearance?"

"That's what we're going to find out." Brett jotted down Garcia's full name, then the address for Leo's father. "First we'll pay a visit to Hicks Howard, then we'll go see Garcia."

An engine rumbled outside, then quieted, and Brett

heard the front door open and slam. He flipped off the computer, ushered Willow over to the table and picked up his tea.

The door to the office screeched open, and Maddox filled the doorway, his broad shoulders squared, that air of superiority and disapproval radiating from him.

"What's going on here?"

Brett shrugged. "Willow stopped by to pay her condolences about Dad."

Maddox tipped his Stetson toward Willow in a polite greeting. "Hey, Willow. Nice to see you. How's your boy?"

Willow's eyes darkened with pain, but she quickly covered her emotions. "He's growing up fast."

Maddox smiled at her, but looked back at Brett. "You're having lunch in Dad's office?"

Brett shrugged and said the first thing that entered his head. "Thought I'd feel closer to Dad this way."

Maddox's brows quirked as if he didn't believe him, but Brett had spoken a half-truth. He did feel closer to his father in this room. He envisioned Joe resting in his big recliner with his nightly shot of bourbon, a book in his hand, his head lolling to the side as he nodded off.

Maddox gave him an odd look, then at least pretended to buy the lie. Brett was grateful for that.

But he picked up his and Willow's plates and tea glasses and carried them to the kitchen, anxious to leave.

The day was passing quickly, and he didn't want Willow to spend another night without her son.

EARLY AFTERNOON SUNLIGHT faded beneath the gray clouds as Brett maneuvered the long drive to Hicks Howard's farm. The place was miles from nowhere and looked as if it hadn't been operational in years. Run-down outbuildings, overgrown pastures and a muddy pond added to the neglected feel.

If Leo had come here, it had probably been to hide out. But if he was in trouble, whoever he'd crossed had found him anyway.

Willow checked her phone again, willing it to ring with some word on Sam. Why hadn't the kidnapper called yet?

Terrifying scenarios raced through her head, but she forced herself to tune them out. She had to think positive, had to believe that she would bring Sam home.

Willow tensed, her chest hurting. Maybe she should tell Brett that Sam wasn't Leo's now. But…she wasn't ready for his reaction, for the anger, to explain why she'd kept her secret for so long.

Granted, she'd had her reasons. Brett had left her to sow his oats. He hadn't wanted to settle down. If he'd stayed around, he would have known about Sam.

Brett rolled to a stop beside a tractor overgrown by weeds. It looked as if it hadn't been used in a decade. A rusted pickup covered in mud sat under an aluminum shed.

As he approached, a mangy-looking gray cat darted beneath the porch of the wooden house. Boards were rotting on the floor, and the shutters were weathered, paint peeling.

Brett knocked on the door, and a noise sounded inside. Something banging, maybe a hammer. He knocked louder this time, and a minute later, the hammering stopped and a man yelled to hang on.

The door opened and a craggy, thin, balding man leaning on a walker stared up at them over wire-rimmed glasses. "If you're selling something, I don't want it."

"We're not selling anything. We just want to talk." Brett gestured to Willow, and she introduced herself.

"Mr. Howard, I was married to your son, Leo."

"What?" The man grunted as he shifted his weight. "I

hate to say it, honey, but you don't look like Leo's type."
He raked his gaze up and down her body. "My son usually
goes for the more showy girls."

Remembering Doris, she understood his point. "Did Leo
tell you he was married?"

The older man scratched at the beard stubble on his chin.
"No, but he didn't come around much."

"Why was that?" Brett asked.

Mr. Howard wrinkled his nose. "Why you folks asking
about my son? Is he in some kind of trouble?"

"Would it surprise you if I said he was?" Brett asked.

"No. Leo was always messing up, skirting the law. From
the time he was a teenager, he hated this farm. I was never
good enough for him, never made enough money." He gestured at the walker and his bum leg. "When he left here,
he said he was going to show me that he wasn't stupid like
me. That he'd be rich one day."

"Was he?" Willow asked.

Howard shrugged. "About five years ago he came back
with a duffel bag of money, all puffed up with himself. But
when I asked him how he got it, he hem-hawed around."

"You thought he'd gotten it illegally?" Willow asked.

His head bobbed up and down. "I confronted him, and
that's when he came at me." He gestured toward his leg.
"That's how come I had my accident."

Willow's pulse hammered. Leo had caused his father's
accident? No wonder he hadn't told her about him…

THE MORE BRETT learned about Leo Howard, the less he
liked him. "Did he give you an indication as to how he got
the money?"

"At first I thought he probably won it at the races, but
when I was in the hospital after my leg got all torn up, the

sheriff over in Rawlins stopped by and asked me if Leo stole some money from his boss. Some big hotshot rancher."

"Boyle Gates?"

"Yeah, I believe that was his name."

"Gates dropped the charges?" Brett asked.

Howard coughed. "Yeah. Don't ask me why, though."

Brett studied the old man. "You must have been angry at your son for the way he treated you."

"Like I said, he was trouble. I did all I could to help him, but it wasn't ever enough."

"Leo and I were separated for the past three years," Willow interjected. "Have you talked to him during that time?"

Howard shook his head no.

"Do you know any of his friends or men he worked with?"

"No, I think he was too ashamed of me to bring any of them around."

Or maybe he'd been too ashamed of his own friends, since they were probably crooks.

KNOWING THAT LEO had hurt his father made Willow feel ill. How had she not seen beneath his facade?

Family meant everything to her. Not money. But obviously Leo had wanted wealth and would use anyone in his path to obtain it.

Brett left his phone number in case the man thought of someone Leo might have contacted the past year.

"You didn't tell him that he has a grandson," Brett said as they settled back inside his truck.

Willow's heart pounded. She hated to keep lying to Brett, especially when he was helping her. But she needed to find the right moment to tell him the truth.

Suddenly her phone buzzed, and she quickly checked

the number. *Unknown*. Fear and hope mingled as she punched Connect.

"Hello," Willow said in a choked whisper.

"You want to see your son again?"

"Yes. Please don't hurt him."

Brett covered her hand with his, so they were both holding the phone and he could hear. "We need proof that Sam is all right."

"I told you not to call the cops," the man shouted.

"He's not a cop," Willow said, panicked. "He's just a friend."

"You want to see your son alive, do what we say."

"I will, I promise. Just tell me what you want."

"The half million Leo stashed. We'll contact you with the drop."

Willow's stomach contracted. Leo had a half million dollars stashed somewhere?

"Let me speak to Sam," she whispered.

But the line clicked to silent. A second later, the phone dinged with a text.

Willow started to tremble as she looked at the image. It was a picture of Sam on a cot, clutching a raggedy blanket, tears streaming down his face.

Emotions overcame her and a sob wrenched from her throat. *Sam was alive*.

But he looked terrified, and she had no idea what money the man was talking about, or how to find it.

Chapter Nine

Willow pressed her hand to her mouth to keep from screaming.

Brett dragged her into his arms, and she collapsed against his chest, her body shaking with the horror of that photograph.

"*Shh*, it's going to be all right," Brett said in a low, gruff voice. "We'll find him, I swear."

Willow gulped as she dug her nails into his chest. "What kind of horrible person scares a child like that?"

Brett stroked her hair, his head against hers, as if he wanted to absorb her pain. He'd always acted tough, but he was tenderhearted and had confessed how much he'd hurt when he'd lost his mother. And now he'd lost his dad, and she was dumping on him.

If he knew Sam was his, he'd probably be hurting even more…

Maybe it was best she not tell him yet. They needed to work together and if he was mad at her, that might be impossible.

Besides, when she brought Sam home and he grew attached to Brett, it would be even more difficult when Brett left town.

And he would return to the rodeo. Roaming and riding was in his blood.

He rocked her in his arms, and it had been so long since she'd been held and loved that she savored being close to him again. She had always loved Brett and had missed him so much.

Yet when this was over, Brett would go back to all those other women. If she let herself love him again, she might fall apart when he walked away. And she couldn't do that. She had to be strong for Sam.

Her heart in her throat, she forced herself to release him, then inhaled to gather her composure. She could still feel the tenderness in his arms and the worry in his voice.

He'd promised her he'd find Sam, but they both knew he might not be able to keep that promise. That the men who'd abducted Sam were very bad.

"Willow, did you know anything about Leo having a half million dollars?"

A sarcastic laugh bubbled in her throat. "Of course not. Like I said earlier, he claimed he'd made good money before we married, but I never saw it. He said he'd invested it and when the investment paid off, he was going to buy a big spread for us. But things fell apart shortly after the wedding." And now she realized he'd agreed only because he'd married her as a cover for himself.

Brett veered onto the road and drove away from the Howards' property. "What happened?"

Willow shrugged. She really didn't want to talk about Leo. Leo was the biggest mistake of her life.

"Willow, we were friends once. It might help if you told me."

Friends? He'd been the love of her life.

But right now she needed whatever he could give her. "Leo acted stressed all the time. *Secretive.* He left for days, sometimes weeks, at a time. And when I asked about his

trips, he got angry and said he was trying to make it big. I…
told him I didn't care about money, but he was obsessed."

"Just like his father said."

Willow nodded. She didn't care why Leo had stolen
money or that he'd lied about his father.

All she cared about was who he'd angered enough to
take her son.

BRETT STEERED THE TRUCK toward Rawlins, where the state
prison was, hoping Gus Garcia had some answers.

He'd do anything to alleviate Willow's pain. Granted
he didn't have a kid, but if he did, he'd be blind with fear
right now.

And he'd kill anyone who tried to hurt his child.

Hell, he'd kill anyone who hurt Willow's child.

His phone buzzed, and he glanced at the caller ID display. His publicist and agent, Ginger Redman. Knowing
she'd badger him to get back to work, he let it roll to voice
mail.

"Aren't you going to answer that?" Willow asked.

"It's not important," Brett said and realized that for the
first time in years, his career wasn't his top priority. He'd
chased his dreams and become popular and had his picture
taken a thousand times.

But he'd missed years with his father, he and his brothers were barely speaking, and he'd lost Willow to another
man. They should have had a family together.

But…he'd had a wild streak and had to see what was
out in the world.

He glanced at Willow and chewed the inside of his
cheek. He had to admit he'd had a lot of women since he'd
left Horseshoe Creek. Not as many as the tabloids reported,

but enough so that he couldn't remember all their names or faces.

But the only one he'd ever cared about was the woman sitting in the seat next to him.

"Maybe Leo hid that money in his truck," Willow said, her lost expression tearing at him.

"I searched the truck and didn't find any money." Brett gave her a look of regret. "Can you think of anywhere else he'd hide it? Did he have a safety deposit box?"

Willow rubbed the space between her eyes as if she was thinking hard. "Not that I know of."

"How about a gym locker somewhere? Or an office where he could have had a safe?"

"No. But apparently, I was totally in the dark about what he was doing."

Brett hated the self-derision in her voice. "Willow, it sounds like he was a professional liar. You saw what he wanted you to see."

"So that makes me a big fool." Willow rubbed her forehead again. "What's worse is that I allowed him in Sam's life. I trusted him with my little boy, and now Sam's in danger because of my stupidity."

"It's not your fault," Brett said, as he made the turn onto the road leading to the prison.

"Yes it is. I'm his mother. It's my job to protect him and I failed."

"It was his father's job, as well, Willow. He's the one to blame."

Willow looked down at her hands, the wilderness stretching between them as desolate as the silence. Wind whistled through the car windows, signs of winter evident in the dry brush and brittle grass. Trees swayed in the gusty breeze, the wind tossing tumbleweed and debris across the road.

"Sam is afraid of storms," Willow said, her voice cracking.

"Just hang on," Brett said. "We'll find that money. And if we don't, I'll tap into my own resources."

Willow's eyes widened. "I know you've done well, Brett, but you don't have that kind of money, do you?"

Brett gulped. "Not half a million," he said. "But I can put together a hundred thousand. And if push comes to shove, I could sell Maddox my share of the ranch."

Willow's lip quivered, and he wanted to drag her into his arms. But he'd reached the drive to the prison and the security gate, so he squared his shoulders and pulled up to the guard's station, then reached for his ID.

EMOTIONS NEARLY OVERWHELMED WILLOW. Brett had offered to give her the money to save Sam, when he had no idea he was his own son.

Guilt choked her.

She should have told him about Sam. She should tell him now.

But…there was so much to discuss. And at the moment, they had to focus on finding Sam. Then she'd tell Brett everything.

And pray that he'd forgive her.

But would he want to stay around and be part of Sam's life? Or would he head back to his rodeo life with the groupies, late-night parties and the fame?

The guard requested their ID and asked who they'd come to visit, then recognized Brett and practically dove from his booth to shake his hand.

Willow tamped down her insecurities. Brett was a celebrity. She was a small-town mom who sold quilts for a living. They lived different lives now, lives that were too far apart for them to even consider a relationship.

The guard waved Brett through and must have radioed ahead, because when they reached the prison entrance, another guard greeted them with enthusiasm and the warden rushed to shake his hand. It took a few seconds to clear security, then the warden escorted them to his office.

"You want to see Gus Garcia?" The warden's tone was questioning. "May I ask why?"

She and Brett hadn't strategized, so she used the most logical story that came to mind. "I think he might have information about my husband," Willow said. "He left me and my son, and I'm trying to get child support."

"*Ahh*, I see." He motioned for the guard to take them to a visitor's room, and Willow and Brett followed the guard down the hall.

Barring a bare table and two straight chairs, the room was empty. A guard escorted Garcia inside, the inmate's handcuffs and shackles clanging as he walked. Willow's stomach quivered with nerves at the beady set to his eyes.

He was short and robust with a shaved head, a tattoo of a cobra on one arm, and scars on his arms and face. "Keep your hands where I can see them and no touching," the guard ordered.

The beefy man shoved Garcia into a chair, and Brett gestured for Willow to sit while he remained standing, his arms crossed, feet spread. His stance defied Garcia to start something.

"What do you want with me?" Garcia asked.

"My husband was Leo Howard," Willow began.

Garcia looked genuinely shocked. "Howard got married?"

"Yes," Willow said. "Five years ago."

Garcia chuckled. "That's a surprise."

Brett cleared his throat. "We need to know what happened between you and Howard and those other men the police suspected were working with you on that cattle-rustling ring." Brett hesitated, obviously studying Garcia's reaction. "You took the fall for them. Why?"

"Who the hell told you to come and talk to me?" Garcia's eyes darted sideways as if he thought he was being lured into a trap.

"Look, we don't care what you did," Brett said. "But we suspect that you were working with a group, and that Howard was involved. We also believe that Howard took the money you all made, and tried to cut your partners out of their share.

Anger slashed on Garcia's face, and he stood. "I don't know what you're talking about. Now, leave."

"Please," Willow said.

"I don't know where any money is." Garcia waved his handcuffs in the air. "How could I? I've been locked up in this hellhole."

"But Leo worked with you, didn't he?" Willow cried. "Did he promise you he'd keep your share if you took the fall?"

Garcia turned to leave, but Willow caught his arm. He froze, his body teeming with anger. The guard stepped forward, but Willow gave him a pleading look and the guard stepped back.

Willow lowered her voice. "Please, Mr. Garcia. I think Leo swindled or betrayed your partners. Now they've kidnapped my son. If I don't give them that money, there's no telling what they'll do to him."

Garcia's eyes glittered with a warning that made Willow shiver and sink back into the chair. If he didn't have the answers they needed or refused to help her, how could she save Sam?

BRETT TRIED TO get into Gus Garcia's head, but he didn't know what made the man tick. The only reason he could fathom that the man had confessed and covered for his partners was money.

But if he thought his partners had betrayed him, why wouldn't he want to help them now?

"Listen, Mr. Garcia, I don't understand why you'd cover for Howard or anyone else, but if you tell us where Leo hid the money or who's holding it, I'll write you a check myself. How does a hundred thousand sound?"

Garcia heaved a breath, sat down, looked down at his scarred hands and studied them as if he was wrestling with the decision.

When he lifted his head, his eyes were flat. "I told you I don't know where any money is. Maybe he hid it in that house he lived in at the time."

"What house?"

Garcia shrugged. "Some place in Cheyenne."

Anger shot through Brett. He would find this house, but he wanted more. "Listen to me, a little boy's life may depend on us finding that cash."

A gambit of dark emotions splintered Garcia's face. "Leo was a liar and a thief. I ain't heard from him since I was incarcerated."

Brett stood with a curse, then tossed his card at the man. "If you think of anything that can help us, call me."

Willow looked pale as the guard led Garcia out.

"What do we do now?" she asked.

"Find that damned house where Leo lived. Maybe he did hide it somewhere inside."

Frustration knotted Brett's insides, though. Finding the money there was a long shot. And they were running out of leads.

If they didn't turn up something soon, he'd contact his financial advisor to liquidate some funds. It wouldn't be the full ransom, but it might be enough to fool the men into releasing Sam.

GUS'S GUT CHURNED as the guard led him down the hall and shoved him back into his cell.

He wanted to punch something, but that guard was watching him with eagle eyes, and if he misbehaved they'd throw him in the hole. Worse, it would go on his record, and so far he'd managed to stay clean this past year.

If he messed up, he wouldn't make parole. And making parole meant everything to him.

But dammit, nothing was right.

Leo and those other two sons of bitches that he took the fall for were supposed to lay low and give him his cut when he was released.

But it sounded as if Leo had betrayed them and run off with the money.

He gritted his teeth as the cell door slammed shut. He hated that sound.

Why had he let them coerce him into lying for them?

His wife's and little girl's faces flashed in his mind and his heart felt heavy. He knew why. He'd had no choice.

They'd threatened Valeria and his kid. That was the only reason he'd helped them with the rustling operation in the first damn place.

And the woman claimed they might hurt her little boy if they didn't get what they wanted.

Indecision tormented him. McCullen had offered him enough money that he could take his family far away and live the good life, if he talked.

But if he talked, they would go after *his* family.

All he had to do was wait out one more year of his

sentence, and he'd be a free man, then he'd be released and he'd protect them.

They were the only thing in the world that he had to live for.

Chapter Ten

Willow fought a sense of despair as they drove away from the prison. "Do you think Mr. Garcia is lying? Holding out for his share of that half million?"

Brett started the engine and drove through security. "I don't know. I think there's more to the story. If he thinks his partners, or Leo, are trying to cut him out, he probably would have taken the hundred thousand I offered him. That's a lot of money for an ex-con."

He was right. Which worried her even more. If Garcia didn't know where the money was, how could *they* find it?

"Do you know the address of the house where Leo lived after you separated?" Brett asked.

Willow racked her brain. "I think I can find it. A few bills came after Leo left and I forwarded them to him." She searched her phone, but she hadn't entered it in the contact information.

Frantic, she accessed her notes section and scrolled through them. "Here it is. 389 Indian Trail Drive. It's outside Cheyenne."

"It'll take us a while to get there," Brett said. "I know you didn't sleep last night, Willow. Close your eyes and rest while I drive."

Willow looked out at the desolate countryside with the

mountain ridges in the distance and the rocky barren land, and fresh tears threatened.

Where was her little boy? Was he cold or hungry? Were the men holding him taking care of him?

The storm clouds were thickening, growing darker. Sam would be getting anxious about the weather, about not coming home. He needed her.

BRETT WAITED UNTIL Willow's breathing grew steady, and she'd fallen into a sound sleep. His phone buzzed again. *Kitty. Dammit*, she was persistent.

He ignored it and phoned his financial planner and manager, Frank Cotton.

"What's up, Brett? Do you have some new investments you need handling?"

"Not exactly. I want you to see how much cash I can liquidate and how quickly."

A tense silent moment passed. "You want *cash*? May I ask the reason? Are you planning a big trip somewhere? Are you purchasing property?"

No, but he might need to sell to Maddox. Only if he asked Maddox, his brother would want an explanation. He could approach Ray, but he doubted Ray had the money to buy him out.

"I'm not ready to discuss my plans yet," Brett said. "But it's important. And Frank, keep this matter confidential."

"Brett, don't tell me you knocked up some young girl."

Brett ground his molars. Was that what Frank thought of him? What others thought about him? "Thanks for the vote of confidence, Frank, but it's nothing like that. Just do what I ask and keep your mouth shut." Furious, he hung up.

Snippets of his past flashed back. The rodeo groupies clamoring after him after his rides. Throwing themselves at him in hotels and bars. All wanting a piece of the celebrity.

Girls with no real clear dreams of their own, except to bag a man and live off his money.

Unlike Willow, who'd built her own life and was devoted to her little boy. Shy Willow who'd stolen his heart, but hadn't made demands on him when the itch to leave Pistol Whip had called his name.

No wonder Frank thought he might have knocked up some young thing. He had left a trail of women across the states. But he didn't remember their names or faces.

Only they'd filled that empty void in his bed, when he'd craved loving from a woman, and Willow wasn't there.

His father's praise for following his dreams echoed in his ears. He'd always thought he and his daddy were alike, that his father had regretted marrying and settling down so young. Had regretted being saddled with three boys to raise.

Brett had been determined not to make the same mistake.

But now he'd achieved success and fame, and plenty of money, but this past year he'd been restless as hell.

Lonely.

How could he have been lonely, when all he had to do was walk into a bar and he'd have a pretty woman in his bed for the night?

He glanced over at Willow, and the answer hit him swift and hard. He was lonely because none of those women were Willow.

His phone buzzed. *Maddox.*

He took a deep breath and connected the call. "Yeah?"

"What the *hell* were you looking for on my computer?"

Brett gripped the steering wheel as he veered onto the highway toward Cheyenne. "I just needed to do some research. What's the big deal?"

"The big deal is that you used my password to access police files. Why were you looking at arrest records?"

Brett's temper flared. "You checked up on me?"

"I knew you were lying earlier, so I checked the browser history." Maddox released an angry sigh. "Now tell me what you were doing? Are you in some kind of trouble?"

First Frank, now his brother. And here, he'd considered confiding in Maddox.

"Can't you just trust me for once?" Brett snapped.

A heartbeat passed. Brett didn't know if Maddox planned to answer.

"Listen, Brett, if you are in trouble, tell me. I know we don't always see eye to eye, but I'll see what I can do to help."

Emotions twisted Brett's chest. Would Maddox put himself on the line to help him?

Maybe, but he couldn't take the chance. Not with Sam's life.

"Actually I might need you to buy me out of the ranch."

A longer silence this time, one that reeked of disappointment. "So that's it? You made a fortune out there on the circuit, but you've blown it all. What are you into, Brett? Gambling? Women?"

His words cut Brett to the bone. "I'm not into anything."

Maddox didn't seem to hear him, though. "I knew you didn't care about Dad or me or Ray, but I thought you might have some allegiance to Horseshoe Creek."

His brother's disgusted voice tore at Brett. He *did* care about all of them. And he wanted part of that land more than he'd realized. Horseshoe Creek was his home. His roots.

Where he'd always thought he'd return once his wild days ended. Of course, like a fool, he'd thought Willow would be waiting...

Maddox heaved a breath. "How soon would you need to be bought out?"

Brett's gut churned. "As soon as possible."

Maddox cursed. "All right. I'll see what I can do. If I see Ray, I'll mention it to him, in case he wants part of your share."

Brett hated the thought of selling out to his brothers. Even more, he hated that Maddox thought he didn't give a damn about Horseshoe Creek.

But if they didn't locate the money Leo had stolen, he would sell his share in a heartbeat to save Willow's son.

WILLOW STIRRED FROM a restless sleep as Brett rolled to a stop in front of a small brick ranch house set off the road with a garage to the left and a barn out back. The house looked fairly well kept, although the barn was rotting and obviously wasn't being used for farming.

"Was Leo living here with someone else?" Brett asked.

"I don't know. It's possible."

Brett turned to her. "Were you the one who asked to get out of the marriage, Willow?"

"Yes." She reached for the doorknob. "But he didn't argue. He wanted out. That much was obvious." Doris's words echoed in her head. Leo needed a respectable wife so nobody in town would ask questions.

But respectable to *whom*? He hadn't told his father about her or Sam.

"He was the fool for not wanting to be with you," Brett murmured.

Willow swallowed hard. "You left me, too, Brett." She regretted the words the moment she said them.

Brett's eyes flickered with pain and truth of her statement.

"It doesn't matter now," Willow said. "All that matters is getting Sam back."

Brett's gaze latched with hers, and he started to say

something, but she opened the door and hurried up the sidewalk. This was not the time for a personal discussion of the past.

That would come. But first she had to bring Sam home.

Brett caught up to her just as she punched the doorbell. He surveyed the property as if looking for signs of trouble. The door squeaked open, and a middle-aged woman in a nurse's uniform appeared at the door. Behind her, Willow noticed a white-haired woman in a wheelchair.

"Can I help you?" the woman asked.

"My name is Willow James, and this is Brett McCullen." Brett tipped his Stetson in greeting, and Willow forged ahead. "We'd like to talk to you, Miss…?"

"Eleanor Patterson," the woman said. "What's this about?"

Willow offered her a tentative smile. "I was married to a man named Leo Howard who lived in this house. How long have you lived here?"

"Just a few months. We needed a one-story, so we found this place."

"Did you know Mr. Howard?" Brett asked.

Eleanor angled her head toward Brett, her eyes narrowed, then lighting up in recognition. "You look familiar."

Brett's handsome face slid into one of his charming smiles. "You might recognize me from the rodeo circuit, ma'am."

She snapped her fingers. "That's where it was. My goodness, you're more handsome in person than you are in the magazines."

Irritation nagged at Willow.

"Thanks," Brett said with a smile. "Ma'am, we don't mean to bother you, but did you know Leo Howard?"

"No, the house was vacant when the Realtor showed it to me."

"Did the previous tenant leave anything here when he left?" Willow asked. "Maybe some boxes or papers."

"I really don't know." Eleanor gestured toward the older woman in the chair. "Now if you'll excuse me, it's time for her medication."

"Please think hard," Willow said. "I'm looking for some important documents that I think he put somewhere."

Eleanor looked back and forth between them, then sighed. "The house was basically empty, but now that I think about it, there were a few old boxes in the attic."

"Would you mind if we take a look?" Brett gave her another flirtatious smile, and she waved him toward the hallway where a door led to an attic. Willow followed him, uneasy at the way the woman in the wheelchair watched them, as if she thought they intended to rob her.

Dust motes drifted downward and fluttered through the attic as they climbed the steps and looked across the dark interior. Three plain brown boxes were stacked against the far wall, a ratty blanket on top.

They crossed the space to them, and Brett set the first box on the floor. Willow opened it and began to dig through it while Brett worked on the second box. Flannel shirts, jeans and a dusty pair of work boots were stuffed in the box Willow examined, along with an old pocket watch that no longer worked, and a box of cigars.

Odd. Leo hadn't smoked.

"There's a couple of fake IDs in here," Brett said. "A few letters, it looks like from Doris, but Leo never opened them."

Willow spotted another envelope in the box and removed it. Inside, she found several photographs. "Look at these." She spread them out—a picture of Leo's father, then Doris, then Gus Garcia and two other men. Were those Leo's partners?

He slid another box over between them and lifted the top. Inside lay a .38 caliber gun and some ammunition. Beside it, he found another driver's license under the name of Lamar Ranger, yet it bore Leo's photo.

Oddly another pair of boots sat inside. Curious, Brett searched inside the boot but found nothing. Still wondering why the boots were stowed with the gun instead of the other box of clothes, he flipped the boots over and noticed one of the soles was loose.

"What is it?" Willow asked.

Brett removed his pocketknife and ripped the sole of the shoe off and found a folded piece of paper inside. He opened it and spread it on the floor, his heart thundering.

"A map."

Willow leaned closer to examine it. "You think this map will lead us to the place where Leo stashed the money?"

"That's exactly what I'm thinking." He folded it and put it in his pocket, then set the gun and fake ID in one box to take with them. They might need them for evidence.

Willow brushed dust from her jeans as they descended the steps and shut the attic.

Eleanor appeared in the hallway, her brows furrowed. "Did you find what you were looking for?"

"Not really," Brett said. "But we're taking this one with us. The boots are special to Willow."

Willow thanked her, then she and Brett hurried outside to his truck. She hoped Brett was right. If that map led them to the money, she could trade it for Sam and bring him back home where he belonged.

BRETT'S PULSE HAMMERED as he drove away from Eleanor's. He waited until they'd reached the dirt road he'd seen on the map, then pulled over, unfolded it and studied it.

"Where is it?" Willow asked.

Brett pointed to the crude notations on the map. Symbols of trees and rocks in various formations that must be significant, signs that would lead the way to his hiding spot.

"If it's there, and we find it," Willow said, "maybe we can end this tonight."

Brett gave a quick nod, although he was still worried that the kidnapper would hurt Sam.

He fired up the engine again, and turned onto the dirt road while Willow pointed out the landmarks.

"There's the rock in the shape of a turtle." A hundred feet down the road. "Those bushes, they form a ring." Another mile. "There's the creek."

He made each turn, the distance growing closer until he spotted the ridge with water dripping over it creating a small waterfall. Willow tapped the map. "Hopefully it's in this spot, hidden under the falls."

Brett pulled over and parked, then got out. The shovels they'd used to bury Leo were still in the back, so he retrieved them and carried them along the trail to the ridge overhang.

Willow knelt and they both examined the wall of rock. She pointed to an etching of a star. "I think the money may be buried here."

Brett propped one shovel by the rock and began to dig. Willow yanked her hair back into a ponytail, and jammed the second shovel into the dirt.

For several minutes they worked, digging deeper, but suddenly a gunshot sounded and pinged off the rock beside him.

Brett threw an arm around Willow and pushed her down, just as a second bullet whizzed by their heads.

Chapter Eleven

"Who's shooting at us?" Willow cried.

"I don't know, but the shot is coming from behind that boulder." Brett gestured toward the bushes beside the falls. "Run behind those bushes."

Willow remained hunkered down, but crept toward the left by the brush. Another shot pinged off the rocks at their feet, and he grabbed her hand and dragged her from the ledge behind some rocks.

"Stay down, Willow."

"What are you going to do?"

"Find out who the hell is firing at us."

Willow grabbed his arm to hold him back. "Please don't go, Brett. I don't want you to get hurt."

"I'm not going to wait here like a sitting duck." Brett ushered her down to the ground, then grabbed his shovel and circled back behind more bushes and trees so he could sneak up on the shooter.

Rocks skittered and a man scrambled down a path. Brett chased after him, but the man veered to the right and cut through a patch of brush to a black sedan parked behind a boulder.

Brett looked back and motioned for Willow to meet him at the car. She took off running, and he jogged down the path, trying to catch up with the shooter. By the time they reached the truck, the sedan roared away.

Brett tossed the shovel into the back of the truck, grabbed his rifle and started the engine. Willow jumped inside, looking shaken. He hit the accelerator and sped behind the sedan, determined to catch him.

"Can you see the tag number?"

Willow leaned forward and squinted as the driver spun onto a side dirt road. "SJ3... I can't see the rest."

The truck bounced over ruts in the road, spitting dust and gravel as he closed the distance. Tires squealed and the driver sped up, trees and brush flying past as he maneuvered a turn. A tire blew and the car swerved. The driver tried to regain control, but he overcompensated and the car spun in a circle, then careened toward a thicket of trees.

The passenger side slammed into the massive trunk, glass shattering and spraying the air and ground.

Brett grabbed his rifle as he slowed to a stop, and motioned for Willow to stay inside the truck.

"Be careful, Brett. He tried to kill us."

He certainly had, and Brett aimed to find out the reason. And if the bastard had Sam, he'd shove this rifle down his throat.

He raised the gun in front of him, scrutinizing the car as he inched forward. The passenger side was crunched, but the driver's side was intact. Still, the front windshield had shattered, and he didn't see movement inside.

Instincts as alert as they were when he climbed on a bull, he crept closer, his eyes trained on the driver. Daylight was waning, the sun sinking behind clouds that threatened rain, the temperature dropping.

He kept the gun aimed as he carefully opened the car door. It screeched, but opened enough for him to see that the driver was alive. Blood dotted his forehead where he'd hit his head.

Brett jammed the gun to the man's temple, then snagged him by the shirt collar so he could see his face. White, about forty years old, scruffy face, scar above his right eye.

"Who the hell are you?" Brett asked.

The man groaned and tried to open his eyes. He wiped at the blood with the back of his hand. Brett jammed the tip of the rifle harder against his skull, and the man stiffened.

"Don't shoot, buddy. Please don't kill me."

"You tried to kill me and the woman I was with." Anger hardened his tone. "I want to know the reason."

"I wasn't going to kill you," the man said, his voice cracking. "I just wanted to scare you off."

Brett clenched his jaw but kept the gun at the man's head. "Why?"

"Because Eleanor called and said she thought you knew where the money was."

So Eleanor had lied. "Was she working with Leo or *sleeping* with him?" Brett asked.

"Neither, I'm Eleanor's husband, Ralph," the man said. "She takes care of Leo's grandmother. Leo stayed with her for a while, then moved out."

"Where did he move?"

"I don't know. He told Eleanor he'd pay her to be the old lady's nurse, but then he left her high and dry, and me and Eleanor have been trying to pay the bills."

"I thought she said she didn't know Leo."

"She didn't. They set it up over the phone."

Unfortunately he believed the man. Leo had been scum through and through.

The man fidgeted. "Did you find the money?"

"You know about the money?" Brett asked.

"Leo's grandmother told us he had a big bagful. She wanted it to help us. And Leo owes us—"

"We haven't found any cash," Brett said. "And before you ask, I was not working with Leo. He's a dirt bag who *stole* that money. He married the woman you were shooting at and lied to her, then he turned up dead. The people he betrayed kidnapped her son."

The man's eyes widened in shock. "Leo's dead."

"Yeah and if I don't find that money, that little boy may be, too." Brett gripped him tighter. "Do you know where he is?"

The man shook his head back and forth, his eyes panicked. "No, I like kids. I'd never do anything to hurt one."

"What about the men Leo was in cahoots with? Did you know them?"

"No, I swear. When Leo called Eleanor to hire her, she said he seemed nervous. But she likes geriatric patients and wanted to help the old woman."

"She didn't mention a name, or maybe a place Leo said he was going when he left that house? Maybe another address?"

He shook his head again. "If he had, I would have paid him a visit myself. When you showed up, we thought you might lead us back to him."

Brett released the man with a silent curse.

He turned and walked back toward Willow, hating that he had no answers yet.

WILLOW COULDN'T BELIEVE her eyes. Brett was letting the man who'd tried to kill them go.

"Who was he?" Willow asked as soon as he returned to the truck. "Why was he shooting at us?"

"Eleanor's husband. The woman in the wheelchair was

Leo's grandmother. He hired Eleanor as a caretaker, but ran off without paying her."

"He really was awful," Willow said, her heart going out to the elderly woman.

"Apparently Eleanor and her husband were desperate financially. They thought you and I knew where Leo was, or at least where his money was, so he followed us. He wasn't trying to kill us, just scare us off so he could take the cash."

"So Leo wrecked that couple's lives, just like he did mine." Willow grimaced. Of course it was her fault for trusting him, for allowing him to be around Sam.

Brett started the truck and drove back toward the falls. When he parked this time, he managed to get closer to the area where they were digging. He carefully scanned for anyone else who might have followed.

"You can stay in the truck, Willow. I have to see if the money is there."

"No, I'm going with you."

Again, they grabbed the shovels and strode to the ridge, then ducked below the falls. The hole they'd started was still there, so he jammed the shovel in and continued to dig for the money.

Minutes ticked by, the wind picking up as rain began to fall, slashing them with the cold moisture. By the time he'd dug a few feet, the shovel hit rock. "It's not here."

"It has to be," Willow said, desperate.

Brett wiped his forehead with the back of his sleeve. "Let me try a different spot."

They spent the next hour digging around the original location, but again and again, hit stone.

Finally Willow leaned against a boulder. "If he put it here, someone must have already found it."

"Or he moved it," Brett said.

Willow shivered from the cold and the ugly truth. Another night was setting in.

Another night she'd have to wonder where her little boy was and if she'd ever see him again.

THEY MADE THE DRIVE back to Horseshoe Creek in silence. Brett hated the strain on Willow's face, but he understood her fear because he felt it in his bones.

He'd been certain that map would lead them to the money.

But Leo could have already retrieved the cash and moved it. Only where had he put it?

Maddox's truck was parked at the main house, so Brett bypassed it and drove straight to the cabin. "Was there any place that was significant to Leo? A place he liked to go riding?"

Willow rubbed her forehead. "Not that I know of."

"How about a place he took you and Sam?"

She looked out the window, as if she was lost in thought. "Honestly, Brett, Leo never spent much time with Sam."

He gritted his teeth. The poor kid. He needed a father. And it sounded like Leo hadn't been one at all.

Brett thought about his own father and how much he missed him now. They'd clashed over the years, but even when Joe McCullen was hard on him, Brett had known it was because his old man cared about him. That he was trying to raise him to be a decent man.

They walked up to the cabin together, and he unlocked the door. He ached for his father, for Willow and for her son, who was probably scared right now and wanted his mother.

"I'm sorry he let you down, Willow." He turned to her, his heart in his throat. "I'm sorry I let you down, too."

Willow's face crumpled, and tears trickled down her eyes. "Brett, what if—"

"Shh." He pulled her into his arms and stroked her hair. "Don't think like that. These guys want that money. If we don't find the cash Leo stole, I'll pay. I already called my financial manager and he's working on liquidating some funds."

Willow looked up at him with such fear and tenderness that he knew he'd do anything in the world to make it right for her. Then she lifted her hand to his cheek, and he couldn't resist.

He dipped his head and closed his mouth over hers.

Overwhelmed with affection for her, he cradled her gently, and deepened the kiss, telling her with his mouth how much he cared for her. How much he'd missed her.

How much he wanted to alleviate her pain.

Willow leaned into him and ran her hands up his back, clinging to him just as she once had when they were friends and lovers. Regret for the years he'd missed with her swelled inside him.

He stroked her hair, then dropped kisses into it, then down her ear and neck and throat. She rubbed his calf with her foot, stoking his desire, and he cupped her hips and pressed her closer to him.

Need and hunger ignited between them, and their kisses turned frenzied and more passionate. He inched her backward toward the sofa.

But his phone buzzed, and they pulled apart. Their ragged breathing punctuated the air as he checked the caller ID. *Unknown.*

He punched Connect. "Brett McCullen."

A second passed.

"Hello?"

"Mr. McCullen, you talked to my husband, Gus, today at the prison."

Brett straightened. "Yes. I was hoping he could help me. Did he give you my number?"

"Yes, although he didn't want me to call. But he explained to me about the little boy. I'm…sorry."

Brett frowned.

"I…think I might be able to help."

"You can help? *How?*"

"I can't discuss this over the phone. Can you meet me?"

"Of course. Just tell me the place."

"The Wagon Wheel. An hour."

The Wagon Wheel was a restaurant/bar near Laramie. "I'll be there."

Chapter Twelve

"Who was that?" Willow asked when Brett pocketed his phone and reached for his hat.

"Gus Garcia's wife. She wants to meet me tonight."

Willow's heart jumped to her throat. "She knows where Sam is."

Brett grabbed his keys. "She didn't say. But if she has any information that might lead to that money, I need to go."

Willow reached for her jacket, but Brett placed his hand on her arm.

"I can handle this if you want to stay here and rest."

Willow shook her head. "No way. Besides, if this woman holds back, maybe I can appeal to her on a woman-to-woman basis."

Brett's mouth twitched slightly. "I can't argue with that."

The wind splattered them with light raindrops as they ran to his truck. As Brett drove toward The Wagon Wheel, silence fell between them, thick with fear for Sam. Still, Willow couldn't help but remember the kiss they'd shared. A hot, passionate, hungry kiss that only made her crave another.

And reminded her how much she'd loved Brett.

And how painful it had been when he'd left her years ago.

She couldn't allow herself to hope that they could rekindle that love. And when Brett discovered Sam was his...

She'd face that when they got her little boy back.

It took half an hour to reach The Wagon Wheel, a bar/restaurant that specialized in barbecue and beer. Pickups, SUVs and a couple of motorcycles filled the parking lot, the wooden wheel lit up against the darkness.

Willow pulled her scarf over her head as they hurried to the door. Country music blared from the inside as they entered. The place was rustic with deer and elk heads, saddles, saddle blankets and other ranch tools on the walls. Wood floors, pine benches and tables, and checkered tablecloths gave it a cozy country feel.

Willow dug her hands in her jacket pockets. "How do we recognize her?"

Brett shrugged, but his phone buzzed with a text. When he looked down, the message said, Back booth on the right.

"That way." Brett led Willow to the rear of the restaurant where a small Hispanic woman with big dark eyes sat with her hands knotted on the table.

"Mrs. Garcia?"

She nodded, her gaze darting over Willow, then she looked back down at her hands as if wrestling with whether or not to flee.

Willow covered the woman's hand with her own and they slid into the booth. "I appreciate you meeting us. My name is Willow. Tell me your name."

"Valeria," the woman said in a low voice. "I...my husband will be upset that I come."

Willow squeezed her hand. "I don't want to cause you trouble, but my son is missing, Valeria, and I need help."

Valeria gave them both a wary look. "You don't understand. My husband...he not talk because he scared for me and little Ana Sofia."

Willow's heart pounded. "Ana Sofia?"

"Our little girl. She's eight." Valeria pulled a photo from her handwoven purse and showed it to them. "She…is so sweet and so tiny. And Gus went to prison so those bad men wouldn't kill us."

Willow tensed. "Someone threatened your little girl?"

Valeria nodded and curled her fingers into Willow's. But she looked directly at Brett, her eyes pleading, "If I talk to you, you take us some place where they can't hurt us?"

Brett spoke through clenched teeth. "Yes, ma'am. I promise. I'll pay for protection for you myself."

BRETT HAD NO patience for any man who would hurt a woman. "Who threatened you and your daughter, Valeria?"

"If I tell you, they may hurt my Gus."

"He's in prison," Willow said.

Brett understood Mrs. Garcia's fear, though. If someone wanted to get to Gus, they could.

"No one will know about this conversation," Brett assured her.

"Just tell us what happened," Willow said softly.

Valeria pulled her hand from Willow's and twisted them together in her lap. "*Sí.* I do this for the little boy, miss. I cannot stand for anyone to hurt children."

"Neither can I," Willow said, a look of motherly understanding passing between the two women.

"You see, Gus, he work for this rancher named Boyle Gates. Mr. Gates have big spread, but some say he cheat and steal so he be biggest, wealthiest rancher in Wyoming."

"What exactly did Gus do for Gates?" Brett asked.

"He was ranch hand," Valeria said. "Gus proud man. He work hard. But one day Mr. Gates accuse him of stealing money from his safe in house. My Gus not do it, but man named Dale Franklin say he saw Gus take it."

"Dale Franklin? He died, didn't he?"

"Yes." Her voice quivered. "Gus think they kill him. He was working with a rustling cattle ring. They tell Gus they do same to him and us if he not help them."

"What exactly did they want him to do?" Brett asked.

She dabbed at her eyes with a colorful handkerchief. "Steal cattle." Her lip quivered. "Gus not want to, but they say they fix things with Mr. Gates so he keep job and they pay him, too. He still say no, but then they talk about hurting me and our Ana Sofia, he go along."

"And when the men were caught, Gus took the fall to protect you."

She nodded, her eyes blurring with tears. "Gus try to be good in prison so he get out one day. That reason he not talk to you."

"You said *they*, but you only mentioned a man named Dale Franklin. Who else was involved?" Willow asked.

Valeria looked nervous again, but Brett assured her once more that he would protect her and her child. "I'll also do whatever I can to help Gus get paroled. Just give me the men's names."

Valerie heaved a big breath. "Jasper Day and Wally Norman."

"Do they still work for Mr. Gates?" Brett asked.

She shrugged. "I think Mr. Norman, he wind up in prison, too. Not sure he still there."

"Valeria, whoever is holding Sam believes Leo Howard had that money and stashed it somewhere. Do you or Gus know where he would have hidden it?"

She shook her head no. "Mr. Howard was leader. Gus said he was brains."

Brains without a conscience.

Brett wished the bastard was still alive so he could beat

the hell out of him. Because of him, Willow's little boy was in danger.

"Valeria, where is your little girl now?"

"At Miss Vera's. I clean her house."

"Let us follow you and pick up Ana Sofia. There's an extra cabin on my family's ranch where the two of you can stay. You'll be safe there."

Willow took Valeria's hands in hers. "I promise, no one will look for you at Horseshoe Creek."

Brett's gut tightened. He should discuss this with Maddox first, but Horseshoe Creek was as much his land as it was his brother's.

That is, until he sold his share to Maddox. Then he would have no stake in the land. No ties to it himself.

Was that what he wanted?

No, but he'd do it for Sam.

WILLOW FOLLOWED VALERIA inside the small shack where Valeria lived. Ever since her husband had been incarcerated, the poor woman had been cleaning Ms. Vera's house, as well as rooms at a motel to put food on the table.

Willow didn't condone Mr. Garcia's illegal activities, but if he'd been coerced to help the other men out of fear, she could understand. Just look at the lengths she had gone to in the past couple of days for her own son.

Little Ana Sofia was a tiny dark-haired girl with waist-length black braids and the biggest brown eyes Willow had ever seen. She clung to her mother's skirt as Valeria explained that they were taking a trip for a few days.

The child's questioning look only compounded the turmoil raging inside Willow.

How could she ever have married a man who would threaten a family like Leo had?

Had she been that desperate for a father for her baby?

No…she'd been desperate to forget Brett. She'd seen the tabloids of the women throwing themselves at him and had needed comfort. And Leo had stroked her ego—at first.

All part of his ruse to cover up the fact that he was a criminal.

"This is Miss Willow," Valeria said. "She and Mr. Brett are going to let us stay on their ranch."

Not *her* ranch. Brett's and his brothers'. But Willow didn't comment. At one time she'd fantasized about marrying Brett and the two of them carving out a home on a piece of the McCullen land.

But that dream had died years ago.

"Hi, Ana, you have beautiful hair." Willow stroked one of her braids. "And beautiful big eyes."

"They're like my daddy's." Ana's lower lip quivered. "But I don't get to see him anymore."

Valeria looked stricken, but Willow patted the little girl's back. "Well, maybe one day soon, you will. And you can tell him all about the horses and cows you see on Mr. Brett's ranch. Would you like that?"

"I like horses," the little girl said.

Valeria hugged Willow. "Thank you, Miss Willow."

Willow's throat closed. "No, Valeria, thank you."

Because of Valeria's courage, they might have a lead on how to find the money Willow needed.

WILLOW HELPED VALERIA and her daughter settle into a cabin near the one where Brett and Willow were staying. The sound of an engine made him step outside the cabin, and he cursed.

Maddox in his police SUV. What was he doing here?

Wind battered the trees and sent a few twigs and limbs down, a light rain adding to the cold dreariness as evening set in.

Brett jammed his hands in his pockets and waited, contemplating an explanation as Maddox parked and strode up to the porch. Rain dripped from his cowboy hat and jacket as he ducked under the roof.

"What's going on, Brett?"

Brett tensed at his brother's gruff tone. Maddox had a way of saying things that reeked of disapproval even without using specific words.

"I decided to stay in that cabin over there. And a friend of mine needed a place, so she's staying here."

Maddox arched a brow. "A woman? She's not staying with *you*?"

Brett swallowed back a biting retort. He'd be damned if he'd admit that Willow was staying with him. "No, she just needs a safe place for her and her little girl for a few days."

Maddox crossed his arms. "Brett, is this woman one of your conquests?" He lowered his voice. "Is the kid *yours*?"

Anger slashed through Brett. "You *would* think the worst of me, wouldn't you?" He squared his shoulders, making him eye to eye with Maddox. "I wouldn't do that to a woman. And if the child *was* mine, I'd take responsibility."

Animosity bubbled between them, born of years apart— and the years they'd fought as kids.

"I'm sorry," Maddox said quietly. "I guess I jumped to conclusions."

Brett released a tense breath. Maddox didn't apologize often.

"She's in trouble," Brett said in a low voice. "Can't you just trust me for once, Maddox, and let her stay here without asking questions?"

Maddox studied him for another full minute, then gave a clipped nod. "Okay, little brother. Do you want me to have my deputy or one of the ranch hands drive by and check on them tonight?"

Brett shrugged. "Maybe one of the ranch hands. I don't think the deputy needs to come." Sweat beaded on his brow. What if the deputy drove around and found Leo's grave?

"Okay, I'll tell Ron to swing by."

"Thanks, Maddox."

Maddox made a clicking sound with his teeth. "I guess it's time we both start trusting each other, right?"

"Right." Brett's gut knotted with guilt as Maddox strode back to his SUV. Maddox would kick his butt when he learned what Brett had done.

It would also destroy any chance of a reconciliation between him and his brother.

WILLOW BATTLED TEARS as she listened to Brett's conversation with Maddox. Brett wouldn't have abandoned a child.

She should tell him about Sam.

After all, he was putting his relationship with his brother on the line for her. She owed him the truth. But he cut her off before she could speak.

"I'm going to see that rancher tonight. Stay here with Valeria."

Willow glanced down at her phone, willing it to ring. But the picture of little Sam that the kidnapper had sent stared back.

She wrapped her coat around her. "No, I'm going with you. I want to see his reaction to the picture of my son."

SAM PUSHED ASIDE the grilled cheese the man set in front of him. "I want my mommy."

"Well, your mommy's not here, kid. Now eat the sandwich."

Sam picked at the burnt edge, then set the plate on the floor "It's black. And it gots the crust on it and Mommy cuts the crust off."

The man's pudgy face puffed up like a big fat pig's. Then he picked up the sandwich and shoved it toward Sam's mouth.

Sam's stomach growled, but he hated the man, and he wasn't going to eat the nasty thing so he turned his head away.

The mean man probably put roaches in the sandwiches or spiders or maybe he even spit tobacco in it. He'd seen him spitting that brown stuff in that can.

"Fine, you little brat. Starve." He hurled the sandwich at the wall. It hit, then fell to the floor, a mangled mess.

Sam fought tears. "When are you gonna take me back?"

The man glared at him, then slammed the door. Sam heard the key turning and threw himself at the door, beating on it. "I wanna go home! Let me go!"

He beat and beat until his fists hurt, and snot bubbled in his nose.

Don't be a baby, he told himself. *Cowboys don't cry.*

He wiped his nose on his sleeve and looked around the dingy room. He needed to find a way out, but those windows were nailed shut.

He hunted for something sharp to use to stab the man with if he came back. A knife or a nail or a pair of scissors. But he couldn't find anything but a broken plastic comb.

The rope they'd first tied his hands with was on the floor. It wasn't long enough to make a lasso like the cowboys used.

He wound the rope around his fingers and tried to remember the knots he'd seen in that book he sneaked from the library. It had pictures of roping calves and horseback riding and trick riding.

His mama had another book in the table by her bed, too. She pretended she didn't like rodeos, but he'd seen her looking at pictures of that famous rodeo star. Only those pictures made her cry.

He laid the rope in his lap and twisted and turned it, then tried again and again. If he could trip that mean man, and tie him up like a calf, he could run and run till he found his mommy again.

Chapter Thirteen

Brett waited until the rancher showed up to guard Valeria and her daughter.

"Is she running from a husband?" Ron asked.

Brett shrugged, not wanting to explain. "Something like that."

"I'll make sure no one bothers her tonight."

"Thanks." Brett shook the man's hand. One thing he could always count on was that Maddox hired good men.

He met Willow at the truck. His phone buzzed again as he drove toward Gates's ranch. *Kitty.* He ignored the call.

Why couldn't she take the hint? A second later, his phone rang again.

"Aren't you going to answer that, Brett?"

"No, it's no one important."

Willow's brows lifted. "It's your girlfriend, isn't it?"

Brett's pulse clamored. He didn't want to discuss the women in his past with Willow. "I don't have a girlfriend."

Willow released a sardonic laugh. "Oh, that's right. You have a different woman in every city."

He hated that she was right. "Where did you get that idea?"

"Pictures of you and your lovers are plastered all over the rodeo magazines. How could I *not* know? Let's see. There was Bethany in Laredo, Aurora in Austin, then Carly in Houston, Pauline in El Paso—"

Brett held up a hand. "Okay, so I've dated a few women. *You* got married." And had a child with another man. And within a year after his last visit home. A visit that had made him think they might have a future.

But she'd squashed that with her wedding.

"You're right. I guess we both moved on."

Had they? Or had he just been biding time, hoping one day to reconcile with Willow?

The rain fell harder, slashing the windshield and roof, forcing him to drive slower through the rocky terrain.

"By the way, congratulations on all your success, Brett." Willow looked out the window as she spoke. "You followed your dreams and became exactly what you always wanted to be."

Brett gripped the steering wheel as he sped around a curve and headed down the long road toward Gates's spread, the Circle T. Willow's words taunted him.

He had achieved success on the circuit. And he didn't have to go without a woman. There were plenty of groupies out there. But they wanted the same thing—the fame, the money, the cameras…

All carbon copies. *Shallow.*

None of them wanted the real Brett or cared to know about his family. Or that sometimes he regretted leaving Pistol Whip and the chasm between him and his brothers. That when his mother died, he'd fallen apart and missed her so much that he'd cried himself to sleep every night.

That he wanted to be as perfect as Maddox, but he hadn't been, so he'd joked his way through life. That the only thing he'd been good at was riding.

He'd certainly screwed up with Willow.

Willow gestured toward the turnoff for the ranch. "There's the sign for the Circle T."

He'd read about Gates's operation. He owned thousands of acres, raised crops and had made a name for himself in the cattle business.

At one time, Brett's father had wanted to make Horseshoe Creek just as big. He'd wanted him and Ray to help Maddox—with the three of them working together, it might have been possible.

But Brett had needed to stretch his wings. And Ray... he'd had too much anger in him. He couldn't get along with Joe or Maddox.

Willow grew more tense as they approached the house, and kept running her finger over the photo of Sam that the kidnapper had texted.

Brett put thoughts of Horseshoe Creek and his own problems behind. He could live with Maddox hating him when this was over.

As long as he put Sam back in Willow's arms.

EVEN THOUGH IT was dark and raining, Willow could see that the Circle T spanned for miles and miles. She'd heard about the big operation and that Gates was a formidable man.

Had he earned his money and success by being involved with crooks like Leo?

She tugged her jacket hood over her head, ducking against the wind and rain as she and Brett made their way to the front door. A chunky woman in a maid's uniform answered the door and escorted them to a huge paneled office with a large cherry desk, and corner bar. Dozens of awards for Gates's quality beef cattle adorned the wall.

The maid offered them coffee, but she and Brett both declined. Her stomach was too tied in knots to think about drinking or eating anything.

A big man, she guessed around six-one, two hundred and eighty pounds, sauntered in wearing a dress Western shirt and jeans that looked as if they'd been pressed. An expensive diamond-crusted ring glittered from one hand, while a gold rope chain circled his thick neck.

Brett introduced them and shook the man's hand. Gates removed his hat and set it on his desk in a polite gesture as he greeted Willow.

Gates pulled a hand down his chin. "McCullen, you're one of Joe's boys, the one that's the big rodeo star, aren't you?"

"Yes, sir."

"I was sorry to hear about your daddy," Gates said. "He was a good man."

"Yes, he was." Brett's expression looked pained. He obviously hadn't expected condolences from the man.

"Care for a drink?" Gates gestured toward the bar, but Brett and Willow declined.

"So what do I owe the honor? You here to find out my trade secrets?" Gates emitted a blustery laugh.

Brett laughed, too, but it sounded forced. "No, sir, although if you want to share, I'm sure my brother Maddox would love to talk."

Gates harrumphed. "I guess he would."

Willow squared her shoulders. "Mr. Gates, did you know my husband, Leo Howard?"

Gates's mustache twitched with a frown as he claimed a seat behind his desk. "Name don't ring a bell."

"How about Gus Garcia?" Brett asked.

Gates's chair creaked as he leaned back in it. "That bastard tried to steal from under me. Why are you asking about him?"

"We believe that the men Garcia partnered with were in cahoots with Leo Howard."

Willow watched for a reaction, but the man didn't show one. "I don't understand. Garcia confessed and is in prison. I don't know about any partners. But since they locked Garcia up, I haven't had any more trouble."

"You knew a man named Dale Franklin was killed during the arrest? Two other men, Jasper Day and Wally Norman were also involved."

Gates planted both hands on the desk. "All I know is that after they put Garcia away, I cleaned house around here, brought in a whole new crew of hands."

He'd cleaned house to protect his business from corruption? Or to eliminate suspicion from himself for illegal activities?

Brett leaned forward, hands folded. "Do you know where we could find Day or Norman?"

"No, and I don't want to know."

Willow stood and approached his desk. "Mr. Gates, I think my ex-husband and those men rustled cattle and made a lot of money doing it, that they stashed the money somewhere, and I need to know where it is."

Gates shot up from his seat, his jowls puffing out with rage. "What the *hell*? You think I had something to do with them? Listen here, woman, they stole *from* me, not *for* me."

"Mr. Gates," Brett said, holding out a calming hand. "We aren't accusing you of anything. We just want to know if you have any idea where either of those men are."

"No." Gates started around his desk. "Now you two have worn out your welcome."

Willow flipped her phone around and jammed it in the man's face. "Look, Mr. Gates, someone kidnapped my little boy. His name is Sam. I think Day and Norman are responsible. They're demanding the money Leo made off the cattle rustling in exchange for my son. If I don't find it, I might not see my son again."

BRETT STUDIED GATES for telltale signs that he was behind the kidnapping. Gates was a formidable man. If Leo had stolen from him, he had motive for murder.

But Gates paled as he studied the photograph. "You think those men sent that to you?"

"The man didn't identify himself," Willow said. "But he said he wanted the money Leo stole. And if I don't find it, they'll hurt my little boy."

Gates pinched the bridge of his nose. "I'm sorry about your child, miss, but I don't know anything about a kidnapping or any money. And that's the gospel."

"Are you sure?" Brett asked. "You've built an empire awfully quickly. Maybe we should have your herd checked to make sure some of your cattle weren't stolen?"

Gates whirled on Brett in a rage. "How dare you come to my house and suggest such a thing. Now, get out."

"Mr. Gates," Willow cried. "If you have any idea how to find my son, please help me."

Gates's tone rumbled out, barely controlled. "I told you, I don't know anything."

Brett crossed his arms. "Think about it, Gates. Kidnapping is a capital offense. If you help—"

Gates stepped forward and jerked Brett by the arm. "I said get out."

WILLOW WAS TREMBLING as she and Brett left the Circle T.

"Do you think he was lying about knowing Leo?"

Brett's brows were furrowed as he drove away. "I think he's a ruthless man who's made a lot of money fast."

"What are we going to do now?" Willow asked. Her hopes were quickly deflating.

"I've been trying to think of another place where Leo might hide the money. You said his mother died. Where is she buried?"

Willow wrung her hands together. "I don't know. He didn't like to talk about her."

The windshield wipers swished back and forth as the rain fell, the night growing longer as she imagined little Sam locked in some scary place alone.

Brett punched in a number on his phone. "Mr. Howard, this is Brett McCullen again. Can you tell me where your wife was buried?" A pause. "Thank you."

He ended the call and spun around in the opposite direction. "She's in a memorial garden not far from Laramie."

Willow closed her eyes as he drove, but rest didn't come. Images of Sam flashed through her mind like a movie trailer. Sam being born, that little cleft chin and dimple so similar to Brett's that it had robbed her breath.

Sam, the day he'd taken his first step—they had been outside in the grass and he'd seen a butterfly and wanted to chase it. A smile curved her mouth as she remembered his squeal of delight when he'd tumbled down the hill and the butterfly had landed on his nose.

Then Christmas when he'd wanted a horseshoe set. And his third birthday when she'd taken him to the county fair, and he'd had his first pony ride. Dressed in a cowboy shirt, jeans and hat, he'd looked like a pro sitting astride the pony.

He would have loved to watch Brett at the rodeo.

But she'd known watching Brett compete would be difficult.

Every time she'd seen a tabloid with his photograph or a picture of a woman on his arm or kissing him, she'd cried. So she'd finally avoided the rodeo magazines.

Although how could she escape Brett when each time she looked at Sam, she saw his father's face?

Exhausted, she must have dozed off because when she stirred, they'd reached the graveyard. Rain and the cold made the rows of granite markers and tombstones look even more desolate.

Brett parked and reached for the door handle, but she caught his arm. "You aren't going to disturb that poor woman's grave, are you?"

A dark look crossed Brett's face. "We put Leo in the ground, Willow. I'll do whatever I have to in order to save Sam."

Tears blurred her eyes. She thought she'd loved Brett before, but even if he walked away when she got Sam back, she would always love him for what he'd done to help her.

"WHAT THE *HELL* have you done?"

He clenched the phone, his knuckles white. "I did what I had to do."

"You kidnapped a kid? What were you thinking?"

"I was thinking about getting that damn money. Howard refused to tell me where he hid it."

"So you killed him?"

"He came at me and tried to grab the gun from me. It just went off."

"This is some screwed-up mess. I don't want to go to prison for kidnapping."

"What about me? I could be charged with murder." His breath quickened. "That's the reason I took the kid. I need that money to skip the country. And I figured Howard must have told his wife where it was."

"But she claims she doesn't know. She's hooked up with one of those McCullen boys and they're asking questions all over the place."

"The woman has to be lying. Let her sweat a little over the kid and she'll give it up."

Chapter Fourteen

Brett felt as if the walls were closing in. Like the fear that chewed at his gut before he rode a bull these days. The fear that he might not come out whole… Or even alive.

But he didn't care if he died, if Willow got her son back.

Still, he was playing a dangerous game. Burying dead bodies, hiding the truth from the law, desecrating a grave when he'd been taught all his life to respect the dead.

Surely Leo wouldn't have dug deep enough to disturb his mother's coffin, and he would have needed equipment if he actually stored the cash inside the casket. So it made sense that he would have dug a shallow hole.

The rain splattering the grave marker reminded him of Willow's tears and the fact that they'd just buried his father, and his tombstone hadn't been ready at the funeral. Maddox had ordered it.

He wondered what Maddox had written on the headstone.

Pushing his own grief aside, he examined the dirt on Mrs. Howard's grave, looking for signs that it had been disturbed lately. Of course, Leo could have buried the money here when he'd first married Willow.

Then he'd sat back biding his time until interest in the

cattle rustling case died down and no one was looking
for him.

Rain dripped off his Stetson and down into his shirt collar as he dug deeper, raking the dirt aside. Another shov-
elful of dirt, and he moved slightly to the right to check
that area. The wet dirt was packed, but he dumped it aside,
only to find more dirt.

Questions about Leo pummeled him as he continued to
explore one spot then the next. Could Leo have hidden the
money in Willow's house? No…she said she'd rented that
place after they'd separated…

But he had gone back to see her the day he'd died…

Irritated that he had no answers, he kept digging, but
forty-five minutes later, he realized his efforts were futile.

Leo had not buried the money in his mother's grave.
Maybe he had some kind of moral compass after all.

Whispering an apology to the woman in the ground,
he covered the grave with the dirt again, making quick
work of the mess he'd made, then smoothing it out to show
some respect.

Finally satisfied that he hadn't totally desecrated the
memory of the woman in the ground, he wiped rain from
his face and strode back to the truck. Willow sat looking
out the window over the graveyard, her eyes a mixture of
hope and grief.

He wanted to make her smile again. Fill her mind with
dreams and promises of a happy future, the way they'd once
done when they sneaked out to the barn and made love.

"It wasn't there, was it?" she said, her voice low. Pained.
Defeated.

"I'm sorry." He climbed in and reached for her, but she
turned toward the window, arms wrapped around her waist,
shutting down.

That frightened him more than anything. If they didn't

find Sam tonight, it would be the second night she'd been without her son. The second terrifying night of wondering if he was dead or alive.

WILLOW WAITED IN the truck as Brett stopped by the cabin to check on Valeria and Ana Sofia.

When he returned to the truck, he waved to the rancher Maddox had asked to watch the woman and her child. Ron had parked himself outside the cabin and seemed to be taking his role of bodyguard seriously.

"I'm glad she's safe. She was a brave lady to help me," Willow said, her heart in her throat.

Brett drove to the cabin where they were staying. "Don't give up, Willow. I'm still working on liquidating some funds. At least enough to make a trade and satisfy these men."

She murmured her appreciation, although hope waned with every passing hour.

Brett tossed her an umbrella and she ran through the sludge up to the cabin door. As soon as they entered, she ducked into the bathroom and closed the door. Tears overflowed, her sobs so painful, she couldn't breathe.

She flipped on the shower water, undressed, climbed in and let the hot water sluice over her, mingling with her tears. When the water finally cooled, she forced herself to regain control, dried off and dragged on a big terry-cloth robe. She towel dried her hair, letting the long strands dangle around her face, took a deep breath and stepped into the den.

Brett was standing with a drink in his hand, his eyes worried as he offered her the tumbler. "Drink this. I need to clean up."

She hadn't noticed how muddy and soaked he was, but

he'd been out in the freezing rain digging for that money for over an hour. He had to be cold and exhausted.

But he still looked as handsome as sin.

She accepted the shot of whiskey and carried it to the sofa where he'd lit a fire. Tired and terrified, she sank onto the couch and sipped the amber liquid, grateful for the warmth of the fire and the alcohol that burned from the inside out.

The flames flickered and glowed a hot orange red, the wood crackling as the rain continued to beat like a drum against the roof. The shower kicked on, and she imagined Brett standing beneath the water, naked and more virile than any man had a right to be.

It would have been romantic, if she wasn't so worried about Sam.

The door opened and Brett walked in, his jeans slung low on his lean hips, his chest bare, water still dotting the thick, dark chest hair. Her breath caught, her body ached, the need to be with him so strong that she felt limp from want and fear.

If she allowed herself to lean on him, she would fall apart when he left.

"Let me grab a shirt." He ducked into the bedroom, saving her from herself. But a light knock sounded on the door.

Assuming it was Maddox, or perhaps Ron, bringing Valeria and her daughter over, she walked over and opened the door.

A blond-haired woman in a short red dress and cowboy boots stood on the other side aiming a pistol at Willow's heart.

BRETT JAMMED HIS ARMS in his shirtsleeves, determined to dress before he wrapped Willow in his arms and dragged her to bed. She looked so sad and frightened and desolate on that couch. And her tear-swollen eyes when she'd emerged from the bathroom had torn him inside out.

He was buttoning the first button when he stepped back into the hallway and saw Kitty at the door. His heart began to pound. What was *she* doing here? How had she found him?

"Who…are you?" Willow whispered. "What do you want?"

Brett inched closer, shock hitting him at the sight of her fingers wrapped around that pistol. "Kitty? What the *hell* are you doing?"

Kitty waved the gun in Willow's face. "You *bitch*. You can't have Brett. He's mine."

Willow lifted her hands in surrender. "You… I saw your picture with Brett."

Brett gritted his teeth. The gossipmongers made it look as if he and Kitty were a hot item. That he was constantly entertaining women in hotels and his RV, even in the stables between rides. That he even indulged in orgies with women he met online and at the honky-tonks.

"You can't have him," Kitty screeched. "I love Brett and he loves me, don't you, sugar?"

Brett recognized the psycho look in Kitty's eyes. It was the same look she'd had the night she broke into his hotel room and he found her waiting in his bed, naked and oiled, crying and threatening suicide if he didn't marry her that night.

He inched closer, watching her for signs that she intended to fire that gun. "Kitty, it's all right. Just put down the pistol. This is not what you think."

She glared at him, then at Willow. "Not what it looks like? You're both half-naked and alone in this cabin." She waved the gun at Willow. "But you can't have him. Brett and I are meant to be together."

Willow lifted her chin. "Brett is just an old friend. Nothing is happening here. I swear."

Just an old friend? Was that how she saw him?

Kitty's hand trembled, and she fluffed her long blond curls with her free hand. "Is that true, Brett? She means nothing to you?"

Brett swallowed hard, and gave Willow a look that he hoped she understood. One that silently encouraged her to play along. "That's right. Willow and I knew each other in high school. I'm just helping her out with a problem."

Kitty moved forward, hips swaying as she curved one arm around Brett's neck. "Then you've told her about us?"

Brett kept his eyes on the gun.

"I saw the pictures of you two together, Kitty," Willow cut in. "You're a lucky girl to have Brett."

"No, I'm the lucky one." Brett lifted a hand to stroke Kitty's hair and pasted on his photo-ready smile. Even the times he'd been sick or bruised and half-dead from being thrown, he'd used that smile. "Come on, honey. Let's go outside and take a walk. I'll show you my ranch."

Kitty gave Willow a wry look as if to say she'd just won a victory, and Brett ushered Kitty toward the door. "You'll love Horseshoe Creek."

Kitty batted her lashes at him, her eyes full of stars. Or maybe she was high on drugs.

She leaned into him, and he stepped onto the porch with her, then escorted her down the steps. When they'd reached the landing, he made his move. He grabbed the gun from her, then twisted her arm behind her back, and pulled her against him so she couldn't move. "This is it, Kitty. You've gone too far."

She struggled to get away, but he kept a strong hold on her arm and yelled for Willow. The door screeched open, and Willow poked her head out.

"Brett?"

"Call Maddox," he said between gritted teeth. "She's going to jail."

WILLOW WAS STILL trembling when Maddox arrived. She tightened the belt on her robe and waited inside while Brett explained the situation to his brother.

The rain had died down enough for her to hear Brett's explanation through the window. "She's been stalking me for months, Maddox. But tonight she went too far. She pulled a gun on Willow."

Kitty jerked against the handcuffs, her sobs growing louder. "How can you do this to me, to *us*, Brett. I love you! I thought we were going to get married!"

"We had two dates, that was it," Brett said to his brother. "I swear. I didn't lead her on, Maddox. There was never anything between us."

Maddox raised a brow. "Willow's here?"

Willow ducked behind the curtain. She didn't care if Maddox knew she was visiting Brett, but she didn't want to face him. He probably thought she was cheating on her husband with Brett.

Worse, if he asked questions about Leo, she didn't want to lie.

"Yes," Brett said. "But that's not what this is about. I need you to take Kitty into custody. Contact her family and tell them she needs psychiatric help."

Maddox hauled Kitty into the back of his police SUV. Tears streaked her face, and she was still screaming Brett's name as Maddox drove away.

Willow braced herself as Brett strode in. His hair was damp, his jaw rigid, that spark of flirtatiousness in his eyes gone. He looked angry and worried and...so damn masculine and sexy that her heart tripped.

"You've been breaking hearts everywhere you go, haven't you, Brett?" She regretted the words the moment she said them. The bitter jealousy in her tone gave her feelings away.

THERE WAS NO way Brett was going to let Willow believe that he'd been in love with that deranged woman.

"Willow," he said, his teeth clenched. "I swear, we went out twice, then I realized she was unstable. After that, she started stalking me."

"I saw the pictures, Brett." Her voice cracked. "*Everyone* saw them."

He strode toward her, water dripping from his hair, his eyes luminous with emotions. "You can't believe everything you see in the tabloids. They're trying to sell copies."

"But you slept with her."

"Twice and I was half-drunk at the time. A week later, she broke into my hotel room and was waiting in my bed naked. When I told her to leave and pushed her out the hotel door, the press snapped a picture and turned it into something lurid."

Her eyes glittered with anger and something else... *jealousy*? Was it possible that Willow still cared for him?

"So all the pictures of you and the women were fake?"

His heart hammered as he closed the distance between them. He knew she was scared for her son and frustrated, and so was he. But he couldn't allow her to think that he didn't care. That he hadn't wanted her every damn day he was gone.

So he tilted her chin up and forced her to look into his eyes. "I wasn't a saint, Willow. But know this, I never kissed a woman without wishing she was you."

Then he did what he'd wanted to do ever since he'd ridden back into town.

He dragged her into his arms and kissed her with all the hunger he'd kept at bay for the past few years. Except this time he wouldn't stop at kissing as he had before. This time he wanted all of Willow.

Chapter Fifteen

Willow clung to Brett's words. None of those women had meant anything to him. When he'd closed his eyes, he'd seen her face.

Just as she had imagined Brett holding her when she was in Leo's arms.

Leo had known that she hadn't loved him. He'd felt it. Not that she had anything to feel guilty about. Apparently he'd never loved her either.

Of course he'd acted like he had. He'd showered her with attention and gifts and affection at a time when she'd been most vulnerable.

But it had all been a lie.

Brett's lips fused with hers, and she welcomed the sensations flooding her. Anything to soothe the pain and fear clawing at her heart.

Brett stroked her hair, then ran his hands down her back, pulling her closer to him so she felt the hard planes of his body against her curves. Her pulse raced, need and desire mingling with the desperateness that she'd felt since he'd walked back into her life.

He'd come the minute she'd called. Would he have come sooner if she'd had the courage to ask?

He made a low sound in his throat, and her hunger

spiraled. "Willow, I want you," he said in a gruff whisper against her neck.

She tilted her head back, shivering at his breath on her skin. "I want you, too."

Brett swung her up into his arms and carried her to the bedroom. She kissed him frantically, urging him to do more, and he set her on her feet, then looked into her eyes.

"I've wanted you every day since I left Pistol Whip."

"I've wanted you, too, Brett." It had always been him. No one else. There never would be.

But her voice was lost as he nibbled at her lips again and drove his mouth against hers. They kissed, the passion growing hotter as he probed her mouth apart with his tongue. Lips and tongues mated and danced, his fingers trailing over her back, down to her waist, then one hand slid up to cup her breast.

Her breath caught and her nipple stiffened as he stroked her through her robe. She wanted him naked, touching and loving her everywhere.

Her whispered sigh was all the encouragement he needed. He cupped her face and looked into her eyes again, and for a second, the young boy she'd fallen in love with stood in his place.

All their dreams and fantasies, whispered loving words, kisses and secret rendezvous… She was back in the barn with Brett, hiding out with the boy she loved.

Then there was the night he'd come back to Pistol Whip. He'd shown up on her doorstep and she'd taken one look at him standing in the rain and invited him into her bed.

They'd made love as if they'd never been apart. They'd also made Sam that night.

Her robe fell to the floor, cool night air brushing her skin. His breath rasped out with appreciation as he cupped both breasts in his hands.

"You're so beautiful," he murmured.

She blushed at his blatant perusal, but shyness fled as he lowered his mouth and drew one stiff nipple into his mouth. Willow moaned as erotic sensations splintered through her, and she threaded her fingers in his hair, holding him close as he laved one breast, then the other.

Aching to touch him, she popped the first button on his shirt, then the second. He pulled away from her long enough to toss his shirt to the floor. His bare chest was broader than she remembered, dusted with dark hair, his skin bronzed from the sun, although a few scars lined his torso. She wondered how he'd gotten each one of them, but didn't ask. She didn't want to talk.

She wanted to be in his arms, loving him the way she once had when life had been simple and she'd had dreams of a future.

She unbuttoned his jeans, the sound rasping in the silence, and he kicked them off. Her body tingled as his hands skated over her hips. His eyes grew dark and needy, and he pulled her against him.

Her breasts felt heavy, achy, the tingling in her thighs and womb intensifying as he kissed her again and she shoved his boxers down his legs. Finally he stood naked in front of her. Powerful muscles flexed in his chest, arms and thighs, and his sex was thick and long, pulsing with excitement.

She trailed her fingers over his bare chest, and he moaned, then cradled her against him and walked them to the bed. Her head hit the pillow, her hair fanning out, as he nibbled at her neck again, then raked kisses along her neck and throat, moving down to her breasts where he loved her again until she begged for more.

NEED PULSED THROUGH Brett as he coaxed Willow onto the bed. His body ached for her, but the need to assuage her pain was just as strong.

He closed his mouth around one turgid nipple and suckled her, his sex hardening as she moaned his name. She stroked his calf with her foot, raking it up and down as she dug her hands into his hair.

Her hunger spiked his own, and he trailed sweet hungry kisses down her belly to her inner thighs.

"Brett…"

"*Shh*, just enjoy, baby." He flicked his tongue along her thigh, finding his way to the tender spot that made her go crazy. She tasted sweet and erotic, just as he remembered, and he teased her with his tongue until she clawed at his arms, begging him to come to her.

"I need you, Brett," Willow whispered.

He flicked his tongue over and over her tender nub until her body began to quiver and she cried out in release.

"Please, Brett."

Brett's heart pounded with the need to be inside her as he lifted himself and covered her with his body. For a moment, he lay on top of her savoring her tender curves against the hard planes of his chest and thighs. But she rubbed her hands down his back, then splayed them on his hips and butt, and his sex surged, needing more.

He tilted his head and looked into her passion-glazed eyes, then braced his body on his hands, and grabbed a condom from his jeans' pocket. She helped him roll it on, her fingers driving him insane as she touched his bare skin. When he had the protection in place, he kissed her again, deeply, hungrily, then rose above her and stroked her center with his erection. She groaned again, then slid her hand down and guided him home.

The moment he entered her, he closed his eyes and hesitated, forcing himself to slow down or he was going to explode. She lifted her hips and undulated them, inviting him to move inside her, and he did.

In and out, he thrust himself, filling her, stroking her with his length, pumping harder and faster as they built a natural rhythm. Sweat beaded on his forehead as he intensified their lovemaking, his release teetering on the edge.

Willow clutched at him, rubbing his back as she moved beneath him, then groaned his name as another orgasm claimed her. He kissed her again, then lifted her hips so he could move deeper inside her, so deep that he felt her core. She breathed his name against his neck.

It was the sweetest sound he'd ever heard, a sound he'd missed so much that it tipped him over the edge and his release splintered through him.

WILLOW CLOSED HER EYES and savored the feel of being in Brett's arms. Erotic sensations rocked through her with such intensity that she clung to him, emotions overwhelming her.

Tears burned the backs of her eyelids. She had told herself not to fall in love with Brett again, but that had been futile.

Because she'd never stopped loving him.

Fear made her chest tighten again. She'd barely survived the first time he'd left her. How would she survive this time?

A deep sigh escaped her as he rolled them sideways and tucked her up against him. Brett kissed the top of her head, then disappeared into the bathroom for a moment. She thought he was going to dress and leave her alone, and she already missed him.

But he crawled back in bed with her, pulled her into his embrace and rubbed her arm. His body felt hot against hers as his breathing rasped out. She wanted to stay in his arms forever.

"Willow?"

She tensed, knowing she should confess the truth about Sam.

"I've been thinking. Wondering why Leo came to your house the day he died."

Willow went still. "I hoped he was going to drop the signed divorce papers by."

Brett took a strand of her hair between his fingers and stroked it the same way he had when they were young and in love. "But why that *particular* day? What if he really came back for the money? Maybe he retrieved it from the original place he'd buried it."

Willow turned to look into his eyes. "You think he had it with him that day?"

Brett shrugged. "Maybe he knew his partners were onto him, so he decided to hide it at your house. It wasn't in his truck. And we didn't find it where that map led us or at his mother's grave."

Willow's pulse kicked up, and she shoved the covers back. "Then we need to search my house."

Brett nodded, although before she slid from bed, he pulled her back and kissed her again. Her heart fluttered with love and hope.

When they found the money and Sam was home, would Brett forgive her for keeping her secret? Was it possible that they might be a family someday?

Her cell phone buzzed, and she startled. Sam?

Brett handed her the phone from the nightstand and she punched Connect. "Hello."

"Do you have the money?"

Panic shot through Willow. "No, but I think I know where it is."

"Where?"

She swallowed, struggling for courage. "Meet me at my house in an hour. Bring my son to me, and you can have it."

BRETT YANKED ON his jeans and shirt while Willow vaulted from bed and threw on her clothes. He hoped to hell he was right, that the money was hidden somewhere at Willow's.

But just to be on the safe side, he grabbed the duffel bag he'd used to bring his clothes in, then packed some newspaper in the bottom.

"What are you doing?"

"If we don't find the money, I'll use this as a decoy until we rescue Sam." He retrieved his rifle from the corner in the den, wishing he had that money from his accounts to cover the newspaper, but hopefully they'd find Leo's money, and he wouldn't need this bag. And if they checked it…well, he had his rifle. He'd do whatever he had to do to get the boy.

He snatched his coat and handed Willow her jacket.

"Let's hurry. I want to look for the money before this bastard arrives." His phone buzzed, though, and he tensed. Maddox.

What if he'd somehow discovered Leo's body on the ranch?

Exhaling slowly, he punched Connect while Willow tugged on her jacket and boots. "Hey."

"Brett, what kind of trouble are you involved in?"

"I told you that woman was stalking me. End of story."

"I'm not talking about her," Maddox said sharply. "I want the truth about what you're doing. You're looking into Willow's husband, aren't you?"

Brett gritted his teeth. Did he know Leo was dead? "Why would you ask that?"

"I've been investigating a cattle-rustling ring that a man named Garcia is serving time for. It's his wife and kid you brought to the ranch, isn't it?"

He should have realized that would arouse Maddox's suspicions. "Maddox—"

"Just shut up and listen. I know you've always had a thing for Willow, and she's at that cabin with you. But her husband is dangerous."

"What do you know about him? Did he hurt her?"

"That's my guess. Dad talked to me one day and said he was worried, that something was off there."

If he'd been around, he would have known himself. And Willow never would have suffered.

Maddox cleared his throat. "He was in with some bad people. That's the reason you were looking up prison records, wasn't it?"

Brett glanced at his watch, impatient. "Yes, Maddox, but I have to go."

"Brett, let me handle the situation. I think Howard was involved with those cattle rustlers. I don't have proof but I'll get it. In fact, I'm trying to locate him to question him now. Does Willow know where he is, Brett? Because if she's covering for him, she could go to jail, too."

Willow looked panicked and tugged him toward the door. "I'll tell her if she hears from him to call you."

He didn't wait on a response. He hung up with a curse. Maddox was smart; it wouldn't take him long to figure out what was going on.

Willow followed him outside where the rain was still beating on the roof as they hurried to his truck.

Wind and rain battered the windshield as he drove, blurring his vision of the road. He flipped the wipers to High, his nerves on edge as he turned onto Willow's road.

The truck bounced over the ruts, mud spewing. He looked over his shoulder to make sure no one was following.

Hell, for all he knew, Maddox might be on his tail.

Willow twisted in the seat, obviously agitated. "They *will* bring Sam, won't they?"

Brett's gut contorted. He'd wondered the same thing.

If Sam could identify them, they might have already ditched him, then planned to take the money and run.

His fingers curled around the rifle on the seat beside him. If they had hurt Willow's little boy, he'd kill the bastards.

WILLOW SCANNED THE OUTSIDE of her house in case the kidnappers had arrived early. Her throat ached from holding back tears.

She was going to see Sam again. She had to see him.

But what if she and Brent were walking into a trap? What if they'd never intended to give her back her son?

Fear almost paralyzed her. Determined not to give up, though, she forced the terror at bay. She had to stay strong.

Brett parked and got out, carrying his rifle and the duffel bag with him. Memories of finding Leo dead in her bedroom flashed behind her eyes, and nausea climbed her throat. But she forged on, determined to hold it together.

They slogged through the rain and she unlocked the door, her shoulders knotted with anxiety. The den looked just as she'd left it, and so did the kitchen.

Although it felt as if it had been years since she'd been home. She didn't know if she could ever live here again.

"I don't know where he would have hidden it," Willow said.

"I'll search the closets. You search the kitchen. He could have taped an envelope with a key to a safety deposit box under a drawer or table."

Brett strode to the hall closet and began to dig through it. She checked the cabinet and drawers in the kitchen and the desk, under the drawers and table, and on top of the cabinets. The laundry room came next. Her movements were harried as she ripped through plastic storage containers and checked beneath and behind the washer and dryer.

She searched the pantry, but yielded nothing, so she hurried to the bedrooms. Brett was in her room. The sight of the bloodstains was still so stark that it made her stomach turn.

Sucking in a sharp breath, she darted into Sam's room. Sam's toys and clothes were still scattered about as they'd left them. Knowing time was of the essence, she dropped to her knees and searched beneath the bed. Her hand connected with a toy superhero and she pulled it out, along with several odd socks, a ball and a candy wrapper.

Her thoughts raced as she pulled down his covers and checked below his mattress, the bottom of the box spring and the back of the headboard.

Panic was starting to tear at her, and she threw the closet door open and searched the floor. Shoes, toys and a cereal box. On the top shelf she found the extra blankets and sheets she'd folded along with a flashlight, Sam's Halloween costume and boxes of rocks they'd collected at the creek.

She dug through the corner of the closet and found a stack of magazines—rodeo magazines. Her throat closed as she spotted a picture of Brett on the front of one of them. He must have found this in her nightstand drawer.

"Any luck, Willow?" Brett's voice jerked her from her thoughts and she stuffed the magazines back inside.

"No, nothing. You?"

Brett scowled. "No, but I'm going to look around outside."

"I'll check the attic."

He nodded and she rushed to the hall and climbed in the attic while he stepped outside. The rain had slackened, although droplets pinged off the window where the wind shook it from the trees.

Several boxes of old clothing and quilt scraps were

stored on one wall. She went to the antique wardrobe and opened it. It would be a perfect hiding place. In fact, Sam had hidden inside it once when they were playing hide-and-seek. After that, she'd made sure that it couldn't be locked so he wouldn't get trapped.

She swung the door open and found fabric scraps from her projects along with boxes of photographs of her and Brett in high school.

But there was no money anywhere.

Outside an engine rumbled in the distance, and she looked out the attic window and saw lights flickering. Was it them?

Did they have Sam?

BRETT FOUND NOTHING in the garage, so he scanned the side of the house for a crawl space or a hiding place but didn't see one.

The sound of the car engine made his nerves spike. He hurried inside and grabbed the rifle along with the duffel bag. Willow raced down the steps from the attic and clutched his arm. "Brett, what are we going to do?"

"Play along with me."

She nodded, although terror filled her eyes. Brett stepped onto the porch, deciding to use the darkness to camouflage the bag. A black sedan pulled up, lights turned off.

He held the rifle beside him, hand ready to draw, the duffel bag in his other hand. Willow's nervous breathing rattled in the quiet.

The sedan door opened and a man wearing a ski mask stepped from the backseat. The driver remained behind the wheel, hidden in the shadows.

The silver glint of metal flickered against the night. "The woman needs to bring the money over here."

"First, we see the boy," Brett said in a tone that brooked no argument.

A hesitation. The wind hurled rain onto the porch and caused a twig to snap and fall in front of the man. He didn't react, except to reach inside the car and snatch something.

Brett feared it was another weapon, but a little boy wearing a jacket appeared, his body shaking. He couldn't see his face well for the shadows, but he cried out for Willow.

"Mommy!"

Willow stepped onto the porch. *"Sam!* Honey, I'm here. Are you all right?"

"I wanna come home!" Sam yelled.

Brett caught Willow, before she barreled forward.

"Send the boy over, then I'll throw you the money," Brett ordered.

A nasty chuckle echoed from the man. "No way. The woman brings the money. When I see it, I release the kid."

Brett's fingers tightened around the rifle. He was a damn good shot. But this was a dangerous game.

Willow's and her son's lives depended on him.

"Fine." Willow grabbed the duffel bag.

"Willow?" Brett reached for her but she shook off his hand.

"I have to do this," Willow said. "I'll do anything for Sam."

Brett's gut churned as she slowly walked down the steps.

"Send the boy," Brett said.

The man took Sam by the collar and half dragged him across the yard. Brett inched down a step, but the man aimed the gun at Willow. "Stay put, McCullen, or they're both dead."

Chapter Sixteen

Willow soaked up the sight of her little boy's features.

His dark eyes were big and terrified, but he was alive. And she didn't see any visible injuries or bruises.

"Are you okay, honey?" she asked softly as she approached Sam.

He gave a little nod of his head, but his chin quivered. "I wanna come home."

"You *are* coming home," Willow assured him. There was no way this man would leave with her son. She'd die first.

The man's gun glinted as she neared him, but that ski mask disguised his face.

Willow clutched the duffel bag to her side. "I have what you came for. Now let my son go."

The man glanced down at the bag. "Closer."

Willow inched forward, but kept the bag slightly behind her, determined to lure Sam away before the man realized the bag was empty.

She hesitated a few inches from him, then stood ramrod straight, her chin lifted. "Let him go."

The man met her gaze, then shoved Sam. "Go on, kid." At the same time, he reached for the bag.

"Mommy!" Sam ran toward her, and she hugged him

to her and threw the bag at the man's feet a few inches from him.

She gripped Sam by the arm just as he ripped open the bag to check the contents. "Run back to the house, Sam!"

He was crying and clinging to her, and she turned to run with him, but the man lunged at her and snatched her arm. "You lying bitch."

"Run, Sam, *run!*" Her head snapped back as the man caught her.

Brett was coming down the steps, his rifle aimed. "Let her go!"

Sam stumbled and fell, crying out for her. "Mommy!"

"Save him," Willow shouted to Brett.

The second man in the car fired his gun, and Brett jumped back slightly, then pressed his hand on his left shoulder. Blood began to ooze out and soak his shirt.

He'd been shot.

"Please let me go," Willow cried. "I don't have your money, and my son needs me."

"Shut up." The man jammed the gun to her head, but Brett started forward again so the man spoke to Brett. "Move another inch and I'll shoot her."

Brett kept his rifle aimed, but froze a few feet from Sam. "Listen, man, she tried to find the money. But she doesn't know where it is."

A litany of curse words filled the air. Sam pushed up from the ground and shook his little fists at the man. "Let my mommy go!"

Sam started to run back toward her, but Brett snatched him by the neck of his jacket. "Stay still, son. I'll handle this."

The man kept the gun to her head and dragged her back toward the sedan. She wanted to fight, but the cold barrel against her temple warned her not to mess with him. She didn't want to die and leave Sam motherless.

Sam was sobbing, so Brett picked him up. Willow saw the moment he looked into Sam's face and realized he was his.

His gaze flew to hers, questions mingling with shock.

The driver of the sedan fired at Brett's feet, though, and he dodged the bullet, protecting Sam with his body.

The kidnapper opened the sedan door. Willow shoved at him, but he grabbed her around the throat, then pressed the barrel of the gun to her head again.

"Don't hurt her. I'll get you some money!" Brett shouted. "I have a hundred thousand of my own I'll give you in exchange for her."

"Get it and we'll talk." The man shoved Willow inside the car.

Willow tried to crawl across the seat to escape out the opposite door, but he slammed the gun against the back of her head, and the world went black.

BRETT'S HEART WAS pounding so loudly, he could hear the blood roaring in his ears. The driver of the sedan spun the vehicle around. The other man fired at Brett again to keep him from chasing them, and Brett clutched Sam and darted behind a tree to protect him.

"Mommy!" Sam screamed as the sedan accelerated. *"Mommy!"*

A cold knot of fear enveloped Brett as the sedan disappeared with Willow inside.

Sam wrapped his arms around Brett's neck and clung to him, his little body trembling with fear.

Sam. *His son.*

The words echoed over and over in his head. Sam was his little boy.

All this time, these years, the past few days—Willow hadn't told him. Had kept the truth from him.

Why? Because she thought he wouldn't have been a good father…

"I want my mommy!" Sam sobbed.

Brett patted the little boy's back, his heart aching for the ordeal Sam had suffered. For the fear and trauma, for the murder he'd witnessed.

And now his mother was gone, snatched at gunpoint in front of his eyes.

He pressed Sam's head to his shoulder and rocked him in his arms. "*Shh*, son, it'll be all right."

"My…mommy…"

Sam's sniffles punctuated the air, wrenching Brett's heart. "I know you're scared, son, and you've been through a lot." Brett's shoulder was starting to throb, and blood soaked his shirt. "But I'm here now. I'm here and I'll make things right."

I'm your father, he started to say. But he didn't want to confuse Sam now. Besides, what had Willow told him?

Sam thought that bastard Leo was his dad…

Rage heated Brett's blood. He would rectify *that* as soon as possible. As soon as he brought Willow home.

Then they would sit down and have a damn long talk.

Sam's cries softened, but his fingers dug into Brett's neck as Brett walked toward his pickup. He needed to take care of the bullet in his shoulder before he passed out. If he did, he wouldn't be any good to Sam or Willow.

They were his priority now.

But how was he going to remove this bullet without seeing a doctor or drawing suspicion from the law?

He carried Sam around to the passenger side of the truck, his lungs squeezing for air when Sam looked up at him with those big eyes. Eyes that looked exactly like his. The cleft in his chin, the dimple…he was a McCullen through and through.

How had he not seen it before?

Because you didn't look.

In the photo he'd seen of Sam, the boy was wearing a cowboy hat. It had hurt too much for him to think about Willow having another man's son, so he hadn't paid attention to the child's features.

But this boy was *his*.

He fastened Sam's seat belt, soaking up his face for a moment, and thinking about what he'd missed. All those baby years. The first time he'd walked. Christmases and birthdays…

Sam wiped at his nose and looked up at Brett. The fear there nearly stalled Brett's heart. "You helping those mean men?" Sam whispered.

Brett nearly choked on a sharp denial. But he didn't want to scare Sam any more than he already was. "No, son." He gently raked a hand over the child's hair, emotions nearly overwhelming him. "I'm a friend of your mommy's. I've been helping her try to get you back from those men."

Sam's eyes narrowed as he looked at Brett's shoulder. "They shot you like they shot Daddy."

Leo was not his father. But Sam *had* witnessed the murder. "Yes, but I'm not going to die, Sam. And I'm not going to leave you." Not ever again. "I'm going to get your mother back. I promise."

Sam's chin quivered, but he gave Brett a brave nod.

Knowing time was working against him, he walked around to the driver's side and climbed in. He reached inside his pocket and removed a handkerchief, then jammed it inside his shirt over the wound to help stem the blood flow.

Then he cranked the truck and drove back toward Horseshoe Creek.

He was starting to feel weak, and he needed help. Someone to remove this damn bullet and someone to watch Sam, so he could get hold of that cash and trade it for Willow's life.

He didn't know where to go. Who to turn to.

Maddox would be furious when he found out what Brett had done.

But he was the only one who could help him now.

He'd probably lock Brett up when all was said and done.

He glanced over at Sam who was watching him with those big sad eyes.

But Sam was his son, and if there was anything that Maddox cared about, it was family.

Brett would pay the consequences when this was over and go to jail if it came to that.

But he'd save Willow first.

WILLOW STIRRED FROM UNCONSCIOUSNESS, but her head was spinning and nausea rose to her throat. She lifted her hand to the back of her head and felt blood. The car bounced over the rocky road, jarring her and making her feel ill.

She struggled to sit up, but the car veered to the right, throwing her against the side.

"Be still, bitch, or you're going to get it again."

A sob welled inside her, but she sucked it down. "Please let me go. My little boy needs me."

He barked a sinister laugh. "You're the one who screwed up. You should have given me the money instead of getting greedy."

Willow pushed herself to a sitting position. "I'm not *greedy*. I told you I didn't know where the money was and I *don't*."

He grabbed her arm, clenching it so tightly that pain shot through her arm and shoulder. "We know Leo came to see you, that he took the money from where he'd first hidden it. He was supposed to meet us that day with it, but he stopped off at your house first."

"Leo and I have been separated for years," Willow cried. "He came by to drop off divorce papers, not give me money."

"Because you were already keeping it for him," the man snarled.

Willow shook her head back and forth. How could she convince them that she was telling the truth?

And what if she did and they killed her because she was of no use to them anymore?

Then she'd never see Sam again, and he would grow up without a mother…

She closed her eyes and said a prayer. Even if she didn't make it, Brett had recognized that he had a son. He would raise Sam as a McCullen.

Sam will be all right.

Except she wanted to be there to see him grow up, to learn to ride a horse, to play ball and graduate from school and get married one day…

BRETT IGNORED THE PAIN in his shoulder and focused on driving back to the ranch. He had to get Sam to Horseshoe Creek where he'd be safe.

Dark clouds hovered above, threatening more rain, and he took a curve too quickly and nearly lost control. Sam's little face looked pale in the dark, and Brett reached out and squeezed his shoulder.

"I know you've been through it, little man, and you miss your mother, but hang in there a little longer."

"You said you knew her?" Sam said in a small voice.

"Yes," Brett said. "We were friends back in high school." *Friends and lovers. And I'm your father.*

Although Sam obviously had no idea.

Sam suddenly tilted his head to the side. "You're that rodeo star aren't you? I saw your picture in that magazine Mommy had."

Willow had a magazine with his picture in it.

Of course she had. She'd seen pictures of him and Kitty. She thought he was sleeping with a different woman every night.

And he had, he admitted silently.

But would he have if he'd known he had a child? That Willow had delivered his baby?

Regret and heartache ballooned inside him as he turned onto the road leading back to Horseshoe Creek.

Sam sat up straighter, his little face turned toward the window. "Where are you taking me?"

The poor kid had been kidnapped. He probably was wondering what Brett was going to do to him. "We're going to my ranch," Brett said. "Your mommy likes it there. And I have two brothers and a nice lady named Mama Mary who took care of me when I was little. She'll take care of you till your mommy is home."

As soon as he said the words, he felt better. Maddox would be angry, but Mama Mary would love Sam unconditionally with no questions asked.

"You gots horses?"

Brett's mouth twitched. "Yes, buddy. Do you know how to ride?"

"Not really." Sam's voice dropped to a low whisper. "Mommy said I was too little."

Brett rubbed his hand over Sam's head again. "Well, you look pretty big to me. And I know you're tough. So I'll teach you to ride soon. Sound good?"

Sam nodded, and for a moment, Brett saw himself when he was little. Anytime he was upset or mad, he'd ridden across the ranch and the world had seemed better. He could pass that on to his son.

The farmhouse slid into view, and for once, he was relieved to see Maddox's SUV in front of the house. He parked, pressing his hand to his bloody shoulder as he hurried around to help Sam.

The little boy took his hand and jumped to the ground, and Brett held on to him as they walked up the porch steps. When he opened the door, Maddox was standing in the hall, his expression dark.

"Brett, I need to talk to you. This evening I found something—"

Brett cut him off. He had to get the words out fast. "I have to talk to you, too." Brett swayed slightly, his head light from blood loss.

Maddox's gaze took in Sam, then he noticed Brett's bloody shoulder. "Good grief, you've been shot."

Brett nodded and stumbled forward, and Maddox caught him. "It's worse, Maddox. I need your help. Two men... they kidnapped Willow."

Chapter Seventeen

Willow struggled against the bindings around her wrists and feet as the man tossed her into a dark room. A sliver of light managed to peek through the curtains, and she dragged herself on her belly to the bed and slowly clawed her way on top of it.

She pushed the curtain aside, and hoped to escape through the window, but it was nailed shut.

A sob welled in her throat, and she slumped back down on the bed. Was this the room where they'd kept Sam?

She mentally searched for strength. If her little boy had held it together long enough for her to save him, she could do it long enough for Brett to find her.

The most important thing was that Sam was safe.

Safe with his father who probably hated her now for keeping his son from him all these years.

That didn't matter either, not now. Sam was okay and if she died tonight, Brett would take care of Sam. He'd teach him how to play baseball and skip stones in the creek behind the ranch, and how to saddle a horse and trick ride.

Although one day he might teach him to ride a bull and she wasn't so sure about that.

She would miss it all if she was dead, but Sam would be happy with his father. He would raise him to be an honorable, brave McCullen man.

She rolled to her side on the bed and looked across the room. A ratty stuffed animal lay on the floor, along with a piece of rope.

Sam had been here. He'd twisted the rope into the letter *S*. Her heart warmed as she remembered him pretending to rope cattle like the cowboys on TV.

Brett would teach him how to rope calves one day, too.

She wanted to be there for him and see all those things.

She blinked, and struggled to untie her hands, but the ropes cut into her wrists. Frustrated, she drew her knees up and tried to reach her ankles with her hands to untie her feet, but the knot was so tight, she couldn't budge it.

Outside, footsteps pounded and voices echoed through the wall. She forced herself to be very still so she could hear, although it was difficult over the sound of her own roaring heart.

"You took the woman now? What the hell are you doing?"

Willow tensed. That was a woman's voice. It sounded familiar, but it was too muffled for her to place.

"I thought she was lying about the money."

"But what if she doesn't know where it is?"

"That cowboy said he'll pay us. It won't be half a million, but it'll be enough to get out of the country so we can lie low for a while."

"All right. But give the man a deadline. The longer you wait, the more likely we are going to get caught."

"Twenty-four hours. That's the deadline. If he doesn't produce the money by then, kill her."

BRETT'S KNEES FELT like they were going to cave in.

"Brett, who shot you?" Maddox caught him just before he collapsed. "Mama Mary, Rose, hurry, I need help!"

Sam was still clinging to Brett, looking scared to death.

"It's okay, son," Brett murmured in a soothing voice as he lowered him to the floor. "I'll be fine. Maddox is my brother." He gestured toward the badge on Maddox's shirt. "He's a good guy, the sheriff. He'll help us find your mommy and get rid of those bad men."

Mama Mary and Rose rushed in, both startled by the blood on his shirt.

"Oh, my word!" Mama Mary cried. "What's going on?"

"This is Willow's son, Sam," Brett said. *And my son, too.*

"Brett, this is Rose," Maddox said.

Brett muttered that he was glad to meet her. "Take care of Sam, Mama Mary. Two men took Willow and I need Maddox's help."

Rose gasped. "They took Willow?"

"You know her?" Brett asked.

Rose nodded. "I sell her quilts at my antiques shop."

Mama Mary dropped to her knees, her big bulk swaying as she rubbed Sam's arms. "Come on, little one. I bet you're hungry and tired aren't you?"

Sam hung on to Brett's leg. "I want my mommy," Sam said in a haunted voice.

Tears glistened on Mama Mary's eyelashes, but she didn't hesitate to comfort Sam, just the way she'd comforted him when he was little and his mother died.

"I know you do, sugar," Mama Mary said. "And don't you worry. Mr. Brett and Mr. Maddox are the two finest men in Wyoming. They'll have your mama back in no time." She dried his eyes with her apron. "Now your mama would want you to eat."

Sam leaned in to the big woman's loving arms. "Come on, little one. Mama Mary will whip you up some mac and cheese. I bet you like mac and cheese, don't you? It was Mr. Brett's favorite when he was your age."

Sam nodded against her, and Brett ruffled Sam's hair.

"It's okay, bud. I'll be right here. My brother's going to patch me up."

Sam seemed to accept what he'd said, and Mama Mary carted him to the kitchen where Brett knew he was in good hands.

Maddox helped him into the den and onto the couch. "Rose, get some towels so we can stop this bleeding. Then call Dr. Cumberland. We have to remove this bullet."

"There's no time," Brett argued.

"Listen to me, Brett," Maddox said in a deep voice. "You won't be any good if you die on me."

Rose dashed from the room, and Maddox poured two whiskeys. He returned and handed Brett a glass, then took a swig of his own, his eyes dark with rage and worry.

"Now, what the *hell* is going on?"

Brett rubbed his hand over his eyes, then swallowed his drink. "You aren't going to like it."

"I know that." Maddox walked over and sat down beside him. "But I'm your brother, man. And if you need my help, I'm here. But I need to know everything."

Brett nearly choked on his emotions. He'd just found out he had a son. And now his brother was ready to help him.

Of course Maddox didn't know what all he'd done.

But it was time for him to come clean. He'd take whatever punishment came his way. As long as Maddox helped him save Willow.

"The night of the funeral," he began, "Willow called me, hysterical."

Maddox leaned his elbows on his knees. "This has to do with her husband, Leo, doesn't it? Did she know he was a crook?"

Brett shook his head, a bead of perspiration trickling down his brow. "They were separated, but he was supposed to come by her house and drop off divorce papers.

On the way he picked up Sam. When Willow arrived home, she found Leo dead. And the men who'd killed him had abducted Sam."

Maddox muttered a curse, and let a heartbeat of silence pass. "Go on."

"They told Willow that if she called the law, they'd kill Sam."

"That's the reason you were snooping around on my computer?"

"Yes. The kidnappers said that Leo had a half million dollars. They wanted the money in exchange for her son." *His* son.

"What's the connection with the prisoner?"

"I think the kidnappers worked with Leo, they were his partners and he betrayed them so they killed him."

"His partners? You're talking about the cattle-rustling ring?"

"Yeah. When the police became suspicious about it, the leaders threatened Garcia's family, so he took the fall for all the charges."

Rose ran in with some towels, and Maddox cut Brett's shirt off to examine the wound. They pressed towels to the bloody area, then applied pressure.

"So where's Leo's body?" Maddox asked.

Brett gritted his teeth at the pain. "I buried him, Maddox. Just until we could find Sam."

Maddox exploded and stormed across the room. Rose offered Brett a sympathetic look, folded another towel and pressed it to his bloody shoulder.

Brett cleared his throat. "I'm sorry, Maddox, but I didn't know what else to do. I did try to preserve evidence."

"How could you preserve evidence when you buried him?" Maddox crossed his arms as he stopped pacing.

"Brett, do you realize what kind of position you've put me in?"

Brett let the silence fall. He could never live up to Maddox.

"Yes, and I'm sorry," he said honestly. "But Willow was terrified, afraid they'd kill Sam because we think he witnessed Leo's murder."

Maddox pinched the bridge of his nose.

Brett's lungs squeezed for air. "There's something else."

Maddox shoved his hands through his hair. "What?"

Brett swallowed hard. He couldn't believe it himself. But it was true. "Sam is my son."

WILLOW CLENCHED THE PIECE of rope that she'd found on the floor in her hand as if that piece of cord tied her to Sam.

She picked up the stuffed animal and pressed it to her nose. Sam's sweet little-boy smell permeated the toy just as his infectious laugh and insatiable curiosity filled her with love.

Footsteps echoed outside, then the door squeaked open. Remembering they'd set a deadline before they killed her, she barely suppressed tears.

They had removed their bandannas this time, revealing harsh faces, rough with beard stubble and scars. Faces that were now imprinted in her brain.

Which meant they were definitely going to kill her.

The bigger man with beefy hands strode over to her with a gun in his hand. The taller one stepped into the room with his phone.

The bigger guy grabbed her by her hair and jammed the weapon to her head. Willow cried out at the force, but froze when she felt the cold barrel at her temple.

Were they going to kill her now?

BRETT GRITTED HIS TEETH as the doctor removed the bullet, then cleaned the wound and stitched his shoulder.

"I didn't know doctors made house calls anymore." Although he knew this man had taken care of his father and had been friends with Joe McCullen.

Dr. Cumberland chuckled, but his eyes looked serious beneath his square glasses. "I usually *don't*, but this is a small town, and your brother is the sheriff."

"Yeah."

"He's a good man," the doctor said. "He takes care of this town and the people in it."

Guilt nagged at Brett. Unfortunately, Brett had put him in a terrible position.

From the doorway he heard Maddox discussing the situation with Rose. "I know he had reason," Maddox said, "but this is a mess. I have to retrieve Howard's body and have the crime scene processed."

"What about Willow?"

Maddox made a low sound in his throat. "We'll figure out a way to find her."

Dr. Cumberland handed Brett two prescription bottles. "Take these for pain when you need them. The other is an antibiotic to prevent infection."

Brett waved Maddox over. "I've already called my business manager. He should have a hundred thousand ready for me by morning."

Maddox scowled down at him where he lay on the couch. "Okay, but even if you give them the money, they may still kill Willow."

Brett clenched the pill bottles in one hand. "I won't let that happen."

Maddox studied him for a long moment while Rose watched, her expression concerned. "I want these guys,"

Maddox said. "Leo Howard was a crook. He was the leader of a cattle-rustling operation across the state. Our town isn't the first one he hit."

"Willow didn't know anything about it," Brett said earnestly.

"I don't doubt that. But he even stole from Horseshoe Creek, Brett. So this is personal."

More personal to Brett because the man had threatened Willow and Sam.

"Do you know who Leo was working with?" Maddox asked.

Brett thought hard. "There was a man named Wally Norman who was questioned about the cattle rustling."

Maddox nodded. "Yeah. Norman went to prison later on other charges. I think his partner was a man named Jasper Day. Day disappeared after Norman was locked up. I suspect he was lying low until the heat died down and he could get his hands on his share."

"I think Boyle Gates might have been involved, too," Brett said. "Willow and I talked to him, but he threw us out."

"Gates?" Maddox pulled his hand down his chin. "I wondered how that SOB grew his spread so quickly. Probably filled it with stolen cattle."

"He's smart, though," Brett said. "If he's involved, he helped set Gus Garcia up to take the fall." He tried to sit up, but he swayed slightly. Maddox steadied him, and Brett set the pills on the table. He didn't intend to take anything to impair his judgment. He needed a clear head to save Willow.

"I'll send a team to process Willow's house," Maddox said. "If we can match prints to whoever was there, maybe we can use it to track down the men who have Willow.

Knowing their identities may lead us to a location where they're holding her."

Maddox reached for his phone. "I'll also get my deputy looking into Day's and Norman's whereabouts."

Brett started to thank Maddox, but his phone buzzed. His shoulder throbbed as he shifted and dug it from his jacket pocket. A text.

Fear ripped through him at the sight of the photo of Willow with the gun to her temple. Below the picture, the kidnapper had typed a message.

Twenty-four hours or she's dead.

Chapter Eighteen

Brett wanted to punch something. If those jerks hurt Willow, he'd *kill* them.

Maddox yanked on his jacket. "I'm meeting my head CSI guy, Hoberman, at Willow's. If the kidnappers left prints, we'll find them and get an ID."

Brett gripped the edge of the sofa to stand. "I'll go with you."

Maddox laid a hand on Brett's shoulder. "No, Brett. Let me do my job. You aren't going to be any good to anyone, if you don't get some rest."

Maddox leaned over and planted a kiss on Rose's lips. "I'll be back later."

"Be careful," Rose said softly.

Maddox's eyes darkened as he kissed her again, and Brett looked away.

He'd always seen his brother as the strong one, the one who didn't need anyone, but watching him with Rose gave him a glimpse of another side.

Maddox was just as vulnerable as he and Ray had been. Only Maddox had been the oldest, and his father had relied on him to be strong for his little brothers.

No wonder Maddox had resented the two of them when they let him down.

Mama Mary appeared at the door with Sam by her

side. The gleam in the older woman's eyes told Brett all he needed to know. She'd fallen in love with the little boy at first sight.

Mama Mary was fierce and loving, had steered him back on track a few times when he'd strayed, but she always did it with a loving hand.

His heart twisted as his gaze rested on his son. His chin, those eyes, the dimple, even that cowlick reminded him of himself. And Sam looked just as lost as he had when his mother died.

But he was not going to let Sam lose Willow. Not as long as he had a breath in his body.

"Mr. Brett, he wolfed down that mac and cheese, but I believe this boy needs some sleep. I'm gonna take him upstairs. Which room do you want him in?"

Brett smiled at Mama Mary and pushed himself to stand. "My room. I'll take him."

Mama Mary's eyes twinkled with understanding. "There's a box of some of your old clothes in the storage room. I bet I could find some pajamas in there that would fit Sam."

"That would be great." Brett's shoulder throbbed as he made his way over to Sam, but he ignored the pain. "Come on, buddy. I'll show you my room."

Sam gave Brett a brave nod and slipped his small hand into Brett's.

Emotions flooded Brett.

A pity that now he'd come home, Brett's father was gone. And that Sam would never know his grandfather.

Sam tightened his fingers inside Brett's palm, and he squeezed his son's hand, amazed at the protective instincts that surged to life.

He would not let his kid down.

Together they climbed the steps, Brett walking slower

to accommodate Sam's shorter stride. When they reached the landing, he took Sam to the last room on the right, his old bedroom.

Sam's eyes widened when he entered. Brett felt a sense of pride at the fact that his father had left all his rodeo posters on the walls. Men who'd been heroes to Brett and inspired his drive to join the circuit.

"Did you go to all those rodeos?" Sam asked.

Brett grinned. "Every last one. My daddy took me when I was little. And I'll take you."

Sam looked up at him in awe. "I wanna go, but Mommy always said no."

Brett stooped down to Sam's eye level and rubbed his arm. "Well, maybe together we can change her mind." Although hurt and anger with Willow gnawed at him—she'd deprived him of the first four years of Sam's life.

He pushed aside his own feelings, though. Sam would have to come first.

"You really think she'll let me come to one of your rodeos?"

To *one* of his? "I promise we'll work something out. Maybe I can teach you some tricks one day. Would you like that?"

Sam bobbed his head up and down, fighting a yawn.

Mama Mary appeared with a pair of flannel pajamas with superheroes on them. "I think these will fit."

Brett took them from her and thanked her. "Will these do, little man?"

Sam nodded and began to peel off his jeans. Brett squatted down to help him change, worried as he looked for bruises on the boy. "Sam, I know you were scared of those bad men. Did they hurt you?"

Sam pulled on the pajamas. "They locked me in that dark room and wouldn't let me out."

The quiver in his voice tore at Brett. He helped Sam slide on the pajama shirt, then folded down the quilt, and Sam crawled into bed. Then he sat down beside him and tucked the covers up over Sam.

"Do you know where you were? Was it a house or a barn? Was it in town or on a farm somewhere?"

Sam sniffed. "It was a house, but the windows was nailed shut."

Anger made Brett clench his jaw. "When you looked out the window, what did you see? Another building? Cows or horses?"

Sam twisted the sheet with his fingers. "Woods. There was trees and trees everywhere."

Brett sighed. "How about noises? Did you hear anything nearby? Maybe a train or cars? Or a creek?"

Sam scrunched his nose in thought. "I can't remember. I just heard that big man's mean voice. He tolded me to eat this gross sandwich, but I didn't want it, I wanted Mommy. And he got mad…"

Sam's voice broke and tears filled his eyes.

Brett held his breath. "What did he do when he got mad?"

"He yelled and throwed the food, and then he shut the door and locked me back up."

Brett hated the bastard more than he'd hated anyone in his life, but he softened his tone. "It's over now, little man. You'll never have to see those men again."

Sam collapsed into his arms again, and Brett rocked him back and forth, soothing him until the little boy's breathing steadied. He eased him back down on the bed and tucked him in again.

Sam's sleepy eyes drifted to the shelf, and Brett saw the stuffed pony he'd slept with as a boy. He took it down and handed it to Sam.

"This was my best friend when I was your age. His name is Lucky. He gets lonely up here. Can he sleep with you?"

Sam nodded, then took the pony, rolled to his side and tucked it under his arm. Brett planted a kiss on his head, his heart filled with overwhelming love.

"Night, little man."

Tomorrow he had to bring Willow home to his son.

But Willow hadn't told him about Sam, because she obviously thought he wouldn't make a good father.

How would she feel about letting him be part of Sam's life now?

WILLOW STRUGGLED AND FOUGHT to untie her hands and feet. Her fingers and wrists were raw, her nails jagged from trying to tear the rope in two. Finally, she fell into an exhausted sleep just before dawn.

But she dreamed Leo was standing over her with blood spewing from his chest while he held a gun against Sam's head. She motioned for Sam to stay still and begged Leo to let him go, but he waved the gun at her and ordered her to get on her knees and crawl outside.

Terrified for Sam, she did as he said. He shoved and kicked her until she reached the grave he'd dug for her. A sliver of moonlight illuminated the deep hole where snakes hissed and crawled along the edges, their tongues flicking out as if waiting to take a bite out of her.

Then Leo kicked her hard and she fell, tumbling down, fighting and clawing as she tasted dirt and the snakes slithered over her body and bit her, poison shooting through her blood as she screamed.

A man's loud voice boomeranged through the room as he burst through the door. Willow jerked upright, disoriented.

Reality quickly interceded as he rammed his face into hers. "Shut up or I'll shut you up."

Willow bit her tongue. She'd obviously been scream-ing in her sleep.

She sucked in a breath and stared at him, determined not to show fear.

Tense seconds passed as he glared at her, daring her to make a sound.

More footsteps, then the thinner man appeared. "We need to set up the meet."

"I'll handle it."

Willow shivered as they slammed the door and left her tied up and alone again. Terrified they'd kill her even if Brett found the money, she started to work on the knots again.

If she could just free herself, when one of them came in again, maybe she could get past him and run.

BRETT DOZED FOR a couple of hours, but couldn't sleep for worrying about Willow. Every hour that passed intensified his fear that he wouldn't be able to save her.

He called first thing about the money, and his manager said all he had to do was pick it up at the bank in Pistol Whip. Brett took a quick shower and checked on Sam, but he was still sleeping, so he grabbed a cup of coffee and breakfast.

Maddox came in, looking tired and stressed to the hilt.

"My manager called. I'm meeting him at the bank to pick up the cash he liquidated for me," Brett told him.

Maddox accepted a cup of coffee from Mama Mary, then joined Brett at the table. "We found prints at Willow's. Jasper Day's and Wally Norman's. Norman escaped prison last week. He shanked a guard and killed him, then took his uniform to escape. We believe he contacted Day and they came hunting Howard."

"And when Leo refused to give them their share of the profit from the stolen cattle, they killed him."

"Exactly."

"And Willow and Sam got caught up in it because she married the jerk." Brett grimaced. She wouldn't have if he'd stayed around.

But you didn't. You left her alone and pregnant.

That realization made him feel like a heel. While Willow had been raising their little boy, he'd been sleeping around and smiling at cameras.

It was a wonder she didn't hate him.

"Hoberman will let me know if they turn up anything else useful. But finding those prints is enough to obtain a warrant for the men. I need Howard's body, though."

Brett stood and pushed his chair back. "All right, I'll show you where he is." He poked his head in the kitchen and called Mama Mary's name. "I have to go with Maddox. Will you take care of Sam this morning?"

"Of course. Rose is here, too. She loves kids and Sam knows her from when Willow stopped in at her store."

"Tell her I said thanks. We'll be back in a bit."

He grabbed his jacket and followed Maddox to his SUV.

"I wish you'd come to me before," Maddox said.

Brett winced as his stitches pulled. "I'm sorry, Maddox. I didn't want to put you on the spot."

"Didn't want to put me on the spot?" Maddox said gruffly. "You don't think burying a body and covering up a crime put me on the spot?"

"I know it did," Brett said. "But I couldn't let anything happen to Sam."

Maddox cut his look toward him. "Did you know he was yours?"

Pain rocked through Brett. "Not until we rescued him, and I saw him for myself."

Maddox mumbled something low beneath his breath. "He is definitely yours," he finally said with a small smile.

Pride ballooned in Brett's chest. "He is, isn't he?"

A silent understanding passed between them. Sam would be raised a McCullen from now on.

"Where is the grave?" Maddox asked.

Brett pointed to the east and gave him exact directions. Maddox had the ME and Hoberman waiting to meet them, and a few minutes later, Brett walked the ground and showed him the grave.

The CSI team began to dig, turning the damp earth, and Brett checked his watch.

He had less than twenty-four hours now to save Willow.

WILLOW'S SHOULDERS AND FINGERS ached from twisting and turning, and fresh tears of frustration threatened. She couldn't work the damn knot free.

The door opened again, and the thinner of the men appeared with a plate of scrambled eggs on it. He set a bottle of water beside it.

"I have to go to the bathroom," Willow said. Maybe there would be something in the bathroom she could use as a weapon.

He cursed, but gave a little nod, then jerked her up from the bed. "I can't walk," Willow said. "Please untie me so I can use the bathroom and eat."

His beady eyes met hers. "If you try to run, we'll kill you."

Fear nearly choked her, but she whispered that she understood. "I won't run. Brett will get you the money. I know he will."

"He'd better. We're out of patience."

He removed a knife from his pocket and cut the ropes. She shook her hands free, then wiggled her toes as he untied her feet. He gestured toward the hall, and she ducked in and used the facility, then did a quick desperate search for a razor or pair of scissors. Anything to defend herself.

But the cabinet was empty, the bathroom dingy and old, as if the house had been vacant for a long time.

That would make it harder for Brett to find her. She'd already looked out the window and realized they were off the grid and surrounded by woods.

The man pounded on the door and she opened it, trying to play meek as she glanced to the living area and kitchen. She didn't see the bigger man, so decided that he might be gone.

Getting away from one man would be easier than two.

He grabbed her arm, but she lifted her knee and kicked him in the groin. He doubled over and yelped in pain, and she ran toward the kitchen. She spotted a kitchen knife and grabbed it, then flung open the front door.

Cold wind assaulted her, then a man's fist came toward her face. She tried to scream as the man behind her yanked her hair, but her jaw screamed with pain from the blow the bigger guy had landed.

Another blow to her shoulder blade and she dropped the knife and crumpled, writhing in pain. The bigger guy hauled her up over his shoulder, and the world tilted and spun as he carried her outside.

A second later, he opened the trunk and threw her in. Her head hit something hard, a tire iron maybe, and she saw stars.

"I warned you what would happen if you tried to run," the thinner man snarled.

The trunk door slammed shut, pitching her into darkness. She tried to stay conscious, but nausea flooded her.

The last thing she thought before the car engine started

and the car jerked away was that they were going to kill her and bury her just as she'd done Leo.

Except they'd do it out here in the middle of nowhere where no one would ever find her.

Chapter Nineteen

Brett's life flashed behind his eyes as he watched the men digging up Leo Howard's body.

A month ago, *hell*, two weeks ago, he'd been grinning for the cameras, at the height of his career, with his future bright in front of him. His agent had even suggested him for a part in a Western movie.

Now he'd not only discovered he had a son but he'd become an accessory to a murder and might be facing charges of tampering with evidence and covering up a crime.

Instead of riding for a living or starring in a movie, he might soon be sitting in a cell.

The plastic he'd wrapped around Leo came into view as the diggers dumped wet soil beside the grave. One of them paused when his shovel hit something. "He's here."

Brett breathed out in relief. For a fraction of a second, he'd actually been afraid that someone might have discovered Howard's body and moved him.

Maddox angled his head toward him. "You wrapped him in plastic?"

"And a rug." Brett grimaced. "I tried to preserve him as best I could."

Maddox motioned for the men to continue while he stepped aside. "Tell me exactly how you found him."

Brett inhaled sharply. "I can do better. I took a picture," Brett said. "I was planning to tell you everything once Sam was safe."

Maddox muttered a low sound. "All right. Let's see."

Brett pulled his phone from his pocket and accessed the picture. "Willow said Howard picked Sam up from a neighbor's then brought him home. We think the men must have been following him or watching the house, and confronted him about the money. When he refused to give it up, they shot him in the chest and took Sam."

Maddox studied the picture. "I'll have forensics process his body and compare evidence from the house to corroborate her story." His brows furrowed. "Did Howard have visitation with Sam?"

"I don't think so. Willow said he didn't want to be a father." Maybe because he'd known Sam wasn't his. Had Howard resented that fact? Had he taken his temper out on Sam?

"Then why did Leo pick Sam up and take him back to the house?"

Brett stewed over that. "Maybe he knew his partners were after him, and he intended to use Sam as leverage."

The breeze picked up dead leaves and dirt, scattering them at his feet. Brett rubbed his hands together against the chilly wind.

"What did Sam tell you about that night?" Maddox asked.

Brett swallowed hard. "Nothing. I...didn't ask him about it. I figured he'd been through enough."

The diggers had uncovered the length of Howard's body along with the bag of bedding. Two of the men climbed in the grave to hoist him from the hole where they'd laid him in the ground.

"I understand why you don't want to upset Sam, but he might have seen where Howard stashed that cash."

Brett's pulse pounded. He hated to make Sam relive that horrible day.

But if he'd seen where Leo hid the cash, he had to talk to him.

Willow's life depended on it.

CLAUSTROPHOBIA THREATENED TO completely panic Willow. She was suffocating in the trunk of this car.

The constant rumbling and bumping over rocky roads intensified her headache and made her nauseous.

She reminded herself to breathe in and out and remain calm. Brett would bring the money and rescue her. And if he didn't…he'd take care of Sam.

The car finally jerked to a stop, brakes squealing. The sudden change in movement propelled her across the car trunk, and she rolled into the side. Doors slammed.

The men were getting out.

Terrified they'd carried her someplace in the wilderness to kill her and leave her body, she frantically ran her bound hands across the interior of the trunk. It was so dark, she couldn't see, but there had to be a release lever inside.

Although with her hands and feet tied, how in the world would she escape?

A noise sounded, then voices. "What are we going to do with her?"

"Get rid of her."

The female again. And she sounded so coldhearted.

"We need the money first."

"All right. Then do it. And kill that cowboy, too."

Willow's stomach knotted. Who was that woman?

Doris, Leo's former girlfriend? Or Eleanor, his grandmother's nurse? Maybe she'd lied and she had been involved with Leo.

"What should we do with the bodies?" one of the men asked.

"There's an old mine near here," the woman said. "Dump their bodies in there, then close up the opening so no one will ever find them."

Tears blurred Willow's eyes. If they killed her and Brett, what would happen to Sam?

BRETT WATCHED AS the medical examiner, a young woman named Dr. Lail, knelt beside Howard's body. One of the crime workers photographed the way he was wrapped in plastic and the rug, then folded those back so she could examine the body.

Brett ignored the pinch of guilt he felt over burying the man in the cold ground. Howard hadn't deserved any better.

"I'll do an autopsy," Dr. Lail said. "But judging from the gunshots, he probably bled out."

Maddox thanked her and supervised while they carried Howard's body to the ME's van to be transported to the morgue.

"We have to notify next of kin. Did he have relatives?" Maddox asked Brett.

"Father and grandmother." Brett gave him their names and addresses.

"I'll ask Deputy Whitefeather to make the notification."

"I need to go to the bank," Brett said. "Then I'll have a talk with Sam." A talk he dreaded, but one that needed to happen.

Maddox gave a clipped nod. "Call me when you hear from the kidnappers. You aren't meeting them alone."

Worry nagged at Brett. "Maddox, if you come with me, they'll kill her."

Maddox stepped closer to him. "You can't afford not to have my help." Maddox lowered his voice. "Trust me for once, little brother. They won't know I'm there. But you could be walking into a trap. What would happen to Sam if you and Willow both got killed?"

A sick knot thickened Brett's throat. But his answer was immediate. "I'd want you and Rose to raise Sam."

Maddox's gaze met his, a sea of emotions in his eyes. "Of course I would raise him, he's a McCullen, but we aren't going to let anything happen, Brett. Not if we work together."

It had been a long time since they'd worked together on anything. But Sam and Willow were more important than any petty problem they'd had between them.

So he followed Maddox to the SUV, and they drove into town. Brett went in the bank while Maddox walked across the street to the jail to talk to his deputy about making the death notification.

Brett spotted his business manager, Frank Cotton, waiting in a chair outside the bank president's office. Cotton stood and greeted him with a worried expression, one hand clutching a leather bag.

"Are you going to tell me what this is about now?" Cotton asked worriedly.

Brett motioned for him to keep quiet and they moved against the wall. "I'm sorry, but I can't."

Cotton tugged at his tie. "Listen, if you're in trouble with one of those rodeo groupies, just tell me and I'll make it go away."

Brett jerked his head back. "What are you suggesting?"

"I'm here to do whatever you need, Brett. If you want a girl run off, I'm your man. If you need a lawyer to, say... draw up a confidentiality agreement or adoption papers for a kid, or pay for an abortion, I'll handle it. We won't let anything stand in the way of your career."

Brett stared at him, disturbed by the offer. At one time, his career had been all that mattered. But now he didn't give a damn about it.

All that mattered was Willow and Sam.

And he'd just reconnected with Maddox. Granted they still had things to work out—whether or not Maddox would arrest him—but he wanted to be part of Maddox's life.

And part of Horseshoe Creek.

"Thanks," he told Cotton. "But I'm not paying off a girl. If I need a lawyer, I'll let you know."

He took the leather bag, then glimpsed inside. Cash, just as he'd requested. "Just keep this between us, Cotton."

"Of course."

Brett turned to leave. "Your agent's been calling," Cotton said. "She wants to talk about your schedule this spring."

"I'll get in touch with her," Brett said.

He stepped outside the bank and started to cross the street, but a truck whizzed by and he jumped back as a bullet flew toward him.

Chapter Twenty

Brett ducked behind a pole, just as another bullet whizzed by his head. Who was shooting at him?

He tried to get a look at the driver, but the truck roared down the road in a cloud of exhaust. Then someone slammed something hard against the back of his head, and he stumbled and went down. He tried to hold on to the bag of cash, but someone snatched it from his hands and raced away.

"Everyone get down!" Maddox yelled as he jogged from across the street, his gun drawn, his gaze sweeping the area for the shooter.

A few locals on the street screamed and darted in different directions. Brett pushed to his hands and stood, cursing as he hunted for the person who'd just stolen the cash. But he'd come out of nowhere and disappeared just as quickly.

Maddox was breathing hard, his gaze still surveying the street as he approached Brett. "Are you hit?"

"No. The shooter drove off, but another guy punched me and stole the money."

Maddox pivoted again. "The shooter was a decoy meant to distract you so the other man could sneak up behind."

"Yeah, and he succeeded."

"Did you get a look at either one of them?"

"No, not really. The license plate on the truck was

missing. The one who took the money was big and wore a hoodie."

Brett's manager stepped from the bank, looking terrified. "Brett, man, are you all right?"

"Yeah, but he stole the money." Brett scraped his hand through his hair, frustrated. "I can't believe this is happening."

Maddox narrowed his eyes at the manager. "Did you see anything?"

The tall man fiddled with his bolo tie. "No, I heard the gunshot, and like everyone in the bank, we dropped to the floor and hid. We thought someone was coming in to rob the bank."

"It had to be the bastards who have Willow," Brett said. "They must have followed me here, and decided to take the cash and run."

His heart stuttered. Which meant that they might have given up on the other money and killed Willow.

AN HOUR LATER, Brett entered the farmhouse. Anxiety churned in his gut. Maddox had canvassed everyone in the bank, the street and business owners, but no one had seen anything.

Once the first shot had rent the air, panic had set in. It was a small town. The locals weren't used to high crime or random attacks…or murder.

But they would know soon enough that a kidnapping had occurred and that a man had been shot to death right here in their safe little town.

Rose greeted Maddox with a big hug and kiss. If Brett hadn't been so fraught with fear for Willow, he would have laughed at the mushy look on his big brother's face as he locked lips with her.

Sam raced in from the kitchen. "Did you get Mommy back?"

Brett's lungs squeezed for air. He'd never look at life the same way now that he had a little boy.

Maddox, Rose and Mama Mary gave him sympathetic looks.

"We were making cookies to surprise her when she comes home," Mama Mary said, wiping flour from Sam's cheek with a gentle hand.

"And Sam made her a card," Rose added with a smile.

Brett stooped down to Sam's level. "She's not with me now, but we're going to find her, little man. And she's going to love the cookies and card."

Sam's face fell into a pout. "We're making peanut butter. That's Mommy's favorite."

Emotions nearly choked Brett. He remembered that about Willow. One time she'd eaten half a dozen of Mama Mary's famous peanut butter cookies. He clasped Sam's hand in his. "Come in here with me a minute, bud. I need to talk to you."

Sam clamped his teeth over his lip, but followed him to the den. Brett wanted to wrap his arms around his son and swear to him that everything would be all right.

But he had to find Sam's mother first or he would be making empty promises.

"Sam, I'm trying to figure out where those bad men are keeping your mommy. Do you remember anything else about the place?"

"No. Just that it was dark, and it smelled bad." The little boy dropped his head and picked at the button on Brett's shirt.

"How about your daddy? What can you tell me about him?"

Sam turned his face up toward Brett. "He was mean to Mommy and he didn't want me."

The breath left Brett's lungs in a rush. He lifted Sam's chin with his thumb. He wanted to assure him that he wanted him, but that would take an explanation he didn't have time for right now. But it would happen. "You know, that's not your fault. You are a wonderful kid."

Sam simply stared at him with big frightened eyes. "Daddy didn't think so. He said I was a baby, and I was in the way."

Brett wrapped his arm around his son. He wished Leo was alive so he could kill him. "That's not true, Sam. You're very special and your mommy loves you with all her heart." *And so do I.* "I care about you, too."

Sam looked up at him. "I see why my mommy liked you when she was in school. You're nicer than Daddy. He yelled at Mommy all the time."

"That's because he was a bad man."

Sam looked down again. "But if he was bad and the other men killed him, why did they take me and Mommy?"

"Because your daddy stole money from them, and they're greedy and want it back."

"There was lots of it?" Sam said.

"Yes." Brett rubbed Sam's back. "Did you see your daddy with any money?"

He shook his head.

Brett hesitated, trying to word his questions carefully. "Daddy picked you up at your mommy's friend's house that day?"

"Yeah. I didn't wanna go with him, but Miss Gina said I should."

Brett chewed the inside of his cheek. "What happened when you and Leo got back to your house?"

Sam kept tugging at Brett's button, his little body trembling slightly. Brett rubbed Sam's back. "I know it's hard to think about, but buddy, it might help."

A long moment lapsed between them, then Sam's breath wheezed out. "We went inside, and he tolded me to hide in my room."

"What? Why?"

"He said some men followed him."

So Leo had tried to protect Sam. That was something.

"Did he have anything with him?"

Sam scrunched his nose. "Like what?"

"Maybe a briefcase or suitcase."

Sam's eyes lit up. "He gots a big gym bag and brought it in the house. Then he pushed me in the closet and shut the door and told me not to come out."

"You stayed in the closet?"

Sam nodded. "I was scared. I just wanted Daddy to go away. But he said he had to get some stuff he left with Mommy."

"Did she say what stuff?"

"No, and Mommy said she throwed the stuff he left away. But he said he hid it there. I was scared he'd get mad about that, so I didn't tell him."

Smart boy.

"After you got in the closet, what did your father do?"

Sam's finger twisted the button harder. "He took my toys out of my toy box and throwed them on the floor."

Brett imagined the scene, questions ticking in his head. He and Willow had searched the house, but what if Leo had stowed the money in that toy chest?

"Then someone busted in. I heard the door cracking, then those awful men shouting and Daddy gots up and tried to talk to them."

Brett cradled Sam in his arms, holding him tight.

"They yelled and said ugly words, then Daddy jumped on one of them and…the gun went off."

His heart ached for his little boy. To witness a murder

at such a young age was bound to affect him, maybe give him nightmares. Possibly for years to come.

He needed his mother to help him through the trauma. He also needed a father.

"I'm sorry you had to see that, Sam, but you're very brave to tell me about it." Sam shivered, and Brett hugged him with all the love in his heart.

Then he cupped Sam's face in his hands. "I need you to be strong just a little while longer, okay?"

Sam nodded, the trust in his son's look nearly bringing Brett to his knees.

WILLOW'S BODY ACHED from being tied up and bound in the trunk of the car. She was suffocating.

But they didn't seem to be in a hurry to let her out. In fact, it had gotten quiet for a while and she thought they might have left her.

The sound of another engine roaring rent the air. Tires screeched. Then more doors slammed.

"Where have you two been?" the woman asked.

"We got that money McCullen promised."

"He found Leo's stash?" the woman asked.

"No, the money McCullen withdrew from his own funds. With that and Leo's money, we'll all be set for a long time."

"You idiot," the woman said. "He's liable to call the cops."

"And tell them what?" the man barked. "That someone stole ransom money? That he buried Leo's body? I doubt that rodeo star wants that in the papers."

"It's time for us to make the meet," the other man said. "If McCullen doesn't bring the cash Leo stole this time, let's get rid of the woman and get out of town before things heat up.

The trunk opened, and Willow clenched her teeth as the bigger guy hauled her to the ground. She stumbled, then gasped when she saw the woman.

Gina, her neighbor. The woman she'd thought was her friend.

Dear God... "Why?"

Gina gave her a nasty grin. "Because Leo was supposed to be mine. And so was this money. And with you out of the way, now it will be."

The big guy, Norman she'd heard him called, punched a number on his cell phone. It must be Wally Norman. A minute later, she heard Brett's voice.

"Hello. This is Brett McCullen."

"I'm texting you an address. If you want to see the woman again, bring the cash and come alone."

"Let me speak to Willow first," Brett said.

Willow shuddered as the big guy pressed a gun to her temple. "Say hello, honey."

"Brett, I'm okay, just take care of Sam!"

The man jerked the phone away, then whacked her on the back of the head again and shoved her back in the trunk.

Tears caught in her throat. The drop-off was a trap.

Chapter Twenty-One

Brett left Sam to finish the cookies and card with Mama Mary and motioned for Maddox to join him in the hall. "Maddox, I received a text about the drop."

"Where?"

Brett angled the phone for Maddox to see the address. "Do you know where that is?"

Maddox shrugged. "Yeah. It's not too far from here."

"I also may know where the stolen money is."

"Where?"

"Sam said that when Leo picked him up, he had a bag with him, and that he was digging around in Sam's toy chest."

"Did you look there before?"

"I saw the chest but all that was visible was toys. Maybe he hid it under them."

"Let's go." Maddox grabbed his keys, but Brett put a hand to his brother's shoulder.

"Not in your SUV, Maddox. If they see you, they'll kill Willow."

Maddox exhaled. "You're right. We'll drive your truck."

Seconds later, they raced to Willow's house. Crime-scene tape marked the house and fingerprint dust coated everything inside.

Worse, the house smelled of death and emptiness, not

like a home, but like a place where a terrible wrong had been done. Would Willow want to return here?

"The toy chest?" Maddox asked, jarring him back to the moment.

Brett pushed all thoughts aside and hurried into Sam's room. Knowing Sam was his son made the toys and posters on the wall seem more personal and they tugged at his heart.

Toys had been dumped and scattered across the floor from the toy chest. A football, toy trucks, plastic horses, a plastic bat and ball.

"You see it?" Maddox asked behind him.

"No." He quickly emptied the remaining toys, then felt along the bottom and discovered a piece of plywood. Had that board come with the toy chest?

A nail felt loose, and he pulled at it until the board loosened, then he yanked it free. "I found it!" Cash was neatly stacked and spread evenly across the bottom.

Maddox handed him the duffel bag, and Brett quickly filled it with the money.

Nerves tightened his neck and Brett watched for another ambush as he carried it out to his truck. Seconds later, Brett sped from the house.

"Listen, Brett, when we get there, I'll stay down until we see what we're dealing with."

Maddox checked his gun, and Brett grimaced. His rifle lay on the seat between them. If he needed it, he'd use it in a heartbeat.

Dark clouds rolled overhead, the wind picking up as he turned down the road into the woods. Trees shook and limbs swayed as he neared the cabin, and he searched for signs that Willow was there.

"What do you see?"

Brett squinted through the dark. "An old cabin, looks

like it's been deserted for a while. I don't see anyone. One light on in the house from a back room."

"How about a vehicle?"

"A dark sedan. Tinted windows. I can't see if anyone is inside."

"Park and sit there for a minute. Wait and see if anyone comes outside."

Brett did as he said, his senses alert as he scanned the exterior of the cabin. An old weathered building sat to the right. It appeared empty, but someone could be hiding inside.

A sound to the left made him jerk his head to see what it was. A deer scampered through the woods.

He hissed a breath, then reached for the door handle. "It's time. I have to see if she's here."

Maddox caught his arm and looked up at him from the floorboard of the truck. "Be careful, Brett. This could be a setup."

He knew that.

But he had to take that chance.

He eased open the door and slid one foot from the truck. Clutching the duffel bag with the other hand, he lowered himself to the ground. He visually surveyed the area again, his stitches tugging as he slowly walked toward the cabin.

"I've got your money," he shouted.

The front door to the cabin opened, and he braced himself for gunfire. If they killed him, at least Maddox was armed and could save Willow and take her home to Sam.

WILLOW FELT DIZZY from being locked in the trunk of the car and inhaling the exhaust as they'd driven.

The car jerked to a stop, and she forced tears at bay. Crying would do no good. These people didn't care about her.

All they wanted was money.

The trunk opened, and she squinted, blinded by the sudden light. Then a cold hard hand clamped around her wrist and dragged her from the car again. She stumbled, dizzy and disoriented.

"Day should be meeting with McCullen now," the man named Norman said.

Gina gestured to the right. Willow looked around, sick when she realized that they were in the middle of nowhere.

And that Gina was pointing to an old mine. Rusted mining equipment sat discarded, piles of dirt scattered around along with metal garbage cans and tools.

"How can you do this, Gina? Sam is just an innocent little boy. He needs me."

"He'll survive," Gina said.

"Did you kill Leo?" Willow asked.

"He deserved it. He tried to betray me, just like he did Norman and Day."

"Why did Leo take Sam to my house?" Willow asked. "Why didn't he just get the money and leave?"

Gina hissed. "He knew Norman broke out of jail, and he and Day were onto him."

Hate swelled inside Willow. Leo had taken Sam with him as insurance.

"And you followed him to my house and killed him," Willow said, piecing together the most logical scenario.

"No, that was Norman," Gina said. "He said Leo attacked him."

"So when he died that day, you kidnapped Sam?"

"We earned that money the hard way." Gina waved a hand toward the mine. "And when Jasper gets back with it, we'll flee the country and live the good life."

Panic clawed at Willow. Norman reached for her and she tried to run, but with her ankles bound together, it was futile. She stumbled, then he threw her over his shoulder like a sack of potatoes and carted her toward the mine.

BRETT PAUSED AT the foot of the steps. A thin man with a goatee and tattoos on his neck appeared, a .38 pointed at Brett. Jasper Day.

"Toss the money on the porch," Day ordered. "And you'd better not try to cheat us this time."

"You're the crook and the murderer, not me."

Day's laugh boomeranged through the silence as he waved the gun. "Throw it now."

Brett clenched the bag tighter. "First, I want to see Willow."

Day shook his head. "Not going to happen. I'm calling the shots here."

Brett had a bad feeling this was going south. That Willow wasn't here. If she was dead…

"Either you bring her out here, or I walk back to the truck."

Day cursed. "You're a fool. I've got a gun pointed at your head, and you think you can bluff your way out of this."

"I don't care about the money," Brett shouted, "but I'll give my life for Willow. Now show me that she's alive."

Day's hand shook as he took a menacing step toward Brett. "Put the bag down now, McCullen. This isn't one of your rodeo games."

Brett held his ground and yelled for Willow. "Is she in there?" He gestured toward the cabin, and Day glanced sideways with a cocky grin.

Brett took advantage of that small sideways look, swung the bag and threw it with all his might. The bag slammed into Day with such force that it threw him backward. But he managed to get off a shot before he fell.

Brett dodged the bullet, then Maddox jumped from the

truck and fired at Day. One bullet into Day's chest, and he crumpled to the ground with a bellow. His gun skittered to the ground beside him as the man's arm fell limp.

Brett and Maddox ran toward him, then Maddox kicked the gun away, knelt beside the bastard and handcuffed him to the porch rail. Brett started toward the house, but Maddox called his name. He was right behind him, holding Day's gun. "Take this."

Brett snatched Day's revolver and inched up to the house. Maddox motioned for him to let him enter first, and Maddox eased through the door. He glanced in all directions, then gestured for Brett to go right and he'd go left.

Brett gripped the weapon with sweaty hands and inched across the wood floor. A bedroom to the right made his heart stop. A single metal bed sat by the wall, ropes discarded on the floor, a food tray, a ratty stuffed animal...

This was where they'd held his son. And they'd probably brought Willow to the same room.

But no one was inside now. He looked for blood but didn't see any. That had to be a good sign, didn't it?

He stepped into the hall and found Maddox frowning. "There's no one here, Brett."

Fear knotted his insides. "Where is she, Maddox?"

"Let's ask Day. He'll know." Brett followed him back outside but Day was barely conscious.

Brett dropped down beside him and snatched the man by the collar. "Where did your partner take Willow?"

The man looked up at him with glazed eyes. "Doctor..." he rasped.

Brett held up his phone. "I'll call for help when you tell me where they took her."

Day spit at him. "Go to hell."

Brett lifted Day's own gun to the criminal's head. "No, that's where you're going if you don't talk."

Chapter Twenty-Two

"You won't do it," Day rasped.

"You're sure about that?" Brett said darkly. "Because that little boy you kidnapped is my son. And his mother means everything to me."

The man's eyes bulged, and he coughed up blood.

Maddox aimed his gun at the other side of Day's head. "Where is she, Day?"

"The old mine off Snakepit Road."

Brett shoved away from the man, sick to his stomach. That mine had been shut down for years. And the road was dubbed Snakepit Road because miners had complained about the hotbed of snakes in the area.

"I have to go," Brett told Maddox.

Maddox looked down at Day. They both knew he wouldn't make it, but could they just leave him?

"Go ahead. I'll call for an ambulance and be right behind you." Maddox caught his arm. "Be careful, little brother. Don't do anything stupid. Wait for me to move in."

Brett muttered that he would, although if he had to go in on his own to save Willow, they both knew he'd do it.

Without Willow and Sam, his life meant nothing.

WILLOW SHIVERED WITH cold and fear as Norman tossed her to the ground inside the mine. She'd grown accustomed to the dark trunk, but this dark cavern wreaked of decayed animals and other foul odors she didn't even want to identify.

Norman cast his flashlight around the hole where he'd put her, and she cringed at the sight of the dirt walls. He must have dragged her a half mile inside. Wooden posts that supported beams inside the mine had been built when the mine was being worked, and Norman dragged her over to one and tied her to the post. Rocks and dirt scraped her arms and jeans, the jagged edges of loose stones cutting into her side.

"I wouldn't fight it too much," he said with an ugly sneer. "These beams are old and rotting. If one comes down, the whole mine may cave in."

"Why are you warning me?" Willow demanded. "You're going to leave me here to die anyway."

His thick brows drew together in a unibrow as he looked down at her. Then he turned and left her without another word. A snake hissed somewhere in the dark, and she pressed herself against the mine wall and pulled her knees up to her chest, trying to make herself as small as possible.

Not that the snake wouldn't find her anyway.

The light faded as Norman disappeared through the mine shaft, and she dropped her head forward, fighting despair.

Brett would have no idea how to find her. She was going to die here in this hellhole, and he would never know how sorry she was that she'd kept Sam from him.

Or that she'd never stopped loving him.

BRETT SCANNED THE DIRT road and deserted mine ahead as he sped down Snakepit Road.

There were no cars, no trucks, nothing to indicate anyone was here.

Fear seized him. Had Day lied to them? Had they taken Willow somewhere else?

His tires screeched as he barreled past the sign that marked the mine and threw the truck in Park. He jumped out, shouting Willow's name as he ran toward the opening of the mine, but just as he neared it, he noticed dynamite attached to the door and some kind of trigger, as if it was set with a timer.

Terror clawed at him, and he rushed to tear the dynamite away, but he was too late. The explosion sent him flying backward against some rocks, the sound of the mine collapsing roaring in his ears.

For a moment, he was so disoriented he couldn't breathe. Dust blurred his vision. His ears rang.

But fear and reality seeped through the haze. Was Willow inside that mine? Was he too late to save her?

He shoved himself up from the ground, raking dirt and twigs from his hair and clothes as he raced back toward the opening. "Willow! Willow, are you in there?!"

He dropped to his knees and started to yank boards away, but when he did, all he found was dirt. Mounds and mounds of it…

She might be buried alive in there…

Tears clogged his eyes and throat, and he bellowed in despair. But he lurched to his feet, ran to his truck, grabbed his cell phone and punched Maddox's number.

"I'm on my way, Brett."

"Get help!" Brett shouted. "They're gone, but there was dynamite outside the opening of the mine and it just exploded. I think Willow's inside."

A tense moment passed, then Maddox's breath rattled over the line. "I'll call a rescue crew and an ambulance," Maddox said. "Just hang in there, man."

Brett jammed the phone in his pocket and ran back

toward the mine, yelling Willow's name over and over and praying she could hear.

It seemed like hours later that Maddox arrived. His brother Ray shocked him by showing up on his heels. "Just tell me what to do," Ray said, his dark eyes fierce.

"We have to get her out," Brett said. "She has to be alive."

"A crew is on its way with equipment," Maddox said. "We need an engineer, someone who knows the mine, Brett, or we could make things worse."

How in the hell could they get worse? Willow was trapped, probably fighting for her life.

Ray cleared his throat. "Let me take a look. Maybe there's another entrance. Another way inside."

Ray's calm voice offered Brett a glimmer of hope, and he followed his younger brother, hoping he was right. They walked the edge of the mine shaft following it for half a mile, searching brush and rock structures for a second entrance.

"There had to be an extra exit for safety," Ray said.

He walked ahead, climbing a hill, then disappeared down an embankment. Brett was just about to give up when Ray shouted his name. "Over here. I found it!"

He looked up and saw Ray waving him forward. The sound of trucks barreling down the graveled road rent the air, and he looked back to Maddox who was waving the rescue crew toward the site.

"I'll tell Maddox I'm going in this end and check it out," Ray said.

Brett nodded and waited until Ray went down the hill, then he dropped to his stomach and crawled inside.

He couldn't wait. Every second that passed meant Willow was losing oxygen and might die.

The mine shaft was so low at the exit that he had to slide

in on his belly. He used his pocket flashlight to light the way and slithered on his stomach, dragging himself through the narrow tunnel until he reached a taller section that had been carved under rock. It was a room with supports built, giving him enough room to stand up.

"Willow! Can you hear me?"

He waved the light around the tunnel, searching for other crawl spaces, and spotted one to the left. He dropped down again, ignoring the dust and pebbles raining down on him, well aware the whole damn thing could collapse in seconds.

"Willow!" He continued to yell her name and search until finally he heard a sound.

"Willow, can you hear me? If you can, make some noise!"

Please let her be alive.

He crawled a few more feet, then reached another clearing where more supports indicated another room, although it appeared the roof had collapsed in the center. Willow must be on the other side. "Willow!"

"Brett!"

He breathed out in relief. "Hang in there, honey, I'm coming."

He started to dig with his hands, but realized tools would make the process faster, so he crawled back the way he came. It seemed to take him forever to reach the exit. He sucked in fresh air as he crawled out and raced down the hill to where the other men were starting to get set up.

"I told you to wait," Ray said.

Brett blew off his concern. "I found her. But I need a shovel or pick to dig her out."

"We've got this, Mr. McCullen," one of the rescue workers said. "It's too dangerous for you."

Why? Because he was a damn celebrity. "I don't care. I have to save her."

"They're the experts." Ray stepped up beside him. "One wrong move in there, Brett, and you could bring the whole mine down."

Maddox placed a hand on his back. "Brett, let them do their jobs. Besides, it won't help Sam if you get yourself killed."

"Who's Sam?" Ray asked.

Brett rubbed a hand down his face and began to explain to his younger brother that he had a son.

WILLOW FADED IN and out of consciousness. She couldn't breathe, couldn't find the air.

What had happened? One minute she'd been tied down here, praying Brett would find her. Then…something had exploded.

The roof had come tumbling down, rocks and dirt pummeling her. She'd tried to cover her face and head, but it had happened so quickly, and now dirt and rocks covered her. She tried to move her legs but they wouldn't budge.

Either she was paralyzed or the weight of the dirt was too heavy…

Her head lolled to the side, and she forced herself to inhale shallow breaths to conserve air. She thought she'd heard Brett calling her name.

Or had she been hallucinating because she was so close to death?

She closed her eyes and tried to envision someone rescuing her. Pictured Brett carrying her to safety and fresh air. Saw the two of them walking with Sam in the pasture, sharing a picnic, then telling Sam that Brett was his father.

Next, Brett was proposing, promising her they'd be the family they should have been all along.

The earth rumbled, some loud noise sounded and the mine began to tremble and shake again. She closed her eyes and mouth against another onslaught of debris, but when she opened them, her head was almost completely covered, and she choked on the dirt.

WITH EVERY SECOND that ticked by, Brett thought he was going to die himself. Maddox let the rescue crew take charge of finding Willow, while he issued an APB for Wally Norman. Authorities were alerted at airports, train and bus stations, and the police in states bordering Wyoming. He even notified border patrol in Mexico and Canada, although they didn't intend to let Norman get that far. Tire marks indicated that he'd been driving a sedan, although he could ditch that anywhere. *Hell*, he could have changed vehicles already and picked up a disguise.

"We're almost through!" one of the men shouted. They'd set up a man on the outside with receivers to communicate, as the two other rescue workers crawled inside.

Brett paced by the exit, grateful when an ambulance arrived.

"I can't believe you have a kid," Ray said.

"Me either." And he'd almost lost him and Willow.

But he was grateful Maddox and Ray were here. They hadn't exactly spent any time together since he'd returned. The three of them had retreated to their separate corners, just as they had as kids.

Except now Maddox had put his job on the line for him. And Ray...well, he'd come to his aid, no questions asked.

"They've got her!" one of the men shouted.

Brett rushed to the outside of the exit, desperate to see Willow. Ray stood behind him, silent but strong, as if he'd be there to catch him if he fell apart. It was an odd feeling, one he hadn't had in a long time.

Everyone in his business and the rodeo wanted something from him, wanted to build off his fame, wanted his money, wanted a part of him. But his brothers were here, just to support him.

Their father would have been proud.

Another agonizing few minutes stretched by, but finally one of the men slowly emerged, dragging a board through the opening.

A board with Willow strapped to it.

She was so filthy and covered in dirt and bruises that he could hardly see her face.

He held his breath as he dropped to her side and raked her hair back from her cheek. Her eyes were closed, and she lay terrifyingly still. "Willow?"

He looked up at the rescue worker, desperate for good news.

The man looked worried, his expression bleak as his partner emerged from the mine.

Brett cradled Willow's hand in his as the men lifted the board to carry her to the ambulance.

"Get the paramedics!" one of the rescue workers yelled.

More shouts and two medics ran toward them.

Brett whispered Willow's name again. "Willow, please wake up, baby. Sam and I need you." Suddenly he felt a tiny something in his hand. Willow's fingers twitching, grasping for him.

Brett choked on tears as she finally opened her eyes and looked at him.

THE NEXT TWO HOURS were chaos. Brett rode with the ambulance to the hospital, whispering promises to Willow that he wouldn't leave her side. She was weak and had suffered bruises and contusions and possibly a concussion. She also needed oxygen and rest.

"Gina," she whispered. "My friend."

"What? You want me to call her?"

"No. She was in on it," Willow rasped. "She was helping Leo. She told Norman to kill me."

"I'll tell Maddox to issue an APB for her, too."

She broke into a coughing spell, and he helped her sip some water. "Sam."

"He's home with Mama Mary," Brett said. "I called and told them you're all right. I'll bring Sam to visit tomorrow."

Willow clung to his hand. "No, I'll go home and be with him." A tear slid down her cheek. "Only I don't know where home is. I can't go back to that house where Leo was killed."

"Shh." Brett stroked her cheek. "Don't worry about anything tonight, Willow."

She breathed heavily, then looked up at him again. "About Sam, Brett…"

"I told you not to worry about anything," he whispered. "We'll find a way to work it out."

Although, as she faded into sleep again, Brett laid his head against the edge of the bed and clung to her hand. She had kept Sam from him once and bitterness still gnawed at him for what he'd missed.

Still…he loved Willow and wanted to be a father to his son.

But would Willow want him now after he'd let her down all those years ago?

Chapter Twenty-Three

Willow lapsed in and out of consciousness all night. She dreamt she was dying and that Brett saved her. She dreamt that he left her and walked away and was marrying someone else.

Every time she looked up, though, Brett was there. He stayed by her bed holding her hand and reassuring her she was all right. He fell asleep in the chair. He gave her water when she was thirsty and wiped her forehead with a cool cloth and held her when she woke screaming that she was drowning in dirt.

But sometime in the early morning, she stirred and heard him on the phone.

"Yes, Ginger, I know the movie offer is a big deal." Pause. "I realize it's a cowboy part, that it would take me to a new level."

Willow closed her eyes, her heart aching. Brett was already planning to leave her just as he had before. Except this time when he left, he would know he had a son.

She steeled herself to accept his decision. She would no more trap him now than she had five years ago.

And she'd never let him see how much he'd hurt her.

BRETT HAD NEVER prayed so much in his damn life.

Even when they'd finally moved Willow from the ER into a room, he'd been terrified she'd stop breathing.

Her screams of terror had wrenched his heart.

The nurse checked her vitals, the doctor appeared to examine her and Brett stepped out to call home. Maddox answered on the first ring.

"How is she?"

"All right. How's Sam?"

"Asking about her, but Mama Mary and Rose are feeding him funny-face pancakes and he's gobbling them up."

Brett had always loved Mama Mary's funny-face pancakes. Especially the chocolate-chip eyes.

"There's more. We caught Norman and Gina. They're being transported back here to face charges."

"Thank God." He swallowed hard. "What about me and Willow?"

"I explained everything to the local judge. And this morning I arrested Boyle Gates. Seems Day spilled Gates's involvement and the way they framed Garcia. Gus is going to be released. I offered him a job here on the ranch, so he and his wife and daughter can have a fresh start."

"You've been busy."

"I just like to see justice done. And Garcia needs a second chance."

Maddox was a stand-up guy. "Dad would be proud of you."

"He'd be proud of you, too, little brother."

"I don't know about that. Willow would never have gotten in this mess if I'd stuck around."

A second passed. "Maybe not. But that was then. What are you going to do *now*?"

Brett glanced back at the hospital room. "I'm going to fix things, if I can."

He ended the call and went in to see Willow. She was sitting up in bed, but her expression was guarded, her eyes flat.

"How are you feeling?"

"I need to go home and be with Sam."

"I'll tell Mama Mary to bring you some clothes and if the doctor releases you, I'll drive you back to the cabin."

Willow shook her head. "I can't go back there, Brett. Not with you." She hesitated and averted her eyes. "Our time has passed."

Brett's lungs squeezed for air. She wasn't even going to give him a chance?

He couldn't accept that. "Willow, you've been through a terrible ordeal. We all have. I was terrified that I'd lost you. Maybe you blame me for that, for everything."

She slipped from bed, hugging the hospital gown around her. "Don't, Brett. I'd appreciate it if you'd ask Mama Mary or Rose to bring me some clothes so I can shower and get Sam. Then we'll find a place to stay on our own."

Brett watched with a hollow feeling in his gut as she stepped into the bathroom and shut the door.

He phoned Mama Mary, and she agreed to bring Sam and some clothes. Willow must have gotten soap and shampoo from the nurse. By the time she was finished showering in the bathroom and in a clean hospital gown, Mama Mary was there.

She knocked and peeked in the door with a smile. When Willow saw Sam, her face lit up. She opened her arms and he fell into them.

The two of them hugged like they hadn't seen each other for years.

Suddenly Brett felt like the outsider. Like an intruder who didn't belong.

He stepped outside to gather his composure, his emotions in a tailspin. He'd thought he and Willow had gotten close again, that she had feelings for him. But had he hurt her too much for her to forgive him? Didn't she want him to be part of Sam's life?

Mama Mary patted his shoulder. "I'm sorry, son. But Willow asked me to drive her to a hotel. I don't understand what's going on between you two, but she probably just needs some time."

Or maybe he'd lost his chance years ago and Willow would never love him again.

THREE DAYS LATER, Willow was still miserable. She and Sam were temporarily staying in a small apartment above the fabric store in town. The lady who commissioned several of her quilts had been generous, and Willow had jumped at the chance to be close to town. Somehow she felt safer knowing the sheriff's office was down the street.

But she missed Brett, and so did Sam.

She pushed the boxes of pictures that she'd brought with her into the closet. *Out of sight, out of mind.*

Except she couldn't get Brett out of her mind. Which made her furious at herself.

Brett was probably packing to leave for his big movie role. Planning a hot, sexy, wild night with that woman, Ginger.

She would be only a whisper of a memory to him once he got to Hollywood and the sophisticated women who were probably dying to have a cowboy in their bed swarmed after him.

Sam lined his toy ponies on the floor, then pretended to gallop them around the pasture. How could she not look at her son and see Brett?

Worse, she didn't know what to say to Sam. How to explain why they weren't staying at the ranch anymore.

They still hadn't told Sam that Brett was his father. Brett hadn't pushed either.

Maybe he wanted it that way. If that was the case, it was best that Sam stay in the dark.

Determined to distract herself, she sorted through the mail. A white envelope written in calligraphy caught her eye. She opened the envelope, surprised to find a wedding invitation to Maddox and Rose's wedding.

It was to be a simple affair, just family and a few friends, and would take place at Horseshoe Creek.

She tucked the invitation back in the envelope, her heart aching. She wasn't family, but Sam was. Only he had no idea that he belonged to the McCullens.

Could she deprive him of that?

BRETT HAD TRIED to take Mama Mary's advice and give Willow time. But every day without her and Sam in his life was so painful he could barely breathe.

But today was his brother's wedding, and of course it made him think of Willow and the wedding they'd never had. The one they should have had.

The one he wanted.

But after all Maddox had done for him, he had to put his brother first today.

Chaos filled the house as Mama Mary ushered everyone around. The caterers, florist, the vendor with the tables and tent they'd ordered for the lawn.

And of course, him and Ray.

She'd insisted they wear long duster jackets and bolo ties, since they were standing up for Maddox.

Brett was his best man.

He felt humbled and honored and so damn glad to be home at Horseshoe Creek that he never wanted to leave.

The realization hit him, and he stepped into his old room and called his agent to tell her he was going to refuse the movie deal. He was done putting on shows.

He would stick around here and help Maddox run the ranch. And one day he would win Willow back.

Determination renewed, he left a message for Ginger, then strode down the steps. Maddox looked nervous but happier than any man had a right to be. He'd invited the ranch hands, Gus Garcia and his family, and Deputy White-feather, who seemed standoffish to him and Ray, though he didn't have time to contemplate the reason.

The weather had warmed today, a breeze stirring the trees, but the sun was shining, the flowers Rose had chosen dotting the landscape with color.

"Come on, brothers. It's time," Maddox said.

Brett and Ray followed Maddox and found the guests already seated in white chairs by the creek. Mama Mary and Rose had created an altar of flowers between two trees where Rose stood, looking like an angel.

The smile she gave Maddox sparkled with love.

Maddox was a damn lucky man.

Ray fidgeted with his tie, as if it was choking him, but Brett pasted on his camera-ready smile. As he and Ray took their places, he glanced at the guests and saw Willow and Sam sitting by Mama Mary.

His heart nearly stopped. She looked so beautiful in that pale green dress with her long hair billowing around her shoulders. Gone were the bruises and dirt from the mine, although her eyes still held remnants of the horror.

Was she still having those bad dreams? Who was holding her at night and soothing her when she did?

How about Sam? He looked handsome in that Western shirt and bolo tie. It was almost like Brett's. But did he have nightmares at night, too?

He was so enamored with watching the two of them that for a moment the ceremony faded to a blur and he imagined that he and Willow were the ones declaring their love.

Ray poked him. "The ring, brother."

He jolted back to the present and handed Maddox the simple gold band he'd bought for Rose.

Maddox and Rose exchanged vows, then kissed and cheers erupted. He and Ray turned to congratulate them, yet all Brett could do was wish he and Willow were the ones getting married today.

Champagne, whiskey, beer and wine flowed at the reception on the lawn by the creek that the ranch had been named for, and he took a shot of whiskey for courage, then went to talk to Willow before she could run.

He wanted her and Sam, and he didn't intend to back down without a fight.

He found her standing with Sam by the creek. She was trying to teach him how to skip rocks, but she had it all wrong.

He picked up a smooth stone, squeezed Sam's shoulder and then showed him the McCullen way. Willow's gaze met his, sadness and regret flickering in the depths.

But for a brief second, he saw desire spark. Enough desire to warm his heart and give him a second jolt of courage.

Sam squealed when the water rippled at his next attempt, and Brett patted his back. "Good job."

Sam stooped to collect more stones, and Brett brushed Willow's arm. "You look beautiful tonight."

A sweet blush stained her cheeks. "I thought you'd be gone by now," she finally said.

Brett shrugged. "Maybe I don't want to go."

She gestured toward Maddox and Rose who were dancing in the moonlight while the wedding guests watched. "I'm sure Maddox is glad you stayed for the ceremony."

"That's not the reason I stayed."

Sam picked up another stone, raised his hand and sailed it across the creek.

"Good job, Sam."

Sam grinned. "You still gonna let me ride your horses like you promised?"

Willow laid a hand on Sam's shoulder. "Sam, honey, we'll get you lessons somewhere. Brett is a busy man. He has to leave soon. He's going back to the rodeo, and he's going to star in a movie."

Brett's smile faltered. "Where did you get that idea?"

Willow leaned down to speak to Sam for a minute. "If you want a cookie, you can go get one now."

Sam bounced up and down with a grin and ran toward the table with the cookie tray.

"I heard you on the phone with that woman, Ginger. I'm sure she's waiting for you with open arms."

Brett chuckled. Was that a note of jealousy in Willow's voice? "Ginger is my publicist and agent, Willow. Nothing more."

She averted her gaze. "Well, I'm sure there will be lots of women in Hollywood."

"What if I don't want Hollywood?"

"I know you, Brett, you always had big dreams. You belong in the limelight, not here."

Brett squared his shoulders. "You don't want me to be around Sam?"

"That's not what I said."

He cleared his throat, changing the subject. He had to get this out in the open. Had to know the truth. "Why didn't you tell me about him, Willow?"

She closed her eyes for a brief second, her breath unsteady. When she opened them, he saw regret and some other emotion that he couldn't define.

"Why, Willow? Because you didn't think I'd be a good father?"

"*What?* No." Her eyes flared. "You wanted to leave."

"You didn't give me a chance to choose the right thing."

"*The right thing?* What was that, Brett? What was I supposed to do, tell you I was pregnant and trap you into staying?" She waved her hand around the air. "You would have resented me for asking you to give up your dreams and it would have killed any love you had for me."

He hated to admit it, but she had a point. He had been young and restless. And he might have felt trapped.

But he'd changed. Grown up. Seen what was out there and figured out what was important in his life. "I'm sorry I wasn't the man you wanted, that you needed back then."

Sadness tinged her eyes. "I'm sorry that I didn't tell you about Sam, but I honestly didn't want to hold you back. Then you would have hated me, Brett, and I couldn't have stood that."

"I could never hate you, Willow." He lifted her hand into his. Hers was trembling. Or maybe it was his.

"I'm sorry for so many things, for not being here for you, for leaving so that you let Leo into your life, and into Sam's."

"That's not your fault," Willow said. "That was my mistake."

Brett kissed the palm of her hand. "We both made mistakes, but Sam is not one of them. And I'm not going back to the rodeo or starring in a movie."

Willow's eyes widened in surprise. "You're not?"

"No." Brett's heart swelled with love for her and his brothers and the land he'd once called home. He'd had to leave it to know how much it meant to him.

"I already told my agent, I'm done with rodeo, and that I don't want the movie deal."

"But Brett, it is a good opportunity for you."

"Maybe. But…I've wasted enough time. I want to be here."

"In Pistol Whip?"

He nodded. "I'm going to help Maddox run Horseshoe Creek." He grinned just thinking about his plans. "Being here will give me more time for you and Sam." He glanced at Sam, his heart nearly overflowing. "I promised him I'd teach him to ride."

Tears glittered on Willow's eyelashes. "He'll like that. That is, if that's what you want."

Brett took her other hand in his and drew her closer, then looked into her eyes. "What I want is *you*, Willow." He kissed her fingers one by one. "I love you and always have."

"But you're a wanderer, Brett. A dreamer."

"We can wander together," he said. "And I have lots of dreams." He pulled her to him and kissed her. "I've been dreaming all week about marrying you and the three of us living on the ranch. That cabin is pretty small and Maddox and Rose are in the big house, but I have enough money to build us a house of our own."

"But you gave up your money to get Sam back."

Brett shrugged. "That was just a small part of my savings. Besides, when Maddox made the arrests, he retrieved the stolen money. A portion of it will go to Eleanor, who has agreed to continue caring for Leo's grandmother."

"What about her husband?"

"I told Maddox not to bother pressing charges. The man wasn't bad, just desperate."

"That's generous of you, Brett."

He shrugged. "I guess I understand what desperation can do to a man. The rest of the cash will be divided among the ranchers the men stole from. He also recovered my hundred K."

Willow licked her lips. "I...don't know what to say, Brett."

"Say you love me, Willow," he said huskily. "That you'll be my wife."

Willow's mouth spread into the smile that he remembered as a young man; the adoring, loving one she'd reserved only for his eyes.

She looped her arms around his neck. "I love you, Brett. I never stopped." She stood on tiptoes and kissed him tenderly. "But you're giving me so much. What can I give you?"

"You've already given me the greatest gift of all. A son."

Willow toyed with the ends of his hair. "He is pretty special. I think he looks like his dad. He acts like him, too, sometimes."

Brett chuckled. "Then we're in for trouble."

Her look grew serious. "Are you sure, Brett? You won't get tired of being here? Of me?"

"I could never get tired of you, Willow. You're the only woman I've ever loved." He nuzzled her neck. "And there is one more thing you can give me."

Willow laughed softly. "What?"

He laughed and kissed her again. "A little girl."

Willow smiled and kissed him again, passion sparking between them just as tender and erotic as it always was when he touched her.

"Mommy, Brett, I gots cookies!" Sam raced toward him with cookie crumbs all over his mouth and they both laughed, then took his hand and walked along the creek.

Tonight they would tell Sam that Brett was his father, and that they were finally going to be a family.

And Sam would grow up a McCullen on Horseshoe Creek.

Brett could almost see his father smiling down at him from Heaven.

He would teach Sam to be a man just as his father had taught him.

Epilogue

Ray watched his brothers congratulate each other. Maddox married Rose. Brett was back with the woman of his dreams and had a son.

He wanted to pound their backs and wish them good luck. Tell them he was happy for them.

Find that kind of love for himself.

But the bitterness he'd felt for years ate him up inside like a poison.

Maddox and Brett still thought their old man hung the moon.

If they knew the truth, would they feel the same way? Or would they understand the reason he and his father had fought?

Maddox raised a glass of whiskey to make a toast, and Ray slipped into the shadows where he'd tried to stay all his life. He'd protected his brothers by keeping his father's secrets and lies.

As soon as the reading of the will was over, he'd leave Horseshoe Creek again. If he stuck around any longer, he might be tempted to tell them the truth.

But the old saying about the truth setting you free was a lie.

* * * * *

"Get some rest. You want to be alert when we make a break for it tonight."

"Will you rest, too?" she asked.

"I'll keep watch," he said. "I won't let anything happen to you."

He buried his face in her hair and inhaled deeply of her floral-and-spice scent. She made him feel more vulnerable than he ever had, yet at the same time stronger. A man who had spent his life avoiding complications, he welcomed the challenges she brought. She made him think what the future might look like with her in it.

She stirred, and he pushed away his musings. She opened her eyes, then smiled. "Does this mean the wonderful dream I was having is real?" she asked.

"What was the dream?"

Her smile widened. "It involved a big feather bed and you and me—naked."

He indulged himself with a kiss, fighting the urge to take her there on the hard ground. "We'll have to see about making that dream come true later."

BLACK CANYON
CONSPIRACY

BY
CINDI MYERS

Published in Great Britain 2015
by Mills & Boon, an imprint of Harlequin (UK) Limited,
Eton House, 18-24 Paradise Road, Richmond, Surrey, TW9 1SR

© 2015 Cynthia Myers

ISBN: 978-0-263-25317-7

46-0915

Harlequin (UK) Limited's policy is to use papers that are natural, renewable and recyclable products and made from wood grown in sustainable forests. The logging and manufacturing processes conform to the legal environmental regulations of the country of origin.

Printed and bound in Spain
by CPI, Barcelona

Cindi Myers is an author of more than fifty novels. When she's not crafting new romance plots, she enjoys skiing, gardening, cooking, crafting and daydreaming. A lover of small-town life, she lives with her husband and two spoiled dogs in the Colorado mountains.

For the Western Slope Writers of RMFW

Chapter One

The sound of the explosion reverberated through the underground tunnels. Lauren tried to run, terrified the rocks would collapse around her, but her legs felt as if they were mired in sand. She fought to see in the murky darkness, choking on rising dust, her ears ringing from the aftershock. She opened her mouth to scream, but no sound emerged.

A strong hand grabbed hers, pulling her toward the light. Gunshots sounded behind them, even as rock chips flew from the wall beside her head, the fragments stinging her skin. The man with her pulled her in front of him, shielding her with his body. "Go!" he commanded, and shoved her harder. "Run!"

She ran, dodging piles of rubble and fresh cascades of rock. The dim light ahead began to grow brighter. Footsteps pounded behind her and she started to scream again, but it was only the man, his embrace warm and reassuring. "It's going to be all right," he said. "You're strong. You can make it."

He sounded so certain that, despite all the evidence to the contrary, she believed him.

Another tremor shook the cavern, and larger boulders crashed around them. One struck her shoulder, knocking her to her knees. The man pulled her up, into his arms, and kept running, dodging the falling rock, taking the blows and moving on, always forward, toward freedom.

The cool night air washing over her brought tears to her eyes. She stared at the blurred stars overhead and choked back a sob. The first stars she'd seen in weeks. A taste of freedom she'd feared she might never know again.

"Can you walk?" the man asked, setting her on her feet, but keeping his arm firmly around her, supporting her.

She nodded. "I can."

"Then, we've got to go. We've got to stop him."

Hand in hand, they raced toward the castle situated improbably in the middle of the Colorado desert. She seemed to fly over the ground, her feet not touching it, only the firm grip of the man's hand in hers anchoring her to the earth.

She heard the helicopter before she saw it, the steady *whump! whump!* of the rotors beating the air. Then they ascended a small hill and stared at the chopper lifting off, soaring into the pink clouds of dawn. *No!* she silently screamed.

LOUD, OUT-OF-TUNE CHIMES from the doorbell pulled Lauren from the dream—one she'd had too often in the weeks since her escape from the abandoned mine that had been her prison for almost a month. The details sometimes changed, but the results were the same as reality—her captor, Richard Prentice, escaping into the night as she watched, powerless.

"I don't think she's awake yet," she heard her sister, Sophie, tell whoever was at the door.

Lauren struggled into a sitting position and checked the clock. Almost eleven. How had she slept so late? "I'm awake," she called. "Give me a minute to get dressed."

She threw back the covers and sat up. She was safe in the apartment she shared with her sister in Montrose, Colorado. The words of her rescuer still echoed from the dream. *You're strong. You can make it.*

In the living room, she found Sophie with two other women. Emma Wade, a tall redhead who dressed to show off her curves in flowing skirts and high heels, stood beside Abby Stewart, a sweet grad student whose shoulder-length brown hair was cut to hide most of the scar on one cheek, the result of a wound she'd received while in the army in Afghanistan. The two women had befriended first Sophie, then Lauren, after the sisters' arrival in Montrose.

"Sorry to disturb you, but we've got something here you need to see." Emma handed Lauren a newspaper. "Maybe you'd better sit down before you read it."

"What is it?" Sophie asked, and followed Lauren to the couch, where Lauren sat and focused on the newspaper, nausea quickly rising in her throat as she read the headline.

Former Top News Anchor Released read the headline on the small article in the *Denver Post*'s entertainment section.

Lauren Starling, twice voted most popular news anchor in the *Post*'s annual "best of" selections, has been released from her contract with station KQUE, effective immediately. Station president Ross Carmichael asked for the public's support and understanding for Ms. Starling "at this difficult

time. Lauren's illness is affecting her ability to perform her job, so we thought it was in her best interest to release her from her obligations, to allow
her time to seek treatment and recover," he said.

In March of this year, Starling was diagnosed
with bipolar disorder, following several incidences
of erratic behavior on-air. She made headlines
when she disappeared for several weeks in May
and June, eventually turning up at a ranch owned
by billionaire developer Richard Prentice. Starling
has accused Prentice of kidnapping her, a charge
he denies. He says he offered his home as a safe
place for Starling, a longtime family friend, to heal
and recover.

Starling's former husband, actor Phillip Starling,
also issued a statement regarding Starling's accusations against Prentice. "Lauren hasn't been herself
for the past year," he told this reporter. "Her wild
accusations against Richard—a man we've both
known for years—prove how unstable she has become. I hope for her sake she will seek treatment
and I wish her all the best."

Ms. Starling was unavailable for comment.

Lauren smoothed her hand over the paper, trying to
hide the shaking. She could feel the eyes of the others
on her. Were they searching for signs that she was finally cracking up? She was used to people looking at her.
She'd been a cheerleader and a beauty queen, and had
finally landed her dream job of prime-time news anchor
at Denver's number two station. She'd spent most of her
life seeking and gaining attention.

But that was when the looks from others had been

admiring, even envious. Now people regarded her with suspicion. The looks came attached to labels. She was "unstable" or "erratic" or "crazy." She'd admitted she had a problem and gotten help, but instead of sympathy and understanding, she'd only earned suspicion. She didn't know how to handle the stares anymore.

"Lauren, are you okay?"

Sophie, her sister, asked the question the rest of them had probably been wondering. Lauren fixed a bright smile on her face and tossed her head back, defiant. "I'm fine."

"I'm so sorry," Emma, who worked as a reporter for the *Post*, said. "I hated to be the bearer of bad news, but I didn't want you hearing about it from someone who wasn't a friend, either."

"I can't believe Phil would say something like that." Sophie rubbed Lauren's shoulder, just as she had when they were girls and Lauren had suffered a nightmare. "I never did like the guy."

Lauren had loved Phil; maybe part of her still did. Handsome and charming, as outgoing as she was and a talented actor, Phil had seemed the perfect match for her. But maybe two big egos in a marriage hadn't been a good idea. Or maybe he'd sensed something was broken in her long before she'd discovered the reason for her erratic mood swings and out-of-control emotions. When he'd finally come clean about cheating on her with a woman he worked with, she'd taken the news badly. Though in the end, that plunge into depression had led to the diagnosis and work to get her life under control.

"Prentice probably paid Phil off." Abby scowled at the paper. "And now he's using his influence to ruin your reputation."

"So far he's doing a pretty good job." She flipped the paper over and started to fold it, but another headline caught her eye. "Oh, no!" she moaned.

"I didn't want you to see that." Emma tried to pull the paper away, but Sophie took it instead.

"'Task Force Status in Jeopardy,'" Sophie read.

"'Senator Peter Mattheson has called for a Senate hearing to consider disbanding the interagency task force responsible for solving crimes on public lands in the region around Black Canyon of the Gunnison National Park. The task force, more commonly known as The Ranger Brigade, has successfully stopped a drug smuggling and human trafficking ring in the area as well as solved other less sensational crimes, but recently made headlines over charges of harassment brought by billionaire developer Richard Prentice. Prentice, not a stranger to controversies involving various government agencies, filed suit earlier this year against the Rangers, demanding seven billion dollars in damages.'"

"Don't read any more," Abby said. "It's all a bunch of lies."

"This is so awful," Lauren said. "There should be something we can do to stop this guy."

"The Rangers are working harder than ever to do just that," Emma said. "I'm worried Graham is going to work himself right into a heart attack." Captain Graham Ellison, FBI agent and Emma's fiancé, headed up The Ranger Brigade. Other members of the task force included Abby's boyfriend, Michael Dance, and Sophie's boyfriend, Rand Knightbridge.

"What will happen if the task force disbands?" Lauren asked.

"It won't," Emma said. "All of Richard Prentice's money isn't going to keep him out of jail forever. The grand jury is supposed to end its proceedings today. Once they hand down an indictment, all his money and influence won't mean anything."

"*If* they hand down an indictment," Abby said. "Michael is afraid all the expensive experts Prentice has hired will persuade the grand jury that he's as innocent and persecuted as he likes to portray himself in the press."

"They can't ignore all the evidence against him," Lauren said. She had spent two full days last week in the grand jury room, giving every detail of her six weeks as Prentice's captive, as well as information about the investigation she'd conducted into his affairs that had led the billionaire to capture her and hide her away, first upstairs in his mansion, then in an abandoned mine on his property.

"Michael says he heard Prentice hired an expert to testify that the picture you gave them of Prentice with Alan Milbanks was so blurry no one could tell who the men in the photo really were," Abby said.

"Alan Milbanks gave me that photograph himself before he died," Lauren said. The drug dealer had been shot to death in the fish store that served as a front for his smuggling operation only a few days before Lauren was rescued. "He told me Richard Prentice was bankrolling his drug business."

Abby shrugged. "I'm just saying that some people are more easily persuaded than others. The jury might believe Prentice."

They might. After all, Lauren had believed his lies, too, at least at first. He'd portrayed himself as a caring, charity-minded businessman who'd been forced, by circumstance, into the role of champion of individual rights. All his problems with the government were simply misunderstandings, or the result of his defense of personal liberty for everyone.

"I heard the grand jury brought in a lot of other experts," Emma said. "Of course, it's all hush-hush. No one is supposed to know who testifies before the grand jury, and there isn't even a judge present, just the prosecutor. But people talk."

"What kind of experts?" Sophie asked.

"Psychiatrists." Emma glanced at Lauren, then quickly averted her gaze.

"I'm betting they weren't talking about Richard's state of mind," Lauren said.

"You don't know that," Sophie said. "Maybe they were explaining what would lead a man with more money than Midas to want to gain even more illegally. Or why a man known for dating models and actresses would decide to hold you hostage until you agreed to marry him."

"The psychiatrists were talking about me," Lauren said. "I saw some of the jurors' faces when I told them Richard wanted to marry me. They thought I made the whole story up." After all, that had been Prentice's defense from the moment she was found: Lauren had come to him for help. She'd always been free to leave his property, but she'd fixated on him and insisted on staying. He'd only been trying to be a good friend; the poor woman was delusional.

"All I know is that the grand jury is supposed to deliver its decision this morning and I have to get to the courthouse." Emma pulled her sunglasses from her purse. "I've already started working on my story for the next issue of the *Post*. There's no way twenty-three people could hear what happened to you, Lauren, and not indict."

"Call when you know something," Abby said.

"Oh, I will," Emma said. "We might even have to break out a bottle of champagne, once Prentice is safely behind bars."

No one said anything until Emma had left, then Abby turned to Lauren. "Let's forget about Prentice for a little bit," she said. "What are you going to do about your job?"

Her job. For a moment she'd almost forgotten the original reason her friends had shown up this morning. She'd loved the excitement of reporting on breaking news and the feeling that she was involved in important events, a part of the lives of the people who tuned in every day to hear what she had to say. She still couldn't believe she'd lost all of that. "I guess I need a plan, huh?" Though she hadn't the foggiest idea what that plan should be.

"I think you should hire a lawyer," Abby said. "The station can't cut you off with no severance or benefits or anything when they've outright admitted their firing you is related to your medical diagnosis. The Americans with Disabilities Act probably has something to say about that."

"Abby is right," Sophie said. "Threaten to sue them and make them cough up a settlement—and continue your medical benefits, at least until you find something better."

Right. She didn't want to lose the benefits that paid for the medication that was keeping her on an even keel. "Good idea," she said. "I have a lawyer friend in Denver. I'll call him today." She grabbed a notebook from the counter that separated the apartment's kitchen from the living area and wrote that down. It felt good to have something constructive to do.

"And I'm not going to stop going after Richard Prentice, either," she said. "Even with the grand jury indictment, the prosecutor will need every bit of evidence he can get to convict. Prentice thinks his money puts him above the law. I'm going to show him he's wrong."

"Emma will help, I'm sure," Sophie said. "If you both use your skills as investigative reporters, you're bound to turn up something."

"We can all help," Abby said. "I only know about botany, but I'm good at following directions, so if you give me a job, I'll do it." A graduate student, Abby had almost completed her work toward a master's degree in environmental science.

"Me, too," Sophie said. A former government administrator in Madison, Wisconsin, Sophie had given up her job to move to Montrose and search for Lauren.

"Thanks, all of you." Lauren hugged them each in turn. For all the terrible things that had happened to her in the past weeks and months, she'd gained these wonderful friends. They had rallied around her since she'd come to Montrose, and treated her like another sister. That was a blessing she was truly grateful for.

A knock sounded on the door. Sophie said, "That's probably Rand. He said he was going to stop by and take me to lunch."

Lauren answered the door. "Hello, Rand." She smiled at the handsome, muscular man with short brown hair who stood on the landing, then looked past him to the darker, taller man behind him. "Hello, Marco."

"How are you doing, Lauren?" Agent Marco Cruz asked as he followed his coworker into the apartment. His deep, soft voice made her heart beat a little faster. When had she turned into such a cliché, going all swoony over the handsome guy in uniform who'd just happened to save her life? Of course, pretty much any straight woman with a pulse got a little weak-kneed around Marco, who might have been the inspiration for the description "tall, dark and handsome."

But Lauren was not any woman, she told herself. She wasn't going to allow hormones to let her make a fool of herself over a guy who was probably used to women falling at his feet. She was grateful to him, of course, but she refused to be that cliché. "I'm holding my own. Come on in."

She ushered the men into the house. Rand greeted Sophie with a kiss. Since the two had worked together to rescue Lauren, they'd been almost inseparable. "Are we interrupting something?" he asked, looking around the kitchen at the women.

"We were discussing Richard Prentice's latest," Sophie said. "Emma just left. She showed us an article in the *Post*—he's managed to get Lauren fired."

"The article doesn't say anything about Prentice getting me fired," Lauren said.

"No, but I'd bet my last dime that he paid your ex to say you were unstable," Sophie said. "And he probably threatened to sue the station if they didn't let you go."

"Prentice must have a whole team of lawyers working full-time," Rand said.

"We saw that he's suing the Rangers, and his senator friend is agitating to disband the task force," Abby said.

Rand shrugged. "Nothing new there."

"Do you think he'll succeed in breaking you up?" Sophie asked.

"I don't think so. He's just trying to distract attention away from his own troubles."

"Emma told us the grand jury plans to hand down an indictment today," Lauren said.

"That's just the start," Rand said. "Once the indictment is in place, the serious work of doing everything we can to bolster our case really gets started. Even with everything we have, convicting that man is going to take a lot of luck to go along with our hard work."

"What do you think, Marco?" Lauren asked. The DEA agent didn't talk much, but she'd learned he was smart and thoughtful.

"I think we're going to have to get lucky if we want to succeed in bringing down Prentice," he said. "We need to find his weaknesses and target them."

"Does he have any weaknesses?" Sophie asked.

"Lauren was his weakness once," Marco said.

She flushed. When he'd kidnapped her and held her hostage, Prentice said it was to stop her from interfering in his business. But instead of killing her, he'd tried to woo her and persuade her to marry him. "I don't think he feels the same about me now," she said.

"The opposite of love is hate," Marco said. "I still think you matter to him, one way or another."

"Oh, I'd say he definitely hates me now, and he's playing hardball, getting me fired and making the public think I'm crazy."

"You're not crazy," Marco said. "Just stay smart and be careful. And call me if you need anything."

She turned away, not wanting him to see how his assurance affected her. They'd only spent a few hours together, when he helped rescue her from Prentice, but she'd felt safer with him than she ever had with anyone, despite the fact that, to most people, he was pretty intimidating—hard muscles, hard eyes and an expression that said he was untouched by events around him.

Rand checked his watch. "I hate to break up this party, but we have to go. We've only got an hour for lunch, plus I left Lotte in the Cruiser." Lotte was Rand's police dog, a Belgian Malinois who had helped locate Lauren.

"Give her a biscuit and an ear scratch for me," Lauren said. "And we all have to get back to work, me included. I've got a lawyer to call."

"I won't be long." Sophie hugged her goodbye. "Maybe we'll take in a movie later."

The men left with Sophie, and Abby prepared to take her leave, also. "I think Mr. Tall, Dark and Deadly has a thing for you," she teased as she collected her purse and sunglasses from the kitchen counter.

"Marco?" Lauren's face grew warm. "He was just being nice."

"Marco is never 'just nice,'" Abby said. "Not that he's not a decent guy, but he's very reserved. And a little scary."

"Do you think so?" She'd never felt afraid with Marco.

"He was in Special Forces," Abby said. "Those guys are all a little scary. But very sexy, too." She nudged Lauren. "And I think he definitely likes you. You should ask him out."

"I don't need another rejection right now."

"I don't think he'd reject you," Abby said.

"Even if you're right, now's not the time to start a new relationship. I really need to get my life together."

"Maybe Marco would help." At Lauren's scowl, Abby held up her hands in a defensive gesture. "Okay, okay, I'll stop matchmaking. But, you know—keep it in mind."

The apartment felt emptier than ever when the women were gone. Lauren set about putting away coffee cups and wiping down the counter. After she spoke with Shawn, her lawyer friend, she should update her résumé. And maybe see about doing some freelancing. The local university might need someone in their television department.

She returned to her list and began making notes. Was there a way to get hold of Richard Prentice's tax records? Maybe through some kind of public records request? That might be revealing…

Pounding on the door made her jump—not a friendly knock, but a heavy beating against the wood that made the wall shake. She grabbed up her phone, ready to hit the speed dial for 9-1-1. "Who is it?" she called in a shaky voice.

"I have a delivery for Lauren Starling."

She tiptoed to the door and peered through the peephole. A burly man in a tracksuit stood on the landing. "You're not with a delivery company," she said. "Go away."

"I have a package for you." He held up a box about eight inches square.

"I don't want it. Go away."

"I'm going to leave it here on the landing. You need to open it."

"Go away before I call the police."

"Suit yourself."

She watched as he set the box on the doormat and walked away. She waited a full five minutes, heart racing, mind whirling. Who was sending her a package? Was this some kind of joke, or a bomb?

Finally, reasoning there was only one way to learn the answer to her questions, she eased open the door and looked around. The area was deserted. Quickly, she picked up the package and took it inside, where she set it carefully on the table and stared at it.

No return address. No postage or metered label, either. She put her ear to it. No ticking. But would a bomb necessarily tick? She wished Rand and Lotte were still here. The dog could probably tell if the package contained explosives. She could call them, but Rand had enough on his mind right now without worrying about her. The local police might help—or they would just as easily dismiss her as that crazy woman who'd been on television. She couldn't take any more humiliation. Better to handle this herself.

Feeling a little silly, she grabbed a knife and slit open the end of the box. Inside, she glimpsed red foil paper and white silk ribbon. Less afraid now, she worked the knife around until she could lift off the top. Inside the first box was a second, gift-wrapped package. Again, no label.

She carefully worked loose the ribbon on this box and opened the flaps. Inside was a single dried rose and a printed card. "In loving memory," the card read, "of Lauren Montgomery Starling."

Trembling, she turned the card over. Printed in pencil, in neat block letters, were the words, "Such a short life wasted. We'll all miss you when you're gone."

Chapter Two

Marco stood in line behind Rand and Sophie at the sandwich shop, but his mind was still back at the apartment with Lauren. The first time he'd laid eyes on her in that abandoned mine tunnel where she'd been imprisoned, he'd felt a connection to her. Not just physical attraction—any man might have felt that for the blonde, blue-eyed beauty with the killer figure. The affinity he felt for Lauren went deeper than that, to something in his core. Which was crazy, really. They didn't have anything in common. She was a beauty queen celebrity who lived in the public eye. He'd made a life out of skulking in the shadows.

Maybe it was her strength that resonated with him. It was different from the physical power and mental discipline he practiced, but her ability to endure moved him. She'd had to deal with more trouble in the past few months than most people would ever face in a lifetime, but she still managed to keep smiling and keep fighting. The smile had been a little shakier today; losing her job had to hurt. The stress of all that had happened to her was showing; she was drawn and pale. If Prentice was behind this latest attack on her, Marco wanted to find the guy and teach him a lesson he'd never forget.

His phone buzzed and he slipped it from his pocket and glanced at the screen. Pls come. More trble. Don't say anythng 2 others. Don't want 2 upset Sophie. Lauren.

He pocketed the phone once more and tapped Rand on the shoulder. "I'm going to skip lunch," he said. "Something's come up."

"Anything wrong?"

"Nah. I just remembered something I have to do. Anyway, you know what they say about three being a crowd." He nodded to Sophie. "I'll see you soon."

He sauntered out of the shop—Mr. Smooth, not a care in the world. But every nerve vibrated with worry. Lauren wouldn't have contacted him unless she was in real trouble. Though they'd spent some tense hours together when they were trapped in that old mine on Prentice's estate, he was still a stranger to her. But who else did she have to turn to in the face of real danger? Her sister and her friends couldn't handle a real threat, while he'd spent most of his adult life fighting off enemies of one kind or another.

He reached Lauren's apartment a few minutes later and she opened the door while he was still crossing the parking lot. Clearly, she'd been watching for him. "Thank you for coming," she said. She leaned against the door as if even staying upright was an effort.

He took her arm and guided her back into the apartment, then shut and locked the door behind them. "What is it?" he asked. "What's wrong?"

"A man delivered this a few minutes ago." She led him to the kitchen table, where a brightly wrapped box looked like leftovers from a birthday party. "All that was in it was this dried-up flower and that card."

He bent over the card, not touching it, and read the message printed there. "Look on the back," she said.

He flipped the card over, and clenched his hands into fists. "Someone is trying to frighten you," he said.

"It's working." She studied his face, searching for what—reassurance? Hope?

He could give her neither. "We can check for fingerprints," he said. "But we probably won't find any."

"No, I don't think you will. And I didn't recognize the man who delivered it, though I wouldn't be surprised to find out he works for Prentice."

"Why do you say that?" he asked.

"He was the type of guy Richard uses for his private security force—beefy and menacing. Guys who get off on being intimidating." She shuddered, and he fought the urge to put his arms around her, to comfort her. She'd mentioned before that Prentice's guards had tried to bully and take advantage of her, pawing at her when they thought they could get away with it. The idea made him see red. If he ever got one of those guys alone…

Not a productive thought. He needed to focus on the task at hand. They both stared at the small card—a harmless piece of paper that carried such a potent threat. "Is this his way of saying he's going to kill me?" she asked.

"Maybe." No sense sugarcoating the truth. If she was dead, she'd stop agitating for Prentice's arrest. The billionaire had killed before to silence his enemies. Marco was sure of that, even if the task force had never been able to find conclusive evidence to link him to the killings. "You need to show this to the police."

"And tell them what?" Anger flared, the sharp edge in her voice a good sign, he thought. She wasn't going to sink into despair. "Do I say Richard Prentice is threatening me? He'll deny it and issue another statement about how obsessed I am with him and how crazy I am. And they'll believe him, because everyone knows you can't trust an unstable person like me."

He gripped her shoulders, not hurting her, but demanding her attention. "Don't let what people say come true," he said. "You're not crazy or unstable. You're strong. You were strong enough to get away from Prentice the first time. We can outsmart him now."

"We?"

"I'm sticking with you until I'm sure you're safe."

"So you think this is a real threat?" The last word was barely a whisper.

"Yes. And you're right—the police aren't the answer. Going to them is probably exactly what Prentice expects you to do, what he wants, even." He led her to the sofa and sat with her. "As long as he can keep this in the press, he can keep hammering home the idea that you've lost it. By ignoring him, we frustrate him and force his hand."

"But what will he do next?"

"I don't know. But it's why I can't leave you alone."

She laughed, but with no mirth. That was the sound of someone fighting to maintain control. "This is ridiculous. You're not my personal bodyguard. And you have a job. You have to work."

"You're the chief witness in the case we're building against Prentice," he said. "The captain will agree we need to keep you safe."

"Haven't you been paying attention? You don't have a case. Prentice is doing his best to paint me as the crazy woman who can't be trusted. Anything I say against him is obviously a figment of my troubled mind."

"That's what he wants people to think, but we know

it's not true. And other people know it, too. You have to stay strong and not let this get to you."

"Did they train you to give these pep talks when you were in Special Forces? Because it's not working."

"There goes my career as a motivational speaker."

His attempt at humor didn't move her. "Why is he doing this now?" she asked. "It's been almost a month since I escaped his ranch."

"He was hiding out on some Caribbean island, working to get the charges against him dropped and probably hoping you'd go away. You haven't, so he's decided to turn up the heat. You know enough about him that you're still a real threat to him."

"Or maybe I'm a loose end he wants tied up," she said.

"Or maybe he wants revenge because you turned down his advances," he said. "Love can make people do crazy things."

"Oh, please! Richard Prentice doesn't love anyone but himself."

"Maybe *love* isn't the right word… He was obsessed with you, and I don't think people like him turn those feelings off like a light switch. The obsession just… transforms. Turns darker."

"Thanks. Now you're really creeping me out." She rubbed her hands up and down her arms as if warding off a chill. "So what are we going to do? You can't babysit me twenty-four hours a day."

He stood and began to pace, studying the apartment. It was a ground-floor unit in a complex that faced a side street off the main highway. The front door opened onto a large parking lot, and there were large windows on all sides. No security. No guards. Easy in-and-out access.

"Anyone could break in here with no trouble at all," he said. "We need to move you to a safer location."

"I can't afford to move. I'm unemployed, remember?"

"You can't afford to stay here, either."

"Do you really think it's that bad?" she asked. "I mean, would he really kill me? Isn't convincing everyone I'm crazy enough?"

"We don't have the proof we need, but we believe he's had people killed before," Marco said. "There was his pilot—and don't forget that fish seller, Alan Milbanks."

She nodded. "Milbanks's death meant the chief source for my story about Richard Prentice was out of the picture. Very convenient."

"Not having you around would be convenient for him, too. Do you want to take that chance?"

"No." She straightened and lifted her chin, determined. "Do the Rangers have a safe house or something?"

"No. You can come to my place."

"Your place?" She choked back a laugh.

"What's so funny?"

"You live in a duplex. With Rand in the other half."

"Exactly. You'll have twice the protection. And your sister's over at his place all the time anyway."

"No, Marco, I can't. What will people think?" She flushed. "I mean, if your place is like Rand's, there's only one bedroom."

He liked it when she blushed that way—it did something to his insides that he didn't want to think about too much. He'd rather enjoy the feeling. "I'll sleep on the sofa."

"I couldn't."

"Go." He put a hand to her back and urged her toward

her bedroom. "Pack a bag. I know what I'm doing." His duplex wasn't ideal, but it was off the beaten path, had only one street leading in and out, bars on the windows and a reinforced door. And it wouldn't be the first place anyone would look for her. Keeping her there would buy him more time to identify any real threat.

"If anyone but you tried to order me around like this, I'd tell them exactly what they could do with their bossy attitude," she said as she headed down the short hallway off the living room. "But you make me believe you re-ally *do* know what you're doing."

While he waited, he scanned the parking lot in front of the apartment. He focused on a big guy across the street. The man wore a blue-and-white tracksuit and had a pair of binoculars trained on Lauren's front windows. Marco moved closer to the window and raised the blinds. The big guy didn't move. Marco glared. No reaction from the guy in the tracksuit. He might have been a mannequin, except they didn't make mannequins that burly, and after a few seconds, the watcher reached up to scratch his ear.

Marco moved quickly down the hall to Lauren's bed-room and stopped in the doorway, stunned at the sight of her up to her elbows in lace and satin. She'd appar-ently dumped the contents of her dresser drawers on the bed and was sorting through the pile of panties, bras, stockings, negligees and who knew what other items of feminine apparel.

She glanced over her shoulder at him. "It was easier to just dump everything and sort through them this way." She grabbed up a handful of items and danced over to an open suitcase in the dresser and dropped them inside, then spent some time arranging them, smoothing them out and humming to herself.

"There's a man standing out front, watching your apartment," Marco said. "He's not even trying to hide it. He has this huge pair of binoculars, like a bird-watcher would use."

"Maybe he is a bird-watcher." She giggled, a high-pitched, unnatural sound.

"Come look and tell me if you know him."

"All right."

She glided down the hall ahead of him, still humming, and went to the window. "Oh, yes, I know him." She waved like someone greeting a friend at the airport.

"How do you know him?" Marco asked.

"He delivered that package." She waved idly toward the box on the table.

"All right. Go ahead and finish packing. We should leave soon."

"Yes, I'll do that. I have a gorgeous new dress. I was in the mall yesterday and saw it and just had to have it. I'll take it in case we go someplace nice."

Marco frowned. "Are you feeling all right?" he asked.

Her smile didn't waver, though to him it seemed forced. "Why wouldn't I be feeling all right?"

"You've been under a lot of stress." He spoke carefully, watching her eyes. Her gaze shifted around the room, as if frantically searching for something. "Most people would be anxious in a situation like this."

"Yes. I am anxious." She twisted her hands together. "I just… I'd love to go for a run now. Burn off some of this extra energy." She turned to a dresser and began pulling out exercise tops and shorts, adding them to the pile of clothing on the bed.

Now was not the time for a run. He had to get her

away from here, away from the guy in the parking lot, to some place safer. "Would you like me to call Sophie?"

"No! No, don't call Sophie! She's always so worried, worried I'm going to go off the deep end or do something stupid. Something…crazy." She whispered the last word, standing still with a tank top dangling from one hand.

"You're not crazy." He kept his voice calm in the face of the agitation rolling off her in waves. After he'd met her, after he carried her in his arms out of the collapsed mine on Richard Prentice's estate, he'd gone online and done some reading on bipolar disorder. He'd learned that stress and even variations in routine could trigger a manic episode. Lauren's life had been nothing but stress these past months, and she had no more routine—no job or real home or any certainty about the future.

"Maybe…maybe I should call my doctor." She looked at the clothes piled on the bed and the open suitcase. "I took my medication," she said softly. "I always do, even though, sometimes, I don't like the way it makes me feel."

"Maybe the medication just needs…adjusting."

She nodded. "Right. I…I'll call him."

He waited in the bedroom while she went into the living room. He wondered if he should remove the clothes from the bed—pack for her. But no. That was too personal. Too patronizing, even.

He backed out of the room and rejoined her as she was hanging up the phone. "I talked to the nurse," she said. "She suggested I take more of one of my pills, and she's calling in another prescription I can take if I need to."

He nodded. "Do you need anything from me? Help with packing? Something to eat?"

"No, I'm good. I'll just, uh, finish up back here."

"I'll keep an eye on our friend."

"Friend?"

He nodded toward the parking lot. "The bird-watcher."

She laughed again, and the sound continued all the way down the hall. The sound worried him a little, but it also made him angry. Why did such a beautiful, vibrant woman have to be plagued with emotions that veered so easily out of control? Why was she at the mercy of a disease she hadn't asked for and didn't want? He'd spent his life fighting off physical enemies, first in a street gang, then the military, now as a law enforcement officer. But what could he do to help her?

THE MEDICATION BEGAN to work quickly, a numbing fog slipping over the anxiety and agitation that were the first signs of a climb toward mania. Lauren hated this lethargy and *not feeling* as much as she dreaded the extreme highs or lows of her disease. Why couldn't she just be normal?

She finished packing her suitcase, stuffing in clothes without care, putting off having to go back into the living room and face Marco. This hadn't been a bad episode. She hadn't burst into song or taken off her clothes or made a pass at him—all things she'd done before her diagnosis had provided an explanation for her bizarre behavior. But she'd waved her underwear around in front of him, and laughed at the idea of a man stalking her.

He was so solemn and unemotional. What must he think of a woman who, even on her best days, tended to feel things too deeply?

In the end, she didn't have to go to him; he came to her. "Are you ready to go?" he asked. "We can stop and get some lunch on the way."

"Sure." She zipped the suitcase closed and looked at the disarray of the room.

"It's all right," he said. "You can clean this up later." He picked up the suitcase. "Do you have everything you need?"

"Yes." She grabbed the two pill bottles from the top of the dresser and cradled them to her chest. "I'm ready."

She put the pill bottles in her purse and followed him to the door. Sophie had rented the apartment when she'd decided to relocate to Montrose to be with Rand, and Lauren only stayed there because she had no place else to go. She couldn't claim to be attached to the place, but still, it felt bad to be leaving so soon, to face more uncertainty.

Deep breath. Center. She closed her eyes and inhaled through her nose, the way the therapist at the psychiatric hospital had shown her. She could deal with this.

When she opened her eyes, Marco was watching her. She saw no judgment in his calm brown eyes. "Are you ready?" he asked.

She nodded. "Is the bird-watcher still out there?"

"He left a few minutes ago. I guess he'd done his job."

"What was his job, do you think? Besides delivering the package."

"He was sending the message that you were being watched. His job was to intimidate you."

"The note did that."

"I guess Prentice likes to cover all the bases."

"What about the package?" She looked around for the creepy gift. "I don't want Sophie finding it when she comes back."

"I've got it." He indicated the shopping bag he must have found in the pantry. "I'll have someone check it out. Maybe we'll get lucky and learn something useful. Come on." He opened the front door and started across the lot, toward the black-and-white FJ Cruiser he'd parked closest to her apartment.

"I'll follow you in my car," she said.

His frown told her he didn't think much of that idea. "You should ride with me."

"I can't just leave my car. I can't be stuck way out at your duplex with no transportation." The idea ramped up her anxiety again, like something clawing at the back of her throat.

"Then, we'll take your car and I'll send someone back later for mine."

"All right." Relief made her weak. When they reached the car she hesitated, then handed him the keys. "You'd better drive. Sometimes the pills make me sleepy."

He nodded and unlocked the trunk and stowed her suitcase and the shopping bag, then climbed into the driver's seat. "What pharmacy do you use?"

Her prescription was ready. Once they'd collected it, he swung by a sandwich shop for lunch. She wasn't hungry—another side effect of the medication—but she ordered to avoid explaining this to him. Finally they were on the highway headed to his place. She put her head back against the headrest and closed her eyes. Maybe when they got to his place she'd take a nap. But she'd need to unpack, and she still had to call her lawyer, Shawn…

"Have you had any trouble with your car lately?"

She opened her eyes and sat up straight. "No. What kind of trouble?"

"The brakes." He pumped the brake pedal, but the car only sped up, down a long incline that curved sharply at the bottom.

"What's wrong with the brakes?" She leaned over to

study the speedometer, the needle creeping up past seventy miles an hour. "Why are we going so fast?"

"I think someone may have tampered with your car." His voice remained calm, but the fine lines around his eyes deepened, and his knuckles on the steering wheel were white with strain.

She covered her mouth with her hand and stared at the highway hurtling toward them with ever-increasing speed. At the bottom of the hill was a curve, and beyond the curve, a deep canyon. If their car went over the edge, they would never survive.

Chapter Three

Marco didn't look at Lauren, but he could hear the sudden, sharp intake of her breath and sense her fear like a third presence in the car. He tried pumping the brake pedal, but nothing happened. He pressed it to the floor and downshifted to first gear. The engine whined in protest, and the car slowed, but not enough.

"Hang on," he said, raising his voice over the whine of the protesting engine. He pulled back on the lever for the emergency brake and the car began to fishtail wildly. He strained to keep hold of the wheel. Lauren whimpered, but said nothing.

They were well out of town now, empty public land and private ranches stretching for miles on either side, with no houses or businesses or people to see their distress and report it. Not that anyone could do anything to help them anyway. If they had any chance of surviving a crash, he had to try to regain control of the car.

They continued to accelerate, racing toward the curve at the bottom of the hill. He steered toward the side of the road, gravel flying as the back wheels slid onto the shoulder. The idea was to let friction slow the car more, but the dropoff past the shoulder was too steep; if he kept going he'd roll the car.

Back on the roadway, the car continued to skid and sway like a drunken frat boy. The smell of burning rubber and exhaust stung his nose and eyes. If they blew a tire, he'd lose control completely; the car might roll. He released the emergency brake and grabbed the steering wheel with both hands. "Brace yourself against the dash and lean toward me!" he commanded.

She didn't argue. As she skewed her body toward his seat, he could smell her perfume, sweet and floral, overlaying the sharp, metallic scent of fear. He wanted to tell her everything would be all right, that she didn't have to worry. But he couldn't lie like that.

He came at the guardrail sideways, sparks flying as the bumper scraped the metal rails, gravel popping beneath the tires. The scream of metal on metal filled the air, making him want to cover his ears, but of course he couldn't. He kept hold of the wheel, guiding the car along the guardrail.

Friction and a gentler slope combined to slow them, and as the guardrail ended, he was able to use the emergency brake to bring them to a halt on the side of the road. He shut off the engine and neither of them spoke, the only sounds the tick of the cooling motor and their own heavy breathing.

He had to pry his hands off the steering wheel and force himself to look at her. "Are you all right?" he asked.

She nodded, and pushed the hair back from her face with shaking hands. "My car isn't, though. What happened?"

"The brakes failed."

"I had the car serviced before I came out here," she said. "My mechanic said it was fine."

"It sat at that overlook in the park for a few days, and

then at the wrecking yard for a few weeks. An animal—a rabbit or something—could have chewed the brake cable." He didn't really think that was what had happened, but he didn't want to frighten her.

"But I've been driving the car for weeks now and it's been fine." She turned even paler. "What if this had happened when I was alone?"

What, indeed? He unfastened his seat belt. "I'm going to take a look."

He had to wrench the hood open, past the broken headlight and bent bumper. He fixed the prop in place and stared down into the tangle of hoses and wires. After a moment, she joined him.

"I couldn't open my door, so I crawled over the console," she said. "Can you tell what went wrong?"

He leaned under the hood and popped the top over the master cylinder reservoir. It was completely dry, only a thin coating of brake fluid left behind. That explained why the brakes had failed, but why had the fluid drained?

He walked around to the side of the car and knelt beside the front tire. He reached over the tire and grasped the flexible hose that led to the brakes. It felt intact, but as he ran his finger along the hose, he found a moon-shaped slit—the kind of damage that could be made by someone reaching over the tire and stabbing the brake hose with a knife.

"What is it?" she asked, following him around to the other side of the car.

He knelt and checked that hose. "Someone punctured the brake line on both sides," he said. "The brake fluid drained out, and that caused the brakes to fail."

She steadied herself with one hand on the fender of the car. "The bird-watcher?"

"Maybe. Or it could have been done while we were at lunch." Big failure on his part. He should have taken the physical threat to her more seriously.

"The parking lot at my apartment has a surveillance camera," she said. "I mean, don't they all, these days?"

"Maybe, but a lot of places use dummy cameras that don't really film anything." He'd bet her apartment complex fell into that category. "And whoever did this is probably smart enough to avoid any cameras."

"We should call the police," she said.

He glanced around them, getting his bearings. Drying rabbit brush covered an open expanse of prairie, only the occasionally stunted piñon providing shade. Here and there purple aster offered a surprising blot of color against an otherwise brown landscape. "This is the edge of national park land," he said.

"Ranger territory." She completed the idea for him and managed a weak smile. "Well, that's something. I wasn't looking forward to talking to the police."

He pulled out his phone. "I'll call someone to give us a ride, then get a wrecker to haul the car to headquarters where we can take a closer look at it."

Her hand on his wrist stopped him. He looked down at the slender, white fingers, nails perfectly shaped and painted a soft pink. "Before anyone else gets here, I just wanted to say thank you," she said. "You saved my life—again."

He covered her hand briefly with his own. "It's going to be okay," he said. "Everything that happens brings us one step closer to stopping Prentice."

"Thank you, too, for not freaking out about my illness," she said. "I'm getting better at working at controlling it, but sometimes…"

"I know. It's okay."

Her head snapped up, her gaze searching. "How do you know?"

"I did some reading." He shrugged. "I like to understand what's going on around me."

"There's nothing understandable about this disease."

"No, but you're doing great. A lot of people would crack under the stress you've been under, but you're hanging in there. You're tough."

"Yeah, I'm tough as a marshmallow." She moved her hand away and squared her shoulders. "But I won't let that stop me. And I won't let Richard Prentice stop me. Maybe he's done me a favor, getting me fired from the station. Now going after him is going to be my job."

"I'm already on it," he said.

"Then, with both of us on his case, he doesn't stand a chance."

LAUREN WISHED SHE was as confident as Marco sounded. She'd meant what she'd said about making convicting Richard Prentice her full-time job. She desperately needed the focus on work to quell her anxiety and tamp down the threatening mania, but the idea that the man she was investigating wanted her dead shook her to the core.

All she wanted was a normal life—a job and a husband and maybe a family one day. But all those things seemed so out of reach. Her own brain had betrayed her, and while the doctors and therapists had assured her that she could live a normal, productive life with bipolar disorder, she suspected them of lying to make her feel better. Or was that just the depressive side of her disorder pulling her down? She couldn't even trust her own thoughts these days.

While Marco contacted Ranger headquarters and summoned a wrecker, she walked around to the other side of the car and phoned Sophie. "Hey, I was just on my way back to the apartment," Sophie said when the call connected. "I thought maybe we could take in a movie or something."

"I'm not there."

"Where are you?"

"With Marco. My car broke down and we're headed over to Ranger headquarters."

"What happened? What's wrong with the car?"

"Marco thinks someone sabotaged the brakes. We're okay," she hastened to add. "The car's kind of beat up, but we're fine."

"Was Marco with you when it happened?" Sophie asked.

"Yes. I'm going to stay with him a few days."

"With Marco?" Sophie's surprise was clear.

"He thinks it will be safer. There was someone watching our apartment earlier." She didn't tell Sophie about the package with its implied death threat. Thank goodness Marco had taken it with them. She didn't want to upset her sister, but also talking about the note made it too real.

"I'm sure it is safer." Sophie sounded amused. "That should be interesting. I think he's attracted to you."

She shifted her gaze to Marco. Did all her friends think that he was interested in her? Then, why couldn't she see it? He stood with his back to her, giving her a great view of his broad shoulders, muscular arms, narrow waist and admittedly perfect backside. He looked like the after photo in the advertisement for a workout program. Physically fit and totally together. The perfect match for a basket case like her—not. "He wants to get Prentice," she said. "I'm the quickest route to that goal. It's nothing personal."

"I don't know about that. He's good at hiding his feelings, but he's bound to have some, somewhere beneath that stoic facade."

"You should consider staying with Rand," Lauren said. "At least for a few days." She didn't want someone coming to the apartment looking for her and finding Sophie there alone.

"Not a bad idea," Sophie said.

"Make him go back to the apartment with you to get your things," Lauren said.

"Do you really think it's that dangerous?"

She glanced at her destroyed car, the paint scraped from the side in a jagged, violent wound. "Yes," she said simply.

Marco tucked his phone back into his pocket and turned toward Lauren. "I have to go," she said. The last thing she wanted was for him to overhear Sophie's analysis of his potential as a love interest. "I'll call you later."

"Someone will be here to pick us up in a few minutes," Marco said once she'd hung up. "Everything okay?"

"Yes. I was just letting Sophie know what was happening."

"Good idea." He leaned back against the car and scanned the horizon. He had a stillness about him she envied, as if whenever he wanted he could quiet all the busyness and distraction that plagued her.

"What are you thinking?" she asked.

"That it would be hard for a sniper to position himself here. The country's too open."

Her knees went weak, and she joined him in leaning

against the car. "You think someone might be out there, ready to shoot us?"

He shook his head. "It's not a good location."

She closed her eyes. This was too real. Someone— probably Richard Prentice—wanted her dead.

"I'll feel better when we get out of the open," he said. "Someone will probably come along soon to see if we crashed—to make sure we're dead."

She swallowed hard. "Can we talk about something else, please?"

He didn't take his gaze from the horizon. "What do you want to talk about?"

"Do you have any brothers or sisters?"

"I had six older sisters."

"Big family." She envied him. Sophie was the only family she had. "Do you see them often?"

"Not really. They live in California." He fell silent for a moment, then added, "Only four of them are still alive."

"Oh. I'm sorry."

"One sister died of an overdose. The other disappeared. We don't know what happened to her."

And here she'd thought she was the only one with troubles. "That must be hard," she said. Not the innocuous conversation she'd hoped for.

"It is what it is." He straightened. "Here's our ride."

A Cruiser identical to the one Marco usually drove made a U-turn and pulled in behind Lauren's disabled car. Montrose County sheriff's deputy Lance Carpenter, the local representative on the task force, left the vehicle running as he stepped out of the driver's seat and pushed his Stetson back on his head. "Trying out for the demolition derby?" he asked.

"Very funny." Marco shoved the car keys into Lance's

hands. "Give these to the wrecker driver—and make sure nobody touches anything around the brakes until the techs have gone over it." He took Lauren's hand and pulled her toward the Cruiser.

"Where do you think you're going?" Lance asked.

"I need to get Lauren out of here before whoever cut those brake lines shows up to admire the results of his handiwork."

"What am I supposed to do?" Lance asked.

"Wait here for the wrecker driver."

"Should we have left him?" Lauren asked as Marco gunned the engine and they headed toward the park.

"The wrecker will be there any minute now, and I wasn't comfortable with you standing around out in the open."

"The idea that I have a target on my back doesn't seem real to me."

"The trick is to balance the awareness of danger with the need to keep from panicking." He glanced at her. "Not easy, I know."

"I think I'm glad I got the extra meds."

"I want to stop by headquarters and talk to the captain, then we'll get you settled at my place."

"I left my bag in the car."

"Lance will bring it."

"You seem pretty sure of that. Do you Rangers communicate via ESP or secret code or something?"

"He's got my back." He glanced at her. "Now you're with me, so he's got your back, too."

His words—and the certainty with which he spoke them, sent a different kind of heat curling through her—part old-fashioned lust and part the unfamiliar warmth of acceptance. Her disease had separated her from others for so long. How ironic that a threat to her life had involved her with a community of friends again.

Half a dozen Cruisers filled the spaces in front of the task force headquarters building. "Something's up." Marco parked along the side of the road and was out of the vehicle before Lauren had even unbuckled her seat belt.

She hurried after him, running to keep up. Inside the building, uniformed officers crowded the small, low-ceilinged rooms. "What's going on?" Marco asked.

"You'll find out as soon as everyone's here."

The captain retreated to his office, shutting the door behind him.

"Any idea what this is about?" Lieutenant Michael Dance, Abby's boyfriend, asked.

Everyone shook their heads. "All I know is, the captain has been on the phone most of the morning," Carmen Redhorse, an officer with the Colorado Bureau of Investigations, said. "Whatever this is about, he's not happy."

Twenty minutes later, Graham finally emerged from his office and surveyed the room full of officers. "Where's Lance?"

"I'm here." Lauren looked over her shoulder to see the deputy in the doorway. He made his way over to them and handed Lauren her overnight bag, then gave Marco a slip of paper. "The car's on its way to the impound lot."

"Did you take a look at the brake lines?" Marco asked.

"Yeah. They look cut to me, but we'll know more when the techs are done."

"If I could have your attention." Graham stood at the front of the room and held up one hand. A hush settled over the crowd. Lauren clenched her hands into fists and fought to keep still; the tension was contagious.

The captain cleared his throat. "The grand jury has failed to indict Richard Prentice of any of the charges against him," he said.

Chapter Four

Lauren blinked, sure she had heard the captain wrong. He must mean the grand jury had indicted Richard Prentice, right? She turned to Marco, his face the stone mask of an Aztec warrior. "What's happening?" she asked.

"Somehow, Prentice managed to get off," he said.

"I don't understand," she said, still dazed. "He kidnapped me. He held me prisoner. You saw where he was keeping me."

"We saw." Rand's expression was as grim as everyone else's. Even Lotte, who stood by his side, looked upset. "We know you're telling the truth, not just about the kidnapping, but about the other crimes he's involved in."

"At least you believe me," Lauren said. "The jury obviously didn't. They believed Richard when he said I was making everything up."

"Maybe it wasn't you," Marco said. "Maybe it was something else."

"They didn't believe me because they think I'm crazy," she said. "I'm mentally ill, so of course I must be a liar, too. I made the whole thing up. It was a wild fantasy I concocted just to get attention." Online columnists and bloggers had already wasted plenty of bandwidth speculating on the reasons for Lauren's "obsession" with the billionaire. Because of course, why would he ever be obsessed with her? Sure, she was pretty, they said. But she had a history of wild behavior. So of course, her side of the story couldn't be trusted.

"Prentice is trying to distract people by making this case about you," Marco said. "It's a game he's playing, but it's a game he isn't going to win."

"What will you do?" she asked.

"We'll have to start over." Captain Ellison joined them. "We're going to work the case as if it's brand-new, reexamining every lead, taking a second look at every bit of evidence. I want everyone focused on this. It's going to take a lot of long days and hard work, but we'll build a case the prosecution can't deny."

Around her, heads lifted and shoulders straightened. The anger they'd felt moments earlier transformed into determination to see justice done. Lauren wished their energy was contagious, but she was still reeling from the knowledge that what had happened to her had been so easily dismissed by the twenty-three members of the grand jury. She touched Marco's arm. "I'll go now and let you get to work."

"Let me go with you," he said. He pulled keys from his pocket.

"No, you're needed here." She looked around the room. Already, members of the task force were pulling out files and booting up computers, ready to get to work.

"It's not safe for you to be alone," Marco said.

"I'll be fine. I'll call Sophie to come pick me up." It wasn't as if she could drive her wrecked car. "Now that he's swayed the grand jury, Prentice knows I'm no threat."

He was going to argue with her, she could tell, but

the door burst open and Emma stalked in, the heels of her stilettos striking the tile floor so hard Lauren expected to see sparks. Jaw clenched, eyes blazing, she looked ready to punch someone. "Hello, Emma," Graham said, as calm as ever. "I take it you heard the news about Richard Prentice."

Emma set her bag down on the edge of a desk. "Officially, I'm here to get your statement on this turn of events for my story," she said. "Unofficially, I need to vent to someone who understands my frustration. How could they do this? How could they ignore all the evidence you had against him?"

"We'll never know for sure, but I'm guessing they interpreted everything as circumstantial," Graham said. "We don't have fingerprints, tape recordings or any written records, and only one eyewitness."

"Whom they don't consider reliable," Lauren said. She blocked any protests they might have made. "Don't deny it. I'm not."

"He is doing a smear campaign against you," Emma said. "My editor sent me a copy of the press release Prentice issued this afternoon."

"What does it say?" Michael asked.

She leaned against the desk and pulled up the press release on her phone. "There's a bunch of malarkey about justice being done, proves his innocence, blah, blah, blah." She waved her hand. "But here's the part about Lauren. 'It is painful to know my friend Lauren Starling is so ill. I can find no other explanation for why she would attack the one man who truly tried to help her. I hope she will find the help she needs to get well. On her behalf I am making a generous donation toward mental health research.'" She made a face. "Excuse me while I vomit. The man is disgusting."

Everyone gathered around Emma to examine the press release and rehash the grand jury's ruling. Lauren took the opportunity to slip outside, where she texted Sophie to pick her up at Ranger headquarters.

She slipped the phone back into her purse and walked over to the gazebo at the far end of the parking lot, which offered a view of the canyon that gave the park its name. The Black Canyon of the Gunnison plunged more than twenty-five hundred feet down to the Gunnison River. Sun penetrated the bottom for only a few hours each day, giving the canyon its name. The land around the gorge shimmered in the early August sun, wind rustling the silvery leaves of sage and rattling the dry cones of stunted piñons.

When Lauren had first arrived here over two months ago the harsh landscape had repelled, even frightened her. She saw nothing beautiful in dry grasses and empty land. The quiet and emptiness of this place made her feel too small and alone.

But her weeks of captivity had changed her opinion of this place. With nothing to do in the early days of her stay at Prentice's mansion—before he moved her into the abandoned mine—she'd spent hours staring out at the prairie. She'd learned to appreciate the stillness of the land, which had called forth a similar stillness within her. She began to see beauty in the thousand shades of green and brown in the grasses and trees. Now the emptiness that had once repelled her calmed her.

The squeal of brakes announced the arrival of a car. Lauren turned to see Sophie's blue sedan pulling into the lot. She hurried to her sister and slid into the passenger seat.

"I can't believe it," Sophie said before Lauren could speak. "Rand just called and told me Richard Prentice is getting off scot-free."

"I guess so." Lauren buckled her seat belt and leaned back against the headrest.

"What are we going to do?" Sophie asked.

Lauren closed her eyes. She was so tired. "Right now, I just want to go home," she said.

Sophie put the car in gear and backed out of the lot. "Is something wrong?" she asked after a moment. "Are you not feeling well?"

"I'm okay. I took an extra pill and it's making me a little sleepy." She hoped that was all it was. Sometimes lethargy was a sign of depression.

"Why did you take an extra pill? Should you be doing that?" Sophie's voice rose in alarm.

Lauren opened her eyes. "It's okay. That's what the doctor said to do."

"You talked to your doctor? Why?"

She knew better than to ignore the question. Sophie wouldn't let it go. She'd always been like that, never giving in on anything. Lauren should be grateful; Sophie's refusal to give up on her had led to her coming to Montrose and prodding the Rangers into finding her.

"I had a minor manic episode this morning. Nothing big, and it's under control now."

"When was this? What happened?"

"After you and Emma left. After Abby left, too. I think it was just the stress of finding out about my job." Though her life had been nothing but stress for months now.

"What happened?"

"Nothing. I just got a little…giddy. Feeling out of control. Marco was there, and he helped calm me down."

"Marco was there?"

"I called him when I realized someone was watching the apartment."

"That must be why he left the café in such a hurry," Sophie said. "Who was the watcher?"

"I don't know. Marco didn't know him, either, and the man left. But there was something else—something I didn't tell you before."

"What's that?" Sophie kept her eyes on the road, her expression calm.

"The guy who was watching delivered a package. Like a gift box, but all it had in it was a dried-up flower and a note."

"What did the note say?"

"It was like one of those memorial cards you sometimes see at funerals, with the words *in memory of* written on it. It had my name on it." She shuddered at the memory. "The Rangers are going to look into it, but I doubt they'll find anything. Someone was trying to scare me."

Sophie didn't say anything for a long while, taking it in. Lauren closed her eyes again.

"I'm glad Marco was with you," Sophie said. "The guy doesn't say much, but he's deep. And any bad guy would think twice before tangling with him."

That was true enough. Beyond his physical strength, Marco had perfected an intimidating attitude. Which made his gentleness with her all the more touching.

"Hey, I thought you were going to stay with him," Sophie said.

"I was, but we've had a change of plans. He needs to

devote himself to the investigation. And now that Richard has gotten the charges against him dropped, I'm no longer a threat."

"Aren't you?" Sophie asked. "You aren't going to give up because of one grand jury's mistakes, are you?"

"I don't know." She was just so tired—of always fighting, of having to be strong when she felt so weak.

"You can't give up," Sophie said. "Giving up means he wins—that the lies he's told about you are true."

She opened her eyes again and forced herself to sit up straight and look at her sister. "Then, what do we do?"

"We do what we can to help with the investigation," Sophie said. "We talk to people, find out what they know."

"Who do we talk to?" Her one contact on the case, Alan Milbanks, was dead.

"Why don't we start with Phil? We'll find out if Prentice paid him to tell the press those lies about you."

The last person Lauren wanted to see was her ex-husband, but Sophie's reasoning made sense. Talking to Phil was a smart and relatively safe place to start. "All right," she said. "We'll talk to him."

"Do you know where he's staying?"

She took out her phone and scrolled through her list of contacts until she found the address of the rehab facility in Grand Junction where Phil was staying. She read it off to Sophie.

"Great. We can be there in an hour." She punched the address into her GPS. "Why don't you take a nap while I drive? I'll wake you when we get there."

Lauren closed her eyes again and tried to get more comfortable in her seat. If only she'd wake up from her nap to find the past few months had been nothing but a nightmare—not the awful reality she had to keep surviving.

LATER THAT AFTERNOON Marco trained the high-powered binoculars on Richard Prentice's mansion. The gray stone castle, complete with crenellated towers and a fake drawbridge, was the billionaire's way of giving the finger to the county officials who had thwarted his plans to sell the park in-holding to them at inflated prices. The castle blocked a park visitor's best view of the Curecanti Needle, a famous rock formation. Now, instead of marveling at the beauty of nature, visitors standing at the Pioneer Point overlook in the park saw this monstrosity.

"See anything?" Rand asked, crouched next to Marco on a rocky outcropping of land just across the boundary line from Prentice's ranch.

"Nope." He swung the binoculars to the left and focused on two muscular men in desert camo, who lounged against a tricked-out black Jeep. One of the men had an AR-15 casually slung over one shoulder. "The troops are taking it easy," Marco said.

Rand grunted. "Their boss is probably feeling pretty secure since the grand jury let him off the hook."

"Something tells me insecurity isn't one of Prentice's problems, ever." He shifted the binoculars farther to the left, to the pile of rubble that marked the entrance to the mine where Lauren had been held. No telling what other illegal booty had been stored in the maze of tunnels. Prentice had been worried enough to order his men to set off explosives and collapse the mine, almost trapping Lauren and her rescuers inside.

Rand must have been thinking about that night, too.

"Why didn't the grand jury believe Lauren when she told them what he'd done to her?" he asked.

"People are afraid of mental illness. Prentice and his experts played on that fear."

"What about you?"

Marco lowered the binoculars and stared at his friend. "Are you asking if I'm afraid of Lauren?"

"Not afraid, but do you worry about getting involved with someone who's dealing with something like this?"

He shifted his backpack from his shoulder and stowed the binoculars. "I don't lose sleep worrying about it."

"Sophie told me you volunteered to be her bodyguard. I thought maybe it was because you were interested in her. You know, romantically."

Marco zipped up the pack and shrugged back into it. "She needs protecting. I can protect her. That's all." That was all there could ever be between him and Lauren Starling.

"So you're just above all those messy emotions the rest of us mortals have to deal with," Rand said.

"I don't have time for them." Those "messy emotions" brought complications and distractions he didn't want or need. He turned back to the view of Prentice's castle. "We have a job to do."

Rand stiffened and put a hand on the pistol at his side. "What's that noise?"

The low whine, like the humming of a large mosquito, grew louder. Marco looked around, then up, and spotted what at first looked like a toy plane or one of those radio-controlled aircraft hobbyists flew. "I think it's a drone," he said as the craft hovered over them.

Rand scowled at the intruder. "Is it armed?"

"No, but I think it's spotted us."

"The captain said Prentice had one of these. What do you think it's doing?"

Marco trained the binoculars on the craft. "It looks as if there's a camera attached to the underside, so I'd say it's taking pictures."

"Pictures of what?"

"Of us. Evidence that we're harassing the poor little rich guy."

"Nothing wrong with being rich." Rand gave a big, cheesy smile and waved up at the drone.

Marco lowered the binoculars, resisting the urge to make an obscene gesture at the camera. "No, but there's a lot wrong with being a jerk." And a jerk who used a beautiful, vulnerable woman in his sick games had to be stopped.

Chapter Five

The low-slung cedar and stone buildings of the Day-spring Wellness Center looked more like an exclusive vacation resort than a medical facility. Fountains and flowers dotted the lavish landscaping, and the few people Lauren and Sophie saw once they'd left their car in the parking lot were tanned and casually dressed as if on their way to a tennis game or setting out to hike in the nearby hills.

"Maybe we should look into checking in here," Sophie said as they made their way up a paved walkway lined with brilliant blooming flowers. "This is way nicer than our apartment. And we wouldn't have to cook or clean."

Lauren stopped before a signpost with markers pointing toward the dining room, gym, pool and treatment rooms. "This all must cost a fortune."

"Then, how is Phil paying for it? Wasn't he hassling you for money before you disappeared?"

"He wanted me to increase his support payments." Because Lauren had earned more money than Phil, an actor with a small theater company, the court had ordered her to pay him support after their divorce. "But I haven't given him any money in months." While Prentice had held her captive, she hadn't had access to her bank accounts, then she hadn't been working, recovering from her ordeal. Now that she'd been fired, no telling when she'd be able to pay him.

Then again, not having access to her money had forced him to admit that his drug habit had gotten out of hand, and he had to seek help. When the Rangers had questioned him about her disappearance, he'd been living in a fleabag motel on the edge of town. "Maybe his girlfriend came into money." When they'd divorced, Phil had been seeing an actress he worked with.

"Maybe Richard Prentice is footing the bill," Sophie said. "In exchange for a few 'favors.'"

"I don't know."

They headed to a building marked Welcome Center. "We're here to see Phillip Starling," Lauren said.

The receptionist consulted her computer. "He's in Pod A." She indicated a map on the desk in front of her. "Follow this walkway around back and you'll see the groups of cottages are labeled. He's probably in the courtyard. We encourage our guests to spend as much time as possible out of doors, enjoying nature."

Lauren thanked her and they headed down the walk she'd indicated. "What's the difference between a patient and a guest?" Lauren asked.

"Maybe a couple thousand dollars a day?" Sophie guessed.

They found Pod A and walked under a stone archway into a courtyard with padded loungers and shaded tables arranged around a gurgling fountain. Phil, his back to them, sat at one of the tables, talking with a young woman who stood beside a cart next to the table.

As Lauren and Sophie drew nearer, the woman

laughed and playfully swatted Phil's shoulder. "You are so bad," she chided.

"Come back after you get off and I'll show you how bad—and how good—I can be," he said.

She laughed again, then saw the two women. "I'd better go," she said, and rolled her cart away.

"Hello, Phil," Lauren said.

He turned toward her and arched one eyebrow. "You're about the last person I expected to see here."

Hair cut, clean shaven and wearing a polo shirt and pressed khakis, he looked much better than the last time she'd seen him. He had a tan and had put on a few pounds. Her ex-husband was definitely handsome. She waited for the catch in her throat that always happened when she saw him again after time apart, and was relieved when it didn't come. Maybe she was finally getting over him. "You're looking good," she said.

"You, too." He stood and kissed her cheek, and nodded to her sister. "Hello, Sophie."

"Hello, Phil." Her greeting was cool; Sophie had never liked Phil, and when he'd left Lauren for another woman she'd stopped trying to hide her disdain.

"What brings you two here?" he asked. "Did you miss me?"

"We wanted to talk to you about Richard Prentice," Lauren said. No sense being coy.

Some of the cheerfulness went out of his eyes, replaced by edgy caution. "What about him?"

"The grand jury refused to indict him on charges of kidnapping," Sophie said.

Phil's surprise seemed genuine. "They think he didn't do it?"

"Apparently, he persuaded them I made up the whole story," Lauren said.

"That's too bad," he said. "I'm sorry to hear it."

"Oh, please." Sophie folded her arms across her chest and glared at him. "Your comments in the paper—calling Prentice your good friend and practically accusing Lauren of being delusional—didn't help matters any."

"You know how the press can be," he said. "Always taking things out of context."

"Did Prentice pay you to say those things about me?" Lauren asked.

"Is that what you think?" He put his hand on her shoulder. She resisted the urge to shrug him off. "Lauren, honey, I know this is hard for you to hear, but you have to admit that the last few months we were together, you were pretty out there. Not yourself."

"Neither of us was at our best then," she said.

"Maybe so. But at least I didn't suddenly decide to redecorate the whole condo and stay up for two nights in a row ripping out tile and moving furniture, only to abandon the project half-done two days later and start looking at new places instead. And what about the time you bought all that expensive cookware and enrolled in an Italian cooking course? You gave one dinner party, then almost never went into the kitchen again."

Lauren did move away from him then. "None of those things hurt anyone," she said.

"They're not normal, Lauren. All I wanted was a normal marriage. A normal life."

"So that's why you became a drug addict," Sophie said. "So things would be 'normal.'"

He took a step toward her, but Lauren stepped between them. "Back to Richard Prentice. Why did you tell the paper he was such a good friend? You hardly knew him."

"I figured it wouldn't hurt my reputation to be associated with a billionaire, you know?"

"How does Prentice feel, being associated with you?" Sophie asked.

Phil shot her a look and turned back to Lauren. "Maybe you shouldn't be going around asking questions about Richard Prentice," he said. "I mean, haven't you had enough trouble from him?"

"Have you talked to him?" she asked. "Did he say anything about me?"

"I didn't have to talk to him," he said. "All I had to do was look him in the eye. There are dark things going on in that brain of his." He took her arm. "Let's take a walk." He glanced at Sophie. "Just the two of us."

She hesitated.

"Please. We need to talk."

"Go on." Sophie sat at the table. "I'll wait here."

He led Lauren down a path, out of the courtyard into an open area at the back of the compound. Beyond the center's manicured grounds stretched open prairie, the mountains blue shadows in the distance. "It's very peaceful here," Lauren said.

"Yeah." He let go of her and hugged his arms across his chest, squinting in the bright sun. "All this openness makes me nervous, though. A lot of times I feel as if people are watching me." He laughed, a hollow sound. "I think paranoia is one of the side effects of withdrawal, or maybe of some of the medication I'm on." He laughed again. "I guess you and me have more in common than I thought."

"What do you mean?"

"We're both messed up in the head."

"Phil, I—"

He shook his head. "Let's not argue. I brought you back here because I just wanted to say I'm sorry things didn't work out between us. I believe we really did love each other and I hope we can be friends going forward."

"What about your girlfriend?" she asked.

He grimaced. "She didn't stick around." He shoved both hands into his pockets and stared out toward the mountains. "Things are going to be better now. This is a good program and I'm getting it together. My agent has some feelers out. I'm thinking of getting into the movies, or maybe television. I could do really well there."

"I'm glad to hear it," she said. "How did you find this place?"

"A friend pulled some strings and got me in."

"Richard Prentice."

He turned to her. "I'm beginning to think the papers are right and you are obsessed with the guy. Let it go, Lauren."

"I won't let it go. Did Richard pay you off to say bad things about me?"

He glanced from side to side, then leaned toward her, his voice low. "He might have shot a little money my way. But I didn't say anything to that reporter that wasn't true. I just maybe exaggerated."

"What do you know about him and Alan Milbanks?" she asked.

He blinked, and for a moment his face went slack. But he recovered, his expression wary. "What about Milbanks?"

"You bought drugs from him."

"What are you now, a cop?" He stepped back. "Yeah, I made a few buys from him."

"Did you ever see him with Richard Prentice?"

"No. He mentioned Prentice to me once. I don't remember how the subject came up—mutual friends or something like that."

Goose bumps prickled her skin in spite of the sun's heat. "Did you tell the police this?"

"No." He shook his head. "Why would I? Anyway, it was no big deal."

"It could be a very big deal. It's another way to link Milbanks and Prentice. It's the kind of evidence that could help bring him to trial for his crimes."

"I told you. You need to let it go." He took another step back. "Get out of it while you can. Move on with your life."

"I can't move on. Not while he goes unpunished for all the wrong he's done. Please. Come back inside with me and we'll make some calls."

He shook his head and put more distance between them. "No way. I've said too much already I—"

Whatever he was going to say was cut off by the whine of a bullet and a dull thud as it slammed into his body. He dropped to his knees and looked up at her, mouth open and eyes wide in surprise as blood bloomed on his chest. Lauren screamed, then turned and ran, her heart pounding in terror.

Chapter Six

The sign over the entrance to Dayspring Wellness Center welcomed visitors to "a dayspring of new beginnings." But Phil Starling had met his end there.

"A single shot from a high-powered rifle. Looks as if it got him right through the heart." The Grand Junction police detective squinted across the empty prairie behind the lot where crime scene personnel swarmed around Starling's slumped body. "There's a shooting range over there. We sent some officers to interview people."

"This wasn't random," Marco said. Sophie had called him as soon as she'd heard what happened. Rand and Lotte had been summoned to assist with the search for a child who'd wandered away from her family's camp-site in the park, but Marco had come as soon as he could.

The detective's expression didn't change. "Do you know someone who wanted this guy dead?"

Richard Prentice. Sophie had told him the sisters had come to the drug treatment center to question Phil about his relationship with the billionaire. But that wasn't enough basis to accuse a man of murder. "Who was footing the bill for Starling's stay here?" Marco asked. "Maybe they were tired of paying."

The detective nodded. "We'll find out. And he was

an addict—maybe someone he knew from when he was doing drugs had it in for him. But you see a lot of random things in this job. We'll check the shooting range. We'll also follow any leads we get about suspicious persons."

"Let me know what you find," Marco said. He left the detective and made his way to the secluded courtyard where Sophie and Lauren waited. They sat together on an iron bench, Lauren folded in on herself, huddled with her arms around her waist, her hair falling forward to obscure her face.

Sophie looked up at his approach. "What did you find out?" she asked.

"Let's talk over here," he said, indicating the shade of a tree a few feet away. Lauren didn't even look up when her sister left her. She had yet to acknowledge Marco's presence.

"How is she?" he asked, when Sophie joined him under the tree.

"I've asked one of the doctors here for a sedative. Stress isn't good for her, and something like this…" She shook her head. "It's so awful."

"Did she say what they were talking about, before he was shot?"

"No. He asked to speak to her alone and left me here. So it wasn't an accident?"

The question had a pleading quality. People wanted things like this to be accidents. As tragic as random violence was, it was easier to deal with than the idea of deliberate evil. "There's a shooting range behind here, but I don't think this was an accident." The shot had been too accurate, a shot that killed quickly.

"I never even liked him much, but I never wanted him dead. And to die like that, right in front of Lauren…"

He glanced at the bench again. Lauren was sitting up now, staring into the distance, eyes glazed, her beautiful face a mask of grief. "Did she still love him?" He hadn't meant to ask the question; her feelings were none of his business. But he held his breath, waiting for the answer.

"I loved what we used to have together," Lauren said, her voice husky and low. "I loved the idea of us together, of being married and happy. Of being normal."

He moved to sit beside her on the bench, wanting to touch her, but not touching. "I know this is painful," he said softly. "But I need to know what Phil said to you. What were you talking about before he died?"

"He told me Alan Milbanks talked to him about Richard." Her voice grew stronger and she turned toward him, her knees brushing his leg. "The two of them definitely knew each other. I was trying to persuade him to go to the police, to tell them everything he knew. Someone killed him to keep him quiet, I'm sure of it."

"Was anyone nearby who could have overheard your conversation?" he asked.

"No. But Phil said he felt like someone was watching him. He joked that paranoia was a side effect of his treatment, but maybe he was right and someone was watching. Maybe they could read lips or maybe…maybe just seeing the two of us together was enough for them to kill him." Her voice broke and she bent her head.

Marco gripped her hand. "This may have had nothing to do with you," he said. "Someone decided to silence Phil, for whatever reason. It could have been a drug dealer he owed money or something completely unrelated to our case. Don't waste time blaming yourself."

She sniffed and nodded. "You're right. My falling apart doesn't help anyone."

He squeezed her hand and released it, then stood as a young woman in purple scrubs approached. "Dr. Winstead prescribed this sedative for Ms. Starling." She held out a small paper cup containing a pill, and a paper cup of water.

"Thank you, but I don't need it now." Lauren stood and pushed her hair back from her face. "I just want to go home."

"The local police may want to question you," Marco said.

"Detective Cargill spoke with Dr. Winstead and said he would question Ms. Starling later, when she's feeling better," the nurse said.

"Then, I'll take you home," Marco said.

"I can take her." Sophie put her arm around Lauren.

"I'll follow you and make sure you settle in all right," Marco said.

"Thank you," Lauren said. "I'd appreciate that."

He would have preferred to have Lauren in the car with him for the drive back to Montrose, but he realized she'd probably be more comfortable with her sister. He had to be content with following their car, observing what he could through the windshield. The two women didn't seem to be talking much. Was that a good or a bad sign? His impression was that women always talked more, especially when something was bothering them.

His phone rang. He answered it and Graham's voice boomed over the line. "What's going on over there?"

"Starling died almost instantly, from a single bullet to the heart. He and Lauren were talking in the back garden of the treatment center when he was shot."

"Who shot him? Any suspects?"

"Looks like a sniper. The police are questioning people at a shooting range not far away, but this doesn't look like an accident to me. I think someone wanted to shut him up."

"One of his drug connections?"

"Maybe. Or maybe Prentice. Lauren said they were talking about Prentice when Phil was shot. He told her Prentice and Alan Milbanks knew each other. She was trying to persuade him to tell the police what he knew."

"How is she doing?"

He studied the back of her head in the car ahead of him. She looked so still—too still. "She's had a shock," he said. "A doctor at the center persuaded the local cops to put off their interview until later. I don't think she's going to be able to tell them much anyway. She says she didn't see anything."

"Where are you now?"

"Headed to her apartment. She and Sophie are in Sophie's car, just ahead of me."

"Stay as long as you need to. Make sure the place is secure."

"Yes, sir."

He knew he'd be staying awhile when he followed Sophie's car into the parking lot of their apartment building and found it crowded with vehicles, including two news vans with satellite dishes on their roofs. Reporters lined the walkway leading to the sisters' apartment.

His phone rang, and when he answered it he wasn't surprised to hear Sophie's voice, agitated. "Marco, what are we going to do? How are we going to get past those vultures?"

"Is there a back way in?"

"There's a sliding door onto a patio, but the gate and the door are locked."

"Then, we'll have to go in the front. Stick close to me and don't respond to anything, no matter what the reporters ask."

They parked as close to the apartment as they could get, behind the news vans. Marco exited his Cruiser, then opened Lauren's door and helped her out while Sophie came around from the driver's side. With an arm around each woman, he made his way toward the apartment.

When the reporters spotted them, they swarmed around. Lauren angled her body toward his and buried her face in his shoulder. "Ms. Starling, what do you have to say about your husband's shooting?"

"Are they thinking this is a murder?"

"What were you doing at the treatment center? Were you and Phil planning a reconciliation?"

Marco forced his way through the crowd of clamoring men and women, his fierce expression causing more than one of them to stumble back out of the way. He waited while Sophie unlocked the door, then the three of them hurried inside, the reporters' shouts muffled by the slamming door.

"That was awful," Sophie said as she hurried to draw the drapes across the front window.

"They're just doing their jobs," Lauren said. "Trying to get the story." She moved out of Marco's arms. He was surprised at how empty he felt when she moved away, cold in the absence of her warmth.

"I'll make some tea," Sophie said, and retreated to the kitchen.

Lauren sat on the couch and kicked off her shoes, revealing pink-polished toenails. "Thank you," she said. "We would have had a tougher time getting through that gauntlet without you."

He sat in a chair across from her. "How are you feeling?" he asked.

She looked pale, but calmer than before. "I'm not sure," she said. "I think I'm still in shock."

"It was a terrible thing to have to experience."

She hugged a pillow to her chest. "Have you ever seen someone shot before?"

"Yes."

"Abby said you were in Special Forces. I guess you've seen a lot of horrible things."

"Yes." Much of his life he'd spent surrounded by violence—in the midst of gang warfare as a child growing up in Los Angeles, as a soldier in Iraq and Afghanistan and as an officer with the DEA.

"How do you handle it without falling apart?" she asked.

"You learn to wall off your emotions. To not see everything that's there."

"That sounds like an awful way to live."

"Maybe it is."

"All my life I've been accused of being too emotional," she said. "Too sensitive. But I'd rather be that way than not feel anything."

She looked him in the eye, a piercing gaze that made him feel naked in front of her. Exposed. "I feel things," he said. He was feeling a lot of things now—a potent mix of lust and admiration and sympathy and the desire to protect her from anything that threatened her. "But I've learned not to show my feelings."

"I'm the opposite." She set the pillow aside. "I can never hide my feelings. I don't know if that's part of my disease, or just the way I'm wired."

"That's one of the things I like about you," he said. "You're honest. I never have to guess your motives."

"You think that now, but you haven't seen me at my worst."

"I've seen a lot of bad things in my life, but you're not one of them."

She shook her head. "Don't go there, Marco."

"Go where?"

"Don't get involved with me. I'm too much trouble. Too unpredictable."

"Maybe I like unpredictable."

"You might think that, but you wouldn't. Phil reminded me of some of the things I did while we were married. I see now how hard I made it for him."

"That wasn't you. It was your disease."

"They're one and the same. I can't separate the two. For better or worse—like a bad marriage. Except there's no chance of divorce."

He leaned toward her, elbows on his knees, hands clasped in front of him. "You won't convince me you're a bad person," he said. "You're a strong woman, but I'm even stronger. And I like a challenge."

"Why do you care so much?" Her voice rose, angry.

Better anger than despair, he thought. "We have more in common than you think."

Her eyes widened. "Don't tell me you're bipolar, too."

"No. But what you're going through right now—fighting for your reputation against someone who's trying to take you down… I've been there."

She looked skeptical.

He hadn't meant to tell her this; he never talked to anyone about what had happened. He searched for the right words to tell his story as briefly and unemotionally as possible. "When I was first in Iraq, I transferred into a new squadron, so I was the new guy," he said. "For whatever reason, another guy, more senior, decided he didn't like me. He started spreading rumors about me—that I'd been transferred out of my old unit because I was a coward who put other soldiers in danger because I didn't back them up on a mission. It's probably the worst thing you can say about a soldier. Being part of a team means always looking out for the other team members."

"You're not a coward," she said.

"None of these people knew me, so they didn't recognize what the other guy was saying as lies."

"What did you do?"

"I had to prove myself—over and over again. Eventually, the others saw what I was really like, but it took a long time."

"That must have been awful," she said.

"It was, but I got through it. And you'll get through this, too."

"We'll all get through this," Sophie said. She carried a tray into the room and set it on the coffee table between them. She handed Lauren a cup of tea. "There's tea for you, too, Marco, if you want it. But if you need to leave, I understand. Lauren and I will be all right."

"I'm going to stay here tonight, just to be sure," he said.

"That really isn't necessary," she said.

"It's all right," Lauren said. "I'll feel better with you here. In the morning, we can talk about what we're going to do next."

MARCO SPENT THE night on the sofa while Lauren took a sleeping pill that knocked her out for six hours. After she forced herself out of bed and into the shower, she joined Sophie and Marco in the kitchen. They had the newspaper spread out in front of them. Sophie jumped up when Lauren came into the room. "Good morning," she said. "Let me get you some coffee." As she spoke, she folded the section of the paper she'd been reading, then tried to take Marco's from him.

"Leave the paper," Lauren said. She sat in the chair to Marco's left. "I want to see what they have to say."

Sophie bit her bottom lip, her hand still protectively atop the stack of papers.

"Let her see," Marco said. "She needs to know what we're up against."

"I'll get the coffee," Sophie said, and hurried away.

"How are you feeling this morning?" Marco asked, his dark eyes fixed on her. He needed a shave and had slept in his clothes, but the ruggedness only made him look sexier.

"I've felt better," she said. "But I'll be okay." She'd taken her medication and done some of the centering exercises her therapist had given her. At the first sign of anything off-kilter, she would call her doctor. She was determined to stay in control and on top of this.

He slid a section of paper toward her. "Start here," he said. "Some of it's pretty ugly, though."

She took a deep breath. "I'm getting used to that."

The front page of the *Post* featured a shot from her wedding, Lauren in a white veil and gown, carrying a bouquet of roses, Phil in a black tux with a white rose boutonniere. He'd been smiling at the camera while she smiled at him. Maybe a foreshadowing of how their marriage would turn out. The headline over the shot proclaimed Actor Murdered in Front of Ex.

Sophie handed Lauren a cup of coffee and returned to her chair. "The reporter who wrote that article should get a job with the tabloids," she said. "He manages to include every bit of gossip and innuendo he could find."

Lauren scanned the article, which began with the facts—Phil had been shot while standing in the back garden of the treatment center with his ex-wife, who had come to visit him. He was undergoing treatment for drug addiction. Prior to that, he had worked as an actor with a Denver theater company and won several awards for his work. His ex was a popular former Channel 9 news anchor who had a history of mental illness. She had been in the news lately for accusing prominent billionaire Richard Prentice of trying to kill her. The morning of the shooting, a grand jury had failed to indict Prentice for the crimes.

Okay, nothing here she hadn't expected, though she would have preferred the reporter be more specific with her diagnosis. She had bipolar disorder, a fairly common, controllable disease. She wasn't a psychopath, a sociopath, or suffering from any of the other sometimes dangerous disorders that people associated with criminal behavior. She continued reading, but the next sentence made her freeze. "Given her history of erratic behavior, police have not ruled out Ms. Starling as a suspect in her ex-husband's death."

She read the words out loud, her voice breaking on the last syllable. Sophie leaned across the table and covered her hand. "I didn't want you to see that," she said.

"How could anyone think I had anything to do with Phil's murder?" she asked. "I was standing right there when he was shot—by a sniper who wasn't anywhere near."

"I spoke with Detective Cargill this morning," Marco

said. "Someone at the scene speculated that the crime could have been a murder for hire and apparently the reporter took that and ran with it."

"What kind of sicko would hire an assassin, then arrange to be with the intended victim when he died?" Sophie asked.

"Apparently the kind of sicko some people think I am." Lauren pushed the paper away and reached for the coffee with shaking hands. "What else did the police say?"

"They're still questioning people at the gun range," Marco said. "The trajectory of the bullet indicates it was fired from there, or near there."

"They don't really think this was an accident, do they?" Sophie asked.

He shrugged, an elegant movement of his shoulders that made Lauren think of an exotic wild animal—a cheetah or a panther. Like one of those big cats, he seemed so calm and contained, sitting there beside her. Yet underneath the stillness lay something lethal, poised to unleash itself if the situation called for it.

"If they think this is an accident, the police might not take the crime as seriously," Lauren said. "Even if they find the shooter, they won't look into who might have hired him to do the shooting."

"This feels like a professional hit to me," Marco said. "They won't find him."

"So we'll never know if Richard Prentice was behind this or not." The truth of that statement shouldn't have surprised her. Though the Rangers could link people engaged in everything from prostitution to drug trafficking to Prentice, the billionaire always managed to distance himself. Some pointed to this as proof of his innocence, but having spent six weeks as his prisoner, Lauren could never believe it. He had never mistreated her; he'd pampered her, even. But his determination to make her his own, in spite of her protests, had shown her the twisted soul beneath the tailored suits and calm demeanor.

"What are we going to do now?" she asked.

"I don't want you leaving the house alone." Marco shifted his gaze to include Sophie. "Either of you."

"Why?" Sophie asked. "You don't really think we're in danger, do you? The grand jury let Prentice go."

"That sniper killed Phil," Marco said. "But the shooter could just as easily have targeted Lauren."

"Richard said he loved me. He wanted me to marry him. In his twisted way, I think he meant what he said. He wants to frighten me into keeping quiet, but I can't believe he wants me dead. I don't think he wants me dead." But the memory of Phil falling at her feet, blood blooming at his chest, sent an icy chill through her, and she had to set aside the coffee. "What am I supposed to do?" she asked. "I can't hide in here forever."

"The offer still stands for you to come stay with me," he said. "And Sophie could move in with Rand."

"I appreciate the offer, but that's no real solution," she said. "I wouldn't be able to come and go at your place, either, and I'd feel guilty about inconveniencing you."

"That's really sweet of you, Marco," Sophie said. "But Lauren doesn't need the stress of trying to get comfortable in a new place. She needs routine and familiarity and calm."

Right. And the last thing she wanted was for Marco to see her when she wasn't coping well.

"Then, you can stay here," he relented. "But don't

go out unless I can be with you. Or Rand or one of the other Rangers."

"You couldn't protect me from a sniper," she said.

"Maybe not, but I can keep you safe from other closer attacks."

She believed he wanted to protect her, and the idea touched her more than she wanted to admit. But how could one man, even a law enforcement officer who'd been in Special Forces, protect her from an enemy she couldn't see and wasn't even sure she knew? "I heard the captain yesterday—you have work to do," she said. "You probably shouldn't even be here now."

"After the shooting yesterday, I'm sure the captain would agree protecting you is important to our case."

The captain might also think she was more trouble than she was worth.

A knock on the door made them all jump. Marco quickly moved to the window and pulled back the curtain a scant inch. Then he relaxed. "It's Rand."

He opened the door and Sophie embraced her lover, who was dressed casually this morning in khakis and a blue polo shirt. "Where's Lotte?" Lauren asked. She didn't often see Rand without the police dog.

"She's at the groomer's. Technically, it's our day off, though I'm still working on the case."

"Marco's been scaring us with all his warnings about danger," Sophie said.

"I hope it worked." He kissed her cheek, then nodded to Lauren. "What's the latest?" he asked Marco.

"The Grand Junction police think the bullet came from that firing range behind the treatment center," Marco said.

Rand nodded. "Perfect place for the shooter to blend

in. By the time anyone figured out he was aiming at more than the range targets, he could be long gone."

"Any new developments on your end?" Marco asked.

"Prentice gave another press conference this morning in Denver, where he's attending a board meeting or something. Senator Mattheson was with him and they took turns going on about what a nuisance The Ranger Brigade is to public safety and how much we are costing the taxpayers every day we're allowed to continue our efforts to usurp local authority."

"He said *usurp*?" Marco asked.

"That and a lot of other five-dollar words. The reporters were eating it up, from what I could see of the television footage."

"How did the captain react?" Marco asked.

"He looked as though he wanted to cut out Prentice's liver and eat it for lunch. But he'd never let anyone outside the Rangers see how upset he is."

"The press will have us under the microscope now," Marco said. "Waiting for us to make one wrong move."

"Speaking of being under the microscope, did you know someone is watching this place?" Rand asked.

"It's probably one of those reporters," Sophie said. "When we got back from Grand Junction last night there must have been a dozen of them camped out by the door."

"The reporters were gone when I checked this morning," Marco said.

"Come check this out." They all followed Rand to the kitchen window. "The gray SUV, parked on the corner," he said.

Marco stood a few inches back from the window and looked in the direction Rand indicated. Lauren came to stand behind him, her hand on his broad, warm back. Touching him this way made her feel steadier—anchored. "It looks like a regular car to me," she said.

"Look again," Rand said. "There's a guy in it and he's definitely keeping an eye on this place."

"Not the same one who was watching you the other day," Marco said. He moved toward the door, Rand close behind him. "Let's find out what this guy is up to."

Most Suitable Woman

ment. The number was from the door: A7 Laurea ...
Cannon said.

What the hell, Sophie said, the ...
Marco chased the note before he'd finished shape ...
read said.

Another time look at Richardson, she wrote, then
Sam/Marco wrote the message into the apar ...

He was too far away to be understood. The para ...
walking down the street with a note ...
Lauren replied, yes. Richard stood ...

Chapter Seven

Shoulder to shoulder, Lauren and Sophie stood at the window and watched Rand and Marco saunter down the street—two friends on their way to get coffee or take in a movie, deep in conversation as they walked. When the Rangers reached the SUV, they suddenly veered over, one on each side of the vehicle. Marco leaned in and said something, and then the driver got out of the vehicle.

"Anybody you know?" Sophie asked.

Lauren shook her head. "He's not one of Richard's guards." They were all big, strong men. This guy was slight and at least six inches shorter than Marco. He had thinning brown hair in need of a trim and dark-framed nerd glasses.

The man was gesticulating now, hands waving, head shaking. Marco and Rand said little, listening. "I wish we could hear what they're saying," Sophie said.

"Nobody looks upset," Lauren said. Rand and Marco were alert, but not rigidly tense. Rand was even smiling now.

After a moment, the man handed Marco something, got in his car and drove away.

The two Rangers made their way back to the apartment. The women met them at the door. "Who is he?" Lauren asked.

"What did he want?" Sophie chimed in.

Marco closed the door behind him, then handed Lauren a card.

"Andrew Combs. Co-Lar Productions," she read, then gave Marco a questioning look. "I don't get it."

"He says he runs an online news network. He wants to offer you a job as their news anchor."

"The face of *Exposed News*," Rand said.

"Exposed News?" She made a face. "I've never heard of it."

"There's a website listed on the card," Marco said. "He certainly made it sound legit."

"If he's so legit, why is he parked out there spying on us?" Sophie asked.

"He said he knew reporters had been hassling you and he didn't want you to think he was one of them," Rand said. "So he planned to wait until you came out to run errands or something, and he'd meet up with you then."

"On neutral ground," Marco said.

"And he said he wanted to offer me a job. For real?"

"He said he could offer you top pay and all kinds of media exposure," Rand said. "That he'd take your career in a new direction."

"That sounds great," Sophie said. "And online, it would be a national audience, right? Not just Denver. This could be a great thing for you."

Sophie's enthusiasm was contagious. Lauren stared at the card, a giddy feeling of excitement bubbling up in her chest. She did have a lot of experience. Maybe this could be a big break. "Let's take a look at the website," she said.

They trooped to her laptop on the coffee table. She

booted up the computer, then brought up the browser and typed in the address for *Exposed News*. "You must be eighteen or older to view this website," came the warning page. "That's strange," she said.

"Maybe they're just being overly cautious," Sophie said. "I mean, news is full of sex and violence, right? Probably not something you want little kids accidentally surfing to."

Lauren clicked the box to verify she was over eighteen and hit Enter. A video loaded, and after a moment they were staring at an attractive young woman reading a report on fighting in the Middle East.

"Am I hallucinating, or is she naked?" Sophie asked.

"Definitely naked," Rand said.

"Yep," Marco said. "Fully exposed."

LAUREN BEGAN TO LAUGH. Not the hysterical laughter of someone on the verge of losing it, but a melodic chuckle that flooded Marco with warmth. He smiled, and the others joined in the laughter.

"It's nice to know I have something I can fall back on," Lauren said. She shut down the website. "But I don't think I'm ready for naked news just yet."

"No wonder the guy was nervous about talking to you," Sophie said. "The idea is so ridiculous."

"Life is pretty ridiculous sometimes," Lauren said. "Or haven't you noticed?" She turned to Marco. "What now? I know you said you didn't want us going out alone, but the two of you must have work to do."

"I don't think you should stay here alone, either," he said. "This apartment is too vulnerable."

"What do you mean?" Sophie asked.

"It's too accessible from the front and the back," Rand

said. "The front door isn't reinforced. Almost anyone could kick it in. You don't have an alarm system or a security camera focused on the door."

"We should go back to our original plan of you two staying with us until we're sure the danger has passed," Marco said.

"It will be easier for us to work if we know you're somewhere safe," Rand said.

Marco looked away from the tender expression his friend directed at Sophie. He might have said the same words to Lauren, except he wasn't one for expressing his feelings in public. Not that he knew exactly what his feelings for the beautiful newscaster were. He'd been assigned to protect her the day he rescued her from Prentice's ranch and he still felt obligated to that duty, but there was something else going on between the two of them that he hadn't yet figured out. Physical attraction definitely played a part, but he also felt an emotional connection with her he hadn't experienced with any other woman. His natural inclination was to back off and not pursue his feelings any further, but the more time he spent with Lauren, the more difficult to do he found that.

"Pack what you need for a few days and come with us," Rand continued. "If you hate it, we'll try to find a safe house or some other place you can stay."

"All right." Sophie took Lauren's hand. "Come on. It can't hurt to go along with them." She winked at Rand. "It might even be fun."

While the women prepared to leave, Marco and Rand went outside to wait. Rand leaned against the side of the building, hands in his pockets, and gazed across the half-empty parking lot. "Naked news." He chuckled. "It would definitely make dull stories about politics and economics more exciting."

Marco tensed, waiting for his friend to say something about Lauren being a good fit for the job, but Rand was smart enough not to go there. Instead, Marco's own mind conjured an image of a naked Lauren reading a news story. His mind went fuzzy as he focused on this picture of her gorgeous breasts and shapely hips...

With great effort, he forced his mind away from the enticing fantasy and discreetly shifted position to accommodate the erection the daydream had produced. "It's a crazy idea," he muttered, and turned away.

After a moment the women emerged, suitcases in hand. "I'll take Sophie to Ranger headquarters with me," Rand said. "Carmen and I are going back over all the evidence we collected at Prentice's ranch the night we rescued Lauren. We're hoping we can find something to counter the stories Prentice has been floating in the press, and tie him to criminal activity."

"I want to stop by the motel where Phil was staying before he went into rehab," Marco said.

"We'll meet you at the station when I'm done there."

"What are you hoping to learn at the motel?" Lauren asked when she was buckled into the passenger seat of Marco's Cruiser.

"I'm curious who might have visited Phil while he was in town."

The motel was a low-slung, old-fashioned motor court, the white paint faded and flaking. The doors to the rooms, each set back slightly from the next in line, had once been blue, though that, too, had faded to almost gray. Marco parked the Cruiser in front of the office.

"I hadn't imagined it would be this bad," Lauren said.

"Not his usual style?"

She shook her head. "I guess he really was in financial trouble." Her eyes grew shiny and she blinked back tears. "I'm sorry." She ducked her head. "It's just hard, realizing he's gone."

Marco handed her a handkerchief. "He was a big part of your life," he said. The words sounded inadequate, but he couldn't bring himself to say more. He knew Lauren and Phil had been married for seven years, but he hated to admit she'd loved a guy like that—one who was so weak.

She dabbed at her eyes, careful not to smear her makeup. "Things were over between us a long time ago," she said. "But I still cared about him. Not the way I cared when we were first married, but just because he'd been important to me once." She glanced at him. "Have you ever been married?"

"No."

"Why not?"

He could have told her the answer was none of her business, or dismissed the question with a cliché about not having met the right woman. But too many people had lied to Lauren; he didn't want to be one of them. "The work I do is dangerous. Adding someone else into the mix, someone I care about and need to protect, complicates things. I might make a mistake because I'm thinking of that person instead of the job."

"Or maybe knowing that person was supporting you, wanting you to come home safely, would inspire you to even greater success." She folded the handkerchief and handed it back to him. "I don't think relationships are ever all good or all bad. Sometimes it's a matter of perspective."

No one had ever skewed his perspective the way she

had; he didn't know if he liked it or not. He tucked the handkerchief back into his pocket and opened the door of the Cruiser. "Let's go see who we can find to talk to."

The only person in the office was an older man in a stained white T-shirt. He scowled at the badge Marco showed him, glanced at Lauren, then back at Marco. "What do you want?" he asked.

"You had a man staying here for almost four weeks in June and July," Marco said. "Phil Starling."

"Don't know him."

"Maybe this will refresh your memory." Marco handed over a copy of that morning's paper with Phil's photo and the news of his death on the front page.

The old man grunted. "Him. So he got shot." He shoved the paper back across the counter. "Nothing to do with me."

"I want to know if anyone came to see him while he was here," Marco said.

"What? You think I keep tabs on my guests? What they do is their own business."

Marco glanced out the window to the right of the front desk, at the row of rooms with blue doors. "You've got a pretty good view here. You strike me as a man who keeps an eye on things."

The man stood up a little straighter. "I don't want any trouble. I run a clean place."

"So you would have noticed if Mr. Starling had visitors."

"He didn't. He kept to himself."

"So no one ever came to see him the whole time he was here?" Marco asked.

"I didn't say that. People stopped by a couple times."

"What kind of people? Can you describe them?"

The guy shrugged. "A couple of big fellows. Football linebacker types."

"How many times did they visit?"

"What's it to you?"

"We're trying to find out who killed him." Not exactly true. That case belonged to the Grand Junction cops. Marco was looking for any connection to Richard Prentice, who was known to hire beefy guys as his private security guards. "How many times did these big guys come to see Phil Starling?"

The old man looked down at the newspaper. "Twice. Once a few days before Starling moved out. The second time, he left with them, but not before one came in and paid his bill."

"How much was the bill?"

"One hundred and seventy-three dollars with tax. I was ready to throw the bum out for being so behind. He kept telling me he'd get the money, and I guess he was right."

"Did the man who paid say anything?" Marco asked. "Did he give you a name or say who he worked for or anything?" They should be so lucky.

"No. He just asked how much Starling owed and paid up. Cash, from a big wad of bills."

"You didn't think that was unusual, to pay in cash?"

"Some people don't like credit cards."

"Did Starling leave anything behind in his room when he moved out?" Marco asked.

"No. I was expecting it to be trashed, he'd been holed up in there so long, but they must have taken everything with them. Even the garbage. It was clean. I mean, cleaner than it was when he checked in. Looked as if somebody had washed everything in there."

"Anything else you can tell us about Phil Starling?" Marco asked.

"Nope."

Marco handed him a business card. "If you think of anything, call me at that number."

Lauren waited until they were in the Cruiser once more before she spoke. "Phil wasn't that fastidious," she said. "He never cleaned when we were married."

"His two friends might have done the job."

"But why go to all that trouble?"

"I don't know. Maybe to get rid of fingerprints, or anything that betrayed their identity."

"They sound like the type of guys who work for Richard," she said.

"Unless we find something to prove an association, that doesn't do us any good," he said.

"It's so frustrating, how he never does his own dirty work," she said. "His money and his position keep him a safe distance from anything incriminating."

He backed the Cruiser out of the parking spot and turned onto the street. "In this case, there's nothing criminal about paying someone's hotel bill," he said.

"Then, why do it?" she asked. "I can't believe it's because he liked Phil so much."

"Favors like that make people obligated to him," Marco said. "When he needs something from them, they're more likely to go along."

"That's a lot of trouble to go to just to get someone to tell reporters I'm crazy." Her voice cracked and Marco glanced at her, wondering if she was going to cry again. But she stiffened her shoulders and stared straight ahead. "I still can't believe Richard might want to kill me now. He said he loved me."

"His mind is twisted. Unpredictable."

She plucked at the seat belt and worried her lower lip between her teeth. "It was so strange. The whole time I was at his ranch," she said, "he kept telling me he loved me, but I never really believed him. There was something about him… He was too cold and unemotional. He didn't seem capable of love."

"Some people are harder to read than others." He'd been accused of being incapable of love himself. He sometimes wondered if his accusers were right. A lifetime of schooling his emotions left him sometimes unsure of what he really felt.

"Richard wasn't just reserved," she said. "There's something wrong with him. I don't understand why other people can't see it."

"Maybe you're more sensitive to emotions than other people."

"Because I'm so emotional myself?" She made a face.

"No. Because you have a gift for reading people."

Her expression softened and she turned toward him. "Thank you," she said.

He started to tell her she didn't need to thank him for anything, but her next words silenced him. "I'm not thanking you for the compliment," she said. "Though that was nice, too. I'm thanking you for respecting me. For treating me like a sensible adult. That's something this disease has stolen from me. Once people could put a label on me—bipolar—they started treating me differently, as if I wasn't even me anymore, just this sick person."

"I don't see you as a sick person." She had her problems, but everyone did, whether they were out there for the world to see or not.

"I know. And that means a lot to me."

Silence settled between them, charged with the awareness of things left unsaid. Other men—Rand and Michael Dance and even the captain—found ways to navigate the divide between duty and personal feeling, but he didn't know how to manage that. From the time he was a kid in his first gang, obeying the rules had been what had kept him in line. What kept him alive. The rules said you didn't fraternize with witnesses or the people you were charged with protecting. In real life, it happened all the time, but not to him.

His cell phone rang, and he punched the button to answer it. "Cruz."

"Marco, you need to get back to headquarters as soon as possible." Rand's voice sounded strained.

"What is it?" Marco asked. "What's wrong?"

"I don't know. The captain has called a meeting. He wants everyone here ASAP."

"We're on our way."

"What is it?" Lauren asked after he'd hung up.

"The captain's called a meeting. Maybe he's got some news about the case."

"I hope so. It would be a relief to have at least some answers."

The lot was crowded with Rangers' vehicles. Marco found a parking place at the far end, and he and Lauren joined the others inside. "What's up?" Marco asked Rand.

"I don't know. The captain has been in his office all morning."

They stared at the door to the captain's private office. Just then, it opened, and Graham emerged. He looked solemn, angry even. Whatever he had to say, it wasn't going to be good.

He walked to the front of the room and faced them. A hush fell over the crowd. "There's no easy way to say this, so I'll just get this over with." Graham glanced at a piece of paper in his hand—a printout of some kind. "The justice department issued an order this morning disbanding the interagency task force." He looked up, his face grim. "Effective immediately, The Ranger Brigade is no more."

Chapter Eight

Stunned silence followed Graham's announcement, then everyone started talking at once. Lauren touched Marco's arm. "What does this mean?" she asked. "Were you all just fired?" She certainly knew what that felt like.

"Not exactly," he said. "With the task force dissolved, we go back to our regular positions in law enforcement."

"So you're with the DEA, right?"

He nodded, his expression grim.

She looked around the room, at the other men and women, who seemed equally upset. "What happens to the cases you were investigating?"

"Some of them will be turned over to local law enforcement," he said.

"You mean the Montrose police?"

"Or the sheriff's department, or the Grand Junction police."

"So they'll continue investigating Richard Prentice."

"What do you think?"

"I think the chances of that happening aren't very high." Now that the grand jury had failed to bring charges, local authorities had no reason to pursue the case further. Not unless a new crime was committed or new evidence came to light. Without an ongoing investigation, the chances of finding new evidence seemed slim to none.

Not to mention that the local cops didn't have the manpower or the funds to fight Prentice and his phalanx of lawyers. Most of the people she'd met in her brief time in town before Prentice had kidnapped her were intimidated by the billionaire. He had influence over judges and politicians at a state level. Look at how easily he'd persuaded the courts to drop all the charges the Rangers had brought against him.

"But you can still work on the case, can't you?" she asked, struggling to salvage something positive from this latest news. "I mean, at least the drug part of it. Alan Milbanks was smuggling drugs, and I'm sure Prentice was bankrolling him. I know there's proof out there that Prentice was involved in Milbanks's operation. You can keep looking for that proof."

"You don't understand. I won't be here to investigate anything. My duty post is in Denver."

His words hit her like a physical blow. He was leaving her? Alone?

Rand, Sophie and Michael joined them. They looked as poleaxed by the news as she felt. "This changes everything," Michael said.

But Lauren had had too many changes in her life the past few months. She turned to Rand. "You can stay, can't you?" she asked. "You're with the Bureau of Land Management. They have a lot of land in this part of Colorado."

"I can't guarantee where my bosses will send me." He put his arm around Sophie and drew her close. She looked on the verge of tears. "But if I have to, I'll ask for leave."

"An investigation like this takes more than one person," Michael said. "It takes a team."

"A team like we were," Rand said.

Graham joined them. "Where will you go, Captain?" Lauren asked.

"I've been ordered back to Washington."

"Will Emma go with you?" Michael asked.

His expression grew more strained. "I hope so, but her work is here."

"She'll go with you," Lauren said. "This could be her chance to land a job with one of the big national papers."

"Richard Prentice is going to get away with murder now that he doesn't have the Rangers watching him," Sophie said. "It makes me so angry."

"I'll still be watching him," Lauren said. "I'm not going to stop digging into his background and looking into his business dealings."

"You can't do that," Sophie said. "It's too dangerous for you to do that stuff on your own."

"She won't be on her own," Marco said.

They all stared at him. "I'll be with you," he said.

"But you just said you had to report to Denver," Lauren said.

"I promised I'd protect you. With the Rangers disbanded, you'll be more vulnerable than ever."

She could hardly believe what he was saying. She swallowed past the knot that had formed in her throat. "But what about your job?"

"As of right now, I'm taking a leave of absence. I have some unfinished business to take care of."

THIS CHANGES EVERYTHING. Michael's words repeated like a mantra in Marco's thoughts as he cleaned out his locker at Ranger headquarters. Around him, the other members of the team were filling duffels and backpacks with personal belongings.

"Simon, is that smell coming from your locker?" Michael called across the room. "What have you got in there?"

"It's my running clothes." Simon held up a handful of T-shirts. "I haven't had time to do laundry lately."

"They ought to be declared hazardous waste," Michael said.

"Maybe I'll leave them here. A little souvenir for whoever has to clean up this place."

Carmen looked up from the locker next to Marco's. "What do you think will happen to this place?" she asked.

"Don't know. They'll probably haul it someplace and use it for storage or offices."

"I called my supervisor in Denver," she said. "Left him a voice mail that I needed to take some personal time."

"You're staying, then?"

She nodded. "I don't like leaving work half-done."

Rand walked by, a duffel in each hand, Lotte by his side. "What about Lotte?" Marco asked.

He stopped; the dog stopped, too. "What about her?"

"Isn't she government property?" Marco asked.

"She's my partner. If I'm on leave, she's on leave."

"You're not worried they'll reassign her?" Carmen asked.

"They'd have to find her first." He turned to Marco. "You realize we have to clear out of the duplex, right?"

"Why would you have to do that?" Carmen asked.

"It's state property," Marco said. "One of the perks of the job."

"I remember now," she said. "I was ticked I didn't get one of those, but now I'm glad they gave me a housing allowance instead. As long as my savings hold out, I can keep my apartment."

"Don't say that too loud," Rand said. "Or you're liable to end up with roommates."

"Uh-uh. It's one bedroom and my cat has already claimed the couch."

Marco stuffed a last notebook into his duffel and zipped it shut. "I'm done here," he said. Time to focus on the future, on finding justice—and justification for the Rangers.

Lauren and Sophie were waiting in the front room. Emma and Abby had joined them, the four gathered in a worried knot by the door, watching the parade of officers and staff carrying boxes and bags to the parking lot. "I can't believe this is happening," Emma said.

"Are you going to write about it for the paper?" Rand asked.

She shook her head. "I couldn't. I'm too outraged for it to ever make it into print."

"Do you think Richard Prentice and Senator Mattheson are celebrating right now?" Lauren asked.

"I hope they are," Rand said. "If they believe we aren't a threat anymore they'll let down their guard."

"How are you going to continue the investigation without access to your files and records?" Abby asked.

"I'll still have access for a few more weeks, at least." Graham joined them. "I'm staying on for a few weeks to oversee the transfer of records, disposal of the building, et cetera," he said. "I'll try to draw it out as long as possible and if you need me to look up anything for you, I will."

"Then, you're okay with what we're doing?" Rand asked.

The lines on Graham's forehead deepened. "I'm not okay with any of this, but I admire your dedication, and I want to finish the job we came here to do—to stop this crime wave that's threatening to take over public lands."

"Why don't you meet at our place this evening and discuss what you're going to do?" Emma said.

Graham nodded. "Everyone get settled, then come to my house at seven."

"Women, too," Emma said. "We can help."

"Women, too," Graham agreed.

"Meanwhile, Marco and I need to collect our belongings from our duplex before someone remembers it belongs to the state and locks us out," Rand said.

"Would they really do that?" Sophie asked.

"I never thought they'd disband the Rangers," he said. "Now I wouldn't put anything past them."

"Where will you stay?" Emma asked.

"They'll stay with us," Lauren said.

When everyone turned to look at her, she flushed pink. "I mean, Sophie and Rand are practically living together already, and we'll find someplace for Marco…" Her voice trailed away.

"Of course they'll stay with us." Sophie put her arm through Rand's.

"You know Lotte has to come with me," Rand said. "That's okay, isn't it?" Sophie had been terrified of the dog when they'd first met.

She nodded. "I'm okay with Lotte, though, come to think of it, I'm not sure if our complex allows dogs."

"We'll worry about that later." He turned to Marco. "You okay with staying with the girls?"

He nodded, his gaze still focused on Lauren. Maybe she had plans for him to sleep on the sofa. That might work for a night or two, but being in such close proximity to her wasn't going to do anything to lessen the attraction between them. Now that he was on leave, his duty to her was less well defined. Instead of a law officer and a witness, they were just a man and a woman.

As Michael had said, the disbandment of the Rangers changed everything.

LAUREN AND SOPHIE headed back to their apartment. They'd persuaded the men they'd be fine for the few hours it took for them to pack and move their stuff into Graham's garage, where he'd offered to store their belongings.

"Rand tried to get me to bring Lotte with us," Sophie said as she drove the car through town. "I'm a lot more comfortable with her than I used to be, but that still doesn't mean I want to be alone with her."

"We can use this time to get ready for the guys," Lauren said.

"And just where is Marco going to sleep? He's too tall for our sofa."

"I'm sure when he was in Special Forces he slept in places that were a lot more uncomfortable than our living room floor. We can make him a pallet or something." Her face felt as if it was on fire, the curse of being fair skinned and blushing easily.

"Okay. If that's what you want." Sophie's smile was

more of a smirk. "Though I can think of places he might be more comfortable."

"Stop it, Sophie. We're not even going to go there." Though even as she said the words, heat pooled between her legs at the thought of Marco naked and in her bed. *Stop it*, she ordered herself. She was never going to get through this if she didn't keep her libido under control.

"We'd better stop at the grocery store," she said. "The guys are going to want more to eat than yogurt and frozen diet dinners."

"We also have canned soup and your not-so-secret stash of chocolate," Sophie said.

"Hey, that chocolate is for emergencies!"

"We'd better buy more. I feel more emergencies coming on."

They detoured to the grocery store, where they filled their cart with chips and lunch meat and frozen waffles and anything they considered "guy" food. "They'd better be hungry," Sophie said as she pushed the loaded cart toward their car.

"I just thought of something," Lauren said. "What if they're into health food or something? Maybe they only eat tofu and chicken and salads."

Sophie laughed. "Trust me, Rand will eat his share of junk food—and Marco's share, too, if it comes to that."

"So things seem pretty serious between you two," Lauren said. "Do you think you'll get married?"

"Maybe. We've talked about the future—a little. But neither of us wants to rush into anything."

"Good idea. Maybe if I'd been more cautious, I wouldn't have made such a mistake with Phil."

"You're in a better place now than you were then."

She started to answer, but stopped when she noticed

movement beside their car. A tall, broad-shouldered man dressed in black stepped out from the passenger side of a white van parked beside them. Something about him looked so familiar.

A crushing grip around her torso cut off the thought. She struggled against the man who held her. "Sophie, run!" she screamed, before her assailant's other hand closed over her mouth, silencing her.

Chapter Nine

Lauren clawed at the face of the man who held her, wild with terror. She writhed in his arms and kicked at his shins as hard as she could. He swore and squeezed her tighter, sending pain stabbing through her chest and cutting off her breath until she feared she might black out. On the other side of the car, Sophie struggled with the man Lauren had seen getting out of the van. She rammed the shopping cart into him, then began pulling cans and bottles from the cart and hurling them at him. He ducked and grabbed for her, but she kept the cart between them and screamed at the top of her lungs. "Help! Help! Somebody, help!"

Lauren opened her mouth as wide as she could, then bit down hard on the hand of the man who held her, tasting blood. He yowled and loosened his hold on her, enough that she could free one hand to jab at his eyeball. With another yowl, he released her and she lurched away from him, staggering and gasping for breath.

By this time, Sophie's screams had attracted the attention of other shoppers, who gathered in front of the store. "The police are on their way!" someone shouted.

At this, Sophie's attacker dived back into the van. Lauren's assailant lunged after him, and within seconds they screeched out of the parking lot. Two men and a woman rushed forward to help the sisters, offering water and re-assurance, and helping to gather their scattered groceries. Lauren hugged Sophie, tears streaming down both their faces.

A siren announced the arrival of two police cars. The officers, a man and a woman, approached. After determining that Sophie and Lauren were frightened and a little bruised, but not seriously hurt, they asked what had happened.

"We came out of the store with our groceries and two men attacked us," Sophie said.

"They fought like wildcats," one of the bystanders offered. "It was really something."

"Did you know these men?" the male officer asked. "Had you ever seen them before?"

Lauren shook her head. She was pretty sure the man who'd gone after Sophie had worked for Richard Prentice, but she'd share that information with the Rangers, who were more likely to take her seriously.

"The one who went after Sophie was a big guy, with very short blond hair and a cleft chin," she said. "I never saw the guy who went after me, but they were both in a white van. The kind service companies use, but this one didn't have a name or logo or anything on it."

"The man who attacked my sister looked like a wrestler," Sophie said. "Dark hair, not too tall—maybe five-eight or five-nine?"

"Did either of you see a license plate on the van?" the male officer asked.

Lauren shook her head.

"I took a picture," a woman volunteered. She stepped forward to show her cell phone.

The officer studied it. "Looks as if they've smeared mud on the plate, but send it over and our techs will see if they can make out anything."

The officers interviewed bystanders and the store manager, and took down Sophie's and Lauren's contact information. When Lauren gave her name, the female officer did a double take. "You're that newscaster who had that run-in with Richard Prentice," she said.

Lauren stiffened. "Yes."

The officer had very pale, gray eyes and an open, direct gaze. "For what it's worth, I believed you," she said. "But Prentice's money talks pretty loud around here." She tucked her notebook into her pocket. "But you didn't hear that from me."

The male officer joined them. "Will you ladies be all right getting home or would you like one of us to follow you?" he asked.

Lauren hugged her arms across her chest. "It's up to Sophie. I'm definitely too shaky to drive." Now that the adrenaline had faded, she felt almost too weak to stand, and she ached all over.

"Thank you, but we'll be fine," Sophie said, and turned to Lauren. "I texted Rand, and he and Marco are coming to get us."

MARCO KNEW HE had to tamp down the rage that filled him when Rand told him Lauren and Sophie had been attacked in a supermarket parking lot. The women were all right, so the focus now had to be on making sure they were safe. Later, he'd work on finding out who had targeted them and bringing them to justice. *Stay in control and act deliberately, always aware of what the most important task is at the moment. Never let emotion get in the way of doing your job.* These were the lessons that had helped him excel over the years.

But no training or mental discipline could prepare him for the relief that flooded him when he saw Lauren, shaken but safe, standing in that parking lot. His knees almost buckled when he climbed out of the pickup truck that was Rand's personal vehicle, and he had to stand still for a moment, holding on to the door and trying to recover. The knowledge that she could have been seriously hurt, even killed, shook him to the point he couldn't speak, and he fought the urge to crush her in his arms.

So this was how it's going to be, he told himself, trying to accept this new reality. After years of avoiding caring deeply for anyone, he'd found a woman he quite possibly couldn't live without.

After a few seconds, he recovered enough to join Lauren and the others beside Sophie's car. "Hey," he greeted her. "You okay?"

She nodded, then shook her head. "I've never been so scared in my life."

Pulling her to him was as automatic as breathing. She buried her face against his chest and he smoothed her hair and spoke softly. "It's going to be okay," he said. "You're going to be all right."

"Sophie says the guys who went after them were big, beefy types," Rand said after a moment. "They were in a white van with the tag obscured."

"I recognized one of them." Lauren straightened and brushed her hair back out of her eyes. Her expression was strained, but she looked calm. "The one who attacked Sophie. He worked as a guard for Richard Prentice. His name was Al or Hal or something like that."

"You didn't say anything to the police about that," Sophie said.

"No. I figured the minute I mentioned Richard Prentice they'd discount everything I said. After all, I'm the crazy woman who had such a twisted crush on him that I went to his house and refused to leave. Then, when he didn't return my affections, I accused him of kidnapping me."

"Don't say that." Marco couldn't keep the hardness from his voice. "You're not crazy."

"No, I'm not," she said softly. "But I'm tired of always having to defend myself. I knew if I waited and told you two about the guy, you'd take me seriously."

"A lot of other people saw him," Sophie said. "If we can link him to Prentice, it won't be only your word against his."

"Right now we need to make sure he can't get to you again." One arm still around her, Marco urged her toward Rand's truck.

She halted, stumbling. "Do you think they'll come back?"

"If Prentice sent them to kidnap you again and they failed, they'll try to finish the job," Marco said.

"But we'll make sure they don't," Rand said.

"How are you going to do that?" Lauren asked. "You can't stay with us twenty-four hours a day. And next time they might bring four people instead of two, or even more."

"They were overconfident, attacking you in broad daylight," Rand said.

"They thought we'd be too frightened to fight back," Sophie said.

"They probably won't make that mistake again," Marco said. "But next time we'll be ready."

"What are you going to do?" Lauren asked.

"Right now, we're going back to your apartment and put these groceries away," Rand said. "You can change clothes and get something to eat, then we'll meet with the others at the captain's place. We'll come up with a plan of action there."

"What about my car?" Sophie asked.

"We'll send someone to get it later, and have them park it at a hotel or somewhere in town," Marco said. "That will confuse anyone looking for you."

"Why would Prentice want to kidnap me again?" Lauren asked when they were all in the truck. "He's already persuaded the grand jury not to believe me, and he's made me look like an idiot in the press."

"He must still feel you're a threat." Rand started the truck and headed out of the parking lot.

"You must know something that could incriminate him," Marco said. "Something you haven't revealed yet."

"I've told you and the police everything I know about him," she said. "Why would I hold back anything that could lock him away for good?"

"It would have to be something you don't even realize is important," Marco said. "But something that makes Prentice afraid enough to try to silence you, despite the risks."

"I don't believe he thinks there are any risks," Sophie said. "He's convinced he's invincible."

"People who believe that always end up making mistakes," Marco said.

"*Do* you know some secret about Prentice?" Sophie

asked. "Something he'd kill to keep people from finding out?"

Lauren stared out the window, at the storefronts and apartment complexes and passing traffic. She didn't like to think of that dark time, when she'd been so lonely and afraid. "I really wasn't with him that much," she said after a moment. "He kept me locked away—first in an upstairs bedroom, then in the mine. He would visit in the evenings several times a week. A few times we had dinner together. I tried to get him to talk about himself. I thought if I could figure out what made him tick, I could persuade him to let me go. But he evaded all my questions about his past, his childhood, his businesses— anything remotely personal."

"So what did you talk about?" Rand asked.

She sighed. "He spent most of his time trying to convince me to marry him."

"So he was romantic?" Rand's eyes met hers in the rearview mirror, clearly skeptical.

She made a face. "Not at all. His idea of a proposal was to persuade me of the benefits of marriage to him. I could have any material thing I wanted. He'd use his money and influence to buy me any job I aspired to. With his wealth and power and my beauty and ability to persuade the public, there was no limit to the changes we could make in government and society."

"He really said that?" Sophie asked. "About making changes to government and society?"

Lauren nodded. "I think he had this picture of me, installed as the anchor or host of some news show, reporting his ideas about unrestricted property rights and unregulated business and power for the privileged, and everyone seeing the brilliance of his ideas. He's fanatical enough to believe it could happen."

"So no romance." Was that relief she heard in Marco's voice?

"Not really. A few times he made an attempt to be, I guess you'd call it, 'warmer.'" She sat up straighter, a memory she'd pushed aside popping into her head. "One time he asked me to call him Bruno."

"Bruno?" Sophie laughed. "Where did he get that?"

"He said it could be my pet name for him." Lauren shook her head. "I guess that was his idea of romance."

"And he never tried anything physical?" Marco's voice was strained.

All she could see from her seat in the back of the truck was his neck, black hair neatly trimmed over his sun-bronzed skin. She studied the inch of tawny flesh exposed above his collar as she spoke. "He held my hand a couple of times and once he kissed me, but even the kiss was cold." Just thinking about kisses from Marco made her feel overheated.

"He's crazy." Sophie hugged her arms across her stomach. "And he scares me."

"It's easy to dismiss someone like him as crazy," Marco said. "But he's operating according to some kind of internal logic, no matter how skewed. If we knew what that logic was, what really drives him, we would have a better chance of getting ahead of him and anticipating his next move."

"I had a lot of empty hours to spend trying to figure him out," Lauren said. "As far as I can tell, he believes he should be able to do whatever he wants, but I don't know why he believes that."

"He doesn't want the government telling him what he

can and can't do with his property and his businesses," Rand said.

"Right," Lauren said. "But he doesn't believe that kind of freedom should extend to all people, only to ones like him, who already have money and position."

"Those who have, get more, and everybody else is out of luck," Rand said. "What kind of political philosophy is that?"

"I don't care about his politics," Marco said. "I only want to stop him from breaking the law."

"He's getting careless, attacking the girls in daylight, in a public place," Rand said. "We put more pressure on him, he's going to crack, and that's when we'll get him."

"I hope you're right," Lauren said. She didn't want to live a life where she was scared to step out her door every morning.

"He knows you're stronger than him," Marco said. "That's why he's so desperate to silence you."

She didn't feel strong right now, but Marco's faith in her made her feel supported, as if, with his help, she could be strong again. "We'll stop him," she said. "With all of us fighting together, there's no way he can win."

THE MEETING AT Graham's that evening was like dozens of other meetings the Ranger team had held—everyone coming together to discuss a case and a strategy for solving it. But as Marco followed the others into the captain's living room, nothing felt the same as before. For one thing, they were all in civilian clothing—jeans and khakis and T-shirts or polos. Carmen wore a blouse with flowers, her long hair loose and earrings trimmed in crystals and feathers, reminding him that she was actually a pretty woman, not just a cop.

Women were the other big difference in this meeting. In addition to Carmen, Emma, Abby, Sophie and Lauren had joined them, ready to contribute what they knew about Richard Prentice, and their ideas for making a case against him. No longer was this about just what law enforcement could do. Though none of the Rangers had officially resigned their positions, they had taken temporary leaves or were using up accumulated vacation days in order to pursue this private investigation. If knowledge of their activities came to attention of their superiors, a number of them might very well lose their jobs.

"It feels strange, being here with all of you," Lauren said. She'd kept close to him all afternoon, her warm presence and soft scent reminding him of the biggest reason he was taking such a career risk. "Included, I mean."

"You probably know more about Prentice than anyone," Marco said. "You can help us find his weaknesses."

"I'm not sure he has any of those."

Graham stood before a whiteboard in front of his fireplace. To his right, Simon, who wore black jeans, a black snap-button Western shirt with large red roses and black lizard-skin cowboy boots, prepared to take notes. "The attack on Lauren and Sophie in the grocery store parking lot this afternoon was the rash move of a man who's not secure in his position," Graham said. "He's worried we're going to learn something he doesn't want anyone to know. He thinks Lauren could reveal that something."

"I've gone over everything I can remember about my time at his ranch," Lauren said. "And I don't see anything incriminating. I never heard him talk about anything illegal. I never saw him do anything illegal. I never saw anything in his house that wasn't on display for everyone to see."

"Keep thinking," Graham said. "Maybe it will come to you. Meanwhile, we need to come up with a plan for uncovering everything possible about him."

"We've been over and over his background," Carmen said. "There just isn't a lot there. He was raised in Texas by a father who was a real estate attorney. His mother owned a dance studio. Prentice started out small, taking over failing oil companies and selling off their assets. A surge in oil prices made him a millionaire overnight and he began operating on a larger scale, amassing more money and influence. Some of his business decisions may have been unethical, but he's always operated just inside the law, at least in his business transactions."

"There's got to be something incriminating in his office," Lauren said.

"Why do you say that?" Michael asked from his seat on the couch beside Abby.

"Remember how he was shredding all those papers the night I was rescued?" she said. "But Sophie and Rand chased him away before he'd gotten very far into the cabinet."

"He's been back to the house since," Rand said. "He's had plenty of time to destroy any evidence."

"Maybe not," she said. "Remember, he thinks he's invincible. And he kept those papers for a reason. He wouldn't want to destroy them unless it was absolutely necessary."

"I never understood why people would keep incriminating evidence—in writing—around," Emma said.

"Sometimes it's because they're so sure they'll never be caught," Graham said. "But sometimes it's because they need the evidence to hold over someone else."

"You mean—blackmail?" Emma asked.

"Something like that," Graham said.

"Who would Richard Prentice want to blackmail?" Sophie asked.

"Probably lots of people," Michael said. "But one person I can think of is Senator Mattheson. Maybe there's a reason the senator always dances to Prentice's tune."

"It would be interesting to know what Prentice has on Mattheson," Carmen agreed. "But proving blackmail could be tough."

"We won't know what he's hiding in those filing cabinets until we get a closer look," Rand said.

"So we do what—break in?" Simon asked.

"Yes."

"Which makes anything we find inadmissible in court," Simon said.

"We don't take anything but photographs when we go in," Michael said. "But we find out what's there and we give the information to the local police."

"Who do nothing because Prentice has paid them off," Simon said.

"Then, we give it to the feds." Michael looked to Graham. "The FBI will have to act if we come up with convincing evidence."

Graham nodded. "How are we going to get in to look at the files? Prentice has at least two guards on shift at all times, plus surveillance cameras."

"I could go in."

The room fell silent. Marco couldn't believe what he'd heard. He stared at Lauren. She wore the determined expression he was coming to know well, jaw set, chin up, eyes flashing. He both loved the look and hated it, admiring her boldness yet wanting to protect her from danger. "I could do it," she said. "I could go there and tell him

I want to talk about my feelings for him. He wouldn't refuse me, I'm sure. Once we're together, I could put knockout drops in his drink or something. I could search the file cabinets, and anything I saw would be admissible as evidence, right?"

"It's too dangerous," Marco said, before anyone else could speak.

"I've been there before and he didn't hurt me."

"Are you forgetting the package he sent? The death threat? The attack this afternoon?" His voice rose, and he tried to rein in the emotions that made him want to seize her and hustle her out of the room until she came to her senses.

She swallowed. "I haven't forgotten those things. But this is our best chance to get close to him and get the evidence we need."

"I won't let you do it," he said.

"This isn't your decision to make." Her eyes met his, troubled but determined.

"No, but it's mine," Graham said. "I can't let a civilian take that kind of risk."

She stood, steady on her feet, and faced the ranks of officers and friends who sat around the living room. "Let me do this," she said. "If I don't, I won't be able to walk out my door without worrying about someone attacking me. I won't be able to get a job without some new rumor about my sanity popping up." Her gaze came to rest on Marco, silently asking for understanding. "I know you all have a lot at stake here, and that it's important to make your case. But my life is on the line here—not because I'll be in danger if I go to Richard's ranch, but because I won't have a life worth living if I don't."

He stood and moved beside her. He wanted to wrap

his arms around her and never let her go, to tell her she was brave and foolish and too precious for him to lose. But he didn't touch her. "If you do this, let me go with you," he said.

"Richard would never permit it," she said. "He knows you're with the Rangers. If you show up with me, he'll be instantly suspicious."

"He'll know one Ranger will be no match for all his guards, and he'll be curious enough to want to hear what you have to say to let you in, in spite of my presence."

"He might kill you."

"He could kill you, too." His throat constricted around the words. "Are you afraid?"

"Terrified. But I'm more afraid of sitting here and doing nothing."

He took her hand and squeezed it.

"I'm telling you not to do this," Graham said, with the air of a man choosing his words carefully. "But as of four o'clock this afternoon, I'm not your commanding officer anymore."

"I'm just a rogue agent, acting on my own," Marco said. "I understand."

"I'll provide backup." Rand stood.

"We all will." Michael stood also, and then they were all on their feet, men and women alike. They began talking about the steps they'd need to take, equipment they'd need to acquire, when the best time would be to approach Prentice, how they could keep him off guard.

Lauren squeezed Marco's hand and moved closer. "Thank you," she whispered.

He slid his hand under her hair to caress the back of her neck. "You're either the bravest woman I know, or the craziest," he said.

"I think it's a little of both." She looked up at him. "Is that all right?"

"It's more than all right." He wanted to kiss her, but not now. Not with all these people watching. He'd save that moment for later, when he could show her, without words, all she was coming to mean to him.

Chapter Ten

Lauren felt as if her safety belt was the only thing keeping her from levitating in her seat. Nervous energy jittered through her, making her hyperaware of everything around her—the brilliant gold and purple of wildflowers on the side of the road, the smoothness of the leather seat against her bare arm, the subtle spice-and-soap scent of Marco in the driver's seat, the way the muscles of his forearm bunched as he gripped the steering wheel.

Was this nerves or the beginning of a manic episode? She'd taken her medication, done her breathing exercises, sent up prayers. How did so-called normal people—people without this anomaly in their brains or chemical imbalance or whatever you wanted to call it—act in a bizarre situation like this? She had no idea. All she could do was trust her own instincts—and the man beside her—and hope they didn't lead her astray.

"How are you doing?" Marco asked.

She smoothed her hands down her thighs, trying to dry her sweating palms. "I'll be okay," she said. She plucked a loose thread from the fabric. She'd chosen the outfit carefully, opting for a short skirt instead of slacks, hoping to tempt Prentice with a little sexiness, but selecting flat sandals instead of heels in case she had to run.

She fought the urge to laugh, afraid if she started she'd be that much closer to hysteria. Who would have thought she'd ever be debating fashion choices for becoming a potential hostage—or murder victim?

Marco turned his Jeep into the gravel drive that crossed Prentice's ranch and stopped at the gate. A guard emerged from the stone guardhouse and Lauren gasped.

"Something wrong?" Marco asked.

She shook her head. "I know him. His name is Henry." He'd been one of the nicer men who'd guarded her, polite and respectful, unlike the men who'd tried to grope her or treated her with disdain.

"This is private property," Henry said as soon as Marco lowered the driver's side window. "You need to turn around."

"Hello, Henry." Lauren leaned forward so he could get a good look at her. "I need to talk to Richard."

He blinked, clearly thrown off guard, but he recovered quickly. "Hello, Ms. Starling. Do you have an appointment?"

"No, but I think he'll want to see me, don't you?" She gave him her brightest smile, the one she used for pageants and other public appearances. The one that had graced billboards and even the sides of buses all over Denver when she'd been the star of Metro News.

Henry shifted his gaze to Marco. "What's he doing here?"

"Richard has his bodyguards. I decided I needed one, too." She'd lobbied for this frank approach, sure Prentice would see through a lie.

"Wait here." He stepped inside the guardhouse and pulled out his phone.

"He's not going to like my being here," Marco said, keeping his voice low.

"No, but Richard is very big on cost-benefit analysis. The cost of having you along won't outweigh the benefit of seeing me." She was hoping that was true, anyway. If Richard was the one behind the attacks on her, he wouldn't pass up the opportunity to have her where he would think he could easily control her.

Henry returned. "Step out of the car, sir," he ordered. "I need to search you."

Marco stood with arms outstretched and allowed Henry to frisk him. The guard stopped at Marco's ankle, pulled up the leg of his jeans and extracted a small pistol from the holster there. Lauren felt faint; she hadn't even known Marco was armed. "You can pick this up on your way out," Henry said. "Mr. Prentice doesn't allow weapons in the house. I'll also need your phone." He turned to Lauren. "Yours, too, Ms. Starling."

"My phone?" She clutched at her purse, which contained her smartphone.

"New rules." The guard held out his hand. "All visitors must surrender their phones. I'll return it to you when you leave."

She sent a panicked look to Marco. Having a gun wouldn't have made her feel safer, but being without her phone meant being completely cut off from the outside world.

Marco pulled his own phone from his pocket and handed it to the guard. Hand shaking, she did the same.

"Why did they take our phones?" she whispered when Marco rejoined her in the car.

"Another way for Prentice to remind us he's in charge."

She glanced at the guard, who'd carried their phones

and Marco's pistol into the stone guardhouse. "What were you going to do with that gun?" she asked.

"Whatever I had to." He put the Jeep in gear and they followed a second guard down the drive and up to the fake castle Prentice called home.

"He told me this place was designed to look like a famous castle in Germany," she said.

"So he made it this ugly on purpose."

Another guard met them at the front door and escorted them to the library. Marco studied the bookshelves. "Do you think he ever reads any of these?" he asked. "Or are they just for show?"

"I think he told me he likes to read history."

"So you are remembering more things he told you?"

"Yes, but nothing significant, only trivia."

The door opened and Prentice entered. He was dressed casually, for him, a sport coat replacing his usual suit jacket, his shirt open at the collar, with no tie. "Lauren, dear, how lovely to see you." He kissed her cheek and squeezed her arm—too hard, but she forced herself not to flinch, or to show any reaction to him but pleasure.

"It's good to see you, too, Richard," she lied.

He ignored Marco, not even glancing in his direction, and led Lauren to a sofa by the cold fireplace. He sat, pulling her down beside him. "I knew you'd be back," he said.

"You did?"

"Of course. I knew you'd realize we're meant to be together."

She couldn't decide if he really believed this, or if he was saying it to get a rise out of Marco, who had followed them across the room and sat opposite them, stone-faced.

"This is my friend Marco," she said. "I don't know if you two have met."

"I know all about the Ranger." His tone was dismissive. "What can I do for you?"

"I'd love something to drink," she said. "Maybe some coffee?" She had knockout drops in a vial tucked into her sleeve—like some movie spy. Carmen had assured her they were potent enough to down a linebacker.

"Certainly." He picked up the phone on the table beside the sofa. "Please bring Ms. Starling a cup of coffee. One sugar, no cream."

"Aren't you going to join me?" she asked.

"No." Again the dismissive tone.

What now? She had to get Richard out of the way so that she could search his office, down the hall.

"What did you want to talk to me about?" he asked.

Right. They had to talk. The Rangers had drilled her on what they thought she should say to him—meaningless small talk that amounted to verbal stalling. But she decided to take another approach. "I was very hurt by the things you said about me in the papers," she told him.

He sat back, one arm stretched along the top of the sofa, just behind her head. "What things?"

"That I'm crazy. That I'm a liar."

A man arrived with her coffee, and they fell silent until they were alone once more.

"Now, Lauren, I never called you a liar," Richard chided. "I merely felt you gave the press and police an unfair picture of our relationship."

The man really was delusional. "Richard, you kept me a prisoner." Marco stared at her, clearly warning her to be more cautious, but she'd set aside all caution when she agreed to come here. She might as well try to find out what Prentice was thinking.

"I was keeping you safe," Richard said. "When you came to me, I was concerned you might hurt yourself. You needed someone to look after you."

"I'm an adult. I'm fully capable of looking after myself." She picked up the coffee cup, wanting something to do with her hands, to hide her growing agitation, but then she set it down again. She didn't trust Richard not to have put something in the drink.

"Are you really capable of taking care of yourself?" Richard asked. "Then, why did you bring him along?" He glared at Marco, who returned the angry look.

"I brought him because the last time I came here alone, you wouldn't let me leave," she said.

"You were free to go anytime you wanted," he said. "All you had to do was ask."

"I asked." Repeatedly. She'd also tried demanding, crying, running away and fighting. Each time he'd had her restrained, carried away and locked in a room.

He smiled an oily, patronizing look. "You didn't ask," he said. "You begged to stay."

She opened her mouth to argue with him, but the slight shake of Marco's head caught her attention. Right. Don't argue. Go along with him. "I'm trying to rebuild my reputation now," she said. "I'm hoping you can help."

"I've always tried to help you before," he said. "But if we're going to talk about hurt feelings, I'm wounded that you feel you need protection from me."

She leaned toward him. She was taking a lot of risks coming here today; why not take one more? "I had to bring Marco because someone is trying to hurt me," she said. "My car was tampered with, and yesterday I was attacked by two men in the parking lot of a grocery store."

He furrowed his brow, the picture of concern. "That is worrying. But are you sure it was an attack? Maybe they were merely fans who wanted your autograph."

"They were not fans, and they didn't ask for autographs."

"Why would someone attack you?" he asked.

"You tell me. Did you have anything to do with those attacks?"

His expression remained as impassive as ever, not even a glimmer of guilt or concern in his eyes. "I imagine a woman like you would have made many enemies in your life," he said.

"A woman like me?" The way he said the words made the hair stand up at the back of her neck.

"You're beautiful, but unreliable." He moved his hand to cradle the back of her head. "Prone to irrational behavior."

The only thing irrational about her now was the fear that gripped her at his touch. She bit the inside of her cheek to keep from screaming as he rubbed his thumb back and forth across the side of her neck. Across from them, Marco stiffened and leaned forward as if ready to spring up.

"If I'm so irrational, then what do you see in me?" she asked. "How would I ever fit into your life?"

"That would be the beauty of our alliance." He continued stroking, and slid closer, his thigh touching hers. "I could rebuild your reputation. Money and power are transformative. It no longer matters what you did or who you were. All that is important is who people think you are. Build the right image and you can do anything."

"That's what you've done for yourself," she said. "You've built an image, and now you think you can do anything."

"I *can* do anything." His fingers closed around her neck, hard enough that she cried out.

"Let go!" she cried. "You're hurting me."

"Sometimes we hurt the ones we love," he said, increasing the pressure of his fingers.

Her heart pounded painfully and she had trouble breathing. She clawed at him, but he leaned over her, holding her down with surprising force. "Marco!" she cried.

"He can't save you now," Prentice growled. "Don't come any closer, Ranger, or I'll kill her." His hand tightened even more around her neck and her vision clouded. Was he trying to choke her, or to break her neck? She beat her fists against him with no effect. And she was growing weaker...

A weight crushed her, squeezing breath and life from her. Above her, Prentice struggled with someone. Marco? She fought to remain conscious and was dimly aware of the two men grappling on top of her.

Then the pressure released and a strong hand grasped hers and pulled her up. "Come on," Marco said. "We've got to get to the study before the guards show up."

THEY LEFT PRENTICE lying in a heap on the library floor. Not dead, but knocked out from the blow Marco had landed on his chin. "Wh-what happened?" Lauren asked as she stumbled from the room after Marco. "What about Richard?"

"He's out for now. He's lucky I didn't tear him in two."

The sight of the billionaire's hands on her had filled him with rage.

"He was going to kill me," she said, half sobbing now. "Right there in front of you."

"He was arrogant enough to think so," Marco said. "But I never would have let it happen." He pulled her up beside him and put his arm around her. "You're safe now. Come on. We have to get to work."

The door to Prentice's office stood open. Clearly, he felt secure in his own home. "You look through the filing cabinet. I'll search the desk," Marco said.

Though Prentice could have afforded the sleekest designer furnishings, he chose to work at an old-fashioned wooden desk, the top easily five feet across, the mahogany finish scarred and worn. Marco rifled through the drawers, passing over the office supplies, peppermints and scattered sticky notes with cryptic messages: "Talk to JR about Wednesday." He pocketed a few of these, then turned his attention to the file drawer at the lower right-hand side of the desk. It contained stacks of neatly folded blueprints and land surveys, along with brochures for developments he assumed Prentice had an interest in.

"There's just files with names of companies he owns or has an interest in," Lauren said. She stood before the filing cabinet, the top drawer open.

"Don't bother reading through things," he said. "Take anything of interest."

He stood back and studied the desk. Why would a man like Prentice, whose house was furnished in either fine antiques or the latest styles, opt for a desk that looked better suited for the junkyard?

He knelt and began feeling along the underside and backs of all the drawers. Sure enough, behind the top left-hand drawer he felt an indentation, and a hidden spring. When he pressed it, a small wooden box dropped into his hand.

He moved into the light to examine the contents of the hidden compartment. A man in a military uniform stared up at him, from a black-and-white photo as worn and faded with age as the desk. The man in the picture had removed his cap and wore his hair slicked down and parted sharply on one side, a thin moustache above his tightly compressed lips. Why would Prentice hide this? He tucked it into his shirt.

"I may have something." Lauren ran to him, a slip of paper in her hand.

He examined the three numbers written on the paper: 96-14-6. "Is it a date? June 14, 1996?" he asked.

"I think it's a combination," she said. "Maybe for a safe?"

"Then we need to find the safe."

He opened the closet and found nothing but an over-coat and a set of golf clubs. Judging by the dust that covered them, Prentice hadn't played in a while. "I've found it!" Lauren called.

She'd removed a picture above a credenza on the back wall of the office to reveal the slightly recessed door of a safe. "Hurry and open it," he said.

While she spun the dial, he moved to the door and listened. No sign of the guards yet, but he was sure it was only a matter of time before they showed up. Too bad that desk hadn't contained a gun. He looked around for a weapon and had to settle for a letter opener. It looked flimsy and would be no match for the automatic weapons the guards usually carried.

"It's open," Lauren called, and he rejoined her in front

of the safe. She reached in and pulled out handfuls of paper and gave him half.

"These look like deeds to property," she said as she flipped through her stack of documents.

"Mine, too," he said. He stopped at one yellowed square of paper. "And Richard Prentice's birth certificate. And a passport." That would prove interesting reading later.

"Did you hear something?" She looked toward the door, all color draining from her face. A sound like a slamming door, then the pounding of running feet echoed along the hallway.

"We have to get out of here." Marco stuffed his pockets with the passport and other papers. Lauren did the same with her handful of documents.

"Which way do we go?" she asked.

"This way." He took her hand and pulled her toward the room's only window. But when he yanked on the sash, it wouldn't budge. He felt along the frame for a locking mechanism.

"Maybe it's nailed shut," she said.

The footsteps in the hallway drew closer, and now they could hear shouting. "Search the house! Don't let them get away!"

"Stand back," Marco said, and picked up the heavy, rolling chair from behind the desk. He heaved it through the window, the frame shattering and glass exploding with the impact. An alarm began to wail, the deafening Klaxon shrieking right above their heads. A guard burst into the room and gunfire splintered the wood beside Marco's head.

"Come on!" he yelled, and shoved Lauren in front of him out the window, then dived after her in a shower of glass and splinters and flying bullets.

Chapter Eleven

Instincts honed from years of training kicked in as Marco turned to face the two guards who appeared at the window. He had to buy time for Lauren to get out of range of their guns, but he had no weapon of his own.

Correct that—he had no firearm. But he had a quick mind and an agile body, two powerful weapons he could use to his advantage against foes who were certain of the superiority provided by all their hardware.

He dived to one side, out of sight of the guards. "Run!" he urged Lauren. "As fast and as far as you can."

"But I can't leave you," she protested, her face contorted with anxiety.

"I'll catch up with you, I promise. Go!"

She hesitated only a moment more before turning and racing away, her feet pounding over the rough ground. The guards began firing after her, bullets striking the ground with small thuds, little volcano eruptions of dirt marking the spot where each one hit.

One of the guards leaned out of the window, bracing his weapon against the frame for a steadier shot. Marco scooped a rock from the ground at his feet and fired it, a ninety-mile-per-hour fastball to the side of the man's head. It struck with all the force of a missile, dropping the guard to his knees, blood trickling down the side of his head.

The second guard turned and located Marco, aiming point-blank. No way would he miss at this close range. Marco dived sideways and rolled, the bullet whistling past him. He sprang to his feet and ran, dodging and weaving, presenting as difficult a target as possible. He raced toward the sun, forcing the shooter to aim into the glare, and he wove behind piles of boulders and the gnarled trunks of piñons whenever possible. The guard's fire became less and less accurate, until Marco was out of range. He began looking for Lauren.

"Marco! Over here!"

He stopped, and turned to look behind him. She was crouched in the narrow space between a group of scrubby post oak trees and a rounded gray boulder, its surface painted with green, yellow and red lichen. The deep shadows of her hiding place almost completely hid her from view, though as Marco approached, she emerged farther, sunlight gilding her pale blond hair.

"Are you all right?" he asked as he drew nearer.

"Terrified, but I'll be okay. What about you?" She swept her gaze over him, brow knitted.

"I'm good." Better than good. If not for the danger to her, he might have exulted in this feeling of power and strength. The past weeks of the necessary tedium of an investigation had left him feeling dull and slow. Their encounter with the guards had sharpened his senses and summoned all the warrior skills around which he'd shaped his life.

He took her arm and helped her the rest of the way out of her hiding place. "We have to keep moving," he said. "They'll be looking for us."

"Moving where?" she asked, even as she hurried to keep up with the brisk pace he set.

"We need to get to the road. From there we can get to town, or flag down someone with a phone who can help us."

"Which way is the road?"

The landscape around them provided no landmarks, only miles of sun-parched grasses and stunted trees, rocky boulders and the distant green line that marked the canyon, and beyond that the snowcapped peaks of the mountains. "The road is that direction." Marco pointed toward the southwest. "If we keep the sun at our backs, we'll be fine."

"I guess this is the kind of thing they teach in Special Forces," she said as they corrected their course to head east.

"Boy Scouts."

She laughed. "You never struck me as the Boy Scout type."

"A church came into the projects when I was nine and started up a troop. I spent two weeks at camp that summer, learning all about trail finding and stuff. But the next year I guess the church decided it wasn't worth it or they couldn't get volunteers or something. They didn't come back."

"But you liked it? The trail finding and stuff?"

"Yeah." He'd felt at home in the wilderness, in a way he never had on the streets of East LA. He didn't have to play the tough-guy role or play up to people he didn't like, or be afraid when he was on his own in the wild. He could rely on himself and his own skills out there, in a way he'd seldom been able to rely on other people.

He took Lauren's hand. "It's going to be all right," he said. "I know what I'm doing out here."

"I know you do." She squeezed his fingers. "That's why I'm not nearly as afraid as I would be if I was by myself."

"You'd do okay," he said. "You're a survivor."

She laughed again, a more derisive sound this time. "I don't know how you can say that. You haven't exactly seen me at my best."

"You survived six weeks as Prentice's prisoner. You didn't let that defeat you. And you haven't let bipolar disorder defeat you."

"Okay, so I guess I am mentally pretty strong. But that doesn't mean I have the know-how or physical strength to survive out here."

"Well, you don't have to worry. I'll be strong for both of us."

She smiled and leaned into him, in a kind of half hug that made him feel ten feet tall and invincible, but also more vulnerable than he had since he was a small boy. But being vulnerable didn't frighten him when he was with her. Not anymore. He guessed that meant he'd learned to trust her—to trust what he could be with her.

He looked around at the open, roadless prairie. The Jeeps Prentice's guards used could easily travel across country, and in this terrain two people on foot would be visible from a long way off. "We need to find cover," he said. "A draw or creek bed or somewhere we can travel without being so visible." He pointed toward a line of trees about a quarter mile to the north. "Let's try there."

Her sandals, though flat, weren't made for travel in this rough country, not like his hiking boots. But she kept going, grim faced and limping at times. He pretended not to notice. No need to make her feel she was less in his eyes, especially since the opposite was true. He admired her determination more with each step.

Years of runoff from spring snowmelt had cut a narrow ravine through the landscape, choked with scrub oak and tough grasses. The red-brown dirt crumbled as they half slid, half climbed into the depression. Marco put his arm around Lauren's waist to steady her and she leaned into him, breathing heavily. "Do you really think they won't see us here?" she asked.

"We'll be less visible here than in the open." He took her hand and led her through the maze of brush, over rocks and around clumps of cactus. They hadn't traveled more than a few hundred yards when a low, mechanical whine cut the desert silence.

Lauren froze, head up, alert. "Someone's coming," she whispered.

He nodded. The noise grew more distinct—the rumble of an engine in low gear and the popping of tires on gravel. "Just one vehicle, I think," he said. "Headed this way."

"Can they see us?" She looked around at the stunted trees and grasses closing in on all sides.

"They might have seen us headed this way," he said. They probably had; why else would the Jeep head so deliberately in that direction? "But they won't have known where we disappeared to." At least, they wouldn't unless they knew the country very well. He doubted the kind of muscle Prentice favored had spent much of their free time exploring the backcountry wilderness, and their regular duties kept them close to Prentice's mansion. He took Lauren's hand again. "Let's find a place where we can keep an eye on them."

He led the way along the bottom of the ravine until he spotted a side channel cutting the bank, a dense knot of wild plum trees anchoring the spot. They climbed the bank and settled among the close trunks of the plums. He would have liked a pair of binoculars, but even without them he could see the Jeep, a cloud of dust marking its approach.

As it drew nearer, he identified two guards. The man in the passenger seat held a semiautomatic rifle, the stock balanced on his thigh, the barrel pointed upward. He wondered if the man's orders were to bring them in alive—or to shoot them and leave their bodies for the coyotes and other wild animals to scatter.

Lauren pressed up against his back, looking over his shoulder, her mouth next to his ear. "Do you think they see us?" she whispered.

Her warm breath tickled his ear, and when he breathed in he smelled the floral-spice aroma of her perfume, underlaid with the scent of feminine sweat and the sage leaves crushed beneath their feet. Every nerve in his body responded to the feel of her against him—the curve of her breasts pressed against his back, her hip bone against the back of his thigh, her warmth seeping into him. He reached back to caress her side. "They can't see us," he said softly. "They won't see us." But if they did, if they got out of the Jeep and came toward them, he would fight with everything he had to protect her.

The Jeep reached the edge of the ravine and stopped, a few hundred yards south of their hiding spot, at about the place where they'd descended into the depression. The guard in the driver's seat scanned the area with a pair of binoculars, skimming over the grouping of plum trees with no hesitation. He thought Lauren had stopped breathing, her heart hammering against him.

The driver lowered the binoculars and put the Jeep into gear once more and drove on, past their hiding spot, until only a diminishing trail of white dust marked its path.

Lauren sagged against him, her face pressed against his back. "I was so scared," she whispered. He felt her fear as much as heard it in her voice. She trembled against him, and he wondered how close she was to breaking down. She'd been through so much. How long before it all became too much for her to take?

He turned and gathered her close, pulling her tight against him. She wrapped her arms around him and returned the embrace, and when she raised her head to look at him, he didn't hesitate, but kissed her.

LAUREN DIDN'T KNOW how much she'd wanted that kiss until Marco's lips covered hers. She wanted it the way famished people want food or thirsty travelers need water. That kiss reminded her of things that were more important than Prentice and his guards, reasons she would keep going, better things to come on the other side of the terror and worry and fear.

His lips caressed hers, soft but firm, as his hands smoothed along the sides of her body, holding her steady, reassuring her that he appreciated everything he touched. He adjusted the angle of his head and ran his tongue across the seam of her lips, and she opened to him, eager to taste, to give of herself more fully. She arched to him, the hard planes of his chest sending a thrill through her, reminding her of his strength, of the power of his masculinity. She clutched at his back, wanting to be nearer still, to lose herself in the moment.

He pulled away gently, keeping his arms around her, his gaze fixed on her. She blinked up at him, a little dazed, and struggled to regain her composure. Doubt swept in to replace the confidence with which she'd welcomed his embrace. "Were you just trying to take my mind off my fear?" she asked.

"I wanted to kiss you." He brushed her hair back from her forehead, a tender gesture that sent a new surge of desire through her. "I've been wanting to kiss you for a while."

She wanted to answer him with another kiss, but told herself she shouldn't get carried away in the moment. She needed to play it cool until she was more sure of him, sure of them. "And you thought now was an appropriate time?"

Amusement danced in his eyes and tugged the corners of his mouth upward, almost into a smile. "Sometimes it's good to listen to your instincts."

"I like your instincts." She smoothed her hands up his chest to his shoulders, savoring the attraction, drawing out the moment.

But instead of another kiss, he stepped back and released his hold on her. "If we were somewhere else, somewhere more comfortable, safer, I'd like to continue this conversation, but we need to move on before those two come back."

The fear surged forward again, but not as overwhelming this time, diminished by the strength of these feelings between them—feelings she was in no hurry to try to define. "What do we do now?" she asked. "I mean, about getting away."

"We keep going." He nodded ahead of them, indicating the trail through the narrow ravine.

"Aren't we traveling away from the road?"

"For now. If the ravine doesn't curve east soon, we'll look for another route. It's more important to stay out of sight of the searchers."

She fell into step behind him, content to let him choose the path through the choking brush that scratched her bare legs and caught at her sandals. "Richard is probably furious," she said after a while.

"Good. Emotional people are more apt to make mistakes in judgment."

Was he saying that their own judgment might be clouded by the emotions they felt for each other? With his back to her, she couldn't gauge his meaning by the expression on his face. Not that Mr. Inscrutable ever gave her many clues as to what was going on in his head or his heart. "Did they teach you that in Special Forces?" she asked.

"Yes."

"So soldiers aren't supposed to have emotions."

"You learn to sublimate them. To set them aside until a more appropriate time to process them."

"What if an appropriate time never comes?"

"Then, you end up with things you haven't dealt with."

"Do you have things you haven't dealt with?"

"Yes."

She hadn't expected this frankness from a man who was so skilled at remaining cool and somehow outside every fray. The knowledge that he trusted her with even this small confession of weakness moved her. "Maybe you'll tell me sometime," she said.

He stepped over a log, the remains of an ancient

lightning-scarred tree, and turned to help her over, as well. But he didn't release her hand right away. Instead, he squeezed her fingers. "Maybe I will."

She smiled to herself as he turned to lead the way once more and she felt stronger and more confident as they traveled in silence for another half mile or so, when the ravine turned east, and so did they. She let her thoughts drift, content to follow Marco and not think too much about where they were headed or why. As long as he was in charge, everything was all right. Prentice had money and manpower, but Marco had brains and skills.

And she had Marco. For now, that seemed more than enough.

He put out a hand to stop her. She stumbled a little and he caught her. "What is it?" she asked. "Is something wrong?"

"There's water up ahead. It's just a puddle, but it will help us keep going."

At the mention of water, she let out a low moan. She'd been trying not to think about how thirsty she was. She looked around him at the muddy puddle about two feet across, the water the color of milk chocolate. She tried to swallow. "We're going to drink that?"

"We'll strain it first." He reached up and tugged at his sleeve until it tore. Pulling harder, he ripped the fabric at the seams, then knelt beside the puddle. "It would be better if we had some kind of container, but we may have to soak the cloth in the water, then squeeze it into our mouths. It might taste a little muddy, but it should be all right."

She nodded, telling herself she shouldn't be squeamish. This wasn't about taste or hygiene—they were trying to stay alive.

She started to step back to give him more room to work when movement out of the corner of her eye made her freeze. The ground just to her right undulated, then what had at first appeared to be a smear of mud and dried leaves shifted and became the coil of a snake. She gasped and made a choking noise, incoherent with fear.

"What is it?" Marco, still kneeling beside the puddle, looked over his shoulder at her. He glanced at her face, then followed her horrified gaze toward the ground.

The snake raised its head, weaving slightly, tongue flickering, menace in every movement. Its tail vibrated, a castanet clatter of warning. "Is that—?" Lauren couldn't finish the sentence.

"A rattlesnake," Marco said.

Chapter Twelve

Marco stared at the snake, the mottled brown-and-tan coils seeming to emerge from the earth like a mythological beast, born of mud and rotting matter and menace. He tried to swallow, dry mouthed, and struggled to breathe evenly through his nose, to slow his racing heart. He was smart enough to be afraid of many things— enemies with guns, for instance. But some fears went beyond rationality to something more innate and primitive. Chief among these was the fear of snakes. No matter that Michael Dance had assured them that the native prairie rattlers found in the park were much less lethal than their cousins to the south and west—a rattlesnake was a rattlesnake, venomous and terrifying.

All this time he'd been so focused on Richard Prentice and his men, he'd forgotten that they weren't the only enemies he and Lauren had to worry about out here in the wilderness.

The snake flicked its tongue and coiled tighter, ready to strike. Lauren's calf was in striking distance. She stared at the viper, mesmerized, her face drained of color. Marco searched the ground for a rock or a stout stick to use as a weapon, but found nothing.

A memory came to him of a television show he and

Rand had watched one evening about snake hunters in the Amazon, who had killed venomous snakes with their bare hands. He and Rand had joked that they preferred using a pistol, but he didn't have a pistol now. Time to try the snake hunters' method, but he'd only have one chance.

He pulled his key ring from his pocket and tossed it so that it landed about a foot to the snake's right. At the metallic chink on the rocks, the snake swiveled its head away from Lauren. Marco lunged and grabbed the snake by the tail. It was like picking up a heavy garden hose, one pulsing with flowing water. Lauren screamed as he whipped the snake into the trunk of the nearest tree. He released it and jumped back, then stood, breathing hard and staring at the limp body of the predator.

"Is it dead?" Lauren asked from behind him.

"It's not after us anymore," he said. "That's all that matters."

She moved into his arms and rested her head on his shoulder. "I don't think I've ever been so terrified," she said. "It was worse than facing Prentice and his guards, or those men in the parking lot who tried to kidnap me and Sophie."

"There's something about snakes," he said, rubbing his hand up and down her back. The contact calmed him, too. "I think it's a primitive fear, hardwired into our DNA."

She raised her head to study him. "I didn't think you were afraid of anything."

"I'm a man, not a robot."

She smiled. "Good to hear you admit it."

He started to ask what she meant by that, then thought

better of it. He'd spent years learning to hide his feelings from others. Maybe he'd gotten a little too proficient at that particular skill.

Cautious, keeping a look out for more predators, they knelt and drank from the muddy water, straining it through Marco's shirt. It wasn't very refreshing, but it would keep them going a little while longer.

They moved on, making a wide berth around the inert snake, and resumed their trek toward the road. The water had revived them, and maybe the promise of safety soon added energy and purpose to their steps. They'd been traveling an hour or so when the sound of a car made them stop once more. Marco listened, then said, "It's traveling faster. I think we're near the road."

LAUREN'S HEARTBEAT SPED up at his words, hope forming a knot in her throat. The road meant safety and eventual rescue. They began walking again, faster. If the rough terrain would have allowed it, she would have broken into a run.

Another hundred yards along, she saw a bridge up ahead where a paved road crossed over the ravine, which widened and flattened, its sides mostly cleared of vegetation. She started toward this clearing, but Marco pulled her back. "Wait," he said.

Forcing herself to keep still, she waited. Half a minute passed, and then she heard a vehicle approaching. When the familiar Jeep appeared, she stifled a groan. She waited for the vehicle to pass before she whispered, "They're still looking for us."

"They won't give up," he said. "Not until they have to. There's too much at stake."

There was too much at stake for her and Marco if Prentice's men found them, too. She started to ask him if he had a plan B when yet another vehicle approached. This proved to also be a Jeep with two burly men in camouflage fatigues. Five minutes later, a third Jeep passed.

"I didn't know Prentice had that many guards," she said, the whine of the third Jeep's engine fading in the distance.

"He probably called in extra manpower."

"What are we going to do?"

"They're never all in the same area at once. We can time them, find a window of opportunity when we can evade them."

He made it sound so logical. So easy. "We can do that?"

He nodded. "But it will be better if we wait until dark. That will make it easier."

The thought of waiting here, in the heat and dust and cacti, for several more hours until evening made her feel almost too tired to stand. She took his hand again, drawing strength from his calm assurance. "Where do we wait?"

He led her back down the draw, to a place where erosion had undercut the bank of the ravine to form a shaded hollow. He sat and she settled beside him, his arm around her shoulder. She tried to ignore the rock digging into the small of her back, or the thirst that made her lips feel swollen. "I'm still trying to picture you as a Boy Scout," she said.

"We didn't have uniforms or anything. Not really. I think I had one of those little scarf things."

"A kerchief?" She smiled at this image of him as a ragtag little boy in a yellow Scouting neck cloth.

"Were you a Girl Scout?" he asked.

"Oh, no. Girl Scouts weren't cool, and I was always cool."

"I'll bet you were always the most popular girl. And the prettiest one."

"I was. Does that sound terribly vain?" She shook her head ruefully. "I was awful. Selfish. I sometimes wonder if all the bad stuff that has happened as an adult is because I was so terrible and insensitive when I was growing up."

"You were a kid. Kids act out. Sometimes they're insensitive. Besides, I don't believe in that stuff."

"In what stuff?"

"Karma, or whatever you want to call it. We don't get what we deserve in life. If that was true, then little kids would never die of cancer and men like Prentice wouldn't be rich and powerful." He squeezed her shoulder. "You can't change what you did before, so don't beat yourself up over it."

"You're right. So instead of moaning about the past, let's think about the future. Do you think there's anything useful in those papers we took from Richard's study?"

"Why don't we take a look and see?" He shifted and pulled a sheaf of papers from inside his shirt. She withdrew her own collection of documents from her pockets and they spread the papers on the dirt in front of them: a picture, a birth certificate, a passport and what looked like deeds.

She picked up the picture and studied it. "This looks old," she said. The photograph was black-and-white, with a narrow white border all around. The man in it stared sternly ahead, his hair slicked to his scalp, his moustache two smudges above his thin upper lip. "Maybe from the 1940s. That could be a military uniform he's wearing."

"There's writing on the back," Marco said. "What does it say?"

She flipped the picture over. The ink was faded to a pale blue, the looping letters indecipherable. "I don't think it's English," she said. "I can't make it out. Except the name. Bruno Adel." She frowned. "Bruno was the name Richard asked me to call him, but this clearly isn't him."

"Maybe it's a relative," Marco said. He picked up the passport and flipped through it. "He made a lot of trips to Venezuela."

"That's because he was dating a model there. The ambassador's daughter."

"These stamps go back almost ten years. I don't think they would have been dating that long."

"I doubt it. I don't think she was that old."

He tapped the passport against his palm. "So maybe he had another reason for going there so often."

"Maybe he has a business there? He supposedly has property all over the world."

They turned their attention to the deeds. She shuffled through the half dozen pieces of paper, then handed them to Marco. "Nothing here looks familiar to me," she said. "And there are just addresses, not names."

Marco held out one of the deeds. "This one. I think the address is for a house in Denver where a bunch of illegal immigrants were held. I think I remember it from the court documents. And there's another address in Denver—that could be a house we busted as the center of a sex trafficking ring."

"So those are things that could help you make a case against Richard?"

"Maybe." He scanned the papers again. "The deeds are in the name of RP Holdings, Inc."

"Richard Prentice Holdings?"

"Or he might say these businesses have nothing to do with him."

"Then, why was he keeping these papers in his safe?"

"We've already seen how good he is at explaining away evidence." Marco laid the papers back on the pile in front of them. "Good enough to persuade the grand jury."

"But he never appeared before the grand jury," she said. "That isn't allowed."

"He didn't have to testify himself. He used his influence and money behind the scenes to shape the testimonies of the experts who did testify." Marco looked scornful. "Of course, we'll never prove it, but I'm sure that's what happened."

"Then, what we need is something that will undermine his credibility," she said. "The way he's tried to undermine mine." If only Prentice had a history of mental illness, or a criminal record, or anything that would make him look like the lowlife he really was.

Marco folded the papers and tucked them back in his shirt. "Try not to worry about it now. Get some rest. You want to be alert when we make a break for it tonight."

"Will you rest, too?" she asked.

He pulled her down so that she reclined against him, her head nestled in the hollow of his shoulder. "I'll keep watch," he said. "I won't let anything happen to you."

It was absurd, she thought as she closed her eyes, to believe that one man could keep a half a dozen or more guards with guns at bay, that he could stop a murderer who wanted them both dead. But Marco made her believe that she could trust him with anything—with her life. Even with her heart.

MARCO HAD BEEN determined not to fall asleep, but as he'd admitted to Lauren, he was a man, not a robot, and the miles they'd walked, coupled with the stress of the day, had produced a weariness that pulled him under. Hidden in the trees, lulled by the vast silence and drugging heat of late afternoon, he'd slept fitfully, troubled by dreams of giant rattlesnakes and an old drill sergeant, who taunted him that he didn't have what it took to survive.

He woke with a start, the sergeant's mocking words still echoing in his ears. Gray light suffused the air around them, turning the distant trees to charcoal smudges against a washed-out paper sky. He checked his watch—almost eight o'clock.

Lauren rested heavily against his shoulder, her breathing deep and even. He buried his face in her hair and inhaled deeply of her floral and spice scent. She made him feel more vulnerable than he ever had, yet at the same time stronger. A man who had spent his life avoiding complications, he welcomed the challenges she brought to his life. She made him think beyond the next day or the next week, to what the future might look like with her in it.

She stirred and he pushed away his musings. Time to focus on the plan for right now. She opened her eyes and looked up at him, then smiled. "Does this mean the wonderful dream I was having is real?" she asked.

"What was the dream?"

Her smile widened. "It involved a big feather bed and you and me—naked."

Arousal stirred at the image her words painted. He indulged himself with a kiss—a long, slow, lingering caress of mouths and tongues that left him painfully erect and fighting the urge to take her there on the hard ground. "We'll have to see about making that dream come true later," he said.

"Promise?"

He never made promises. If you avoided them, you never had to worry about disappointing others. "How are you doing?" he asked.

"Apart from being hungry, thirsty and tired, I'm okay."

He continued to study her, his gaze almost too intense. She shifted, half turning away from him. "What? Why are you looking at me that way?"

"How long before your medication wears off?" he said. "Before you might begin having problems?"

The question disappointed her. She'd thought he wasn't like the rest, thinking she was crazy and unpredictable. "What, are you worried I'm going to flake out on you?"

"I want to know how best to take care of you."

The sincerity in his voice made her ashamed. She stared at the ground. "Don't worry. I took a pill when we stopped for water. Before we left to talk to Prentice, I put a pill case in my pocket. It's got enough medication for a few days. I remembered the last time, when Prentice kidnapped me. He didn't get my refills for me for almost five days." She shook her head. "Withdrawal was no fun."

"I should have known you were smart enough to think ahead like that."

The compliment unsettled her almost more than his concern. "What do we do now?" she asked.

"It's almost dark," he said. "Time to make our move."

She accepted this nonanswer with good grace, and stood and brushed dry grass and leaves from her clothing. "What is our move, exactly?"

"We wait for the patrols to drive by and time them. Even if they're deliberately trying to be random, there will be a pattern of some kind. People think and act in patterns, even if the patterns are irregular."

"It would help if we had some way to write all this down," she said.

He picked up a stick and handed it to her. "Think of the ground as a big chalkboard."

"Why bother? We wouldn't be able to see it in the dark."

Two minutes later, a distant mechanical whine cut the natural silence. Lauren peered from behind the screen of trees they'd chosen as their lookout. "I don't see anything," she said.

"They're still a ways off."

"Still, the road is pretty straight here. I'd think we'd see headlights."

The droning, mechanical sound grew louder, but the highway stretched empty in either direction. Were they driving without lights? Or did sound carry farther than he'd realized in this emptiness?

Within seconds, it sounded as if the vehicle was right on them, but still the road remained empty. "This is crazy," Lauren said. "It's like they're invisible. I thought cloaking devices were the stuff of science-fiction novels."

Marco closed his eyes and focused on the sound. It

was too high-pitched and steady for an automobile. And it wasn't coming from the road, but from straight overhead.

He grabbed Lauren and pulled her back beneath the trees. "It's not a car," he said.

"What is it?" She looked around them.

"It's a drone." He held back the branch of a tree and pointed overhead. They could just make out the shadowy shape of the unmanned drone, hovering a hundred feet above them.

"I heard Prentice had one," she said. "But I thought the feds confiscated it."

"They had to give it back," Marco said. "It's not illegal to own one. Private businesses use them for all kinds of things, from mapping terrain to aerial photography. Prentice wanted it for security patrols."

"And we're a risk to his security, so of course he's going to use it." She squinted up into the sky. "What's it doing up there?"

"Looking for us, probably."

"You mean, like, with a camera?"

"A camera. And probably infrared technology. It can map heat on the ground. Two warm bodies would be easy to spot on the heat map."

"So it can track us in the dark." She squatted on her heels and hugged her arms around her knees. "So we're toast. All the drone has to do is pinpoint us and the goons can come right to us."

"The drone can only find us if we're in the area where it's searching." Marco studied the object, which looked like a cross between an artist's rendition of a UFO and one of those radio-controlled planes hobbyists used. It made a right turn and headed back up along the road.

"But how do we know where it's going to search?" Lauren asked. "A thing like that can cover a lot of territory."

"It uses fuel like anything else, so the operators have to limit it to a defined area," he said. "I think it's making a grid pattern, searching within a hundred feet on either side of the road for five miles or so."

She stood again, and joined him in watching the craft, which was now moving away from them. "You can tell all that after watching it for a few minutes?"

"It's the plan that makes the most sense," he said. "The one I'd use if I were the operator. Prentice and his men know we have to head to the road to find other people and help. He also probably reasoned that we'd travel at night, when it's more difficult for his patrols in the Jeeps to find us."

"But the drone can find us in the dark," Lauren said. She frowned. "Is it armed? Can it shoot us?"

"There have been rumors. At one time he had a Hellfire missile with which he could have armed it, but that supposedly belonged to his Venezuelan girlfriend. She claimed diplomatic immunity and refused to implicate him. But he could have found another missile on the black market."

"What? Anyone can buy a missile?"

"All it takes is enough money and the right connections. Prentice has those."

"What do we do now?" she asked. "Make a break for it while it's gone?"

He shook his head. "The Jeep patrols are probably still near. And the drone can scan a pretty large area, even when it's not directly overhead."

"We can't just stand here, waiting to be caught— or killed."

"No." He took her hand and led her out from under the cover of the trees. "We have to turn around and head into the park."

"What's in the park that will help us?"

Good question. Black Canyon of the Gunnison National Park contained the canyon that gave it its name—a deep, almost inaccessible gorge that, while breathtaking, didn't offer any avenues of rescue. Away from the gorge lay thousands of acres of wilderness, home to everything from mountain lions to endangered birds, but very few people. The few developments in the park crowded in one corner, bordering Richard Prentice's territory. Ranger headquarters had been there, though the buildings were slated to be decommissioned and moved.

"We have to try to reach the park ranger station," he said. "We can get help there."

"How long will it take us to reach?" she asked.

"A day. Maybe two. I'm not sure how far it is."

For a moment she looked devastated, crushed by the prospect of tramping through the wilderness for two days or more. But she quickly masked the emotion and straightened her shoulders. "Then, we'd better get started."

He squeezed her hand, and they set out. Marco faked a confidence he didn't feel. What he hadn't told Lauren was that, without water and food, they had little chance of reaching park headquarters. As the rattlesnake had proved, Prentice's thugs weren't the only dangers that could kill them in the wilderness.

Chapter Thirteen

Lauren had never been so tired in her life. She had to muster every ounce of will to take each step across the rough ground. Her legs ached, her stomach hurt and only the fear of being left behind kept her stumbling after Marco in the darkness. She was so thirsty she could have wept, but she doubted she could muster the moisture for tears. How many hours had they been walking? She probably didn't want to know. The moon had risen some time ago, bathing the prairie in a silvery light that made every tree and boulder seem larger and more forbidding. Any other time in her life, she might have lay down and demanded someone help her. But Marco wasn't complaining, and he had to be suffering at least as much as she was. If he could take this, so could she.

She stumbled, falling into Marco, who turned to catch her. "Are you okay?" he asked.

She brushed her hair out of her eyes and let out a long sigh. "I don't know," she said. "Maybe not so good. What time is it?"

"Almost midnight. Do you want to stop and rest?"

"I'm afraid if I stop, I might never get back up."

"We could try to get a couple hours' sleep."

"It's not falling asleep I'm worried about."

When he didn't answer, she looked at him, trying to judge his mood in the dim light. "Marco, if I ask you to be honest with me, you will, won't you?"

"Yes." No hesitation. He was either a very good liar, or he meant what he said. She wanted to believe the latter.

"What are our chances out here in the middle of no-where, with no food, no water, with Prentice's men still looking for us?"

He compressed his lips into a grim line.

"Don't tell me you haven't thought about it," she said.

"Right now, I'd say our chances are fifty-fifty. If we can find water in the next few hours, those odds go up."

"I'll admit, even mud soup is sounding good to me now."

He put his arm around her. "One thing they taught us in Special Forces is that a lot of survival is mental. People survive incredible ordeals because they believe they can. Don't give up on me."

"I'm not giving up."

"Good." He clapped her on the back. "Now, what will it be? Rest, or keep going?"

"Keep going."

They began walking again, staying close together, conserving energy by walking around obstacles instead of going over them. Time was difficult to gauge, but she thought they might have walked half an hour when Marco stopped, head up, shoulders tensed.

"What is it?" she asked.

"Look at the horizon."

She looked in the direction he indicated, at the pinkish-white light showing over the tops of the trees and rock outcroppings. "Is the sun coming up already?" she asked.

"Except the sun comes up in the east, and that's north."

She didn't ask how he knew this, with no compass or map; Marco knew things like that. "Then, what's making the light?"

"That's what we're going to find out."

They moved faster now, headed toward what seemed to be the source of the light. Even hiking at top speed, they seemed to draw no closer. Lauren began to wonder if it was all a mirage. But after another hour or so, Marco stopped again. "Listen," he said softly.

She held her breath and tried to concentrate. Past the throb of her own pulse, past the rustle of the night wind in the stunted trees, she heard a low, mechanical hum, steady and even. "What is it?" she whispered.

"Generators," he said. "You need a power source for all that light."

"But where is it?" she asked. "We've been walking for hours and we aren't getting any closer."

"Distances are tricky out here, but we're getting closer, I'm sure."

He'd said he wouldn't lie to her, but still she doubted, until she realized after more walking that the sound of the generators was getting louder. Soon they heard not just engine noises but the clank of metal and muffled voices, like a crowd of people talking.

Still, there was no sign of anyone or anything on the flat, featureless prairie, just the soft glow of light that seemed to emanate from the ground. "Are they underground?" she asked.

"Sort of," Marco said. "I think they're in a canyon. The Black Canyon isn't the only one around here, just the largest."

"I didn't pay much attention to the map the park service gave me the first time I visited," she said. "I'm not really much of an outdoors person." And after today, she didn't care if she never saw a hiking trail or a campsite again.

"Let's keep going," he said. "Stay behind me."

They moved more cautiously as they approached the lights and noises, keeping to the deeper shadows as much as possible. Lauren tried not to think about snakes. They weren't nocturnal, were they?

Marco led the way up a small rise, then stopped. She moved in behind him and looked down on a scene out of a dream. People—dozens of them, all men, milled around a well-lit compound. One group stood in orderly rows in front of another man, who seemed to be instructing them. Another group raced through an obstacle course of stacked tires and ropes. Still others zipped around the compound on all-terrain vehicles or lounged among the rows of tan canvas tents, smoking.

Most of the men wore a kind of uniform—dull brown fatigues and heavy black boots. Many of them had rifles slung over their shoulders. She blinked, trying to make sense of the images. "Are they making a movie?" she asked. She'd seen filming in downtown Denver once, and the scene below had that same sense of busyness, everything brightly lit and everyone bustling about. The action had the same feeling of unreality to it, as if everything they looked at was staged.

Marco shook his head. "I don't think so. The Rangers would have heard about it, since we're on park land."

Her gaze came to rest on something that made her sure this was all a bizarre dream. "Is that—is that a Nazi flag?" She pointed to a flagpole near the center of the compound, from which flew the familiar swastika.

"Looks like it."

"But that's crazy!"

"Some white supremacist groups have adopted it as their symbol."

"That's horrible." She shuddered and leaned forward for a closer look. "What are they doing down there?"

"I think it's a training camp," Marco said.

"A training camp?"

"Like the ones the Taliban set up in remote mountain regions to train their followers to be terrorists. But I think this one is to train domestic terrorists."

"Who would do that? And why here—in a national park?"

"They probably enjoy the idea of thumbing their noses at the federal government—a government some of these groups refuse to even recognize. Plus, though it's only a few dozen miles from a city, the land is roadless and remote. In a year's time probably a single person doesn't come here accidentally. There have been cases of whole communities of people squatting on public land for months, even years, building cabins, growing crops— legal and illegal. Our task force was one attempt to stop some trespassing, but it's impossible with so few team members and so much land."

"But someone would have seen them coming and going."

"They probably perform most of their activities at night, and only leave the compound one or two at a time. They dress like tourists and use the ATVs, so they look like recreational riders. And they've done a good job of camouflaging the camp. Check out the netting over one end of the canyon. With that and the dun-colored canvas tents, they'd be almost invisible to anyone flying overhead."

"Do you think Richard knows about this?"

"I'd bet he's financing it." Marco turned away from the scene below to look at her. "The man has made no secret of the fact that he has nothing but disdain for the government, or that some of his most vocal supporters are white supremacists and domestic militia groups. He has the money to finance this kind of operation. It would also explain his constant supply of burly bodyguards."

"Who are always young and white and perfect physical specimens." She shuddered again, remembering the men who had watched over her while Prentice had held her captive. She glanced back into the canyon, then around them. "We have to remember where this is, so that we can report it when we get to safety."

"We're not just going to remember," Marco said. "We're going to go down there."

She stared, sure she hadn't heard him correctly. "What?"

"We have to go down there," he said. "We need food, water and a phone. They have all of that."

"But it's too dangerous."

"If we leave without at least the food and water, we'll die anyway."

"How are we going to stand up against all those men with guns?"

"We have the element of surprise on our side—they're not expecting us. They think they're safe out here in the middle of nowhere. There are plenty of places to hide down there. If we can steal a weapon, it will even the odds."

As if two people against two dozen or more was anything close to even. "You're crazy."

He didn't look crazy, though. His expression was grim, but calm, his eyes determined. "This is the kind of thing I trained for."

"But I didn't train for this." She swallowed, trying to force down the fear that made it difficult to breathe. "I can't do this."

"Yes you can." He gripped her upper arm. "You're strong, you're smart and you're brave."

His faith in her somehow did make her feel calmer. Stronger. "And I've got you on my side," she said.

"Yeah. Remember I said I wouldn't let anything happen to you."

"Is that a promise?"

No hesitation this time, and his words were all she needed to subdue the fear. "It's a promise."

ALL OF MARCO's training had been for moments like this. He studied the encampment, noting the position of key structures and personnel. He and Lauren had to get in, get water, food and a weapon, and gather as much information about the operation as they could, all without being caught.

He led the way down the canyon, to a spot where the walls were shallow enough for them to descend, but far enough from the encampment that he hoped they wouldn't be noticed. "I'll go first," he whispered to Lauren. "Then let me guide you down."

"You'll have to. I can't see a thing after staring at all those lights."

The sides of the canyon were littered with a loose scree of pebbles and brittle shale. He dug footholds with the heels of his boots and grabbed on to clumps of grass to slow his descent. After he'd traveled a couple of yards, he turned back toward Lauren. "Feel for the steps I made with my boots," he said softly. "Lower yourself like you're climbing down a ladder. It you start to slip, I'll catch you."

She did as he instructed, and in this way they made it almost to the bottom of the canyon. Less than ten feet from the bottom, he caught the glow of an ember out of the corner of his eye and smelled the acrid smoke of tobacco. He put out his arm to prevent Lauren from descending any farther.

"Wh—?" He silenced her by tugging on her shirt, and nodded toward the spot where the end of a cigarette glowed red, a few feet from where they would have landed on the canyon floor. As his vision grew once more accustomed to the darkness, he could make out a fatigue-clad figure, sucking hard on a cigarette.

Lauren grew very still, not even the sound of her breathing breaking the silence. Marco stared at the smoking man, willing him to finish his cigarette and return to the camp.

The man tossed the still-glowing butt to the ground and stepped on it, and then they heard the metallic hiss of a zipper being lowered.

Lauren shifted, dislodging a pebble that bounced its way down the slope, the sound of its descent echoing in the stillness. The smoker froze in the act of relieving himself and whirled around. "Who's there?" he demanded.

But even as he reached for his weapon, Marco was on him. With one move, he'd silenced him forever.

He slid the rifle from the man's hand, then dug

through his pockets and found a Bowie knife, a set of brass knuckles and a cell phone. He pocketed all of these and slung the rifle over his shoulder, then began unbuttoning the man's desert camo shirt.

"What are you doing?" Lauren landed beside him with a soft thud, a little breathless.

"Help me take off his clothes. The boots, too." He finished unbuttoning the shirt and shoved it off his shoulders.

"Are you going to wear them?" Lauren squatted and began untying the laces of the dead man's boots.

"No. You are."

She recoiled. "I can't do that!" Her tone conveyed her horror at this suggestion.

"You stand out too much in those feminine clothes, not to mention a shooter could see that blond hair a hundred yards away in the darkness." He shoved the man's cap into her hand. "Put this on. Stuff your hair underneath. Stuff cloth into the toes of the boots if you have to—they're more practical for this rough terrain than your sandals. Hurry."

He could tell she wanted to argue, but she pressed her lips together and ducked her head. Silently, she collected the clothing he handed her. "Did they teach you to kill that way in Special Forces?" she asked before he could turn away again.

"Yes. And just so you know, it's not something I enjoy doing."

"I'm glad to hear it."

She started to turn away, but he touched her arm. "I'm sorry you had to see that," he said. "I'm sorry you had to be any part of this ugliness. But sometimes, surviving means doing ugly things."

She nodded. "I know. And I don't blame you, it's just… It's hard."

"And I hope it never gets easy for you." He hoped the hardness that had been with him so long he had no hope of ever leaving it behind never touched her. He'd let himself forget, for a little while, why the two of them shouldn't be together. The events of tonight had reminded him that, no matter how much he was attracted to her and even cared for her, he couldn't bring any more pain into her life. "You're going to be okay," he said. "Remember that."

"I will."

She quickly changed into the smoker's clothing. "How do I look?" she asked.

The clothes were too big and sagged on her, but that helped hide her curves. With her hair piled onto her head and mostly hidden under the cap, she could pass for a very young recruit. "From a distance, I don't think anyone will suspect anything," he said.

"They won't suspect you, either," she said. "You look like a soldier, even without their uniform."

"That's what I'm counting on. One more thing." He handed her the knife.

She stared at the blade in her hand. Eight inches long, with a carved antler grip, it looked enormous in her delicate grasp. "What am I supposed to do with this?" she asked.

"Defend yourself, if you have to. For now, tuck it into this sheath and wear it on your belt."

She fastened the knife to her belt and they set out, keeping to the fringes of activity, avoiding any other people. "What are we looking for?" she whispered.

"The mess hall or a commissary. Someplace we can get food and water."

"There are a bunch of trash cans over there." She pointed toward a line of industrial gray garbage bins, lined up outside a building. "You need trash cans near a kitchen," she said.

"Then that's a good place to start," he said.

Keeping to the deep shadows next to the row of Quonset huts, they made their way to the open door beside the trash cans. Light streamed from the doorway, and when Marco looked inside, he saw a lone man standing at a table, peeling potatoes. "This is the place," he said. "You keep watch while I go in and get what we need. Make some kind of noise if anyone's coming."

Before she could answer, he slipped into the building, and out of sight.

Chapter Fourteen

Marco disappeared inside the kitchen before Lauren could insist that he not leave her alone there in the dark. She stared after him, trying to remember to breathe, to not panic. Everything would be okay. Marco had said so. She had to believe him, right?

"Hey, dude, you got a light?"

She plastered herself up against the building and stared at the young man who had spoken. He'd materialized out of the darkness, a cigarette in one hand, his cap shoved back on his head.

"Hey, didn't mean to startle you," he said. He moved closer and wagged the cigarette. "I lost my lighter. You got one on you?"

"Uh, no." She realized her voice was too high-pitched. She forced herself to slump her shoulders and lower her voice. "Sorry."

"Oh. Too bad. I thought maybe you were hiding out over here smoking."

"No, uh, just hanging out." Inwardly, she cringed. How lame did she sound?

"I know what you mean, dude." He settled in beside her, leaning against the wall in the darkness. "Sometimes you just have to get away from the grind. I mean,

I believe in the mission and everything, but these guys never let up for a minute."

What is your mission? She wanted to ask but knew she couldn't. She should find another way to get the information out of him. "When I signed up, I didn't expect there to be so much work," she said.

"Tell me about it. I mean, I came out here expecting them to teach me about shooting and making bombs and all that. Instead, they got us spending days memorizing maps and laws and studying history. If I'd have wanted to waste my time on history classes, I'd have stayed in college."

"History is the worst," Lauren said. *History of what?* "What was the name of that guy? The one they went on and on about?"

"You mean that von Manstein guy—Hitler's military strategist? Don't these guys remember Hitler lost? I mean, he was right about a lot of things, but I don't think learning his strategy is going to help us now. We've got better weapons and intelligence and everything."

Hitler? So that swastika was for real? "When do you think we're going to get to do something besides drill and go to class?" she asked.

"Nobody will tell us the exact date, but I figure we're getting close. And it's not one mission, right? It's a bunch. Like, one group's going to go after transportation and somebody else is going to take out communication. It's going to be chaos." His voice rose, excited. "I mean, it's going to be amazing. People won't know what hit them."

"Yeah. Amazing." Lauren felt sick to her stomach. Marco was right. These people were terrorists. They wanted to destroy and kill.

She glanced toward the door to the kitchen. What was taking Marco so long? And what would happen if he came out and the kid was still there?

"What's up with you?" the young man demanded. "Why are you so jumpy?"

"Oh, I...I just saw one of the officers go in there. I didn't want him to come out and catch me goofing off."

"One of them is in the kitchen?" Her companion laughed. "What, he wanted a midnight snack? Of the pig swill they feed us?"

"Aren't you worried what he'll do if he comes out and finds you?" she asked.

"These old blowhards don't scare me. They like to talk a lot, but they want us to do all the work—take all the risks while they get all the glory. This close to the mission they can't afford to cross any of us in case we go running to the authorities and screw up all their plans."

"You wouldn't do that, would you?" she asked. "Run to the authorities?"

"No way! The authorities are the ones I want to stick it to. But the officers are authorities, too, right? And they don't know what's going on in my head. So I can use that to my advantage." He tapped the side of his head with his forefinger. "I may not look it, but I'm smart. I've got an IQ of one-sixty."

"You don't seem that smart to me, soldier," Marco said from behind them. Before the young man had time to react, Marco put the blade of a large butcher knife to his throat.

Eyes wide, the young man made incoherent choking noises. Lauren was almost as terrified. How had Marco slipped up that way without her seeing him? And what was he going to do with that knife?

What he did was remove the blade from the young man's throat and step back. "What's your name?" he demanded.

"Robinson, sir." Robinson brought his hand up in a sharp salute. "Bradley Robinson, Company Two, sir."

"If I had been an enemy, you would be dead right now, Robinson." Marco didn't look at Lauren, all his attention focused on the young soldier, whose face was still blanched white. Marco's stern expression, erect posture and air of command almost had Lauren believing he was one of the camp officers.

"Yes, sir. Dead, sir," Robinson repeated.

"Instead, tomorrow at eighteen hundred hours you will report to headquarters, where you will have a chance to redeem yourself by volunteering for a special assignment," Marco said. "You are to tell no one about this."

"Yes, sir. What is the assignment, sir?"

"You will find out tomorrow. Now go, before I decide to punish you further."

"Yes, sir." Robinson turned and ran.

When she was sure the young man had left them, Lauren moved closer to Marco. "You even frightened me," she said. "When you stepped out of the shadows with that knife."

He tucked the knife into the plastic bag she now noticed he carried. "I wouldn't have killed him unless I had to," he said. "It was better to frighten him into silence."

She glanced in the direction Robinson had run. "Do you think he will keep quiet?"

"He doesn't know my name. He was so terrified he probably can't even remember what I look like. He won't say anything."

She could believe that. Marco had been terrifying.

She'd known he was a strong man, not given to showing emotion, but seeing him as he'd been tonight, so cold, ruthless even, reminded her there was so much about him she didn't know or understand. "What happens tomorrow evening when he reports to headquarters?" she asked.

"If things go our way, by tomorrow evening this camp will be gone, and everyone in it arrested."

"I found out some of what they're doing here," she said. "You were right—this is a terrorist camp. Robertson told me they've been studying Nazi military history and that they've targeted transportation and communication."

"Food isn't the only thing they're cooking in that kitchen," Marco said. "They've got ingredients for significant explosives."

She wanted to ask what he'd done with the man they'd seen peeling potatoes, but maybe it was better if she didn't know. "Did you get any food?" Her stomach growled and suddenly she felt weak and shaky.

"Drink this first." He handed her a water bottle. "Then eat this." She drained half the bottle in a few gulps, only strong willpower keeping her from moaning at the sheer joy of quenching her thirst. The protein bar he'd handed her was small and dry, but it was as welcome as any meal she'd ever eaten.

"Oh, my gosh, I feel so much better," she said. Maybe part of the shakiness and terror she'd felt had merely been a lack of food and water. She was doubly grateful for the clean water to help wash down her medication. All these necessities taken care of, she looked around. The camp was much quieter now, as if everyone but a few guards had gone to bed. "Can we leave now?"

"There's one more place we need to visit," he said.

"Where's that?" Didn't they have everything they'd come here to get—food, water and information?

"Headquarters. I want to get a look at any plans they have, and see if they have a sat phone."

"Didn't you get a phone off that first soldier?" The one he'd killed.

"It's a regular cell phone. It doesn't work out here where there are no towers. If I can get hold of a satellite phone, I can call Graham and get him to work on sending a force out here to bust this place open. They're probably already looking for us, but this place is so well hidden, they might need some help finding it."

"Won't there be guards at headquarters? And more people—maybe even people working?"

"Yes, but my guess is they've been here long enough to be growing complacent. From the looks of things—the permanent structures and worn paths—it appears they've been here several months at least. No one's bothered them in that time, so they're feeling a little invincible."

But we're *not invincible*, she thought, but didn't give voice to the words. She wouldn't succeed in dissuading Marco anyway. Besides, she knew he was right. They had to get word to someone as quickly as possible. For all they knew, the mission—whatever it entailed—would take place within a few days, or even a few hours. They had to find a way to stop that from happening.

She drained the rest of the water. "What do you want me to do?" she asked.

"Let's find the headquarters building first."

The command center was easy enough to locate, since it was the area with the most activity and people, even at this late hour. People were bustling about as if it was the middle of the day, instead of well after midnight. Marco and Lauren stopped in the shadows a short distance away and studied the large Quonset hut with a row of lighted windows along one side and an armed sentry stationed at the entrance.

"Even if we managed to get past that guard, there are too many people around for us to sneak in and steal a phone," she said. "Someone would shoot us before we'd gone five yards."

"We could create a distraction," he said. "Something that would draw away most of the personnel. We could overpower the remaining guards, grab the phone and get out."

"As soon as they realize there's no emergency, the whole camp will be on us like a swarm of ants," she said. "It's not as if we can have a getaway car waiting for us."

"What about a getaway ATV?" He indicated the side-by-side all-terrain vehicle parked beside the headquarters building, the keys conveniently still in the ignition.

"That won't get us away from here fast enough," she said. "Especially if they have Jeeps or another four-wheel drive automobile."

"Still, if we get separated, head for that and take off as fast as you can," he said.

She shook her head. "I couldn't leave you behind."

He grabbed her shoulders and turned her to face him. "I can look after myself," he said, his expression just as stern as when he'd spoken to the soldier. "Promise me you'll do it."

She shook out of his grasp. "No. I won't promise that. And I'm not some scared recruit, so don't think you can order me around."

The sternness left his face, revealing a sadness that

weakened her resolve in a way that bravado never could. "I'm not worth it, you know," he said.

"What do you mean?"

"You saw me back there. I didn't hesitate to kill a man. It's how I'm wired."

She would never forget how quickly he'd silenced that lone man. "You didn't murder him for fun," she said. "There's a difference. I know that."

"You're a good person," he said. "You have enough to deal with in your life without adding someone like me."

Now she was the one who needed to be stern. "I get to decide that. Not you."

He frowned. "Then, you'd better decide to look after yourself first. If things get hairy in there, I want you to run and not look back."

Maybe she would do exactly that, if it came down to it, but she wanted to believe she was better than that, that she would never abandon him. She hoped she wouldn't have to find out. "So we're really going in?" she asked.

"We have to."

"We could leave now and walk to where you could get a signal for that cell phone."

"That could take a day or more. By then it could be too late."

She bit her lower lip. He was right, of course. "I guess if we're talking about saving the country, I shouldn't worry so much about myself," she said.

"I'll do everything I can to keep you safe, but this is bigger than both of us."

She nodded. "All right. But I think the distraction idea is too risky."

He looked at the headquarters building again. The door was closed now, but the guard still stood in front of it, rifle at the ready. Through the row of windows, they could see people working at desks or milling around conference tables. "I don't have a better plan."

"What if, instead of trying to sneak in, you walked in boldly?" she said. "Act like an officer and demand to use the phone."

"The camp isn't that large. They'd know I wasn't an officer. And what are you going to do while I'm in there?"

"Tell them you're a special envoy, and I'm you're aide."

"An envoy?"

She took a deep breath. This was either the best idea she'd ever had, or the craziest. "Tell them Richard Prentice sent you."

Chapter Fifteen

Marco stared, unsure he'd heard Lauren correctly. "Do you know for sure Richard Prentice is involved with this?" he asked.

"No. But like you said before, it's a good possibility," she said. "If he is, the mention of his name is going to carry some weight. If he isn't, you'll still throw them off guard. They'll be trying to figure out who Prentice is and why you're there. If nothing else, they'll believe you're crazy and unstable, and we could use that to our advantage."

He'd learned a lot about risk assessment in various training classes—how to determine the likelihood of success in an operation, and when the desired outcome was worth the degree of risk involved. By any measure, Lauren's plan was a bad idea. There were too many unknowns—Prentice might have nothing to do with this operation, or if he did, they might not know him by that name. Worse still, the man himself might be inside that headquarters building. He'd made a habit of distancing himself from any direct involvement in his operations, but anything was possible.

"I'm sorry. I never should have suggested it. It's too

risky," Lauren said. "I can't ask you to do that. Forget I mentioned it."

"We'll do it," he said.

"What? No, it's too risky. It was a crazy idea." She put a hand to her temple. "I'm tired, and not eating has my medication all off. Don't listen to me."

"No, it was a brilliant idea."

"No, it's too dangerous."

"It is dangerous. But at this point, I don't think we have a choice." He nodded toward the building. "All the activity in there tells me something big is going down, and soon. We have to stop it before a lot of lives are lost."

Two of those lives might be their own, but he didn't have to say the words out loud. He saw the acceptance of that reality in her eyes. But she pushed the fear away and nodded. "All right. Tell me what to do."

He hefted the plastic bag with the food, water and knife. "We need to hide this."

"We can stash it in those bushes." She indicated a clump of scrub oak near where they were standing.

He brushed off his shirt and straightened the crease in his trousers, then eyed her critically. "You need a little more spit and polish if you're going to pass for an aide," he said. "Tuck in your shirt and cuff the trousers."

She did as he asked; unfortunately, tucking the shirt only emphasized her curves. He frowned. "That's not going to work." He tugged at the fabric. "Maybe you can blouse it out a little."

She grabbed his arms and stood on tiptoe to kiss him fiercely. He returned the kiss, pulling her tightly into his arms and crushing her to him. Despite all his vows to distance himself from her, he needed her now more than ever—he needed her courage and her faith in him.

He needed her belief, however misguided, that he was this honorable and worthy man, one who deserved the love she so freely gave.

After a long moment, they pulled apart. He continued tugging at her shirt, avoiding looking into her eyes. When he felt more in control of his emotions, he stood back and eyed her critically. "Stick to the shadows as much as you can," he said. "I'll do my best to keep all eyes on me."

"They'll be shaking in their shoes." She smoothed her hands down his arms, then stepped back. "Are we ready to do this?"

"Let's do it."

LAUREN COULD FEEL the stares of the men around them as she followed Marco up the walkway to the headquarters building. They were ten feet from the door when the guard stepped out. "Halt!" he commanded.

"At ease, soldier." Once again, Marco had transformed himself into the arrogant, authoritative commander, prepared to mete out punishment to any who crossed him. "Special envoy Henry Hoffman here to see your commander."

The guard hesitated. Up close, he proved to be cut from the same mold as the men who'd watched over her at Prentice's mansion—young, muscular and not necessarily bright. Men programmed to follow orders. "What's the password, sir?" he asked.

"The password is your head on a plate if you don't take me to your commander, immediately."

The sharpness of the words made Lauren flinch, and the soldier paled. "Commander Carroll isn't to be disturbed," he said.

"You'd better disturb him for me," Marco said. "The success or failure of our entire mission rests on the intelligence I've been charged with conveying to him."

"Y-yes, sir." The soldier backed toward the door and opened it two inches. "Captain Peterson," he called. "Someone here to see the commander."

A second soldier stepped out to meet them. A little older than the first, and not as beefy, he nevertheless had a shrewd look of intelligence. "The commander has given orders he's not to be disturbed," he said, eyeing Marco suspiciously.

"He's a special envoy," the guard said.

"Envoy from whom?" the second man asked.

"I have vital intelligence to share with Commander Carroll," Marco said.

"Envoy from whom?" the second man asked again, his voice more strident.

Marco fixed him with a look Lauren was sure could have frozen water. Here was the moment of no return, when their ruse either worked or fell apart. "From Mr. Prentice," he said.

Freckles stood out in relief against the second man's suddenly paper-white skin. He opened his mouth to say something, then closed it. "Come with me," he said after he'd regained his composure. Not waiting for an answer, he turned and led the way through the door.

Marco followed, Lauren close behind him. She kept her head ducked, trying to make herself invisible. But they hadn't gone three steps before their escort turned and fixed her with his scrutiny. "Who is this?"

"This is my aide. Hugo."

She kept her head down, staring at her shoes. *Hugo? That was the best he could come up with? Was it because he thought she had a huge bottom?* She fought back a nervous giggle. Definitely time to adjust her meds.

The officious man must have decided she was beneath his notice, because he turned once more and hurried down the hall. She ignored the curious glances from the men they passed. Most of them were older than the recruits she'd seen on the ground, like the smoker Marco had frightened away. Only about half the men in this building wore uniforms, but they all looked grim, even worried.

Their escort knocked on the door at the end of the corridor. "Who is it?" barked a man on the other side.

"Captain Peterson, sir." He glanced at Marco. "I have a special envoy from Mr. Prentice."

The door jerked open, almost sending the freckled man stumbling into the stocky figure who now stood before him. In his fifties, with close-cropped gray hair and narrow ice-blue eyes, he stared at Marco. "I've never seen you before," he said.

"No. I'm one of Mr. Prentice's South American contacts."

Again, Lauren had to suppress a smile. What better way to explain Marco's obviously Hispanic features to this crowd of white supremacists?

"You'd better come in." The commander held the door open wider. He put out a hand to stop Lauren. "Wait in the hall, soldier."

"My aide stays with me," Marco said.

The two men faced off. Whether intimidated by Marco's superior height, his youth or the sheer force of his glare, the commander stepped back and ushered them in. Captain Peterson brought up the rear, closing the door behind him.

Carroll moved behind his desk, the top of which was almost obscured by papers, folders and a large open case, which contained what Lauren thought might be a satellite phone. "Prentice has been promising me new information for days," he said. "But I was under the impression he was going to contact me in person, not send a third party."

"He prefers to keep a certain distance from day-to-day operations," Marco said.

Carroll snorted. "Yes, and if things go south, he walks away clean. I'm not a green recruit. I know how these things operate. But I'm fighting for a cause I believe in, and that means I'm willing to take risks and get my hands dirty."

"Are you suggesting Mr. Prentice doesn't believe in the cause?" Marco asked.

"He believes. And he's done a lot to sway others to our point of view. He's shown it's possible to give the finger to the government and walk away unscathed. That's good publicity, any way you look at it. I would never question his commitment."

"Only his bravery?" Marco asked.

From his position by the door, Peterson made a choking sound. The commander's lips whitened as he pressed them together. "What message do you have for me, Hoffman?"

Lauren held her breath. They hadn't gotten this far in the plan. What message would allay the commander's suspicions, yet allow Marco to use the sat phone to call for reinforcements? How would he tell the Rangers where they were located?

Marco pulled out a chair across from the commander's

desk and sat, one ankle on his knee, a relaxed, insolent posture. "First, I need coffee. It's been a long night."

The commander scowled, but he turned to Peterson. "Go get us some coffee. And have the mess send up some sandwiches, as well."

Peterson clearly wasn't pleased at being sent on this errand, but he didn't dare argue. Shoulders stiff, he exited the room. Lauren moved farther into the corner, keeping to the shadows as Marco had instructed.

"I don't trust that one," Marco said when Peterson had left. "He's too self-important."

"Peterson is loyal, I'm sure of it," Carroll said.

"I never assume anyone's loyalty," Marco said. "Neither does Mr. Prentice."

Carroll shifted, his chair squeaking in protest. "Say what you came here to say. I don't have time for chitchat."

"Mr. Prentice wants to know what you've done to ensure the success of the mission," Marco said.

"He knows what I've done. Doesn't he read the reports I send?"

"People can say anything on paper. He sent me here to see for myself the preparations you've made."

"The men are trained and ready. We've got the manpower and the support in place to hit more than a dozen targets at once. The state will be practically helpless within hours and the rest of the country will take notice. Our success will persuade others of our power."

"People will think foreign terrorists are responsible," Marco said.

"At first they will, but once we begin our press campaign they'll see things differently. They'll realize this isn't the work of some foreign power, but of their fellow countrymen. True patriots who want to bring the

United States back to the righteous roots from which we've strayed."

As he spoke, the commander's face flushed and his voice lowered to the sonorous tones of a Gospel preacher. Lauren wondered if the words were his own, or ones he'd heard repeated so often they had become doctrine. And she wondered what would make a person so dissatisfied and disgruntled that they'd subvert patriotism into an excuse for destruction and murder.

"Are you ready for a strike immediately?" Marco asked.

"We've been ready for more than a week," Carroll said. "All we need is the go-ahead from Mr. Prentice, and the acknowledgment that he's laid all the ground-work on his end. Give us the time and date and we'll make it happen."

"I'll call him and give him my report." Marco motioned toward the sat phone. "I'll recommend he give the go-ahead now."

Carroll shoved the sat phone toward Marco. "Make the call. I'm ready to get this over with."

Marco took the phone, then nodded toward the door. "If you'll leave us for a moment, Commander."

Carroll stared. "You're asking me to leave my office?"

"I could step into the corridor if you prefer."

He shook his head, but left the room. Lauren breathed a huge sigh of relief, but a warning look from Marco kept her in the corner. He nodded toward the door and she got the message. Just because the commander had stepped into the hall didn't mean he wasn't listening, or even watching through a crack in the door.

He powered up the phone and went to stand by the

window, the antennae extended. After a moment, he punched in a series of numbers and waited.

"I'm here. Yes, the trip was terrible. It took five hours to get here from the ranch house. Excellent location, though. I'd estimate ten miles from the main road and another fifteen from the park. The wash makes good camouflage and Carroll and his men have done a good job of hiding the camp. No one would guess this is a training facility."

Lauren covered her mouth to choke back a cry of delight. Marco had found a way to give the Rangers all the information they needed to find them, all while sounding like the bored messenger he'd been portraying for the past half hour.

"I'm convinced Carroll's men are trained and ready," he continued. "He wants to strike as soon as possible. Yes, all the targets—transportation and communication. With the press campaign immediately after to clarify that this is not a foreign terrorist operation, but the work of patriots here in the US."

He waited, listening. Lauren strained her ears, but could hear nothing of the response. "Yes, sir. I'll remain here to assist the commander. Thank you, sir."

He hung up the phone and looked at her. "It's done," he said, his voice barely audible.

The door opened and Carroll entered, but there was a new stiffness in his posture, a new hardness in his gaze that put Lauren on edge. She stood up straighter, and put one hand on the Bowie knife at her belt.

"Very clever, Mr. Hoffman," Carroll said. "Though I suspect that isn't your real name."

Marco blinked, but kept his arrogant expression in place. "Commander Carroll—" he began.

"Corporal Cruz, we meet again."

Richard Prentice stepped into the room behind the commander. Only instead of his usual business suit, the billionaire wore a crisp khaki uniform, a field jacket belted tightly about his waist, twin pistols in holsters on his hips. He wore tall black boots polished to a mirror finish, and an officer's cap set at a jaunty angle on his silver-streaked brown hair. He swept a dismissive gaze over Marco, then shifted his attention to the corner. "Lauren, so nice to see you again," he said, with a smile that sent a chill through her. "But I must say, that outfit doesn't become you. We'll have to see if we can find you something more flattering. It would be a shame for a beauty like you to die dressed as a common private."

Chapter Sixteen

Marco carefully set the phone aside, his expression deliberately impassive. He avoided looking at Lauren, though he sensed her fear. Help was on the way, but it would be hours before Graham could marshal his resources and locate the canyon. He and Lauren might not have that much time.

"Should I kill them now?" Commander Carroll had drawn his handgun and had it trained on Marco. His mouth curved up in a maniacal leer that sent an icy chill up Marco's spine.

"Not yet." Prentice strode into the room. The uniform he wore magnified all his most prominent traits. He'd been arrogant before; now he exuded disdain for all around him. His clipped speech had grown harsher, the words barked out like orders. Even his posture was more haughty, shoulders back, chest up, head tilted to look down his nose at everyone and everything.

He stopped inches from Marco, so that the younger man could smell onions on his breath and the musky aroma of his aftershave. "Who did you call?" he asked.

"The FBI." Marco met Prentice's gaze with a hard look of his own. "They'll be here soon to take apart this camp and arrest you and everyone connected to it."

"They'll be too late," Prentice said. "By the time the players in their giant bureaucracy have analyzed and criticized and compromised and referred the decision up the chain of command until someone finally decides to give the orders to proceed, we will be long gone. But before we go, we'll take out all our targets. Air traffic, highway traffic, telecommunications, even the public water supply will be completely disrupted."

The door opened and they all shifted their attention to Captain Peterson, who entered carrying a tray with a coffeepot and cups. His face reddened. "Sorry I took so long," he said. "The mess was empty. It looked as if the cook left in the middle of peeling potatoes. I had to make the coffee myself."

"Forget the coffee," Carroll said. "Mr. Prentice has identified these two as impostors trying to infiltrate us."

Peterson gaped and set the tray on the desk.

"Destroying everything won't win you any friends," Marco said. "Or any influence. You'll have everyone in the country hunting you down, eager to kill you."

Prentice shook his head. "Maybe for a few days, but in the chaos that follows, people will learn they can't rely on their broken government system for help. Then we'll step in to save them. To show them a better way."

"Why would they trust the very people who caused the chaos in the first place?" Lauren spoke for the first time since Prentice's arrival. She looked less pale now, and her voice was strong—defiant. Marco admired her courage, but if he could he would have told her that defiance probably wasn't the way to lull Prentice into believing she wasn't a threat. Her best hope for escape was to try to remain as quiet and invisible as possible. That would allow Marco to create a distraction and her to run away.

Too late for that now, though. Prentice turned on

her. "Most people are weak," he said. "They value their comfort—their electricity, their running water, their luxury cars and high-speed internet and twenty-four-hour streaming movies—much more than they value principles or ideals. If we take those things away from them, within twenty-four hours they'll be crying and begging and welcoming with open arms anyone who can give them what they want."

"You're wrong," she said. "People will hate you if you kill their loved ones and destroy their lives."

"Some of them," he conceded. "But the beauty of my plan is that none of them will associate what is going to happen with me. An organization—the True Patriots—will claim credit for the destruction, then I will step in to rescue society. With my money and power and concern for people, and my equal disdain for all political parties, I will be their savior."

He struck a statesmanlike pose, head up, one hand with the palm flat over his heart. "After I have stepped in and used my money to restore their creature comforts, most people will be happy to do anything I want. I'll continue to preach the message I've delivered all along of personal property rights, taking power out of the hands of politicians, et cetera. But this time people will listen to me. By the time the True Patriots step forward to support me in the rebuilding efforts, people will see them in a completely new light—not as terrorists, but as reformers—people doing what is needed to get this country back on the right track."

"You're crazy," Lauren said.

He arched one eyebrow. "You would know, wouldn't you?"

Her face flushed even more, but she made no reply.

"Let me kill them now," Carroll said. "They're going to get in our way."

"I have something better in mind for them," Prentice said. He turned back to Marco. "I hear you've gone rogue."

"Then, you heard wrong."

"No? My sources tell me you resigned your commission in the DEA and stayed behind to do what—become a vigilante?"

"Disbanding the Rangers didn't stop us from coming after you," Marco said.

Prentice cupped his chin in his hand and continued to study Marco. "Yes, I'd say you are a vigilante. You fell under the sway of a beautiful woman." He nodded to Lauren. "Her delusions—part of her mental illness—led her to advocate for the overthrow of the government. Disgruntled by your treatment at the hands of your own federal employers, you were happy to join her in her efforts. Together, the two of you masterminded a series of terrorist attacks."

"What are you talking about?" Lauren asked. "You're not making any sense."

"I'm making brilliant sense," Prentice said. "If there was any flaw in my plans to this point, it was that it didn't leave anyone for people to focus their anger on. They couldn't be angry at me, the benevolent billionaire who is paying to put their lives back together. Neither can they remain enraged at my allies in the True Patriots. But some people need someone to hate. With the seeds I have already planted in the media about your unstable nature and propensity for making up preposterous scenarios, they'll be happy to turn their anger on you, and on your deluded consort."

Marco and Lauren exchanged glances. Yes, Prentice was crazy; she wouldn't get anywhere arguing with him.

"You're not going to kill them?" Carroll asked, not hiding his disappointment.

"No, I'm going to leave them alive. In the aftermath of the attacks on the state's infrastructure, they'll be found wandering in the wilderness, out of their minds and protesting their innocence." He addressed Lauren again. "Part of our media campaign following the attacks will be to place the blame for the events on you. We'll be free to manufacture whatever evidence we like, and we'll give people plenty of reasons to discount everything you say. Before you know it, you two will be the most hated people in the country." He reached out and rubbed a lock of Lauren's hair between his thumb and forefinger. "Given what I know about you, that would be a fate worse than death."

"The Rangers won't believe you," Marco said.

Prentice waved his hand dismissively. "The Ranger Brigade is already a defunct task force. Their vendetta against me prevented them from effectively performing the job they were designed to do. Any continued defamation of my character will be dismissed as the whining of poor losers."

The man clearly believed everything he said, and expected everyone else to believe it, too. The depth of his delusion was astonishing—but it also made him more dangerous. If believing you would survive increased your chances of making it out of a life-threatening situation, then believing you couldn't fail also increased your chances of success. And Prentice had already proved he was a master at swaying public opinion in his favor. "You've thought of every angle, haven't you?" Marco said.

"Of course."

Let him believe that, Marco thought. *But he doesn't know me. And he doesn't know Lauren. Not really. We didn't come this far to give up.*

"If we're not going to kill them, what are we going to do with them?" Carroll asked.

"Lock them up for now," Prentice said. "We'll turn them loose right before we leave. With no transportation or way to communicate, it will be hours before anyone finds them, or they find their way to civilization—or what's left of it."

"Where should I lock them up?" Carroll asked.

Prentice turned to scowl at him. "Don't you have a brig, or whatever it's called?"

"We haven't needed one. The penalty for most infractions is death."

No wonder the soldier who'd been caught smoking outside the kitchen had looked so terrified, Marco thought.

"There must be some building with a lock on it," Prentice said.

"Some of the offices have locks on the doors and windows," Captain Peterson offered.

"Then, find one of them to put them in," Prentice said. "It will only be for a couple of hours."

Carroll hesitated.

"Do it, man!" Prentice barked. "We don't have time to waste. Start mobilizing the men. Our mission starts now!"

Carroll shoved the pistol into its holster, then turned to Peterson. "Take them to that empty office down at the end of the hall. Find somebody to guard them. Then report back here immediately."

"Yes, sir." Peterson saluted, then grabbed hold of Lauren's arm and tugged her toward the door.

"Oww! You're hurting me," she protested.

Marco lashed out, striking the captain square on the jaw. Peterson reeled, then reached for his pistol. But Carroll was quicker. He struck Marco on the back of the head with something heavy. The last thing Marco saw before he slid into blackness was Lauren's horrified expression as she stared at him, her mouth open in a scream he couldn't hear.

LAUREN HUGGED HER arms across her chest and paced the length of the small office—five steps across, five steps back. The too-big boots Marco had taken from the dead soldier slapped against the tile floor with a muffled thud, like a rubber mallet hitting a spike.

She clenched her teeth together to keep from chattering and blinked rapidly to clear her eyes of tears she willed not to fall. She'd been alone in this room for fifteen minutes, according to the clock on the otherwise empty metal desk. Where was Marco? Had they decided to shoot him after all? She'd listened, but had heard no gunfire. She told herself this was a good thing, though she knew they might have dragged him far away, out of hearing range.

Though she heard no gunfire, sounds of activity were everywhere—marching feet, shouting voices, the roar of engines. This interior room had no windows, so she couldn't see what was going on, but she imagined men taking down tents, gathering weapons and supplies and mobilizing to spread out across the state to wreak destruction. In the past, terrorists had blown up bridges and power plants and threatened water supplies and communication centers. From what Prentice had said, his organization, the True Patriots—the name made her gag—planned to do all of this and more.

Scuffling in the hallway outside made her jump. She ran toward the door, and narrowly avoided being struck when it burst open and Marco stumbled into the room. He landed on his hands and knees in the middle of the floor, his shirt torn, one eye black, blood dripping from a busted lip. "Stay quiet in here," Peterson ordered. "I'll deal with you later." Then he slammed the door shut, his boot heels making sharp, staccato beats on the tile as he marched away.

Lauren knelt beside Marco and gingerly touched his shoulder. "What happened?" she asked.

"Peterson thought it would be fun to get a little rough," he said. "I'll be fine." But he winced as he stood, and his breath caught as he straightened. He looked at her. "What about you?" he asked. "Are you all right?"

"I'm fine." Sick with worry and fear, but physically, she was untouched. "What are we going to do?" she asked. "How are we going to stop them?"

"The Rangers know we're here now. They'll do what they can to rescue us."

"But they'll never get here in time," she said. "Prentice was right about that. It will take hours to mobilize the officers and the equipment they'll need. From the sounds of all the activity out there, by then everyone will be gone."

Marco leaned against the desk. "We'll have to find a way to get out," he said. "We can't do much locked in this room."

"There's a guard outside the door," she said.

Marco nodded. "I saw him. A big, beefy guy with an AK-47."

"I could try to distract him with my feminine wiles," she said. "Though frankly, after two days in the wilderness, I don't look or smell very sexy." As soon as she was back in the land of indoor plumbing, she wanted a long, hot shower and a shampoo.

"You still look gorgeous," Marco said. "But I don't want you getting near any of these punks." He straightened and began to prowl the room. "There's no window, and no way to cut through the walls."

"Is there just the one guard?" she asked.

He nodded. "They need everyone else to help dismantle the camp and distribute the weapons and explosives necessary for their 'mission.'"

"Then, if you could get him in here, maybe the two of us could overpower him."

He stopped. "That's not a bad idea." He looked around him, then picked up the desk chair, turned it over and pulled off the bottom half, with its five rollers. "I can knock him out with this. But how do we get him in here?"

"I've got an idea I think will work," she said. "Are you ready?"

"What's the idea?" he asked.

"Trust me, this will work better if you're surprised, too. Just stand over there behind the door and when he comes in, hit him hard."

He moved into position then nodded. Lauren stood up straight, took a deep breath, then let out a loud, blood-chilling scream.

Chapter Seventeen

Lauren's throat was raw and her voice was fading by the time the door opened and the guard looked in. "What's wrong?" he demanded.

"He's bleeding to death!" She channeled all the fear and panic of the past twenty-four hours into her voice, and pointed a shaking finger across the room to a spot out of the guard's line of sight. "Help!" Then she began to scream again, loud and incessant and, she hoped, annoying enough to make the guard want to do anything to stop it.

He stepped farther into the room, the rifle cradled across his chest. As soon as he fully cleared the door, Marco stepped out and brought the heavy wheels of the office chair down on his skull. With a single low groan, the guard sank to his knees and toppled over, shaking the floor with the impact of his landing.

Marco grabbed the rifle, then ripped the sleeve from his torn shirt and handed it to Lauren. "Gag him with this," he said. He began tearing the other sleeve to use to tie the man's hands.

By the time he'd trussed the guard's hands and feet and Lauren had tied on the gag, the man was awake. He glared at them, unmoving. "Just lie still," Marco said.

"Probably the best thing for you is to pretend you were out the whole time." He patted the man's shoulder, then nodded to Lauren. "Let's go."

"Where to?" she asked, falling into step behind him.

"Thanks to the guys who beat me up, I know where the back door is," Marco said, even as they reached the closed portal. He pulled it open and she found herself standing in a small, quiet courtyard containing a picnic table, a few chairs and a can of sand studded with cigarette butts. But the space was deserted.

"Now we need to get to the mess," he said.

She stopped and stared at him, hands on her hips. "Marco, I know we haven't had much to eat, but now isn't the time," she protested.

"Not for food," he said. "For explosives."

She blinked. "What are you going to do with explosives?"

"We've got to find a way to keep these guys from leaving this canyon." He took her hand and pulled her across the compound. Half a dozen men raced past, carrying packs and weapons. None glanced their way. In other parts of the compound, soldiers loaded trucks or dismantled tents and Quonset huts. "We need to hurry," Marco said. "If we block their exit with an explosion, they'll be trapped and waiting when the Rangers show up."

THEY RACED TOWARD the mess hall, weaving through marching lines of men headed away from the camp. The Quonset hut that had served as kitchen, mess hall and commissary was deserted, the door standing open. Inside, the pile of half-peeled potatoes and the paring knife still waited on the counter, but the shelves had been ransacked, a trash can overturned, a refrigerator left half-open in the haste to depart.

A door at the back of the building opened onto a large pantry and he led the way there. When Marco had been here earlier, the shelves had been lined with canned goods and cases of MREs, the "meals ready to eat" rations the modern military relied on in the field. But in addition to food, the shelves had also held boxes of blasting caps and bins full of plastic explosives.

Those boxes and bins were gone now, as were most of the canned goods. He felt along the shelves until he came to one that was fitted behind the water heater that supplied the kitchen. Something hard met his fingertips. He pulled out a single box of explosives.

He ripped open the top of the box and they stared at a row of off-white bricks of puttylike material. Lauren took a step back. "Is that safe to handle?" she asked.

"It's harmless until you insert the detonator." He closed the box and searched the shelves for the detonator he'd need. Not finding it, he shoved the box into Lauren's arms and dropped to the floor, feeling under the shelves. As he'd hoped, a single detonator had fallen behind there when they'd swept the shelves clean. He examined the four-inch plastic tube attached to a coil of wire, then tucked it into his pocket.

"Do you really know how to build a bomb?" she asked.

"In theory, yes." He took the box of C-4 from her.

"But in reality?"

"I've never actually done it, no. Maybe you could help."

She clearly didn't appreciate his joke. She crossed her arms over her chest and took a step back. "I can't even make cake from a boxed mix," she said. "If you don't know the recipe for this particular main dish, then I can't help you."

He found an empty backpack in the debris scattered around the room and stuffed the explosives inside.

"It makes me nervous, thinking of you carrying that stuff around," Lauren said.

"We don't have time to be nervous." He added a couple of bottles of water to the pack. "We can't afford to waste a second." Some vehicles had probably already left the canyon, though these would have most likely contained scouts and other people whose job it was to do the advance work and get everything ready for the men who would set the bombs or booby traps or whatever destructive plans the terrorist operatives had made. But the foot soldiers—the demolitions experts and shooters and lookouts—would soon follow, spreading out to their targets, which, from what Prentice and others had indicated, included multiple sites throughout the state.

"Come on," he said. "We're going to have to run." He slung the pack onto his back and they hurried from the kitchen. Outside, the chaos had died down. Whole rows of tents had vanished and two of the Quonset huts had already been dismantled, the pieces loaded into waiting trucks. Only a few people worked dismantling a third hut.

"Where is everybody?" Lauren asked.

"Let's hope they haven't already been deployed on their mission," he said. He broke into a trot, moving quickly across the camp. Again, no one paid them any particular attention; they were just two more soldiers hurrying to put their training into action.

"Where…where are we going?" Lauren asked, a little breathless as she ran after him.

"They must have a way of getting all these vehicles

in here." He pointed to three rows of Jeeps and ATVs parked near the command center. "They must have built some kind of ramp into the canyon. If we can find it and destroy it, they won't be able to drive out. That should slow them down enough to allow the Rangers time to get here."

"How are we going to find it?" she asked.

"We follow the vehicles." He pointed to a line of loaded trucks making their way out of camp. Most of them were smaller trucks, high-clearance and four-wheel drive to handle the rough terrain, but incapable of carrying more than a half dozen men or a few thousand pounds of cargo at a time. They rumbled along in a slow-moving line, men sitting on the sides of the beds or hanging out of the cabs, staring ahead impatiently, anxious to be on their way.

At first, Marco and Lauren raced alongside the trucks, quickly outpacing the lumbering vehicles. But as the canyon narrowed, they were forced to move to the sides, moving up the incline, weaving their way among cactus and knots of brush that slowed their progress. He kept an eye on the line of slowly moving trucks, both to gauge their progress, and in case anyone noticed them and tried to take them out.

But everyone was focused on clearing the area as quickly as possible. Most of the men would have no idea command had captured two prisoners or that those prisoners had escaped. Lauren and Marco were merely two more soldiers, hurrying to accomplish a mission they had all somehow been brainwashed into believing was the good and right thing to do.

"There are so many trucks ahead of us," Lauren said.

She'd moved up beside him, doing a good job of keeping up. "We'll never be able to stop them all."

"We can stop most of them." He hefted the backpack higher on his shoulders. "The ones we can't stop, the Rangers can." One of the first things Graham would have done would have been to set up roadblocks throughout the area to stop anyone who looked suspicious. Even if Marco and Lauren didn't stop every vehicle, they could prevent most of the destruction Prentice had planned.

The trucks in line beside them had stopped altogether now. Lauren touched his shoulder and pointed up ahead. "Look!"

A single vehicle was making its way up a narrow earthen ramp, big, knobby tires biting into the loose soil and rock. Ten feet wide, with at least a seven percent grade, the exit route was treacherous enough that the trucks could only navigate it one at a time, and slowly. One carefully placed charge would be enough to block the exit completely.

He removed the backpack and opened it, and took out a single brick of C-4. After a moment's thought, he added a second brick. He would only have one chance, so he had to get it right the first time.

"How are you going to get down there to plant the bomb?" Lauren asked. "Someone will see you right away and kill you."

She was right. Even if he had someone—and Lauren was the only other person on his side at the moment—lay down covering fire, he'd never have time to move into position and set the explosives up properly, especially given his unfamiliarity with their operation. He frowned at the ascending truck, trying to think of a way—any way—to get to the ramp unseen. The sun was up now, and though shadows still engulfed much of the canyon, sun poured into this eastern end, lighting the ramp like a spotlight.

He slipped the C-4 into the pack and carefully slid it beneath a clump of scrub oak. "You're right," he said. "Time for plan B."

She crossed her arms over her chest. "And what's plan B?"

He slipped the rifle off his shoulder and checked to see that it was loaded. "If I can disable one of the trucks while it's on the ramp, it will block the exit. It will take some time for them to move it out of the way. If I can, I'll disable several vehicles."

"And the minute you start firing, you'll have two dozen guns just like that one shooting this way," she said. "Fired by men who have had nothing better to do with their time for weeks than practice shooting."

"You're right," he said. "But I wasn't planning to shoot from here." He looked up the slope ahead of them. "We need to take a sniper's position, concealed in good cover, probably up on the rim and a little ahead of most of the men, shooting down. And we move before anyone can reach us."

"So we've got to climb," she said.

"Yes, and we need to hurry."

He put her ahead of him and took up a position behind her, his weapon at the ready, aware that if anyone in the line of waiting trucks noticed them, they might think it suspicious that they were taking this difficult route out. At the top, she stopped, bent over at the waist, hands on her knees, breathing hard, her face flushed. He handed her a bottle of water and after a moment she straightened and drank deeply.

From this angle, they could no longer see the trucks and troops below, though he could hear the idling engines and muffled voices. Lauren looked out across the prairie as she drank, squinting into the sun. "It's so tempting to just walk away," she said. "To leave the danger and go back to trying to find help."

"Doing that might mean a lot of innocent people die," he said.

"I said it was tempting, not that I'd do it." She handed him the water bottle. "Come on. Let's find a good place to hide and do this."

He led the way along the rim, keeping low as they approached the ramp. They had to descend a couple of feet to have a good view of the vehicles crawling up the slope. The first truck had almost made it to the top, in perfect position to block all of those waiting to exit behind it. Silently, Marco indicated a boulder amid a clump of scrub. Lauren nodded and moved to crouch behind it. Marco slid alongside her, stretched out with the rifle propped on the boulder. He sighted on the truck, trying to decide whether to aim for the tires or the engine block.

"It's going to be loud," he said softly. "You might want to cover your ears."

She clapped her hands over her ears, and shut her eyes as well, her lips pressed tightly together as if to bite back screams.

The first shot took out the nearside rear tire. The second round of fire peppered the front quarter-panel and hood with holes and exploded one of the front tires. Men shouted and poured out of the surrounding vehicles like ants. Several looked up the slope in their direction and pointed, and raised their rifles.

"We've got to run," Marco said. He leaped to his feet

and pulled her up beside him, then retreated up and back along the rim, out of sight of the soldiers, but not out of hearing range of their shouts.

"Are they going to come after us?" Lauren asked, when they stopped in the deep shade of an overhanging rock to catch their breath.

"They'll send someone," he said. "But we'll make sure they don't find us." He slid down a couple of feet to study the activity below. Lauren moved in behind him, her hands at his waist, her chin on his shoulder. He found himself matching the rhythm of his breathing to her own, calmed by her steadfast presence. He'd worked with many partners on various missions, men he admired and respected, some he hadn't much liked but had learned to trust with his life, a few, like Rand, for whom he felt a deep friendship, But he'd never had a partner like Lauren, someone he felt compelled to protect, yet whom he depended on to prop him up emotionally. He'd gotten through tough missions before by setting all emotion aside, becoming a robot who relied on instinct and training. Lauren made him feel everything from fear to triumph more intently; he wouldn't give up the pleasure she brought him in order to avoid the pain.

"No!" Lauren's cry, the single word half-smothered in his back, startled him.

He whirled around, heart pounding. "What's wrong? Are you hurt?"

"No, but Prentice is getting away." She pointed toward the crowd of men around the disabled truck. A single black ATV negotiated the edge of the ramp, lurching toward the canyon rim. Richard Prentice, bareheaded, with a rifle slung across his back, stood in his seat as he powered the vehicle up the slope. "We've got to stop him," Lauren said.

He was too far away to shoot at the vehicle or the man. He and Lauren would never outrun the ATV. He searched the line of vehicles waiting behind the truck and spotted a side-by-side ATV. He straightened and brushed debris from his clothes, then cradled the rifle and started walking down the slope.

"What are you doing?" Lauren asked, racing after him.

He assumed his commanding officer demeanor and marched straight toward the soldiers, who were so intent on the action ahead that they didn't notice him until he stood beside the driver. "Soldier, I need this vehicle," he said. "I'm ordering you to turn it over to me at once."

The soldier, who couldn't have been more than twenty-two or twenty-three, blond hairs sprouting from his chin and acne scars on his cheeks, gaped at him. "That's an order, soldier!" Marco barked, and hefted the rifle.

"Y-yes sir," the man stammered, and slid out from behind the wheel. His companion fell from the passenger side and scrambled to his feet, trying to regain his balance and salute at the same time. Marco slid into the driver's seat and Lauren raced around to climb in beside him.

"Hang on!" Marco shouted, and gunned the ATV forward, past the stranded truck, on the same course set by Prentice. The vehicle bucked and dipped, but made steady progress up the slope, gaining speed as they neared the rim.

"He's too far ahead!" Lauren shouted over the roar of the engine as they crested the canyon and spotted the dust trail far ahead that marked Prentice's passage.

"We'll catch up to him," Marco said, and floored the

gas pedal. With two people, he had a heavier load than Prentice's machine, but the side-by-side ATV also had a more powerful engine and was more stable than the four-wheeler Prentice drove. They raced in a straight line, bouncing over rocks and cactus, swerving only to avoid larger trees and boulders. Lauren clung to the handhold, her hat long gone, long hair flying out behind her.

"We're gaining on him!" she shouted.

Prentice looked over his shoulder and saw them drawing closer. He drew a pistol and fired it in their direction, the shots wide of their mark, sailing into the scrub around them. He fired until he was out of ammunition, and then he tossed the gun aside, hunched low over the steering wheel and sped on.

"What's that up ahead?" Lauren shouted. "Where is he headed?"

She pointed to a low line of trees in the distance, taller than the surrounding growth, and interspersed with jagged piles of rock. Marco glanced at the sun. They were heading due south now. "I think it's the Black Canyon," he said. "The end that isn't along the park road."

Compared to the Black Canyon, the depression the terrorists had chosen for their camp was little more than a ditch. The steep, jagged sides of the Black Canyon plunged up to twenty-seven hundred feet to the roaring Colorado River below. The national park contained only fourteen miles of the forty-eight-mile-long canyon, though a large chunk of the rest of it was preserved in the Gunnison Gorge National Conservation Area, also part of the Rangers' turf.

But Marco hadn't spent much time exploring the canyon itself. He'd been too preoccupied with crimes in other areas of the park to pay much attention to the gorge that cut a deep slash across a large swath of southwestern Colorado. Now the remoteness and wildness of the area struck him. They'd long ago left the hubbub of the camp behind, and entered this landscape of deep silence and endless vistas, places no man had set foot in years, even centuries.

"He's not stopping!" Lauren shouted as they drew closer to the line of trees that marked the canyon's rim.

If anything, Prentice had increased his speed as he neared the rim. Did he think he could jump it? Even if his ATV had been able to clear the one-thousand-foot distance from one side of the canyon to the other, the rocks and trees that crowded the rim would have prevented him from having a clear shot. If he went over the edge, he would be dashed to pieces on the rocks jutting from the walls, long before he reached the water.

"He's going to drive right over the rim." Lauren covered her eyes with her hands.

Prentice skidded toward the rim, gravel flying up from his tires. At the last possible moment, the ATV came to rest in a tangle of scrub oaks and piñon. Prentice dived from the driver's seat and began running toward the rim. "Does he think he can climb down?" Lauren asked.

"I think he's running for cover," Marco said. "He plans to pick us off from there." He sped up the machine and took it to the edge of the rim, gravel flying from under the front wheels when he braked to a stop, ricocheting off the canyon walls as it fell.

Prentice's first shots whistled in the air around them. Marco shoved Lauren out of the ATV and dived after her. They rolled and scrambled into the cover of trees, then took up a more secure position behind a pile of boulders. Prentice continued to fire from his own position a hundred yards farther west, bullets thudding into the trunks of nearby trees or cutting chips from the rocks.

Marco unslung the rifle from his shoulder and handed it to Lauren. "Can you fire at the rocks around him, just to keep him occupied, while I sneak around the other side?" he asked.

She took the weapon and stared at it. "I don't think I could hit anything. At least not on purpose."

"You don't have to hit anything, just occupy his attention while I move into position."

She gripped the gun more firmly and nodded, her face pale, her eyes determined in spite of her fear. "All right. I will."

He shifted into a better stance to make a run for it when she started firing. She put a hand on his shoulder and pulled him back. When he sent her a questioning look, she leaned forward and kissed him, directly on the mouth and hard enough to bruise his lips. "Be careful," she whispered, then turned away, steadying the gun in front of her, ready to fire.

Chapter Eighteen

He hadn't expected that kiss, Lauren thought as she pulled the rifle's trigger and sent the first of a barrage of bullets in Prentice's direction. Maybe he didn't think this was the time or the place for kissing, but she wasn't going to let him leave her without some way of letting him know how much he meant to her.

She didn't want to think it might be the last chance she'd have to kiss him. They'd survived so many last chances in the past few days. Surely they could make it through a few more.

The gun frightened her, but as she tapped the trigger over and over she began to gain confidence. She sighted down the barrel and aimed the shots to Prentice's right or left. She couldn't really see him, only the flash of his own gunfire as he answered her. He didn't seem to realize they'd changed shooters. She'd lost sight of Marco almost as soon as he'd left her; she prayed he was all right.

Suddenly, she glimpsed him on the rocks above and behind Prentice. She held her fire and stared at him. He crouched like a tiger waiting for a chance to jump. She took her finger off the trigger, waiting.

Prentice continued to fire at her, then silence. Was he out of ammunition? Or had he finally figured out something was going on? She raised the gun and pulled the trigger again, but the response was only an empty click. She was out of ammunition. Why hadn't she made Marco show her how to reload?

She turned her attention back to him in time to see him leap, a superhero without a cape. Prentice screamed and almost immediately the two rolled from behind the obscuring rock, each grappling for a hold on the other. Lauren stood to watch, the rifle dangling useless in her hand. Surely Prentice was no match for the younger, trained man. But desperation must have given him strength. He fought back hard, refusing to surrender.

The two men rolled farther away from the sheltering rock, but closer to the dropoff to the canyon. "Be careful!" Lauren screamed. She took a few steps toward the struggling men. Prentice's face was crimson, his mouth contorted in a grimace as he clawed at Marco's face with one hand and shoved at his shoulder with the other.

"Marco!" she shouted, but he gave no indication that he heard her. His face was set in a stony expression of determination as he thrust one hand under Prentice's chin and shoved, forcing it back at an unnatural angle.

They were only a foot or so from the dropoff now. Lauren screamed as they rolled again and came to rest inches from the edge, Prentice straddling the younger man, driving Marco's head over and over again into the rock.

Lauren looked at the rifle in her hand. If they had swapped places, Marco would have saved a bullet to shoot Prentice. But even if she'd had the ammunition, there was no way her aim was good enough to be certain she could hit the billionaire and not Marco. She dropped the rifle and stooped and picked up a large rock. Maybe she could get close enough to hit Prentice in the head...

With a grunt, Marco shoved upward, hurling Prentice off him, back away from the canyon rim. Both men scrambled to their feet, legs planted, arms at their sides in a wrestler's pose. "Don't come any closer," Prentice said. "I'll jump and I'll take you with me."

"You'd kill yourself just to get back at me?"

"I'd kill myself to save the mission," Prentice said.

"The mission is already lost." Marco took a step sideways, away from the rim, but Prentice didn't follow. "The Rangers are on their way. They know about your plot. You'll never succeed. Come with me. At least then you'll have another chance to talk your way out of trouble."

"You're wrong! We will succeed!" He wore the dazed, wild-eyed expression of someone who wasn't fully present.

Marco took a step forward; Prentice a step back. His back foot teetered on the edge, loose rock falling, before he regained his balance. "Don't come any closer," he warned.

"Richard, don't do this!" Lauren could keep silent no longer.

He looked at her, his expression softening, some of the wildness leaving his eyes. "We could have been so good together," he said. "I would have given you anything you wanted. No one would have dared to say a word against you if you were my wife."

"I didn't want that kind of life," she said. "I didn't need someone to protect me." She only needed someone to love her and to accept her as she was. Someone like Marco. Her gaze shifted to him. He thought he was too dangerous and dark for her, but he didn't realize how much they had in common. They both had things they regretted in their pasts, troubles that would never entirely leave them. But they also had faith in each other. Together, they were both stronger than they were apart.

Movement out of the corner of her eye distracted her, and then a strange, animal yell raised prickles of gooseflesh along her arms. She glanced over in time to see Prentice hurtling toward Marco, a long, sharp stick held in front of him like a lance. Marco doubled over to take the blow on his shoulder, then charged forward, knocking Prentice off his feet. Marco grabbed at the older man as he fell, grasping a fistful of shirt, bracing both feet to haul him back from the edge.

Lauren would never forget the sound of the fabric tearing, or Prentice's screams as he hurtled over the edge, screams that echoed over and over through the still air as he fell.

"Officers on the scene arrested thirty-four men and confiscated more than three hundred pounds of explosives, dozens of automatic weapons and thousands of rounds of ammunition. Roadblocks around the canyon captured another dozen men and trucks and additional explosives and weapons.

"Authorities say the group, which called itself the True Patriots, had plans to blow up five major dams, fourteen highway bridges and five major water-treatment plants, and other intelligence indicates they had also targeted airports and telecommunication towers. Captain Graham Ellison with the FBI, a key figure in the investigation, said at a press conference yesterday if these terrorists had succeeded in carrying out their plans, the destruction would have resulted in the loss of hundreds, even thousands of lives, billions of dollars of damage to major infrastructure, and disrupted life for millions of citizens for the better part of a year. The repercussions would have been felt well into the next decade.

"Investigations are ongoing into the group, though evidence points to billionaire Richard Prentice as a driving force behind the organization, and its chief financier. Prentice died in a struggle with law enforcement while attempting to escape the terrorists' training facility."

Lauren's voice broke on the last words. She took a deep breath and faced the camera with what she hoped was a calm look. "This is special reporter Lauren Starling. For more on this developing story, stay tuned for my special one-hour report tomorrow night on True Patriots, True Terrorists."

The red light on the camera went out and she breathed a sigh of relief and sat back in her chair.

"Great job, Lauren," her producer, Mitch Frasier, said.

"You were terrific." The regular evening anchor, Bradley Eversly, patted her shoulder. "Good to see you back on air."

She accepted more congratulations from others, then retreated to her dressing room to remove her heavy on-air makeup and change into more casual clothes. Her phone rang as she was brushing out her hair. "Hey, we saw you on TV," Sophie's voice greeted her. "You looked fantastic."

"It felt good to be back," she said. "A little strange, too. Where are you? It sounds noisy."

"Oh, Rand and I are at the airport. That's the other reason I called."

"Oh?" Lauren smoothed on pale pink lip gloss and checked her look in the mirror. She'd lost a little weight after her ordeal in the park, but she looked pretty good, considering.

"We're headed to Vegas. We've decided to elope."

"Oh, Sophie!"

"Now, don't be mad. We're hoping you can fly out and stand up with us at the wedding. Rand's trying to get hold of Marco, too, but so far he's not having any luck."

"Rand doesn't know where Marco is?"

"He said he took a couple of days' leave, but wouldn't say why. He must have his phone switched off. You haven't heard from him, have you?"

"No." A cold blackness pinched at her stomach at the words. She hadn't heard or seen anything from Marco since that day at the canyon rim. Helicopters full of soldiers and law enforcement had swarmed in shortly after Prentice went over the edge. One group had led her away for questioning while Marco had disappeared in a crowd of others. In the week since, she'd often thought of calling or texting him, but wasn't sure what to say. She told herself if he'd really wanted to talk to her, he'd have made the effort.

"So will you do it? Can you get away for a few days and come to Vegas?" She realized Sophie had continued talking to her while she'd been lost in thoughts of Marco.

"Oh, sure, I can get a few days off, now that the special is wrapped up. When is the wedding?"

"Whenever you get here. I'll call you later with more details. We have to board the plane now."

Sophie hung up and Lauren ended the call, fighting the sadness that threatened to overwhelm her. She should have been thrilled for her sister, excited about the prospect of a wedding, happy at the positive turn her life had taken. She was working again, as a special correspondent for the number one station in Denver. The public was starting to see that all of Richard Prentice's accusations against her had been false, and that he was the real villain of this tale. Though they might never prove it, the Rangers suspected Prentice was behind the threatening notes, the sabotage of her car and the other attacks on Lauren after she escaped from Prentice's ranch.

She should have been happy, but she couldn't get past this emptiness she felt. Maybe being bipolar made her more susceptible to these black moods, but she had a sense that anyone in her situation would have been blue. The man she loved was avoiding her, and she didn't know what to do about it.

She left the station and drove the short distance to her new apartment in Denver's fashionable lower downtown area. She was crossing the parking lot to her front door when a tall, muscular man stepped out of the shadows. She caught her breath and almost dropped her keys, fighting the urge to run—though whether her legs would take her toward him or away, she couldn't be sure.

"Hello, Lauren," he said.

"Hello, Marco. I didn't know you were in Denver." Amazed by her own strength and composure, she moved past him and began unlocking the three locks on the door to the apartment. Her ordeal with Prentice had definitely made her more security conscious.

"I came to see you. Can I come in?"

"Of course."

He followed her into the apartment, which had seemed spacious enough before, but now seemed too small with him in it. "Can I get you some tea or coffee?" she asked.

She set down her purse and rearranged a trio of candles on the table by the door, suddenly nervous, avoiding his gaze but feeling him watching her, like a caress, hot against her chilled skin. She swallowed, trying to find the words she needed to say to him. Her feelings for him were so mixed up, she didn't know how to even begin to approach the subject.

"I don't need anything." He put his hand on her arm. "Except to talk to you."

She felt weak-kneed at his touch, on the verge of tears, though whether tears of relief, sadness or joy, she couldn't tell. Or maybe the tears were just a sign of hysteria, of her frayed emotions finally giving way. Her skin burned where his fingers brushed against her, and once again she mustered all her willpower to move past him to the beige leather sofa fresh from the showroom. She sat and smiled up at him, composed and aloof. She wouldn't break down, not in front of him. Better to let him think his rejection had not affected her than show him how much she hurt. "How are you doing?" she asked.

She had thought he would take the matching leather armchair across from her, but instead, he sat beside her, scarcely six inches between them. His hair was freshly cut, the smooth skin of his cheeks smelling of some woodsy aftershave. "I've been busy. Things shifted into high gear after law enforcement started moving into the camp. A lot of long days gathering evidence, tracking down leads. You've been busy, too, I understand."

He hadn't really answered her question, had he? He'd told her what he'd been doing, but not how he felt. She could play that game, too. "The station has been very nice," she said. "They're calling me a special correspondent. I get to work part-time, choose the projects that appeal to me. I consulted my doctors and we all decided that would be the best way to get back into work—not too much stress or pressure."

"I saw one of the promos for the special you're doing on the True Patriots."

"What a nest of vipers they are. Half white supremacists, half far-right-wingers, with a sprinkling of guys who seem like World War II reenactors caught on the wrong side. All those quasi-Nazi uniforms and flags, as if Hitler was some great hero. It's so twisted."

"The Nazi thing was mostly Prentice's idea, I think."

"Why do you think that?"

"That old picture we found, of the guy in uniform? Turns out that was his grandfather, Bruno Adel. He worked for the SS under Hitler and fled to Venezuela, where he lived under the name of Ben Anderson. Prentice spent summers with him as a kid and apparently idolized him."

"That explains all the stamps from Venezuela in his passport."

"Adel died ten years ago, but Prentice kept ties with his friends and gradually built up a contingent of deluded sympathizers whose discontent with the US government grew into this plan to wreak havoc and ferment revolution."

"From which Prentice would emerge as the new leader and power." She grabbed a notebook and began writing furiously. "I knew some of this, but we'll have to find a way to work in the new information. It's fascinating, in a very sick way."

He waited until she finished and set the notebook aside before he spoke again. "You look good," he said. He moved his hand near hers, not quite touching.

She glanced up at him, at his beautiful, tense face. "So do you." She looked away again, like someone who moved too near a fire and had to back away. "I heard the Rangers were together again."

He nodded. "We're the big heroes now. Congress is happy to funnel money our way."

"You're the real hero," she said. "I hope people know that."

"You're wrong." He took her hand at last, his grip warm and firm. She drew a shaky breath, her heart beating wildly, forcing herself to go still, to listen to his words and not think about her feelings. "I was doing the job I was trained to do," he said. "You're the one who was really brave. You started the whole chain of events that led to the discovery of the terrorists by volunteering to go and talk to Prentice that afternoon."

"I never could have made it without you," she said.

He rubbed his thumb along the side of her hand, sending tremors through her. "We made a pretty good team, didn't we?"

"We did." She put her free hand on top of his, stilling him. "I wanted to call you," she said. "But I didn't know what to say. I caused you so much trouble, almost got you killed…"

"I thought you were avoiding me because you'd had enough violence and death to last a lifetime."

"I have, but I don't blame any of that on you. And I wasn't avoiding you. I thought you were avoiding me."

"I was going to stay away, but Rand wouldn't let up on telling me what an idiot I was being."

"Good for Rand." Still holding his hand, she scooted closer, more confident with every minute she spent in his strong, calm presence. "I think the feelings we have between us are special. We shouldn't let them go."

His eyes met hers, dark and troubled. "I've never cared about a woman the way I care about you. But that doesn't mean we belong together. I—"

"Hush." She pressed her fingers to his lips. "I love you, Marco. It's a scary feeling, love, but I've had time to think about it, and I'm determined to face my fears. I know there are some dark things in your past. There's darkness in my life, too. Neither one of us knows what the future will look like, but we can be pretty sure it won't always be easy. I have an illness that isn't going to go away. Medication can control it, but things will happen to upset the balance. We'll have to learn to deal with that, and it won't always be easy. But if you can accept that—if you can accept me—then there's nothing in your life that will stop me from wanting to be with you."

He cupped the side of her face and looked into her eyes, spearing her with a gaze full of raw need and longing. "I stopped looking for perfection in my life a long time ago," he said. "But to me, you will always be perfect."

She had no need for more words after that. The love in his eyes, the gentleness of his caress, the intensity of his kiss, told her everything she needed or wanted to know. He pulled her close, fitting her to him as if trying to pull her into him. His kiss was both tender and commanding, claiming her, burning away the memory of every other kiss she'd ever known.

When they finally pulled apart, she was breathless and shaky, but immediately felt stronger when he smiled at her. He so seldom smiled, she delighted in knowing she was somehow responsible for his pleasure and happiness in the moment. She twined her fingers in his and returned the smile. "Let's go into the bedroom." No need to be coy with him; they both knew what they wanted.

She led him down the short hall to the one room of the apartment she had bothered to fully furnish and decorate. The cream-colored satin comforter and lace-trimmed cotton sheets had made up for the deprivations she'd endured in those days and nights in the wilderness. Marco took in the king-size sleigh bed and luxurious bedding. "Better than the bare ground in the desert," he said. "Though I wanted to take you right there, almost more than I've ever wanted anything."

"I wanted you then, too," she said. "But now I'm glad we waited." She wrapped herself around him and they shared another searing kiss, then he slid his hands beneath the soft cotton sweater she wore, skimming her ribs and the sides of her breasts, coaxing her arms up so he could tug off the top. He caressed her breasts through the satin and lace of her bra, his erection hard and insistent against her stomach.

She reached back to unhook the bra, but he stopped her and released the catch himself, tossing aside the garment and bending to take one sensitive nipple into his mouth. She arched against him as he suckled, and moaned softly, her pulse pounding. Blindly, she found the zipper of his jeans and lowered it, feeling his erection jump beneath her fingers. While he transferred his attention to her other breast, she wrapped her hand around him and squeezed gently, smiling against him as he gasped.

Together, they stumbled toward the bed and fell back onto the soft satin, helping each other out of the rest of their clothes as they did so. Naked, they lay side by side, catching their breath and letting their eyes and hands explore each other's bodies. He was everything she'd fantasized about and more—lean muscle and bronzed skin, strength and beauty honed by years of discipline and training. She traced a scar along his shoulder and another by his hip. "How did you get these?" she asked.

"The one on my hip is from a gang shooting a long time ago, when I was a teenager. The shoulder is from Iraq. I don't think about them much anymore."

"The scars inside always last longer," she said, and he stilled, his hand resting on her thigh.

She could feel him pulling away from her, pulling the shutters over his emotions and vulnerabilities. She wanted to shake him, to force him back to her, but settled for placing her palm over his heart, as if she could keep that part of him open to her.

He blinked and he was back with her, looking into her eyes with the openness she treasured. "Yeah," he said, and squeezed her thigh softly. "Those scars stay with you."

"You don't have to hide them from me." She kissed the puckered line of flesh at his shoulder. "You don't have to hide anything from me."

"I'll try," he said. "This is new for me."

"For me, too."

They kissed again, more gently, then he rolled her onto her back and knelt over her. He smoothed the hair away from her face, the calluses on his fingers snagging in the silken strands. "I love you," he said. "I didn't want it to happen, but I couldn't stop it."

"Why didn't you want it to happen?" she asked.

"Because I'll only bring you trouble."

"You could say the same about me." She slid her hands up to caress the sides of his face. "So maybe we belong together after all—two people who know how to handle trouble."

His expression softened. "Maybe we do, at that."

"Now stop talking and make love to me."

"Yes, ma'am." He executed a mock salute, then slid his hand down her body to rest between her legs, over the hot, pulsing center of her need. As he slipped his finger inside her she let her head fall back, surrendering to the onslaught of sensation that battered at her. How was it he knew just how and where to touch her, as if he was reading her mind, or merely attuned to every sensation?

As he caressed and kissed and fondled, she let her hands and lips explore his body, as well. She felt safe in indulging every desire with him, not worried about how she appeared or what he might think. With Marco, she was free to be herself, flaws and all.

When at last he rolled on a condom and slid into her, she felt as if she'd been waiting her whole life for this moment of completion. There had been other men before him, but she could imagine no other man after him. He moved deftly, stroking and caressing, balanced over her until, with a cry, she wrapped her arms around him and pulled him to her, arching to meet each thrust, making love with him, not to him.

Her release shuddered through her, and he followed soon after, their cries of pleasure mingled and fading together. They lay joined for a long time after, breathing hard, letting the sweat dry and their bodies cool.

They slid apart and she slipped out of bed to go into the bathroom to clean herself. When she returned, she thought he'd fallen asleep, but as she climbed into bed beside him he opened his eyes and looked at her. "How's this going to work?" he asked.

"What do you mean?" She rolled onto her side to study him. He lay on his back with his hands behind his head.

"This relationship. How's it going to work, with you here in Denver and me in Montrose?"

"I'm keeping my place in Montrose. I plan to spend most of my time there. I'll only be in Denver when my work requires it, for a day or two at a time. And most of my work for the foreseeable future is going to be reporting on Richard Prentice and the terrorists."

"Then, I can see a lot of you." Did she imagine the relief in his voice?

"I think you should see a great deal of me." She smoothed her hand over his chest. "In fact, I think you should move in with me."

He rolled over onto one elbow to face her. "What about Sophie?"

"She and Rand are on their way to Vegas right now to get married. He's been trying to get hold of you to tell you."

"I turned off my phone. I needed time to think."

"To think about me?"

"About us."

"And what did you decide?"

"That I was all wrong for you. That you'd end up hating the work I do and hating me. That I should turn around and go back to Montrose and never see you again."

"But you came here anyway."

He caressed her shoulder. "Like I said, I couldn't stay away. I love you."

Three simple words, but said by him they meant so much. She buried her head against his shoulder. "I love you, too. Will you come to live with me?"

"Maybe. First, tell me more about Vegas."

"Sophie called me from the airport. They're waiting to get married until I can get there. You should come with me and stand up as Rand's best man. I'm sure that's why he's been trying to reach you."

"I'll do that." His hand tightened on her shoulder. "But there's something else I want to do while we're there."

"What? Do you want to gamble? I'm sure we can do that, too, see some of the sights."

"I want to take a different kind of gamble. You ought to know now that I'm not a man who does things halfway. When I'm committed to a mission, I give it my all."

"Marco, what are you saying?"

He slid from beneath her and turned to face her, his gaze locked to hers. "Marry me, Lauren. We'll do it in Vegas. We can even make it a double wedding if you want."

Her heart turned over. It was a crazy idea. Impulsive. Manic, even.

Marco was none of those things, however. She couldn't think of a person who was more sane and grounded. "You really want to marry me?" she asked.

"I'm in this for life. I want to make it official."

She smiled through the tears of joy that dimmed her vision. "Then, yes. Yes, let's do it. Let's start the rest of our life together now."

* * * * *

 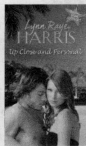  

MILLS & BOON®

Want to get more from Mills & Boon?

Here's what's available to you if you join the exclusive **Mills & Boon eBook Club** today:

✦ *Convenience – choose your books each month*
✦ *Exclusive – receive your books a month before anywhere else*
✦ *Flexibility – change your subscription at any time*
✦ *Variety – gain access to eBook-only series*
✦ *Value – subscriptions from just £3.99 a month*

So visit **www.millsandboon.co.uk/esubs** today to be a part of this exclusive eBook Club!